WOOD'S END IS DEDICATED TO ALL THOSE THAT HAVE
TRIUMPHED OVER ABUSIVE AND CONTROLING CULT-SYSTEMS
IN WHATEVER FORM THEY TAKE.

Wood's End

A Supernatural Thriller of Deliverance and Destiny

DIAMOND HEDGE PRODUCTIONS, LLC

Copyright: October 20, 2009
Published in the United States of America

Second Edition / July 20, 2012 / New Cover

ISBN: 978-0-9847059-8-6 / Soft Cover
ISBN: 978-0-615-51694-3 / E Book

Cover Design by, Brian Churchill / Churchill Studios; Memphis, TN
E-Book Conversion for download by, Paul Mayer: paul.mayer@live.com

WOOD'S END

PART ONE
CHAPTER ONE

ANDREA

I'm leaving, she said,
I have to go,
And he looked out the window,
And watched the wind blow the grass about,
And make of the trees,
Frantic dancing dolls dressed in green.
Okay, he lied and she left,
But not without a piece of him,
In exchange for quite a lot of her.

Andrea felt a tightening sensation in her chest as tears welled in her eyes. *Please God,* she pleaded. *Not now; just not now!* She should be happy, even ecstatic, or so she told herself during the sleepless hours of the night before. Very soon papers would be signed and she could put the nightmare of a failed marriage behind her.

A biting January wind gusted between the tall buildings like a freight train in open country. Andrea Wodsende buried her face deep into the mink scarf wrapped about the collar of a vintage military coat, and jaywalked across Court Street. Despite the traffic, pressed bumper to bumper, she walked with ever slowing step.

Ahead was a bakery and coffee shop. The door opened as she stepped onto the opposite curb, assailed by the comforting aroma of baking smells. How tempting it was to walk beneath the shadowed door of that bakery. She would select a pastry, order coffee, and wait until her one attorney, outnumbered by Dudley's five, gave up on her arrival. They wouldn't expect it. Not from her. Final documents prepared for her signature would be laid out in clinical readiness, to be viewed and signed that very afternoon by a judge. No need for the parties to be present. They would be represented by their respective attorneys. The division of assets was, according to her attorney, the best she could hope for, and generous under the present no fault law.

Andrea took a frigid breath and hesitated outside the building. While others rushed to escape the cold, she preferred the wintry street to this last hollow formality. Soon the fighting would end. There would be no more lacerating accusations from him, and no more emotional rebuttals from her. Dudley would be free to marry her replacement and she would be equally free, but for what?

Her cell phone rang. Was it her attorney? He was never available without a delay of some kind. She hoped he was held up in traffic and wouldn't arrive. She hoped he was unexpectedly due in court on another case. She hoped and almost let the caller go to voice mail. Even as a child she had been more the parent than her mother, and so, ruled by a life time of dutiful habit, she put the phone to her ear on the last echo of the last ring.

"Yes?"

"Andrea? Are you sitting down?"

She recognized the voice and shook her head as though he could see her.

"Cause Babe, do I have news for you?"

In their few conversations, he called her babe, doll, girl, or some other irritating female moniker. She would have asked him to stop, but doubted the relationship would last long enough to set such protocol. He was the private detective her attorney told her she didn't need. Despite that advice, she selected his name from the greater Boston yellow pages in a fit of distrust and what she later reasoned was paranoid delusion.

Feeling humiliated by the necessity, she faxed the list of Dudley's declared assets, social security number, and a recent photo. As she half expected, nothing came of the exchange, and she did her best to forget she'd wasted good money.   Money she would need to buy herself a little recuperation, for clearly she was depressed and fiercely attracted to some indulgent state of immobility augmented by a substantial increase in calories.

"Are you listening?   Hey, Girl, you there?   Cause if you don't hear what I have to say, I swear you'll shoot yourself."

The idea resonated, but Andrea pushed it aside.   She stopped walking and listened with growing disbelief.   Within minutes she did an about face and headed in the opposite direction, cell phone still pressed to her ear.

"Get yourself over to Goldfarb's office, about ten blocks toward the harbor.   Whatever you do, don't go to that meeting without Goldfarb, and don't sign anything he hasn't read."

"But who is he?   I already have an attorney."

"Yeah and fat good he's done.   That one would sell the soap factory and tell you it went bankrupt.   It took awhile. I'd almost given up, but when you see what I've managed to uncover you'll dump him."

"Wait a minute.   I just need a minute to absorb this."

"Yeah and that's why he married you.   Forgive me, Doll, but men like him don't choose smart assertive women, quick on the uptake.   They like them pliable and worshipping. Think about it.   That's how you started.   Am I right?"

"So you're a student of human nature and I'm stupid?   Is that what you're saying?"

"Yeah, well there's different kind of smarts, and forgive me for saying so, but you better acquire the other kind fast."

"He was hiding more than money wasn't he?"

"Yes, but you can talk about that with Goldfarb.   Frankly, I'm done.   You couldn't pay me to dig any deeper.   You understand what I'm saying?"

Andrea stopped in mid-stride.   She did understand.   She understood the sneering threat of suspicion with no real proof.   She understood the addictive penchant to believe a lie, but especially she understood, and had grown all too familiar with that vacant look when anger pulled past restraint and she knew herself to be in mortal danger.   The specifics had become secondary to safety and survival and that was burden enough. But given a little time and, yes, a little more money to buy that time, she might actually forget she had ever been so foolish as to marry Dudley Wodsende.

"This call is so unexpected. I thought we were finished. I was just..."

"Yeah, I know. Going to sign your future away."

"What happened?" Andrea asked.

"I put out a lot of feelers and the right lead came in. The rub was his Euro citizenship and investments there, so I've learned from this. I was too willing to believe he was just a typical doctor type."

"Dudley just keeps surprising me. Thank you," she said and meant it.

"No problem. Women in distress are my bread and butter."

They hung up, and soon Andrea found herself standing before a converted warehouse, fitted with an eclectic blend of Victorian and contemporary features. Elias Goldfarb's office occupied the entire top floor and commanded a spectacular view toward the Boston Yacht Marina in one direction, and over the rooftops toward Quincy Market and Faneuil Hall in the other.

Is that your family?" Andrea asked knowing that it was. The lighted oil painting on the wall of the anteroom depicted a pretty woman with dark brown hair and a little boy she could barely restrain, perched on her lap. The artist had captured the energy, the straining intelligence of the child and although he was the smallest figure in the painting, and the woman elaborately dressed, he was, in every sense, the focal point.

"Yes," Goldfarb said. "That's my wife, Evelyn, and our son, Zach, when he was little."

There was something about the way he said the boy's name that evoked the impression of paternal disappointment, but she wouldn't ask. Once business was conducted, the acquaintance would end. Or so she imagined.

They walked into his office. "Please," he gestured toward a telescope mounted on a stand and pointed toward the harbor.

An expression of frustration pulled at her features. Time was slipping away. Didn't he realize the seriousness of her circumstances?

"I've seen the view," Andrea declined, unable to hide her annoyance. "As much as I don't want to be at that meeting, I hate being late."

"The fact is Mrs. Wodsende, I began working on your documents late yesterday afternoon, and I haven't stopped since. I'm not cheap. I'm expecting you to pay my going rate. We haven't had a chance to work out an arrangement, but I think you'll be happy at what I've uncovered."

Andrea noticed three stacks of file folders neatly arranged on the table behind his desk.

He took her elbow. "Past tax returns and, well, let's just say, that a good visual is worth a thousand words." With firmness he guided her to the window and the telescope. "It's already focused," he said. "You'll want to take a good, long look."

Andrea put her eye to the lens and squinted. What she saw was a beautiful yacht, larger than any of the others moored close by. The size had to be at the Marina's limit. It was the boat Dudley had talked of purchasing sometime in the future, when they could afford to do so. She could see into the cabin's interior and knew that no luxury was spared on décor.

"I don't understand," she said.

"That yacht... Let's just say it's yours if you want it."

Andrea was speechless.

"Incidentally," he asked, "do you have a nick name, something only those who know you really well, call you?"

"Yes, but Dudley liked Andrea. He preferred to be formal and was offended by Andie, even insisting my mother stop using it."

"I'd like him to think we've been working together longer than we have, and perhaps even had a prior acquaintance. So if I call you Andie, you'll know why."

It was mid-morning before Andrea arrived back at her destination. This time the prospect of meeting with Dudley's attorneys did not fill her with dread. She tackled the elevator and walked with an air of purpose into the reception area.

"She just walked in." The receptionist hung up the phone and emitted an audible sigh. "They're waiting for you, Mrs. Wodsende. Follow me please," she said, trying, but failing, to cover her impatience.

To Andrea the woman's attitude seemed like more of the same subtle barrage of disdain she'd suffered from her husband. She couldn't help but wonder if the private detective was right? Was there something about her that sent an unconscious signal to bullies? Weak woman crippled by loss, willing to tolerate rude comments, open to abuse.

Ignoring the receptionist, Andrea veered down the hall and walked into the lavatory. She removed her gloves and recalled the last occasion they had gathered here to hammer out a settlement.

Dudley had tallied the cost of all the jewelry he had given her during their short marriage. With receipts in hand, he wanted the full amount deducted from her part of the settlement. Andrea had managed an emphatic refusal. Her attorney had parroted those words, but an hour later asked her to reconsider. "We'll save our energy," he reasoned, "for more important issues."

Andrea surprised everyone when she stood her ground as Dudley picked up a handy paper weight and threw it in her direction. Only she was not surprised as the heavy object whizzed by her head and broke the glass over a framed print.

Andrea leaned over the sink and stared at her face in the mirror. Her skin was flushed from the cold and her blue eyes were bright with new purpose. Of late, unable to sleep, she had been reading the Bible. Although she often prayed, quick little thoughts and requests, it had been a long while since she had turned to God in any concerted manner. Her mother distrusted the church and had often verbalized intense hatred for all organized religion, which she termed a crutch for weaklings.

In opposition to that intolerance, Andrea had persevered, and since it wasn't safe to talk about anything Christian without suffering a contemptuous tirade, she had cherished her faith in that unassailable place of her soul, where even her mother could not reach.

It seemed only natural, that at this time of distress, she had overcome a kind of block and picked up her Bible, only to be struck by a particular verse about God holding her hand. The concept prompted her to recall a time from her past, as a child of six or seven, when she had called out to Jesus and He had responded with divine protection. The memory was shadowed and painful, and over the years she had pushed it from her mind whenever something familiar from that incident was triggered. Andrea had done a word search that very morning, finding other verses that followed the same theme of God holding the hand of Christian believers.

Andrea came to a decision. As life settled into some kind of normalcy, she would distance herself from her mother and become more her own person. She would ignore Sybil's scornful criticism of all things religious and locate a church to attend. There was a growing desire to know God better; this very Jesus, who had saved her life and her sanity when she was but a small girl.

Andrea opened the palm of her hand and looked at the emptiness there. Until now she had felt oppressed and misunderstood. No one had come to her defense. Not her mother and not even the attorney she had hired. Robert Cohen had come highly recommended, but seemed forever disapproving and irritated by what he called her failure to grasp certain realities.

"Please God," Andrea whispered, suddenly fearful of Dudley's anger. How could she not be? If only she could recall the precise words of that Bible verse. There were several, following the same theme, about a personal God being at her right hand, actually walking with her. *You held my hand once before, Jesus, in even more perilous circumstances, so please do so again. I need you.*

The receptionist knocked and then inched the door open. "Ready?" she asked with false courtesy.

Andrea fought down a rush of anger. Encapsulated in that clenched tone was everything she hated about her circumstances. How long did a divorce normally take? There was no time to think, no time to accept what was happening and plan a new future. She caught the woman's pained expression in the mirror.

"No," she said with a restraint that would belie her next words. "I am not at all ready to pay off those grave diggers you call attorneys. Kindly shut the door."

"Unfortunately, Mrs. Wodsende, we do have a tight schedule today and you are now three hours overdue."

"Really? As much as that? Maybe I'll just leave and we can make it three weeks. Would that meet with your approval?"

"Mrs. Wodsende, we are a very busy firm. You are not the only..."

"My being late is none of your business. Please shut the door."

The assistant glared at Andrea, who counted once again. Dudley with his five lined up against her one and now this new bit of news from Elias Goldfarb. He called himself a forensic accountant slash lawyer. She guessed that meant he was hired to look for money that people had carefully hidden in order to evade the law. Hope lifted her spirits. She didn't want the yacht, but there would now be enough money to purchase her dream of having a small antique shop. She would hire a manager and travel, picking up the pieces she loved and knew others would appreciate.

"I'm just doing my job," the receptionist interrupted her thoughts. "They sent me to get you."

Andrea held the receptionists' gaze in the mirror until the door closed and she was alone. Andrea reached behind her and shifted the lock into place. With slow precision she removed the Air Force blue coat. She took her time as she brushed the windblown tangles from her hair and draped the mink scarf, another expensive gift from Dudley, a reminder of the matching coat he had given her last Christmas.

Why had she decided to wear this gift of his? Did she want to provoke him to recall the expense he had lavished on her during their marriage, which he now considered a waste?

Andrea peered into a small cosmetics bag and selected a particular shade of lipstick. She had meant to throw the sample away when it was given to her with the purchase of perfume some months back. Red wasn't her color. Dudley thought it gauche. She looked at her watch and back at her reflection in the mirror. Red seemed just right. This was a red occasion.

WOOD'S END

CHAPTER TWO

Andrea opened the heavy oak door of the conference room and paused to get her bearings. To a man they conveyed disapproval, but only her attorney, Robert Cohen, furrowed his brow and looked at his watch.

An apology was on her lips, but when she saw his gesture she let it die. "Hello, Gentleman," she said instead. "Shall we get started?"

Andrea walked into the room as the five on Dudley's side of the table, half rose in a lackluster display of courtesy. Only Dudley, heavily flanked on either side, remained seated.

They didn't like her. They didn't respect her, only now she understood why. How could you like the person you were committed to rob blind? If you had half a conscience it would be necessary to rationalize a pretty credible reason.

"We've been waiting for nearly three hours," Cohen whispered loud enough for the opposition to hear. He turned from Andrea and faced the other side of the table. "I know my client has good reason to be late. Nevertheless I'm sorry for the inconvenience."

Andrea noticed several neat stacks of paper, each precisely arranged on opposite sides. Dudley had already read his and with pen poised he was preparing to sign.

"I've gone over these and found everything in order." Cohen held out a pen, hurrying her to the task. Andrea ignored his outstretched hand. Once again, she failed to acknowledge him. A flicker of discomfort rippled across his face. This wasn't the woman he had come to know. Like a first swell over a windless ocean, his mute discomfort was transmitted to others in the room. There was blood in the water and they didn't know to whom it belonged. Only Dudley appeared not to notice.

Andrea turned to Samuel Marstead, Dudley's lead attorney. She had never liked him. When the engagement was first announced, he had approached her about signing a prenuptial agreement, but she had refused and Dudley had not pressed her. She knew that Marstead and her husband had argued. In the end it was Dudley's arrogance, that blind assurance that his will would always prevail, that forced an end to any discussion of such a legal document.

"I'd feel we weren't really married. It's an insult to the institution of marriage, don't you think?" she had told her fiancée.

Looking back on it now she guessed that the doubts she'd been expressing, her hesitation to marry at all, had caused everyone to back off. Now she had reason to regret that failure not to heed the small still voice of common sense that whispered caution.

From the very beginning Samuel Marstead's hostility had been nearly palpable. For reasons she never understood, he disliked, perhaps, even hated her. Dudley seemed to rely on him as a kind of father figure, and when they met socially and she was present, the attorney seemed overly reserved. Once the divorce was certain, whatever façade of cordiality had been present in the beginning fell away, and from then on, Marstead directed the bulk of his conversation over her head unless absolutely forced to address her directly.

Andrea toyed with the pile of documents. She avoided looking at Dudley and addressed her next words to Marstead, speaking with a calmness she did not feel. "I won't be signing anything today."

In the silence that followed Dudley betrayed his impatience, sitting up with heightened alertness. After living with him, Andrea had an intimate acquaintance with the unpredictable nature of his behavior. She knew what triggered him and could read the tenuous balance that determined a verbal or physical outburst, and if she looked at him now... Andrea lifted her head to risk an unabashed glare, face to face, for the first time since entering the room and seeing there, just what she expected to see. Not the suppressed anger boiling beneath the surface that he actually felt, but a mask of solicitous concern.

Oh, she thought, to be free of his many deceptions, threats, and schemes. Since speaking with Elias Goldfarb she now suspected a deeper, more hidden agenda, and she was only grateful that soon none of Dudley's secret life would need to concern her. She would be legally severed, safely removed, no longer connected to him in any way unless one counted the battle scars still fresh.

"The reason being?" Marstead coaxed as if speaking to a dim-witted child, but looking to Cohen for an explanation of his client's behavior.

Andrea forced her gaze from Dudley's face. What some might call a smile, but she knew to be a sneer, played at the corners of his mouth.

"Let's see. Where do I start?" Andrea said, cutting off her attorney before he could speak. Soon she would be joined by Elias Goldfarb, who had stayed behind, making final changes to their draft of a revised proposal.

Andrea scanned the faces of the attorneys lined up across from her. The impeccably tailored suits and scrubbed uniformity made Marstead's compatriots look like clones of one another.

"The assets listed on your disclosure reflect barely a fraction of what my husband owns."

"If you're talking about my family holdings, you can just..." Marstead put a hand of restraint on Dudley's arm.

Undaunted Andrea continued. "For example there is the yacht docked as we speak at the marina; fully staffed and ready for departure. A honeymoon cruise, I imagine."

Against her better judgment Andrea addressed her husband. "And, yes, Dudley, I know you sold the house in Aspen, but it seems you didn't take a beating after investing in a failed enterprise as you claimed. Instead you purchased a villa outside of Milan and, let's not forget, the house on the big island of Hawaii. Then," she paused as though considering, "there is the farm in Woods End. An odd holding really. So close and yet we never visited. Did you buy that farm before we met? Because, Dudley, I consider it curious that I grew up near there and yet you never mentioned that property."

There was something about the way he looked at her then. It was a malevolent stare that discomforted all who saw it. And in that moment, Andrea decided she would have the property. This seemingly insignificant acreage was more than an entry in Dudley's portfolio. It wasn't intended as an annual loss to offset the US tax burden, as Elias had surmised.

"And then," she continued. "There is the stock in at least a dozen Fortune 500 hundred companies. And, yes, the family holdings. Hotels and shopping centers, petrol stations scattered across the continent. There's a pub in Dublin and a glove and shoe factory in Italy. Shall I go on? My attorney will be along shortly with a more complete list."

"Your attorney?"

Andrea turned to face Cohen for the first time. As she scrutinized his face she paused to recall how she had happened to select him as her attorney. Her mother, Sybil had touted his skills. When would she ever learn to stop trusting her mother?

In the last hour Elias had assured her that incompetence at Cohen's level suggested complicity. For all that thought implied Andrea had not wanted to believe it was true. Was Cohen paid off by Dudley? Was he part of what Dudley referred to generally as the family, the network, the firm? There was no other explanation. A penchant for secrecy was so crafted into Dudley's life that she had finally decided she did not, now nor ever, truly know him.

Cohen interrupted her thoughts. "I think you owe me an explanation," he said, his tone impertinent.

"You're fired, Mr. Cohen. Send me a heavily discounted bill and I'll take care of it. Otherwise I may decide to have you disbarred."

"What? I don't understand. You need me. If you've found concealed assets we'll negotiate the changes. And you can keep the jewelry."

Andrea was incensed. She turned and gave him a look of disbelief. "Are you telling me that you've disregarded my instructions and conceded the jewelry to Dudley in what you hoped would be a final settlement?"

In a rare failure of self-control Andrea, lifted the stack of papers and scattered them down the length of the table. "When did you plan on telling me? Or was I just going to discover this as we paged through the settlement?"

"But..."

"You're fired! I'm letting you go. I've hired someone else. Is that clear enough for you?"

He leveled a stare at her. "Wasting time is not something I like, Mrs. Wodsende. You'll get a bill from me and there won't be any discount."

"Be careful Mr. Cohen. I know my husband and it is not unreasonable to suggest that Dudley has already paid you, or that these sharks are in on it."

"That's enough," Marstead interrupted. He gestured to the co-worker nearest the door who, having perceived the inevitable outcome, stood to escort Cohen from the room.

As he left, Elias walked in. His step was brisk, his smile calculated to disarm. He greeted Andrea with a look of solicitous concern.

"Are you doing alright?" he asked. "Someone pour my client a glass of water. She looks a little peaked," as my southern grandmother used to say. He waited as a cool glass of water was deposited at Andrea's elbow, waiting to speak until she had taken a first sip. With deliberate care he removed his coat and cashmere scarf and sat, before taking the time to arrange his papers, making it a kind of extended ceremony to open his laptop, placing a calculator on the table with a thud.

Andrea was amused. She could feel suspicion mount from the other side of the table.

"Andie," Elias addressed her, "do you need anything more? The Marstead firm is known for their hospitality and I'm sure they would want you to be comfortable."

For the first time in days Andrea smiled, knowing that Dudley's growing concern was piqued by the use of the childhood name he hated. She finally had intelligent representation. She felt fortunate that the private detective had found him. And luckier still that Elias Goldfarb was willing to delve into her case, working through the night, even before he had confirmation that she would hire him.

It was all so remarkable really, and then it occurred to her. This had nothing to do with luck. God was watching out for her? Under the table she opened clenched fists locked tight with stress. She spread her fingers and imagined that a personal God she couldn't see held on tight.

"Now gentlemen, shall we get down to business?" Elias reached for four deceptively thin folders. He placed one in front of Andrea and slid another across the table to Marstead; acting as if the posse arranged two to a side, with Marstead and Dudley between them, was invisible. As though an afterthought, he looked at Dudley. "You'll need this," he said handing over the last copy.

Elias addressed Marstead. "I understand your client is committed to a wedding in Milan and honeymoon in the south of France, so we'd better get started."

There was a stunned delay as Marstead opened the jacket and scanned the pages. Dudley was finished first. Andrea knew he read with remarkable speed, with nearly flawless comprehension.

Dudley leaned forward, almost standing. He placed the palms of his hands on the table. Andrea lifted her head and looked back, holding his gaze with a new found confidence, though fully aware that unimpeded he would have traversed the narrow space between them, attacking her with more violence than she had previously experienced.

Dudley would control himself only because he must. Obsessed with a public image, only those he claimed to love would ever see the dangerous truth.

"I think we could all use a break," Marstead said. "We'll order lunch and have time to confer with our respective clients. We can find a vacant office for you, Elias."

"Andie and I have already conferred. So please, review our terms. I think you'll find the proposal fair."

"No need, Elias. I'm sure we can find an empty office for you and deliver lunch there. I've already canceled my morning appointments and hope to finish in time to meet the afternoon's obligations."

"I suggest you clear the afternoon. I've called the club for a table with a special view so Andie can admire that yacht she has so graciously conceded to your client. And who knows," Elias remarked with false gaiety, "she might actually change her mind."

Andrea leaned over and whispered in his ear. As she did so, she felt wary eyes on her.

"There will be one small adjustment to the proposal you have before you." Elias spoke with cool indifference, jotting a note in pencil on the margin of his own document as he spoke. "Mrs. Wodsende would like the property in Woods End."

For the first time Elias spoke directly to Dudley. "I understand you've been blindsided, Dr. Wodsende. This is all a shock to you, so take all the time you want. We can make good use of any and all delay. I want you to understand that given your history, a judge will be issuing an order of protection on behalf of my client." Elias shifted his attention back to Marstead. "If a standard order of protection is an unfamiliar document to your client, please explain it to him."

Dudley stood abruptly, the chair flying out behind him. "Oh, this WILL be settled today. The sooner I'm free of that..." He stopped himself. "Settle it today," he demanded and glared at Marstead. "If you hadn't let us argue about the stupid jewelry this would be done. Settle it!" he demanded again and glared at Marstead before striding from the room.

Andrea understood that Dudley felt compelled to shift blame. In all the years of their marriage he had never said he was sorry or taken minimal responsibility for anything that went wrong. Andrea understood what was coming and almost felt sorry for Marstead. He would become a handy scapegoat for Dudley's violent temperament.

"As we review these documents and reconvene after lunch, I want you to consider one point that your client may have deliberately withheld from you," Marstead volleyed back.

Andrea turned to Elias. "He's talking about the baby Dudley wanted us to have. I just didn't feel our home would be a safe place to raise a child. I wanted to wait, and this is the reason Cohen said I couldn't get a better settlement."

Elias covered her hand, letting her know she didn't need to reply.

"And Mrs. Wodsende deceived my client further when she concealed the fact that she was secretly practicing birth control. This betrayal was extremely painful to a man whose one ambition in life is to be a father."

"Nothing changes," Elias stated simply. "This isn't the first century. Women aren't chattel. And I'd say that close scrutiny of the husband will only prove my client wise for deciding it wasn't safe to bring a baby into this marriage. Further delay means more time to investigate. My client has chosen not to go that route as long as her settlement is generous and not the mere pittance of the current terms."

Elias had thrown down the gauntlet. The message was received, but Andrea was thinking of Dudley. He was gone from the room, and yet an energy left in the wake of his anger remained. It was a bleak and familiar oppression that seemed to poison the very air. Andrea did her best to quell the fear that gripped her, knowing that until she had proof that his vessel had entered international waters, she would sleep with a gun under her pillow.

As Elias and Marstead continued their discussion she rested both hands on her thighs, turning palms up. She needed to experience God's peace; the reality of His sanctuary. A calm assurance filled her and then mysteriously, words she had read only a few times and made no attempt to memorize filled her mind. ***Fear thou not; for I am with thee; be not dismayed; for I am thy God: I will strength thee; yea, I will help thee; yea, I will uphold thee with the right hand of my righteousness (Isaiah 41: 10).***

Andrea watched as feather tips of delicate frost grew between the panes of the industrial strength window, an artful pattern of encroachment against the brightening lights of the city. She felt distracted and restless, and wanted the meeting to end so she could retreat to think and ponder the seemingly impossible turn of events.

Finally they gathered at the door. As Elias held her coat, Marstead made one final, very curious offer. Still refusing to address Andrea directly, he spoke to Elias.

"My client would like to take the Woods End holding off your hands." He went on to report the property poorly maintained with no road access other than a narrow lane that flooded each spring. The mail box was a quarter mile down the drive. Recent tenants had not been able to tolerate the isolation, and abruptly vacated the premises.

Elias pointed out, "There's no mortgage and the taxes are up to date."

"I'm authorized to offer twenty percent above market value."

"My client has no plans to sell anything she hasn't seen. She may or may not get back to you on this."

"What if I offered thirty percent over?" Marstead persisted. "In a depressed market you couldn't hope to do better."

Elias turned to Andrea. "What do you think?"

"Why does Dudley care so much?" she asked.

"Sentimental value I imagine. The farm belongs in the family and I represent them as well. Periodic reunions are held on that site when they can manage to gather. So you see, this is not just Dr. Wodsende making a request, it's his family as well."

"Really?" Andrea was even more intrigued. If a family reunion had taken place during their marriage, Dudley had failed to invite her, although she had often expressed a desire to meet and know his relatives.

"And it would be good to extend the olive branch, don't you agree?" Marstead addressed Andrea directly for the very first time that day. "Perhaps the two of you will end up friends?" His smile was a fixed, robot-like slash across his face and Andrea was reminded of Dudley's sardonic comment that Marstead was always available because he never slept. In spite of herself Andrea shivered.

As Elias appeared to ponder the request, Andrea felt a sudden kinship with him knowing that they shared the same suspicion. She noted a gray pallor beneath Marstead's artificial tan as he awaited their answer. This property mattered. There was significance to its ownership that she didn't understand. Andrea could well imagine the vicious manner that Dudley would have berated his attorney for its loss, having experienced that same verbal abuse herself.

"Entirely up to you, my dear," Elias spoke. "But I don't recommend a quick decision. The divorce has been traumatic and you need time. Rule of thumb; don't make any decisions for at least a year. I tell you what," he now turned to Marstead, throwing him a bone. "If she does decide to sell, she'll give your client first right of refusal."

"I'd like that in writing."

"Of course."

"I'm glad to know the place is habitable. I just might decide to live there," Andrea asserted.

"Not for long..."

Marstead's whisper was a snicker of threatening malice. Andrea looked for Elias, but he was halfway to the door and hadn't heard.

By the time Andrea stepped between the Court Street traffic, retracing the same route that had first brought her to Marstead's office early that morning, she had nearly convinced herself she hadn't heard correctly.

WOOD'S END

CHAPTER THREE

Henry Capra was better looking at fifty, for the white hair and distinguished features, than he'd ever been in his twenties. Following the cult's diversionary strategy for some siblings and not others he had legally adopted a distant family name.

Not athletically inclined, Judge Capra forced himself to exercise and took pride in the result. As he left customs, he shifted his wallet to an inside pocket so as to derail the thieves rampant in the congestion of the common areas of Charles De Gaulle Airport. Except for a valise, stored in an overhead compartment, he had traveled without luggage. As he bypassed baggage claim he thought back to the start of his trip. He had driven through the near empty streets of Boston when his cell phone rang.

"We'll need you on stand-by all day Monday. Andrea and her attorney will be coming by the office to sign the necessary papers. You'll be available to grant the divorce so Dudley can depart as scheduled."

This was not in any way a request. Henry distrusted Marstead almost as much as he did his brother, Dudley, but could not afford the more honest emotion of outright hatred.

"No problem," he said, cell phone pressed to his ear. "As you've already instructed, I've cleared my calendar. Call this line when you're ready for me, I'll be waiting," Henry lied, taking perverse satisfaction in the knowledge that come Monday morning he would not be in the country. Nothing short of the perfect storm over the Atlantic would keep him from this other, so long anticipated juncture of his own. A meeting that no member of his family must suspect had ever taken place.

"Drop me anywhere on the Rue des Barres."

"The Church Saint-Gervais?" his driver replied in English.

"Any corner will do." Despite the flawless French, Henry was glad to be marked a tourist, and as luck would have it, was dropped a mere six blocks from the agreed upon destination.

The elder son arrived first. Henry recognized the angular military-like bearing that had been equally the province of a seven year old. The emotion that besieged him was unexpected and not at all welcome. He willed the tear away with fierce resolve. Mario, still pudgy as though he'd never shed his baby fat, emerged from a doorway where he'd watched the street from a second floor window. Henry had noted the furtive movement at the window, an amateur mistake he himself would never make. His sons had a lot to learn and no time to learn it.

Henry drained the last sip of coffee augmented with whiskey from a miniature airline bottle and ordered another, palming the waiter a hefty tip to reserve his seat and its excellent view of the street until his return. Within minutes he would greet the children he hadn't laid eyes on in twenty-five years. A rush of tenderness, the capacity for which he thought long dead, ambushed him. He was excited yet reluctant, fragile in the face of this long-delayed, bittersweet juncture.

They had never said goodbye. By tacit agreement, in silent communication, his wife had intimated her plans so as to protect him in her rebellion. Playing his part, Henry chose to ignore the signs of preparation. Only when her going was a fact accompli' did he act the outraged husband, bewildered and grieving to a chorus of hypercritical commiseration, which, from that point on and despite family connections, marked him persona non grate.

His boys had called this meeting. *His boys...* Henry tried out the unfamiliar phrase. They were strangers to him now. Guido would be thirty-two and Mario twenty-eight, but in

Henry's atrophied, love-starved memory they remained as he had last seen them.

The three came together at the inner courtyard, with tourists passing to see the famed organ, of which no one in this company was at all interested.

"I remember you," Mario said. "I wasn't sure I would."

"You were only four. Guido seven. Guido remembers. I hope kindly."

"You let us go," Guido replied. "Proof enough that you loved us. Mother remembered you fondly."

"More than I deserve."

Guido acknowledged his father's admission with a nod of his head. "We made a promise to her that if it ever came to this, we would meet you one last time."

"We've connected with quite a few of the others," Mario interjected. "There is a whole network out there. It makes me angry to hear them speak of the childhood we were spared."

"Damaged children, damaged adults. They have always effectively neutralized any threat from that quarter," Henry dismissed.

"You might be surprised," Guido contradicted. "Many have recovered their mental and physical health. Don't underestimate the power of Christ to heal the deepest wounds."

"Spoken like a true prince of the Church. Or is this merely a disguise?" Henry had adopted the deprecating tone of learned prejudice as he gestured to Guido's black trousers and shirt with the starched clerical collar in a show of contempt.

"They found Guido in Rome," Mario offered getting them back to the purpose of their meeting and onto safer territory. Coming had not been Mario's idea. He had suggested to his elder brother that they could be walking into a trap.

As a chef, working quietly in an inauspicious restaurant, Mario might have remained undetected and lived a quite normal existence. He'd been reasonably happy and since eighteen had lived with a girlfriend and their child. They had recently decided to marry, but here he was getting ready to leave her forever. In doing so he was abandoning the child he loved. History was repeating itself, but if Guido could be entirely believed, they had no choice. His son, whose existence remained a secret even to Guido, could only be safe if his father were no longer in the picture.

"So you too are a believer in... Like your mother and brother?" Henry could not bring himself to say the Name.

"Yes, I believe in Jesus Christ." Mario sounded ambivalent. The legacy of a family history he hadn't chosen or created had come to roost and he remained emotionally at war over the necessity to leave behind this other life he'd so carefully crafted.

In stark contrast to his brother, Guido was almost energized by their discovery. He could no longer justify being cocooned in the safety of theological study and practice. There was a wider, more immediate context to what he saw as his calling in life.

For his part, Henry saw the differences between his boys. The one was tested and the other untried. The elder was stalwart and determined, the younger a reluctant passenger. He had sacrificed to give them a life apart from the lineage of Woods End, but in the end he had failed.

Henry unzipped the valise and handed each of his sons a tour guide of Paris. "You'll find an envelope inside with instructions and pass-through to three accounts. You'll find deeds to several properties, and where you can locate ready cash, passports and cyber instructions. As you can see I've prepared for the day when you might need me."

"Blood money," Mario accused.

"Yes, but commandeered for a better purpose. Take it or leave it," Henry replied without betraying his fear for them if they rejected his offer.

"We'll take it," Guido asserted.

"In helping us you've helped your enemies," Mario reminded his father.

"Yes," Henry looked between his sons. He thought them both remarkable, each in his own way, and felt a surge of pride. And yet, he was very worried for them; certain they were inadequate for the challenges ahead.

"Others have been the way that you are going and it didn't work out as planned. So, maybe you could use a dose of reality. Ask yourself; where are these dissenters? Brought back and sacrificed. In jail, homeless or hopelessly addicted. Dead prematurely from a viral brain tumor or mentally ill. Damaged goods, their ravings considered symptomatic of psychosis. Many have multiple personality disorder with alters programmed to self destruct. Every tidbit of worthwhile information so marginalized as to have zero credibility. I can't have that for you. I won't have that!"

"There is a new kind of Christian deliverance that is no longer blind to all this," Guido asserted. "Victims are being restored and healed. Turned from darkness to light."

Henry gestured with a tight little wave of his hand that indicated everywhere and nowhere. "Most people don't recognize our existence. To do so is the last societal taboo of this age. They call us by various names. The architects of a new world order, the illuminati; whatever. Fact is our varied and eclectic activities and peoples defy such a label. I'll do my very best not to give you away, but an Intrinsic will eventually sense a weakness in me and voice a suspicion."

"We'll be praying against that," Guido offered.

"Right now we are safe," Henry continued. "But only because of mass apathy and societal pretensions of tolerance. Safe until the pendulum swings back and we have a moral correction. Comparatively speaking few, if any, epochs of history remain. As countries war the world is blind to the part we play. The dragon time stands panting, a hair breathe from the threshold. It's coming soon."

"You sound as crazy as Mother," Mario's words were laced with bitter sarcasm.

Henry regarded his youngest son in cold appraisal. Mario had secretly harbored expectations of a different outcome; that Henry would play the caring father, the benevolent benefactor, making the inconvenience of all this drama disappear. Henry understood. Aside from wanting his life back, Mario hoped even more to experience, in the fulfillment of these unrealistic expectations, an appeasement of the deep wound wrought by paternal abandonment.

"You pity yourself because I echo the same extremist rhetoric as your mother. Son, this normalcy you feel entitled to, with every mundane accoutrement that such a lifestyle could bring, is just another form of enslavement. I want you to appreciate what your mother sacrificed, how she took every risk that you would be safe and your mind free from programmed controls, to think and determine for yourself."

Mario looked down at his feet. His face had reddened and his fists clenched, but he remained silent.

"From now on that's over. Consider yourself a combatant deep in enemy territory, in a foreign land that has never and will never be your home."

"Such irony... I couldn't have said it better myself," Guido whispered.

But if Henry heard his eldest son, there was no indication. There was something more he must say. The words would be inadequate, stilted. He had such a longing in that moment to tell them the full story of their mother's life, tell them that she was the only person he had ever loved and that in return her love had given him the strength to fight for their escape and survival. But they had minutes and not hours, they had the destitute absence of lives not lived together in all the hushed breadth of what had never been.

"It would be the height of foolishness to imagine that because your mother kept you both safe and undetected, you can easily do the same."

An image flashed to Henry's mind. A picture of what he had avoided thinking of for many years. His wife, her long blonde hair falling wet over her shoulders for the exertion of giving birth. He'd handed over the slippery infant, tiny arms flailing into waiting arms. She had held the infant close, her blue eyes locked with his. She loved her baby instantly, loved him completely and when she lifted her face to his, wordless volumes were communicated and he knew. He would either have to kill her or join her in seeing his family free.

"Your mother was the exception and not the rule. She was forced into the families' enslavement as a young adult. They lacked control of her mind and heart."

So as not to stand out they had slowly migrated to an alcove off the nave. A company of tourists passed the entry and Henry turned to gesture as if giving the two directions. Now his voice was sedate, even sad.

"When you finally leave for good, don't forget. Those you have known must have a plausible explanation; a little truth mixed with fiction. Well meaning associates and friends can be your undoing. Suspicious of an abrupt departure they will unwittingly partner in finding you."

"We've covered that," Guido stated.

"And you must walk out together. One does not linger and endanger the other. Just when you get comfortable, a search will be revived. There are agents, we call them vassals, whose only job is to look for children and adults that have disappeared. Their persistence located Guido and then you Mario, who at least was wise enough to choose a less visible profession."

Henry looked into Guido's eyes. It was a penetrating assault that turned most people off, but left Guido unperturbed.

"Perhaps you would say that being a minister of that other book, is not a mere profession," he probed, wishing that he did not feel a surge of revulsion, that he could see his son only, and not the combatant authority the cross about his neck represented. Several tourists had passed and muttered the requisite, "hello Father," and each time Henry had inwardly winced. "Am I right?" Henry persisted.

Silence carried Guido's answer, an imprint of words more complete than any verbal expression. As an exorcist Guido had stepped into a strong conceptual control of his gift, able to discern through empathic pathways the substantive condition of a human soul, the activity of angels and demons, and God's timing for deliverance.

What the Holy Spirit showed Guido about his father, gave reason to hope. Henry had mounted a quiet, if not passive aggressive rebellion, tested in the unselfish relinquishment of his wife and children. Constrained by the powerful entanglements of a cult he had managed to preserve the sanctity of self so that he might stand at this juncture, offering practical tools and resources that his boys might escape his fate.

On Henry's part, it was a shock that a son of his would choose to take holy orders. That Guido could summon the independence to make such a choice brought into question much of what Henry had been taught to accept as fact. And yet, that very choice invited a level of warfare that he and his wife had hoped their children might escape.

"You might have chosen a less visible career," Henry said. "They hide in the church and you know this very well. Every denomination and sect has their cadre. What you are and what you escaped was marked by spirits and whispered into the minds of marked vassals. You were bound to command attention sooner or later. But you know all this."

"Come with us," Mario interrupted, uncomfortable with the turn of conversation, and saving his brother the trouble of a reply.

Henry was moved. He opened the guide book and buried his head in the pages, concealing a surge of emotion.

"You can never rest," he looked up, a flint-like coldness in his words. "If I wipe the memory of our meeting from my mind, and continue to do my part, you are far safer. It is both harder and easier in this technological age to disappear. I've laid out the steps you must take; the false cyber trails along with instructions; some names and descriptions, the various families and what to watch for. If genuine, the best defense is to be immersed in your kind of prayer. In so doing, a wall of confusion will separate them from you."

Guido nodded his head in agreement.

"I hope your mother told you, you can never have children."

"Then why did you?" Mario challenged thinking of his own son and feeling a prevailing sadness at the loss.

"It's complicated," Henry responded. "Suffice to say your mother and I had no choice. We were brought together as strangers. It was three years before we trusted each other with the ambivalence we felt and more time still for us to lay the groundwork for your escape."

"I don't know," Mario said. "Guido has a vow of celibacy. But with a little time and distance, I'm hoping to build a new identity and start over. I'd like to have a family," he ventured, wishing he could be completely honest.

"Thinking like that will get you or your brother killed. This will never be over unless it dies with the generations. The stain is in your blood. It sings out to those that know it. Even now we are in danger." Henry glanced at his watch. "Anonymity and a few good years to live like other man, that's what I wanted for you."

"It's a lie to think we have any special status," Guido countered. "We're people like everyone else. Trusting in Jesus Christ we've been reborn and if we are to die martyrs so be it. We die in faith under the covering of His blood."

"I thought Dudley was chosen. It's through him," Mario spoke in a rush, ignoring his brother, hoping to extricate his fate from this amalgam of craziness.

"Could be Dudley or it could be through me. Dudley married the carefully selected host. He married Andrea, but those plans have gone seriously awry. Their union was to be legal. A proper birth with the appearance of a traditional marriage. The issue of that union would step into unprecedented wealth and privilege with all the combined power of the various families behind him. All this in deliberate contrast to that other that came over 2000 years ago. He was born to a peasant and lived in poverty. The Dragon's issue is to be born a prince into the time that will be our own, the inverted side of destiny."

"How can you believe all this?" Mario questioned.

"It doesn't matter what I believe. They believe it. Your own Bible foretells much of what is coming. You asked me a question and I'm explaining. The battle begun in the third dimension; the third Heaven will have no equal to what man will suffer when the Dragon rules earth.

"Go on," Guido invited placing a hand on his brother's shoulder, both to quiet and to comfort him.

"For now, all the other progeny are dead, and if they decide they're wrong about Dudley, if something goes awry with these delicate plans, they'll not look to an old man like me. They blame me for your loss. But even so, I am considered more than a man, tolerated because I am a direct woods-son descendant and Dudley's elder brother. If Dudley fails to fulfill the promise, Marstead has only one choice. He will look to one of you."

"Why?" Mario asked.

"Because, as the real head of our family sect Marstead has never been confident of Dudley. Your uncle is reckless. He's too much trouble. Whatever you do, do not have children."

"And then again," Guido deflected. "It may be one of the other families. It may be a sect in Eastern Europe or the Middle East from which this son of perdition will be birthed. It's the height of arrogance to be so wrapped up in family lore. I've studied Bible Prophecy which has shown me a very different outcome."

They separated with no further show of emotion. Mario followed a line of tourists to view the organ. Guido gravitated toward the altar where he knelt to light a candle. Henry walked to the café and reclaimed his seat with its view to the street. It was Guido who passed his way.

"You may have to separate from Mario. He's too unsure."

"Not an option."

Henry didn't reply. There was no need since Guido had already moved off. His son had dropped something on the table. Henry looked down. Guido's clerical collar sat next to his napkin, a white and shinning stain, a clear message. All the preparations for going had been accomplished. Seeing their father was the last task in fulfillment of a promise made to their mother, and even now they were slipping beyond the pale of normal life.

Henry felt a profound pride mingled with admiration. For mere seconds, before doing his best to bleach the memory from his mind, he savored the name like a glass of fine wine. Each had called him, 'father.'

After a suitable delay, Henry walked to the lavatory. Disposing of the clothes he'd arrived in, he donned a sweater and slacks. With valise in hand he joined the crowd on the sidewalk, heading for the underground and taking the train random stops in the general direction of the airport.

In scanning his phone messages, Henry saw that there was nothing from Marstead. Something had happened to frustrate Marstead's plans to be quickly free of Andrea. By some fluke he couldn't explain, by some twist of seemingly random events back at the Marstead firm, it looked to Henry that he would be sitting at his desk in the courthouse on Tuesday morning with no one the wiser.

This begged the question. Did that mean Guido's God had power over his god?

Not until take-off did Henry begin to relax. His thoughts turned to his half brother and their sister, Sybil. In the twist of what had just transpired, there was a kind of thwarted revenge finally realized. Dudley, who had ascended to a position of highest authority, would never have his boys. They would never be robot minions to command as Sybil was. They would not be tokens of sacrifice, awaiting their intended use, as the child, Andie Rose had been slated to be. Nor would they ever challenge Dudley's position, inviting a battle and possible early death at the hands of hedonistic vassals.

The plane had leveled off. A stewardess made her way through the first class cabin. Henry ordered a gin and tonic and watched as she deposited the drink before him. Outside the window, cumulus configurations deepened to shades of lilac and pink tinged with a grayish purple at the outer ends. In the far distance the last rays of light streamed out from that point where the sun would soon dip beneath the horizon.

Tension uncoiled its grip like a physical thing. From deep inside there was a letting go and then something foreign, not experienced in many long years. Henry Capra, born Henry Woods to the clacking of bones and the scream of the sacrifice in a pagan rite on Hallows Eve morn, at Woods End Farm, felt good.

WOOD'S END

CHAPTER FOUR

Elias Goldfarb did not handle family law, and the next day made arrangements for a colleague to preside over the last death grip of Andrea's marriage to Dr. Dudley Wodsende. As they said good bye, he was touched by the tears in her eyes.

The divorce had not taken place as originally planned. Dudley was forced to postpone his wedding and Andrea had a little more time to consider her husband's strange attachment to the farm nestled at the foot of the Berkshire Mountains.

Andrea called her friend, Julie, from the car. "I'll be in town within the hour. What are you doing today?"

Andrea and Julie had graduated from North Adams High together. Their friendship persevered even when Andrea and her mother had moved away, only to return to the same locale several times in succeeding years. Each time, the girls were separated and met again; it was as if they picked up right where they left off. Now that they were adults the pattern had continued.

"I hope I'll be showing houses, my legitimate occupation. You want to meet for lunch?" Julie asked.

"You won't believe this, but it seems that I'm suddenly the proud owner of a house in Woods End. I thought maybe you could meet me there and let me know what I should do with the place. I've already had an offer to sell back to Dudley, so I could use a little professional expertise."

Julie was curious. Woods End was a tiny hamlet not far from Adams. She considered it part of her marketing area. "Which house is it?"

It's about five miles off Ridge Road. I looked it up and there are four or five other houses along that route, but mine is set well back with its own access. It was formally a working farm."

"Can't be."

"Can't be what?" Andrea asked.

"I say take the offer and run. If it's the house I'm thinking of, no good can come from living there. Do you have keys?"

"Of course I have keys. I own the place," Andrea smiled to herself. "The divorce was just made final and I have all the papers to prove it."

"Congratulations. I told you not to marry that bum. Remember what I said? He's crazy. Remember?"

"Yes. I remember. If evil is crazy that would sum up his personality."

"I'm glad to hear you finally admit it. That stubborn loyalty of yours has to stop. How about this? I'll meet you at the end of the drive in about forty minutes. It's so overgrown you'll miss the turn without help."

"Thanks. I look forward to seeing you," Andrea said.

"Apple Orchards."

"What?" Andrea asked.

"At one time they had an orchard. The trees are old, but still there, and beautiful in spring. You can see them from the ridge, and that famous artist from here... Burns Padgett Shiel was his name; he painted the orchard several times. One of the series is at the Adams Public Library. He donated it before his death and provides the insurance coverage through his foundation for as long as they keep it."

"How do you know all this?"

"I stayed home remember. You went off to Boston and I was smart enough to stay right here."

"A famous artist painted my orchard. How charming is that?"

"Trust me.   There is nothing charming about the old Woods place."

"Woods? As in Wodsende? Dudley's attorney said it had been in the family for generations."

"I wouldn't know. It's just what people have called that old farm. My grandmother warned me off. 'Don't go near the old Wood's place,' she would say. It doesn't surprise me that Dudley is related to that family. They called the last man who lived there a devil."

It had snowed during the night.   Dense flakes accumulated at the foundation of abandoned farm buildings and clustered in the angle of wet, barren branches. Following Ridge Road, no longer the Mahican Indian trace it had once been, Andrea scanned the roadside for Julie's white SUV.   Sounding her horn she pulled up behind.   Julie motioned for her to follow; banking a sharp left into what seemed more a well used bridle path than an actual drive.

Almost immediately, access to the ridge road disappeared in her rearview mirror, and Andrea found that the vehicles were hemmed in by a fortress of fir trees. By design or ignorance, the trees were spaced too close together to have grown as healthy and green as they appeared. Squinting into the tree line, it seemed they stood three deep in a parallel line to both sides of the drive with the taller maple, oak, and birch of the wood rising above.

The sharp report of what might have been a hunter's rifle reverberated through the car and seconds later, echoed to stillness.   Andrea jumped, braking to a sharp stop as an avalanche of snow cast the interior into near blackness.

In a stifling wave of claustrophobia she fumbled to open the passenger side window sending a wall of snow, momentarily suspended in place, into the interior of the car. Andrea pushed open the door and breathed in the dry winter air attempting to calm her racing heart. A tree limb had snapped under the weight of new snow and she could see the spider branches of fir spread like fingers over the drive behind.

Up ahead the white SUV had stopped. Julie seemed unperturbed, but Andrea could not dispel a sense of disaster only temporarily avoided. Although her impression seemed utterly ridiculous, she assigned hostile intent to this stretch of wood, and as she drove the car forward she began to search for an opening in which to reverse direction.

Reflecting in later years, she was certain that if she had found that opening, she would have left the farm and not looked back. But trapped in the thrall of a frightening first impression, she told herself that Julie was right. She didn't belong here.

The cars emerged from the darkness of the wood into a clearing and as suddenly as she had felt fear and hostility from her environment she now felt a kind of kindred ease. As though nature were heralding her arrival, the cloud cover lifted, and the scene before her was flooded in a warm golden light. The tightness of her muscles relaxed and she sighed deeply. She was home.

Andrea drank in the details, having immediately fallen in love with the deep angular porch with the fieldstone pillars. This was her porch, the porch she had imagined and always wanted. Inside the clearing the drive was rimmed with a low stone wall, which would be covered in summer with clumps of honeysuckle, and off to the northwest, where the clouds had moved, the slope of Greylock Peak just visible.

As she and Julie exited the cars, Andrea tried to imagine the summer landscape. Her eyes fell over the canopied trellis that sheltered the walk and the twists of old growth that someone had failed to prune in fall.

"What color are those roses when they're in bloom?" she asked turning to her friend as they paused to unlatch the gate.

"I have no idea. As far as I know the old Wood's Place has never been on the market. What do you think so far?" She asked Andrea.

"I love it, but..."

"I know!"

Andrea took a few steps toward the porch and the front door, but Julie took her arm and led her around the side of the house.

"I know what you're feeling. It's creepy, don't you think?"

"No, I think it's charming. I'm just wondering what repairs may be needed for such an old house, and if Dudley kept up with things."

"It's a dump. I don't know how much money you've ended up with, but I can say that the repairs are nearly constant with a house this old. As you can see, there is no clear access to and from the road. You'll have to start by clearing those trees, widening the drive, fixing the bridge, and laying down several tons of gravel. Since services were consolidated, the mail no longer comes here. You'd have to get a post office box."

"Well if you don't mind, I'll take a look for myself."

As she followed Julie around the side of the house, Andrea could almost understand why Dudley had been so intent on keeping this property? Come summer, she could see herself rocking in the porch swing, dozing in the shade with a book on her lap, and Charlie, her Doberman, curled into sleep at her feet.

Taking Elias' advice, Andrea decided to postpone her plan of opening an antique shop. She felt emotionally drained and needed a little rest and relaxation, and this property would provide all the excuse she needed.

That morning, as she prepared to leave for Woods End, she phoned her mother to break the news. Sybil had latched onto the idea of running the antique shop while her daughter combed the world for expensive inventory. Andrea could not trust her mother to feed her dog when she was away overnight, and so knew such an idea was preposterous. The reckoning was overdue, although she always hesitated to incur her mother's brand of sarcastic anger, which tended to include a delayed punch or two arriving when she was feeling especially low and vulnerable.

"Change of plans, Sybil. I've decided to take a year off and consider my options," she announced without fanfare.

"The shop was just a romantic notion and at least right now I don't have the motivation. I may do some writing, but that's it."

"Well! This is certainly a disappointment. I guess it was that new lawyer, that Jew," she spit the word out as if it were particularly distasteful. "I guess he gave you this advice"

"He did, as a matter of fact, and he's been a godsend. I'd appreciate it if you would be respectful of him."

"I imagined myself the proprietor of a nice shop with lots of money coming in," Sybil continued as if she hadn't heard the reprimand.

"I'm driving over to Berkshire County this morning. I want to see what kind of shape the house at Woods End is in. I might decide to live there."

"Are you crazy?" Sybil erupted. "Get back in the saddle. That's what I say. Put that fancy college education to work and forget Woods End. Why would you choose to go back to Berkshire County anyway? We hated that place."

"You hated it. I have many fond memories."

"If only you'd given Dudley a son. Then you might have gotten more money from that husband of yours. How much did you get anyway?"

Andrea had been careful not to let her mother know any details about her more than adequate settlement. Her mother's incessant need for funds would too often magically coincide with whatever those around her happened to have on hand.

"Are you listening to me?" The shrill demand was a startling blast from the past, reminding Andrea of the emergency broadcasting signal that interrupted a good program. As intended, the screech jolted her nerves.

"Yes, Mother."

"Pay attention, baby girl. Men may stray, but when children are in the picture, we can usually force them back. It might not be too late, Andie. You could get pregnant. Make a nice candlelight dinner and..."

Andrea couldn't help but chuckle. "Mother, Dudley has just left for his honeymoon."

"I never give up and you shouldn't either. And I have no family money to leave my only daughter." This last was a plaintive whine.

Yeah, Andrea thought to herself. *And you were counting on me taking care of you so you could continue making the requisite number of trips to the casino each month. With my rich doctor husband out of the picture who will subsidize your losses? Certainly not him! Good riddance!*

Sybil had frequently asked Dudley for "a little extra" to tide her over and he had always accommodated. After her mother's first visit to their home in Boston, where she had managed to extend her stay nearly a month, Dudley had gotten in the habit of offering Sybil a seasonal cruise each year to keep her out of their lives.

It was fortunate for Dudley that Sybil soon met her fifth husband who suffered from advancing emphysema, but with two smart daughters who hated Sybil, fearing that he would die and leave her all his money.

Not that there was much left. Sybil had been systematically raiding his retirement accounts until her step-daughters threatened legal action. Sybil confided that oxygen depletion had dulled her husband's senses. He was soon in the habit of signing almost anything she put in front of him, and the daughters were agitating for power of attorney. This latest crisis had given Andrea a reprieve of sorts from her mother's nagging attentions.

While still quite young, Andrea realized there was not much to like about her mother. Once she'd been given a nosegay of tea roses by one of Sybil's many boyfriends. "Andie Rose... You're as pretty as these posies" he said and Andrea had smiled. Later she asked Sybil, "Did you name me Andrea Rose after these flowers?" In those days she was still hopeful.

"Well of course not. Whatever possessed you of such a thought," was the curt reply. "I always hated that name, but I thought if I named you after Clarence's mother, she might get attached and leave me a little money. That old fart didn't leave me a penny, although she did leave you enough for college, but fixed it so I couldn't touch a penny; not even to feed and clothe my only child." Sybil spoke in a rush, her words streaming together. "I should have named you Clarence. She worshiped that jerk."

"Was Clarence my Daddy?"

"No dear, and don't ask again. You know I don't like to think about what's past. You know what I always say. What do I always say, dear?"

"Don't bring up the past."

"Very good. Not unless you want Sybil to get depressed and take it out on you... Do you want that, dear?"

"No."

"Alright then. Shuuut up!"

In the beginning Andrea appreciated how Dudley kept her mother at a distance. A special ring alerted them to all calls originating from Sybil's place of residence. Most were timed during dinner and they would now, he explained, intrude less. But Andrea came to see that this was his way of controlling their relationship. Was this why she had finally agreed to marry Dudley? He was just arrogant enough to take on her mother's toxic personality and win.

Andrea found it intriguing that her mother, who had an underlying disdain for men, seeing them primarily as a means to an end had clearly worshipped Dudley. And it wasn't just his money. Andrea had been astonished to see the softening of her mother's expression when she looked at him, how she stood as close as she possibly could when they talked. That Dudley hated Sybil was no secret. Sybil knew, but liked him anyway. The contempt in which she held most people just didn't exist where her son-in-law was concerned.

In the beginning of her marriage Andrea had felt grateful to have her mother out of the picture. She liked being taken care of. Dudley was interested in how she looked, and helped choose her clothes and paid for a full-days, weekly visit to the spa, for the kind of pampering she didn't know existed.

In some way that she could not yet express, all his apparent caring seemed to appease the ache of childhood neglect. But at the time she hadn't understood this. At the time she didn't want to see it all that clearly. Above all, Andrea wanted something her mother had never had. She wanted a successful marriage.

Andrea had always made the time to write. This provided just the requisite amount of depersonalization, as she assigned fictional characters all kinds of displaced trauma. In that curious mix of escape and compulsion, sometimes with tears streaming down her cheeks, she felt better for what she'd put on paper. Writing was a panacea, and after what she had been through with Dudley, there was much that begged for form by way of heavy black words against the stark comfort of her computer screen.

In the beginning she hadn't been much interested in Dudley. It wasn't until he followed her home for a visit and had taken an instant dislike to her mother, who had hugely approved of his charm that Andrea began to change her mind.

"Snatch him up while you can," her mother had asserted. "Lord knows what he sees in you, but he's rich enough for both of us."

For his part, Dudley had been appalled by Sybil in a way that bordered on fascination. In his mind, Sybil became the reason that Andrea needed rescuing. Andrea didn't agree, but for some inexplicable reason, and against her better judgment, she had indulged a brief hiatus of passivity. Putting her brain on idle was not smart and yet, just maybe, dangerously familiar.

Yes, dangerously familiar. So now she had to wonder. What was it about abdicating control under the guise of rescue that had appealed to her in the first place? She wasn't a child anymore. Those were the years that had demanded the appearance of complacency in the trade for survival. In those years she needed a rescue that never came.

When she confided bits of her childhood to Dudley, he had raged at Sybil and even, she thought, overreacted, since what she did share was far from the worst of it. Her new husband had put his arm around her and she had rested her head in the warm place between his shoulder and the curve of his neck where a stain of red crept upward, toward the base of his skull. The curious mark extended over the top of his head where it settled like the head of a snake just beyond the hair line at his brow. The detailed birth mark, inflicted by random genetics, was not apparent unless one lived with Dudley. Soon Andrea forgot it even existed and especially since Dudley seemed in no way bothered.

She was proud of how he looked. In summer his hair took on blonde highlights and his blue eyes shown with an intensity that captured attention and drew people to him. On that day he had lifted her chin and kissed her nose and said these words, "From now on I'm taking care of you." And that she guessed, in a nutshell, was her answer. No one had ever offered to take care of her and meant it, and in that one moment she was a little girl and Dudley was her savior, everything she had ever needed.

Dudley invited his family to the wedding, but each one sent their regrets. Return cards and letters had curious postmarks like Dharamsala, Tibet; Trabzon, Turkey; Huttenberg, Austria; Zabkowice, Poland; Mekoryuk, Alaska; Perth Australia; and islands she could not locate on any map off the coasts of Ireland, Newfoundland, Bolivia, or Madagascar. This was such an odd confluence of locations, that she saved the envelopes and when she asked Dudley why his family members were scattered in so many diverse places, his only remark was, "business, but they love you darling. They just can't come."

"How can they love me, they don't know me?"

"They trust my infallible judgment." He smiled. "You are perfect and you'll deliver us the perfect child. They hope for a new addition to the family very soon. Preferably a son to carry on the tradition."

"There's plenty of time for that," she responded feeling pressure at his words.

"I'll want us to have a child right away. You shouldn't get much older. You do want a child, don't you Andrea?"

"Just one?" she asked playfully. The one was all he ever alluded to.

"We'll see. Let's have the first and go from there."

As she recalled this exchange, Andrea felt a cold chill. Sybil had been such a terrible mother that Andrea wasn't sure she could risk following her example. Her deepest fear was that this lack of a maternal instinct was inherited and would be an obstacle she couldn't overcome.

Although a fleeting thought at the time, it came into her mind and lodged there like a stone she could not budge, that Sybil liking Dudley so much should have been warning enough that her marriage to him would end badly. But she failed to heed those first stirrings of alarm and she liked the idea that Dudley could be counted on to protect her from her mother's embarrassing antics.

So now that she was free of Dudley, why would she consider moving back to Woods End? Sybil was no more than forty minutes away and would be visiting far too often.

Through the years a new boyfriend, the promise of a new husband, had spurred Sybil to move them away. Then, as life delivered another disappointment, her mother would move them back to the nearby city of North Adams. It had to be a mere coincidence that, through this property in Woods End, there was an inexplicable connection with Dudley long before they actually met. A connection he never disclosed until a seemingly insignificant line was read in a long list of assets uncovered by Elias Goldfarb, and this secret, if in fact it was a secret, was revealed to her.

It seemed to Andrea like fate, a course decreed by factors beyond her control that she would return to Berkshire County. Woods End was nestled near the very edge of the eastern side of the Berkshire Mountain Range and had never thrived or grown beyond the original borders.

"Local historians say this property used to be a gathering spot for the Mahican on their way to the upper waters of the Hoosic and Hudson Rivers, coming or going to the Salt

Springs between," Julie offered as though she had read Andrea's thoughts.

A kind of excitement buoyed Andrea's spirits as she followed Julie toward the back of the house. Maybe this was just the place to heal from the trauma of her failed marriage.

Andrea's beauty queen rival had met Dudley after starting a new job at the hospital. Andrea knew she was divorced with a young child and couldn't help wondering how Dudley would handle a rambunctious child when he could barely tolerate dust on the dining room table. Her own doubts about getting pregnant had been solidified as Dudley's volatile temperament was revealed to her. Any attempt to talk rationally had been met with intense resistance. As he continued to press for a child, she opted for a passive aggressive solution, settling on the pill.

Before the new Mrs. Wodsende quit her job to plan her wedding, they had come face to face as they entered the same hospital elevator. For a moment Stephanie hesitated and Andrea stepped back, creating as much space as possible, feeling she could read the other woman's thoughts. *Can I avoid this? Will she make a scene?*

Andrea could only imagine how Dudley would have characterized their marriage. At the last moment Stephanie straightened her shoulders in resolve and stepped across the threshold for an interminable descent to the lobby. The two women had exchanged stares, but not words, and Andrea was stunned by what she saw.

It wasn't that her replacement was twelve years younger, with breast implants so tight they failed to move when she walked. It wasn't her blond good looks or the tailored clothes or the understated jewelry that was so much her own taste. It was Stephanie's face, which so closely resembled her own that she had to wonder. *Did Dudley pay for that also?*

It was clear from what she had heard that her replacement was the adoring fan, a role that quickly soured for Andrea. They had argued even on their honeymoon. All too quickly Andrea realized that there was no room in the marriage for any personality or will other than Dudley's. By the time she had discovered his infidelity she could only be grateful that they had never had a child together. At least in this her instincts had been dead on.

As Stephanie stepped out of the elevator ahead of her, Andrea realized she wasn't sad to see the marriage end. Rather it was the loss of a dream, the failure implicit in the weight of her poor selection of a lover and a partner that moved her grief to tears.

Andrea stood in the snow and contemplated the back door of her new house. "And we are not going in the front door because?" she asked, inviting an answer.

Julie stopped and looked down at the worn brick path visible in places where the wind had blown the snow away. She seemed puzzled by the question.

"I don't know. I usually usher my clients through the front door with great fanfare, but of course you're not a client. Still I like the impact of that first impression. I imagined we would enter through the front." She hesitated. "I can't explain it."

"That's crazy."

Julie shrugged her shoulders. "I looked up the history. The same family lived here until the 1950's. They were the original English settlers. Through the years they bought up several adjacent farms. The commonwealth wanted to take part of the acreage as a conservation easement, but in the end the farm remained as it always had. I couldn't find any record that Dudley purchased the land, so my guess is he inherited it. At some point he plowed a bunch of money into the place getting it ready to lease, which he did for a limited time."

"There must be a reason for that," Andrea wanted to turn around and march boldly through the front door. She wanted to get that first great impression. She hadn't seen the interior, but she already loved it.

"The original farm house was a one room log cabin with a loft. You can still see evidence in the low rafters over the kitchen. This land was one of the first in Berkshire County formally deeded to settlers after the Indians were moved west. Over there," Julie pointed. "You can make out the foundation of the old barn."

Andrea looked and saw the stubs of black wet timbers evoking the image of a lost city. Tufts of brittle yellow grass poked out of the snow about the edges of the ruined fieldstone foundation.

"You still have the apple orchard I told you about."

"Right, the one painted by Burns Padgett Shiel. Did he live close by?"

"Yes, his farm is still in the family. It's owned by a nephew, who lives in Boston. A police detective I think. Name is Jared Shiel. Woods End is hoping to cash in on the fame and lure tourists to that nearly deserted township by developing the property with a country store and art gallery."

"So he was that famous?"

"His work is in every major museum and nearly every American embassy. During his lifetime two American presidents gave his work as state gifts to heads of other countries. You can't see the orchard he painted from here," Julie continued, "but you do have a view from the bedroom window that is breathtaking in spring."

With odd reluctance Andrea allowed her gaze to be diverted from where the barn had once stood.

"There has been periodic interest by developers in this place, but your husband... former husband, was pretty closed to the idea. I fielded one of those offers and so got to see the inside of the house at the time. I was told by the family's attorney that they would not consider selling. This was before you married him and of course I didn't make the connection or I would have said something to you. Anyway, I was told there was a sentimental attachment to the place."

The two women stood just outside the back door. Off to one side there was a raised concrete slab, perfectly square. Andrea realized that this would cover the old well that in the days before running water would have been placed just near the kitchen. She recognized a separate outbuilding made of fieldstone with two chimneys at either end, reaching far above the sloped roof. This would be the innovation of a detached kitchen and Andrea felt some excitement as she envisioned this charming space converted to a cozy retreat to work away from the temptation of the Washington Journal and the telephone. She did her best writing in the morning.

Andrea looked at Julie. "But you'd prefer I live elsewhere. Why does everyone want me to sell this place and move on? It's beautiful here."

Julie looked at her. "Okay, you've been away for what, twelve years?"

"That's right, ever since I was stupid enough to marry satan right out of college."

Andrea noticed that Julie failed to laugh. Usually when she referred to her former husband as satan, there was one of two responses. Either people laughed, clearly uncomfortable, or they looked at her askance, judging the politically incorrect assignment of that name.

"There was a suicide here."

"Really?"

"Yes, and before that there was a murder. In so far as gossip can be trusted there has been a long string of bad luck for any who live here. The most recent tenant quit this place in the middle of the night and never came back."

"What happened?"

Julie shoved gloved hands deep into the pockets of her all weather coat and shrugged. She shifted a fallen icicle with the toe of her boot. "I asked the property management company... friends of mine. They didn't really know, but let's just say... If you can bring yourself to change your mind I have a listing in the middle of town that would be perfect for you. I'd defer my commission to see you elsewhere."

"That's nice of you, but I like it here."

"I can even call that developer and see if we can revive his interest in the land."

Andrea was intrigued. Perhaps this charming farm house with the mysterious history was just the catalyst she needed to do some serious writing. "So what do people say? Do people think this place is haunted?"

"Actually they do," Julie responded. "When I talked with Mr. Brown, he told me he had seen an apparition walk from where the barn used to be, right up to the front porch. You can ask him yourself. He's your closest neighbor."

"And what do you say?"

Julie hesitated and looked down at the snow. She crushed the icicle under the heel of her boot. "I hate to be negative when you've been through so much, and I'm not superstitious, but if you're still thinking about living here, I'd phone the priest from St. Patrick's in Williamstown and invite him over to bless the place. I hear there's someone new there who knows what he's doing."

Andrea wanted to laugh, but found she couldn't. Julie was perfectly serious and this surprised her.

"Even when Mother and I lived in Berkshire County, I wasn't aware of this property. Were you?" Andrea asked instead, changing the subject.

"Yes, but only a few brave boys would bike down that drive. There has always been this reputation. On Halloween we would tease each other about coming here for candy. I never did."

Andrea shook her head, but could see there was no convincing Julie that she was wrong.

"Let's go." Julie pushed. "Let me show you that cute little house on Elm Street. It has a porch just as nice. Then we'll have lunch and you can tell me all about your divorce and I'll tell you about my new boyfriend."

"I own this property. I'm responsible to take a look so I can make an informed decision," Andrea quoted Elias. "Let's see if there really is a ghost lurking about. I don't believe in them and I refuse to be intimidated if there is."

Julie took her arm. Only in retrospect did Andrea see that Julie was truly uncomfortable. They entered through the mud room. *My goodness*, Andrea thought. She hadn't heard that word used for ages. Along one wall she could see a line of coat hooks secured to the clapboard interior and a square soapstone sink for washing up. She could easily imagine the farm workers filing in for a huge breakfast after already working since dawn. She reached her hand up to touch one of the hooks; then quickly snatched it back.

"See," Julie said. "You feel it to. This place is creepy."

It was true that Andrea had felt something instinctual. Something her rational mind rejected. Perhaps the house didn't want her.

How ridiculous to think such a thing. This is MY house. If I choose to live here I will, she asserted, forgetting her recent experience on the woodland drive.

WOOD'S END

CHAPTER FIVE

Three weeks later Andrea stood on the porch of the near empty house and watched the moving van disappear toward the summer kitchen. She had hired a service to clean every nook and crevice, installed a new furnace, a restaurant quality gas stove, had the hard wood floors refinished and several windows replaced, and was relieved to hear that none of the service people reported feeling or seeing anything strange.

She had fought with Dudley over such foolish incidentals as the dog he hated, the antique dining room table and sixteen chairs hand carved and shipped from England, which were hers after agreeing to give up a cubist painting by a Dutch artist whose name she could never recall. A woman's breast and elbow and the outline of her spine could be made out in an inelegant pose, more disconcerting for what the imagination proposed.

She had once shared her opinion with Dudley, remarking that the artist was hostile to women. "How do you know?" he had asked, for once interested to hear her reply.

She didn't have room for all the dining room chairs and so put the three leafs and four of the chairs in the attic, two others on either side of a console table in the foyer, and two more in bedrooms. She and Dudley had fought over the silver service and the Minton china. She felt exhausted by the whole ordeal and realized now that while the attorneys kept her focused on such details, she had no energy to reflect on the more important issues.

The dog was the last battle ground before Elias got involved. Although he didn't want or like Charlie, Dudley decided he couldn't live without him so Andrea had conceded more artwork and a collection of snuff boxes.

She hadn't expected to like Charlie so much. The dog was Dudley's idea. She had always felt tentative around dogs and imagined table legs chewed to sticks and dog hair everywhere it shouldn't be. It was fortunate for the puppy, as well as Andrea, that Dudley was out of town when the breeder dropped him off. His ears were bandaged with a head frame holding them upright. She smelled the infection and putting her pathetic whining charge in a basket, had taken him to a vet only to discover what she already suspected. One ear was badly infected. The bandages would need to be removed to facilitate healing. Scar tissue rimmed the affected ear so that it lacked the full stand up appearance admired by Doberman aficionados, reducing Charlie's value. When Dudley returned two weeks later the dog was sleeping on a pallet by her side of the bed and the two had formed a permanent bond.

Andrea loved her new home. Survival had forced on her the necessity of ignoring what she had no power to change, so she concentrated on the details. She could walk a worn foot path to the orchard and fish off a stone bridge, arched over clear mountain water. She hired a service to keep the drive and walkways free of snow in winter and another to mow her lawn and revitalize the ruined flower beds when summer came. She set up her computer in front of a broad window with a view that looked over the broken landscape where the foundation of the barn could still be seen. When spring was a sure thing, she would start renovations on the summer kitchen and tear up the remnants of the barn, using the field stone to repair and extend the wall out back.

The summer kitchen was charming. She discovered a sliding door built into the side that would have been used to pass hot trays of food on their way to the house. But revamping the place to be computer friendly would have to wait. For now it was so stuffed with old furniture and boxes, that when she went to take a look, she could barely budge the door.

With her second cup of coffee in hand, and with Charlie following at her heels, Andrea sat before the scarred oak table, a lovely and warm shade of honey that she had picked up on the coast of Brittany. It had taken so long to arrive that she had almost forgotten, when the container company called from Boston to let her know it had docked and passed customs. She had now commandeered it as a desk, although it had once graced her and Dudley's kitchen. By the time she came to this item on their inventory, she had gotten smart and told Dudley that he could have it, which made him decide he preferred something else.

The doorbell sounded. Leaving her coffee, Andrea walked through the kitchen, through the dining room, turned left down the hall and into the foyer. Charlie stopped abruptly at halls midway point and whined pitifully when she abandoned him at this invisible juncture. If he wanted to follow her up to the second floor bedrooms, he would race up the old servant's staircase off the kitchen. If she lingered in the foyer, he would retreat from that line he would not cross and she would hear his feet scurry overhead until he stopped abruptly to peer down from the top of the stairs. From this better vantage point he would bark and whimper until he'd captured her attention. Not once since they moved in, had he gone up or come down that front staircase.

This idiosyncrasy was no longer amusing to Andrea. She slapped her hip and called to him. "Come on boy. You can do it. You love to greet people at the front door."

Charlie sat abruptly and flattened his ears against his glossy black skull. Stubborn to the end, he refused to budge, refusing to place one paw beyond that invisible dog line that only he sensed.

The doorbell rang again. Andrea passed the staircase letting her gaze admire the elaborately carved wood with birds and bees settled on what looked like over-sized tropical flowers amidst delicate fern leaves. An odd choice of décor, she thought for what had begun as a one room pioneer cabin.

Her house was most unusual. Moving forward she ran her hand over the smooth indentations of the carved wood.

"Look, Charlie, nothing to fear. Now come with me. Come on."

Her coaxing had no effect and, as usual, she walked across the foyer alone. The door creaked slightly, needing to be oiled. Who could it be? Not Julie or her mother since neither stood on ceremony and would normally enter through the kitchen calling out as they came.

Andrea didn't recognize her visitor; a young woman, fresh faced and holding a plate of cookies. *How nice*, she thought, a neighbor, come to welcome her.

"Hello," she said smiling broadly. "Will you come in?"

The young woman hesitated. She looked over her shoulder and then beyond the place where Andrea stood on the threshold. "No, I'd rather not. Do you mind if we sit outside for a few minutes?"

"It's cold, don't you think? We'd be more comfortable inside." Andrea took the offered plate. "Did you make these? I hardly ever bake. They look wonderful."

"I figured the neighbors wouldn't bring you anything."

Andrea managed to reconnect with a few former acquaintances after she joined the Waubeeka County Club, in anticipation of summer and a weekly game of golf, but aside from Julie she saw no other neighbors. Having lived in a city where people were busy and not inclined to make the acquaintance of strangers, she hadn't felt the lapse.

Despite the cold her visitor backed up from the door and sat on a wooden lawn chair. She looked back toward the woods. "You've widened the drive I see."

"Yes."

"Needed to be done. I hated driving through those trees. I used to live here. My husband and I rented the place from your husband."

"Former husband," Andrea gently corrected.

"I never met him. We were saving money in hopes of buying this place. I imagined my husband and me welcoming our grandchildren for Sunday dinner from this very porch."

Andrea looked at her curiously. "And yet you moved without completing your lease?"

"When we finally made the decision, we couldn't move fast enough. It nearly broke us because we rented something and still had to work out the details with your husband's attorney. He wasn't kind to us."

After her experience with Marstead, Andrea knew the claim had to be an understatement.

"We left in the middle of the night. Until now I've not been back." She looked over her shoulder, toward the door.

"If you liked the house so much, why did you go?"

She gave Andrea a hard stare. "Then you haven't felt it?"

"Felt what?"

An expression of vulnerability distorted her expression. She was reaching for the right response. "If I'd known you were going to move in, I would have warned you to stay away. And especially because you live alone."

"I'm not alone. I have my dog."

She gave off a little snort of disdain. "We had a dog, too, and he ran away after the first week. It took us awhile before we realized he could feel and maybe see what we couldn't."

"I'm hoping the gossip about this house will stop. I'm hoping..."

"It won't," her visitor interrupted in flat finality. "I know how I'm going to sound. It's unbelievable really, but I have to tell you anyway. I don't care what you think of me."

Andrea shivered in the wintry air and decided her visitor had to be slightly deranged. "Alright then," she said. "I'll listen."

"Thank you."

More silence. "And I'll keep an open mind. I promise. Now go ahead," Andrea prompted, feeling irritated and impatient to get this meeting over with.

The woman had scooped up a handful of her wool sweater. She twisted the weave into a tight ball until it rose above her waist. Andrea reached out a hand, disconcerted by the woman's anxiety as she now hesitated to speak.

"You'll stretch out your sweater if you're not careful," she said gently, deciding she would listen politely and then escort this former tenant to her car at the first opportunity.

The visitor shifted in her seat as she straightened the sweater.

"Bad things happen to people who live here," she whispered and suddenly pulled back, holding her frame with military stiffness as if resisting an urge to look behind her. "We had all kinds of odd occurrences of seemingly bad luck."

Andrea studied her guest with some astonishment. The woman had now grabbed the sleeve of Andrea's light jacket, twisting the fabric which tightened over her arm.

"I'm sorry. Forgive me." She let go and stood abruptly. "I'm not myself. I'm getting better, but I haven't been myself since we left and now I'm part of the history of this house. The house doesn't like to lose."

"I don't understand."

"The problem is that we left without completing what we were intended to do. We had a Medium come to the house and he told us there were dead people trapped here. He said one was very evil, perhaps even a demon."

"And you believed him?"

"If you'd experienced what we did you would, too, but of course he was wrong about some of it and in the end nothing changed. We were relying more on that Medium and his powers than on God. I know that now. This sounds crazy doesn't it?" she looked at Andrea.

"It does a little. I'm sorry."

"I'm just here to tell you what I've learned since leaving. I don't want you to make the same mistakes we did. Do you believe in Jesus Christ?"

"Yes I do. I wasn't raised in Church. My mother would call herself an atheist. But since I was a little girl I've believed, and recently... with the divorce I've been thinking more about God."

"That's good. You'll need your faith. Read Matthew 17:14-22. It's the story of the father who brings his son to the disciples for healing. They pray over the boy and it doesn't work because his illness is actually caused by demons. It's not a physical illness as the father believed and the disciples failed to investigate and so their prayer was not effective."

"I don't understand what you're trying to say," Andrea replied.

"You can't fight what you won't recognize. The disciples did what my husband and I did. They folded in the face of opposition and fled the field of battle. They didn't persist in prayer as scripture instructs us to do. My husband and I left this house for someone else to handle. Now it will be your problem and for that I am truly sorry."

"But I'm fine," Andrea insisted. "I love my new home."

"After the boy is delivered, the disciple's ask Jesus why their prayers for healing were not answered. Jesus replied, ***this kind goeth not out but by prayer and fasting.'***

"I don't understand what you're trying to say."

"It's harder to be free of some demon strongholds than others; prayer and fasting by the body of Christ is needed. This is not a battle, but a war. No one fights a war without marshalling a force. Get some help. Do you understand?"

She locked eyes with Andrea who couldn't help her response. If this story got out, Andrea knew she would never sell the property, even if she wanted to.

"Will you listen to how foolish your words sound? A house is not a person. A house doesn't have a soul. So a few people have had bad luck? In the long history of this place some must have been happy. It's so beautiful here."

"There was a family that stayed here before us. They were guests of your husband. We were told that the teenage son shot himself in the sun room. And my little boy, well at first we thought he had invented a playmate, an imaginary friend, if you will. We actually thought it was cute. We could see him talking out here in the yard, and when we asked who he was speaking with, he said it was the old time Grandpa." She spit the name out with bitterness.

56

"He told us that Grandpa was a farmer and one day he asked if he could invite him inside. Again, thinking this was innocent, we said yes. That was the turning point. Looking back I believe there needed to be an invitation extended and then accepted. Thinking this was cute and foolish and harmless we sanctioned that request and opened the door for what would follow."

"Children often have imaginary friends. I understand it's fairly common," Andrea said hoping to calm her guest.

"He's only five, but he began to have terrible nightmares and wouldn't go to bed unless my husband or I slept with him. He awoke with scratches that actually bled and got infected. Toward the end, we all slept together on the living room floor. Our pastor said we were hysterical and needed tranquilizers. That's when we called in the Medium. And for a week things were better, but then the house erupted and we were worse off than before. No one could get past the foyer to go up stairs."

For the first time Andrea was attentive. She thought of Charlie, thought about the sunroom. She had filled the space with plants and set up a cozy reading corner where she enjoyed her first cup of coffee each morning with Charlie sitting on her foot. When he became too big for her lap, he settled for her foot. She could not imagine this comfortable retreat as the sight of anything tragic.

"My friend, Julie, told me that someone had died," Andrea offered. "But I didn't ask for details. I could have lived without knowing about the sun room."

"Anyway, I've told you. I'm off the hook. I have to go." She stood abruptly.

Andrea felt relief as she followed her visitor to the car which had been backed into the long drive. This took skill since the drive was narrow and curved over a viaduct with a brook below. It then went some distance toward the house and beyond, stopping at the place where the barn had been, ending at the summer kitchen and back door. Andrea noted that the car was positioned for a quick getaway.

Andrea wanted to reassure her visitor. "Please don't worry about me," she said. "I've found the house to be a delight, just what I dreamed of."

"The house is not what it seems. Dreams dreamt in this house are not innocent. Let me ask you again. You've seen nothing, felt nothing?" She turned her head with a show of great abhorrence, as though looking in the direction of the ruined barn could awaken something.

Andrea took a deep breath. For a moment, and only for a moment, she felt the sense of something alien that she could not define. But the impression was fleeting and she pushed it quickly from her mind. She wouldn't allow this woman to rob her of any enjoyment associated with the house. This was her sanctuary, the place where she would heal from those years with Dudley.

Still, she couldn't resist asking. "Did you hear rumors about this house before you moved in?"

"The Brown family told me. They live up the road and farm some of the surrounding fields. They knew the girl that was kidnapped and forced to marry old man Woods. Despite stories that she ran off with a local boy, a rumor persists that after a child was delivered she was sacrificed in satanic ritual. At the time I laughed in their faces. I failed to see that they were being completely serious."

"I'm planning to have the foundation of the barn leveled when spring comes," Andrea deflected, in a futile attempt to change the subject. "I'd like to use the stones to extend the wall that runs toward the orchard."

Her visitor scrutinized Andrea's expression. "Have you been listening? Do you believe any part of what I've said? I guess I can't blame you. I was the same way. So in love with this place I couldn't see straight. And that's how people get here. They're seduced by logic and perceptions of beauty. It's not what is seems!"

"I'm fine. I feel safe living here. I'm happy."

"Put on the whole armour of God, that ye may be able to stand against the wiles of the devil," Andreas' visitor recited. ***"For we wrestle not against***

flesh and blood, but against principalities, against the powers, against the rulers of the darkness of this world, against spiritual wickedness in high places (Ephesians 6: 11b, 12).

She went on, "It's real and I just want you to be prepared. That Thank God you don't have any children living with you."

But Andrea was thinking how quaint the wall would look built up with the stone from the barn's foundation. Following her gaze the young woman said. "Concentrating on incidentals like moving those stones won't help. If I were you, I'd bring in a backhoe and bury them."

Andrea shook her head, shifting position so that her back was to the barn. She recalled reaching her hand up to touch the old nickel hooks that lined one wall of the mud room and felt something, but couldn't say what. A picture flashed to mind of Charlie refusing to enter the foyer and stubbornly avoiding the front stairs. Was she in denial? Was there something wrong with this house? And then the thought came to her and seemed strangely worth pursuing. Had Dudley ever lived here? And... what, *pray tell, does that have to do with anything rational?*

"Call me if you want, but after today I can't return to this place. My position is weakened because we hired a Medium who had no faith in Christ. We fled in fear. Even now it's dangerous for me to be here."

Andrea was speechless.

"When you decide to leave, please don't sell the house to another family," her visitor continued. "Burn it and tell the insurance company it was an accident. Take the money and run." She lowered her voice to a whisper. "I'll never tell anyone I suggested that."

In a sudden rush of panic, Andrea wanted to ask more questions. But the car was moving forward and she was left to feel foolish and bewildered with a plate of chocolate chip cookies in her hand.

Just as she lifted her hand to wave goodbye the car stopped and the woman opened the door slightly and leaned out. "Don't bother returning the plate," she called. "It's the only thing I took from the house that was here when we moved in. The rest we stored in the summer kitchen out back. The people before us moved out quickly, too. You'll find some of their stuff as well."

With the obligatory warning delivered, the relief to be gone was evident in her demeanor. "Bye," she called, almost cheerful. They might have been discussing something as inane as a book or a recipe.

"Hope to see you around town, Andrea. Welcome to Woods End Township."

Andrea watched the car retreat until it disappeared into the elongated shadows of the wood. She carried the plate back into the house. Charlie was waiting, still worried with his ears plastered against his sleek skull. He looked at her accusing, knowing he had missed something significant. If only he could have gotten beyond the halls invisible barrier and followed his master outside.

Andrea tossed him a cookie, which he expertly intercepted and swallowed in one gulp. She placed the plate on the kitchen counter and took one for herself. The plate was interesting. She emptied the surface, transferring the contents to a plastic container.

With her finger she traced a blood red dragon curled around the center and breathing fire, with a gold scroll trimming the border. She appreciated china and could name many discontinued patterns by sight. This plate was old and of excellent quality. Andrea looked at Charlie who studied her with anticipation, hoping for another cookie.

"No more for you, my man," she said and retrieved one of his treats from a crystal biscuit jar, patting the top of his head as he swallowed it.

She was curious about the plate and decided she would look up the pattern in one of her books, but for now a pervasive exhaustion crept over her limbs. Was she getting sick? It was entirely possible for she had never felt such sudden lethargy before.

Andrea slid open the drawer that housed an assortment of over-the-counter medications and reached for some extra vitamin C, E, and Zinc. All her plans for the day, including a trip to the Adams Public Library, reading up on the house she loved and already felt certain she could not easily abandon, would have to wait.

WOOD'S END

CHAPTER SIX

"This town is called Woods End. Can you imagine why?"

He was the second visitor of the day. He was dressed oddly, she thought, in the Amish or early Mennonite style. His trousers were black and cuffed too short with leather suspenders and a greenish shirt of rough weave.

He repeated the question. "Baby girl," he called her. "Do you know how Woods End got its name?"

"Why don't you tell me?" she invited, and realized he'd come on foot. She knew this because there was no car.

With an avid intensity the man leaned forward, his feet fixed in the impressions left in the snow by her previous visitor. "Place names are important," he said. "They can be portals of introduction and... Well, may I just say, Mrs. Woods? Welcome home."

"It's Wodsende and I'm divorced," Andrea asserted.

"Of course you are. And I've come to leave you this package, my dear." He said, shifting the subject. The friendly tone of his voice was belied by a sneering expression that her mother occasionally adopted when her guard was down and for just a moment, Andrea felt a terror reminiscent of early childhood nightmares. Was she dreaming?

Andrea studied her visitor, noting that his hands were empty. He realized her confusion. "It's there," he said wistfully and with mechanical stiffness, lifted his head in the direction of the steps, and in slow motion higher, ceremoniously, toward the front door with a slow shift left to the porch swing. "The misses and I thought you might like to have some clippings from The Progress."

"The Progress?"

"Yes, the county newspaper back when. Today they call it something different."

Curious, wanting to study him better, Andrea moved to the last step where she sat with her stocking feet in the snow. He nodded his head in approval before turning to go. Andrea stopped him. "You wanted to tell me about the name," she prompted noting the lack of footprints in the snow, proof positive that this was a dream. "Can I make you a cup of hot tea?"

He looked over his shoulder. "Maybe, another time. It's milking soon."

"Milking?"

"Yes, the cows, baby girl; the cows. They won't wait for tea. Perhaps another day?

"Do you live near here?"

"Oh yes. Right over yonder," he replied, his head cocked in the direction of the barn, even as he gazed lovingly toward the house behind her.

Andrea wanted to know more about him. She turned back toward the porch. Lying on the swing she could see a packet wrapped in glossy oilcloth enclosing the clippings he'd brought. It was tied with a bit of burlap and she thought how quaint to use oilcloth in this olden way.

"The misses is making breakfast. She didn't want me to come over so soon to make your acquaintance. But, I'll tell you about Woods End and then I'll return for that cup of tea, if you'll let me?"

There was a pleading quality to the stance of his reed thin figure, but an alarm had sounded in her head and she felt a rush of reluctance.

He waited, not looking directly at her and Andrea realized he had never actually made eye contact. There were practiced layers of deceit in the unspoken weight of his expectation. She swallowed a lump of dread and said, "At some point perhaps I'll meet your wife."

"You will," he said drawing out the words in curious emphasis. "And perhaps you'll have us inside for that nice cup of tea?"

The socially appropriate reply strangled in Andrea's throat. What was it her earlier visitor had said? There needed to be an invitation extended and then accepted. What did her dream have to do with anything that crazy former tenant had to say?

Andrea vacillated. If appearances could be trusted, he seemed such a nice man. Tall and straight with beautiful thick white hair and a face that had aged well. And yet he was, in point of fact, a man without footprints, lacking the necessary substance to make them.

Andrea decided it was time to test her dream theory. She drew her legs up, tucking them tight against her, feeling the cold; not wanting to share the common ground between them. She peered forward, failing once more to engage his eyes with hers.

"Tell me about the name." Her words were not the invitation he wanted or expected. She felt, rather than saw his disappointment.

"The land is a spiritual place of gathering," he explained. "Three times it was wiped out. Twice by marauding Iroguois and once by illness, but settlers kept coming, though they were not wanted. Pursued by Indian warriors above the ridge, settlers and explorers alike sought to escape death. The lower reaches of this valley, extending from Woods End up to the place were the first cabin stood, were covered in early summer with fire flies. Like moths to a flame, the interlopers mistook the glow of fireflies for the welcoming lights of settlement. Here they met death and many scalps were taken. People still hike the old Indian trail."

"The Appalachian Trail," Andrea offered and let her gaze climb to Greylock with its peak gleaming white, the trees blackish-green and an azure sky above. She was intrigued.

"Lots of battles fought here. Indians fighting Indians. Indians fighting Gaul's, Saxons; cast offs and stragglers from the Roman lands beyond the sea. From necessity and persecuted we blended in." He stopped speaking and spit on the ground in distaste though nothing came out. He was an empty man; an empty...

"I've not heard any of this," Andrea said feeling confused and disbelieving.

"Oh, but you have. You are well familiar with the history of your own people. The memory is stamped in your bones and carried to your mind on the very blood that courses through your veins."

Andrea searched for his eyes still hidden under the shadow of the wide brimmed hat. There was the sudden shift of a predatory emergence in his bearing which motivated her to slide her body up yet another step toward the safety of the porch. She tried again to catch his gaze, but he dipped his head, lengthening the shadow even more.

She felt then that he could read her mind and struggled for a single word that might encapsulate the near shape-shift she'd witnessed. And then, as ludicrous as the thought was, she realized he wasn't human. This was an "it." A diabolical, dangerous for life-and-limb kind of haunting visitor, holding out the seductive lure of a lie; an invitation that she might know something unknown and powerful that God's human creation must shun as they await the greater revelations of eternity.

He held out his hand in that moment inviting her to rise from the porch and take his offer of... of whatever it was she must reject. Andrea felt a stab of revulsion so great that she was nauseated; rapt with fear.

She felt his keen interest in her reaction, waiting for it to pass so he could try again. Andrea wanted to rise up from that step and run for her life, but felt imprisoned by a nightmare so real that she could feel the splinters in the wood of the step with her hand.

Newly aware, grateful for the distraction it provided, Andrea felt about for the largest sliver of wood, prying it loose from a crust of snow, positioning it upright.

"Invite me in, baby girl. Invite me... It's time; your capitulation long overdue."

Andrea spoke over the words; shutting out the voice that was now cloyingly invasive. "It's a lovely old porch. When spring comes I'll have it sanded and painted."

"In spring," he began having lifted that word from her mind and noting her hesitation, "I plow up Indian heads. Bloody with the refuse of torn flesh. They smell delicious."

Andrea slammed her hand over the top of the ice encrusted splinter.

Andrea leaned her head over the toilet basin and retched up her morning coffee and the two cookies she had eaten. She gargled with mouthwash and brushed her teeth. Somehow she had fallen asleep only to awaken with the bitter taste of bile burning her throat and cold sweat beading her brow.

She waited for the dream to fade as others did, but at least for now she remembered every detail. Andrea could not resist peering out the window of the sunroom. She could see the corner of the porch and the back of the swing. Maybe the package had shifted. Maybe the wind had blown it out of sight.

"What a foolish thought," she spoke out loud, scolding herself. Dreams didn't have that kind of physicality, and she had squandered the morning, having fallen asleep in this wicker chair, her feet propped on an ottoman.

Giving in to an eccentric compulsion, Andrea walked through the living room and into the foyer. She opened the front door and, feeling utterly foolish, she looked for the package of newspaper clippings that were not there.

Andrea breathed a sigh of relief. She now had two reasons to visit the library. She would see for herself the painting by Burns Padgett Shiel and she would verify the existence of a rural publication called, The Progress.

Still, Andrea could not shake the thought that her dream had held both a threat and a warning. She crossed her arms about her chest pulling her jacket closer for warmth. Charlie came up beside her as she dropped her arms. He slid his head under her hand and licked her palm.

Andrea scratched his bad ear and felt the sting. She lifted her hand and looked. A trickle of blood from a deep puncture wound pooled into the fleshy center of her palm.

WOOD'S END

CHAPTER SEVEN

A sound from the window ledge woke her. The sun had not yet broken over the ridge, but a muted light seeped through the shutters, bringing hazy definition to the red and pink pattern of the duvet cover. Andrea rolled onto her back and stretched. At her window a downy woodpecker drilled through a layer of ice in the gutter and drank. She closed her eyes, wondering if she could sleep a bit longer.

She was just drifting off when the phone rang. She waited for it to stop and when it didn't, she slipped out of bed and reached for the silk robe lined with white terry cloth. By the time she and Charlie stepped into the kitchen, having descended the back staircase, the shrill sound erupted once again.

It had to be her mother. Only Sybil would have the temerity to call this early. Whatever was wrong would be, according to her mother, a dire tragedy of one sort or another that would require Andrea to drop everything and jump to attendance post haste. What could it be this time? A fight with one of her step daughters; lost too much money at the casino and didn't have cab fare home? Feeling indecisive Andrea studied the phone as it rang. Soon it stopped.

She had just pressed the rich coffee grounds into the bottom of the tempered press when it started again. In no hurry she poured the rich liquid, wrapping her cold hands around the cup. She took a sip. Charlie's bowl was empty and he waited patiently by the antique pie safe where she kept his food.

"I see you," she said. "But, first, let's see what Sybil wants." At the sound of her mother's name Charlie's ears went back and he looked forlorn. He didn't like Sybil and the feeling was mutual.

"Hello." She tried again, "Hello."

Andrea felt a surge of impatience. She would hang up and unplug the phones, not answering for the remainder of the day. She might actually get some work done. Yesterday had been a complete waste, since after her morning nightmare she had been unable to shed a pervasive lethargy that had enveloped her in an odd feeling of displacement. After a visit to the library she had tumbled into bed and was asleep by nine, having not opened the cover of the book she had found, its title, of all things, *Haunted Houses of Berkshire County.*

"I'm hanging up, Mother. Unless you acknowledge that you've called me at this ungodly hour of the morning, I'm hanging up."

Charlie made a dog noise of approval and they exchanged a sympathetic glance. "If you don't tell me what is wrong by the time I count to ten, I'm hanging up and I'm not answering the phone for the remainder of the day. And don't bother coming over, Mother, because I won't let you in. I have work to do. One...two...three..."

Charlie whined again and gave her a disapproving look. He wanted her to hang up now. He was hungry and knew that most contact with Sybil unsettled his master. Andrea smiled at her dog. They were thinking the same thing. He didn't smile back.

Andrea had removed the phone from her ear. She was just counting ten. "No, please wait. I just need a minute."

Andrea didn't recognize the voice. "Alright," she said, now curious. She'd wait, but not for long. "Who is this?"

"This is Stephanie Wodsende. Oh, I know I shouldn't be calling you. I know you must hate me, and believe me, I hate myself. If you hang up right now, I'll understand."

Andrea acknowledged to herself that she'd like to hang up. But she didn't hate Stephanie. She actually felt sorry for the woman. They had something in common. Both had been young and vulnerable and succumbed to Dudley's lethal charm believing every lie he uttered.

"Stephanie... What can I do for you?"

"It's about Dudley. Well, I just wonder if there is something you can tell me."

Andrea could not restrain a short laugh of derision. Stephanie opened a door that she had fantasized walking through countless times. She moved to the pie safe as she talked and scooped out a generous portion of dog food from the old tin-lined flour bin.

"You mean other than the fact that he is a self-absorbed two year old with no conscience and a desire to control beyond what any mental health professional would call normal? No, other than that, Stephanie, there is nothing I can tell you that with half a brain you wouldn't already know."

Andrea heard a stifled sob. The dog food clattered into Charlie's bowl. She felt sorry for her harsh words. "I'm sorry, Stephanie. I shouldn't have said that."

"Not a problem. I've thought the same thing and yet I'm struggling to believe there is some good in Dudley. He is sincerely dedicated to medicine and does a lot for his patients. That's about all I can come up with."

Andrea said nothing. She wanted to think there was good in everyone, but felt certain that Dudley was the exception to that rule.

"Could we meet? I have no right to ask. Why should you help the woman who broke up your marriage?"

Andrea couldn't help herself. "You're not that important."

"We need to talk. I can drive out from Boston. I know Woods End is about four hours away. I can get started right now; if you'll let me?"

Andrea hesitated. What was she getting herself into? "It's not possible Stephanie. I couldn't risk it and truth be told, neither should you."

"I have a child. Melody is only six. I'd do anything to protect her. If you can just bring yourself..."

"Sorry, but I couldn't welcome you as a house guest. It wouldn't be smart to insert myself back on Dudley's radar screen."

"You're right. I can't come to you, but you can come here. It would never occur to Dudley in his wildest dreams that we would have anything to say to each other. He imagines that you're jealous of me; that you want him back."

Andrea watched Charlie as he nudged his water bowl against the Lucite strip she'd installed to protect the wall. She made a decision. "I'm sorry, Stephanie. I can't meet you today, or ever."

"How about tonight," she persisted. "Drive into Boston and we can talk while Dudley is at the hospital."

Andrea felt sucked into the past she'd just escaped. Stephanie couldn't drive to Woods End because Dudley would check the mileage on her car. She understood about arranging to meet while Dudley was working his late emergency room shift. Even working nights seemed to be part of his plan. He worked while she, and now Stephanie, slept and there was no getting away from that vigilance.

"Is this necessary, Stephanie? I mean there are shelters for women. There are places to go."

"Yes, but you didn't go, did you? You knew a place like that was no defense against someone like Dudley. You were strong. You stood up to him."

"I wasn't strong at all. If he hadn't already replaced me with you, if he didn't believe I was sterile and couldn't give him a son, I might still be looking over my shoulder every five minutes. By the time he found out about the birth control pills, you were already in the picture. You did me a huge favor and don't get me wrong. I'm still afraid of him."

"Please, Andrea. I know you must hate me, but there are some things I need to understand and only you can tell me."

"My decision isn't personal, Stephanie. Right now I like my life. I'm not counting the hours until he comes home from the hospital, goes to sleep, and wakes up again. I imagine he still requires very little sleep."

Stephanie broke down. Though it was hard and Andrea wanted to hang up she waited until the sobs subsided.

"He promised me so much," Stephanie said. "A peaceful family life. We would travel and go to church together."

Andrea could not help scoffing at this woman's naivety. Even she had been smart enough to realize that a life of domesticity was not something Dudley was up to. "You can't be serious," she said. "I've not met anyone as profane as Dudley. He hates all things Christian and Jewish.

"I know," Stephanie said. "And it isn't anything he says. It's just who he is. The sense of it grew like mold until I couldn't stand him touching me."

"But there was no refusing him was there? And by now you must realize he hates children. And yet, for some reason, feels compelled to produce a son."

"The thought of being connected to Dudley for the rest of my life because we shared a child was just too much to tolerate. I doubt very much I would have been allowed to raise that child." Stephanie stifled a sob. "I'm going to sound paranoid. But... maybe what I have to say won't sound so farfetched. I need to confide in someone before I leave Dudley. I need to tell you and have you say it's all true or I'm in need of medication and a good psychiatrist. Will you? Will you please meet with me?"

"I'll think about it," Andrea said, buying time and hoping the crisis might pass and she could just stay out of it.

"My daughter and I are flying to Memphis tomorrow. I can't talk about this over the phone. It's something I've learned about Dudley and something specific I need to know if there is to be any hope of protecting myself and my child."

"Have you thought that my helping you would enrage Dudley; that meeting is a waste of time?"

"We can know things. We can hold valuable pieces of a puzzle and not realize the importance of what's right before our eyes. Dudley and your mother have known one another a long time. They are connected. I'm begging you. My daughter begs you. Please! I won't ask again."

Andrea took a deep breath. If her mother was involved, nothing Stephanie could say would be any good. And yet Sybil had promised to stay away from Dudley. Andrea believed her wishes had been respected. Her mother had been turning to her for money even before the divorce was final, meaning that Dudley was no longer the free flowing source of ready cash that Sybil had come to rely on.

Andrea found herself gripping the phone so tight that her hand hurt. She thought of Stephanie's daughter and remembered herself at that age.

"I'll leave here before midnight," she said. "That will get me to Boston around three-ish. Is Dudley still on the same schedule? He eats his dinner around three and if there are no patients he sleeps until it's time to close out his charts?"

"Yes, he's a creature of habit. And if he isn't sleeping he'll be attending to a medical crisis," Stephanie offered.

"Seconds after his car is out of sight, go to the garage and let the door up just enough for me to roll under," Andrea instructed. "He'll think it's that pesky garage door again. I was able to convince him that we had a recurring problem and have used that excuse to come and go without him knowing. By the time he reviews the alarm data, maybe you'll be in flight to Memphis."

Stephanie sighed and Andrea felt empathy for the woman she couldn't hate.

"Thank you," Stephanie said.

"You're welcome, but I want you to understand something. I'm not getting involved. If you need a little moral support to protect yourself, I'll do what I can. I like that Dudley has moved on. He doesn't think about me and I want it to stay that way."

"Doesn't think about you?" Stephanie asserted. "You are all he thinks about. He thinks I'm you half the time."

Coldness descended. Andrea shivered and Charlie lifted his head from his bowl and looked at her. She shouldn't go. She shouldn't go anywhere near Boston and Dudley Wodsende. She had jokingly called her husband satan, but it was no joke that she considered him dangerous.

"Will you come?" Stephanie asked, clearly afraid that she had put Andrea off.

Charlie left his food and walked to the mud room door; tucking his tail between his legs. Andrea watched him as she delivered her answer.

"Yes, I'll come. Don't do anything out of the ordinary. If you've been fighting, keep it up. If you've been getting along and tolerating each other, don't suddenly decide to be nice. Don't kiss him or be affectionate. That's a sure tip-off since he doesn't like to be touched unless sex is the outcome and it's his idea. Got it?"

"Perfectly. I think we'll have an enlightening conversation," Stephanie sounded relieved. "Maybe nothing I have to say will surprise you after-all."

Andrea took a sip of coffee and thought about Dudley. Easily enraged by any hint of criticism, the thought of one former wife talking to the unhappy present wife would drive him ballistic. There was no satisfaction in getting back at Dudley. At the end she had been equally afraid and was even now worried that she was opening a door she couldn't close.

"I can't believe you are actually driving to Boston just to meet with that witch."

"Mother, where did you come from?"

"Through that door you failed to lock. I hope you didn't leave it open all night. Crime happens, even here."

"What did you hear?"

"Too bad that stupid dog of yours didn't even bark."

"He recognized your step. He'd only bark if you were a stranger," Andrea said watching as Charlie went back to his bowl and stood over his food as if protecting it from Sybil.

"And to think Dudley sent me on a trip each winter. I hate this town. I'm only staying close because of you."

"You're only here because your bankroll is here, and if he didn't have some smart daughters watching your every move, you'd put him in a nursing home and go on an extended vacation."

"I don't know why I deserve a daughter who doesn't respect her mother. The Bible says you're supposed to respect me."

"When have you ever read the Bible?"

"I'm not ignorant. It's one of the Ten Commandments. Says so on the court house wall."

"Which you just happened to read in a boring moment between divorces or shop lifting cases."

"You are cruel."

"Listen to me, Sybil. Anything you may have heard just now is none of your business. Do you understand? You are not to interfere."

"Oh alright, I won't. But this may be your last chance. If Stephanie is so desperate that she'd call you, then maybe Dudley will take you back."

"Mother! I've said this a hundred times before and you haven't heard me. Must I repeat myself... yet again! I don't love Dudley! I have never loved Dudley, and he happens to be utterly incapable of such an emotion. I will never take him back and he isn't in the slightest bit interested in me."

"That's not what I hear? Are you hungry? I'm hungry. Let's make breakfast together like we used to. It's going to snow later tonight, so I thought I might stay over. You know how I hate being alone."

"What about your husband?"

"Hospice is there and his daughters are hovering about like demented chickens. I told them you needed me."

Andrea gave her mother a hard stare and noticed that Charlie had now vacated the kitchen without finishing his breakfast. She needed to find him and let him out. She guessed he would be hiding behind the oversized rocker in the sunroom.

"If you've been talking to Dudley and I find out about it, I will never lift a finger to help you ever again. I'll pretend you don't exist. Do you understand what I'm saying, Mother? This will be the end of any semblance of a relationship between us. The end!"

"I would never talk to Dudley about you, precious. I know how he hurt you. I wouldn't do that to my one and only baby girl. What did she say, anyway?"

Andrea felt uneasy, but said no more. If she revealed any part of her conversation with Stephanie, it would be like opening a hornet's nest. As it was, Sybil may have heard too much or... just enough to dangerously pique her interest."

"Where are you going?" Sybil asked.

"I'm walking you to the door. I want to be alone if you don't mind, and Charlie needs to finish his breakfast. He won't eat with you around."

"I hate that dog. One of these days I'm going to call the dog catcher and have him picked up. And why do you want to be alone! Since you were a little girl you always wanted to be alone. Me, I hate being alone. I can't stand having just the walls to talk to. Why don't you get rid of that dog? He smells."

"Good bye, Mother. And Charlie doesn't like you either. Spend some time with that husband of yours. Sounds like he needs you."

WOOD'S END

PART TWO
CHAPTER EIGHT

DUDLEY

"We wondered when we'd see you."

"I fell asleep, what's it been, an hour?"

"No, you've slept for at least two hours."

The beginning of a frown crossed Dudley's brow. He looked at his watch. It was five-thirty and if this were a normal morning, he would begin closing out his charts. At seven, when the day shift formally started he would take a shower and dress in street clothes.

Lisa couldn't help noticing that his hair was damp at the neck. A distinct scent of soap carried on the air. Why had he showered so early? This was out of character for Dr. Wodsende whose routine was strictly adhered to. But the question was never verbalized and just as quickly forgotten.

A quizzical look fell over Dudley's features. "It's been less than an hour. You'll recall that I did that phone consult."

No one remembered, but the staff knew better than to question anything Dudley Wodsende said. The in-take clerk handed him a cup of coffee. He looked at her and smiled. She smiled back.

"It's good to see you happy, Dr. Wodsende. We've all been worried about you."

"I appreciate your concern, Lisa. We can be thankful for a *nice quiet night*. Just what I like to see. Not much going on."

"You had to go and say that," Lisa groaned. She looked at her coworkers for confirmation.

Maria Arms, the head nurse, nodded her head. "Have to say you're right, Lisa. Enjoy that coffee, Doctor. It may be your last for a while."

"Now, Maria, how many times do I have to tell you, there is nothing, and I mean nothing, to that superstitious nonsense," Dudley sparred.

"We all know, you're a man of science, but we're keeping records, and if my Eastern European gypsy grandmother were here, she'd convince you differently."

"Write that down!" The male orderly called to Lisa who reached for a tattered three ring binder with a large label emblazoned over the front. *Important Scientific Data – Hands Off.*

"Writing it down as we speak. Date, time, Dr Wodsende said again what he shouldn't. Staff waiting breathlessly."

"Think I'll study while I can," the orderly announced.

"Think I'll eat my sandwich early," Lisa said with exaggerated disapproval as she put aside a garage sale romance novel.

Just lately it had been in Dudley's best interest to allow a certain familiarity with his coworkers. They failed to notice the effort it took to return their friendly overtures. It was especially taxing to maintain vigilance over facial expressions or body language. He had learned from experience that when the widest smile failed to line up with a certain look about the eyes, if his body were stiff or the tone of his voice less than genuine, the message conveyed would not achieve the desired outcome.

Dr. Wodsende looked at his nurse. "Now, Maria, I hope, as an educated woman with some responsibility, you are not going to encourage these two."

"No. Not at all."

"Good!"

"But I do think, just to be safe, I'll make sure all the carts have been properly restocked. Should Legionnaires Disease strike The Parker House or we have a ten-car pile-up outside our gates, I'd want us to be ready." Unable to resist a snicker she headed in the direction of the treatment rooms.

"I can't believe you guys. You actually think you can influence destiny," Dr. Wodsende lectured. "You must stop indulging this fanciful thinking. Just be grateful we have a quiet night, because if we do have a ten-car pile-up, I can guarantee it will have nothing to do with what was said two minutes ago. Casual observations do not cause accidents!" From three different directions his coworkers groaned in unison.

By city standards it had been a quiet night at the private Crest May Hospital and Research Facility located in the heart of downtown Boston, nearly in the shadow of the larger teaching hospital, on several coveted acres of surrounding property. Adjacent to the hospital was a long-term care facility with a rehabilitation wing. Most patients showed up in the ER by referral from attending physicians who had been paged in the middle of the night by their services. After nine in the evening walk-ins were sent elsewhere unless a true emergency existed. Twice a week the small ER received minimal overflow from larger hospitals, but because of their size, they were never the first choice.

The evening shift had dealt with the usual substance abusers and those without insurance who were far sicker than they should have been if medical care had been more available to the poor. Two children with high temps were admitted and the crisis intervention team of the Boston PD had escorted a mentally-ill homeless man to psych via a quick ER visit because he happened to be the son of a staff member. For the last couple of hours even the phone was silent. A cavernous stillness enveloped the night shift. They didn't wish for anything different.

Tired or not, it was the habit of Doctor Wodsende to withdraw to the doctors lounge off the intake area when there was nothing to do. The lounge had a shower, a large TV with an assortment of videos, a place to sleep, and even a limited workout room as well as a private entrance so the doctors could come and go without walking through the ER Lobby.

It was an hour later that they heard the siren. Lisa turned up the volume on her radio. "Trauma patient," she whispered loud enough to be heard by the orderly as he passed the reception desk, text book open and chewing the last remnants of a candy bar.

"Not coming here I hope, because it's not our night for overflow."

"Something about the patient having been here before..." She listened more intently. "They must have called her doctor from the ambulance. And," she paused again, "it's a gunshot victim." Lisa delivered this last to Maria as she moved quickly to knock on the door of the doctor's lounge.

"And *that's* not a coincidence?" the tech called and headed for the drop-off depot area. "Dr. Wodsende can't tell us this is any kind of coincidence, now can he?"

In another minute the ambulance had pulled up to the patient entrance and, with the assistance of the tech, two paramedics wheeled in a gurney. "Which room?"

"Straight ahead," said the tech as he studied the patient, walking fast to keep up. "Can you tell us your name? Do you know where you are?" The series of questions were intended to assess patient alertness. Stumbling slightly, nearly tripping over his feet, the orderly stopped abruptly, a stunned look on his face.

Maria gave him a questioning glare as she ran by keeping up with the paramedics. The routine was well established. Check the airway, is the patient breathing? How is circulation and is the patient orientated to place, time, and circumstance? Now her well trained orderly, a second year pharmacy student who knew better, had stopped in his tracts and entirely backed off. With no time to think, Maria guided the gurney to an even level with the raised stretcher as she and the two paramedics picked up the sheet and slid the patient over.

"BP is 80/39. She's lost a lot of blood. Pulse is irregular. No telling how long she was lying out there in the snow before someone found her and called it in. The cold has slowed the blood loss, but she's in shock and..."

Maria listened to the paramedics and strapped on her own blood pressure cuff. Having regained his senses the orderly began to cut away the clothing attempting to catch Maria's eye, but she was bent over her patient listening for a heartbeat.

"Where is Dr. Wodsende?"

"He's coming, but..."

There was so much blood on the patient's face that Maria wondered if there was a wound she couldn't see. Or had there been spillage from another victim? The paramedics had already started an IV, so Maria dampened a towel with peroxide and water and went to work.

"Find out why Dr. Wodsende isn't here please?" she asked and then called out the basic orders she knew her absent doctor would start with. "We need type and cross match and..."

A spray of blood stained a grey cashmere sweater, while more blood had pooled beneath the left shoulder. With care she lifted away a yellow leaf fragment dried to one cheek and looked more closely at the small even features of her patient before emitting an involuntary gasp of recognition.

Maria's first thought was that Andrea Wodsende was not wearing a bra. The faded blue jeans were stained with urine and what looked like bits of flesh clung in sticky globs to the tips of gray suede hiking boots unlaced and... she noted, on the wrong feet.

"Once we have her stabilized and if she still can't say what happened, I want a rape screen."

"I tried to tell you," the orderly whispered as they rolled the patient so that Maria could examine the shoulder wound.

"Here's the exit wound. Let's get this blood flow stopped. We'll x-ray, but I doubt we'll find a bullet."

"What do we have here," Dr. Wodsende asked, conversing briefly with the medics and appearing to approve the orders already in process before approaching the stretcher. And then...despite the absence of makeup and the unkempt appearance of a woman who was usually perfectly coifed and accessorized, he, too, recognized his patient. For the mere heart beat of seconds an astonished hush fell over their company.

Dr. Wodsende bent low and peered into Andrea's face as though he could not quite grasp the reality of her being among them.

"Andrea, where are you hurt? Can you tell me what's happened?"

Seeing the stunned look on Dr. Wodsende's face both the nurse and orderly took over.

"Andrea," Dr. Wodsende called again. "What happened to you?" But she failed to answer. Her stare was wildly centered elsewhere and the sounds she made were unintelligible and sadly pathetic.

"Lisa, I want you to page Dr. Bloom and ask her to get here stat so that she can take over for Dr. Wodsende. Then call the nursing supervisor."

"No, no. It's not an issue. We're not married anymore. I can treat her. I'm fine," he said emptying the contents of a syringe into the IV tubing.

"That's not the point and you know it very well. Until Dr. Bloom gets here we'll see if there's another doctor on site."

"By the time Bloom gets here Andrea could be dead. So, until she arrives..."

Maria mouthed silently to Lisa, "call Dr. Bloom," but for now she allowed Dudley to continue treating his former wife. When questioned later all that Maria would say was that if anything, Dr. Wodsende was kinder and more solicitous of Andrea than she'd previously witnessed with any other patient.

WOOD'S END

CHAPTER NINE

Fifty year old Betsy Bloom had never shed her fresh, girlish persona. She wore her short hair straight and pulled back with a clone of the same tortoiseshell headband she'd owned since college. Strangers had difficulty believing she was a doctor. An Orthodox Jew, she was devoted to her family and took her responsibility as head of ER and on call plastic surgeon seriously. She called most of her coworkers by their first name and invited others to call her Betsy. She had a caring, but assertive leadership style and was a creative problem solver.

Dudley Wodsende had been the only doctor who had bristled at the informality and Betsy had been puzzled to see how, until recently, he had conveyed a stoic disapproval of nearly every change she implemented.

By the time Dr. Bloom arrived, Andrea Wodsende had already been transferred to ICU. Betsy planned to interview Dudley as soon as she finished with the chart.

"Where is Dr. Wodsende right now," she asked assuming he would have gone home.

"Right now?"

"Yes, right now."

"He's in ICU. Hasn't left her side since they transferred her from ER."

"Whose side?"

"Why, his wife of course."

Betsy picked up the phone and in seconds was talking to the ER charge nurse.

"There is a fifteen minute visitor rule in your department is there not?"

"Yes."

"And Mrs. Wodsende is a gunshot victim?"

"Yes."

"Can you tell me why you are putting this hospital at legal risk by allowing her ex-husband to hover over her bedside after one of the most contentious divorces this city has ever seen?"

"I'm sorry. He's so caring of her, just sitting there. Helped with the IV and the restraints. And..."

"What has that man done to suspend the common sense of my staff?"

"Everything is fine. He's just..."

"I'm sorry to inform you, but I have a different take on the situation. Please escort Dr. Wodsende from your unit. Ask him to join me in my office. Can you do that or should I send security?"

"But, why? What harm can it do? All he's doing is sitting there, holding her hand and..."

"You have to ask, knowing how they fought? How do you think Andrea would feel if she woke up and found him standing over her? She considers him her enemy. I don't care how long they were married, they are not married now."

A sigh came from the other end of the phone. There was an arrogant, forever calculating quality to Dr. Wodsende and no one wanted to be the person assigned to tell him what he didn't want to hear. Too often there was a price to pay if he was provoked or offended. His co-workers, and especially those assigned to his ER shift, had all been stung by his caustic rebuffs.

Though lately, Betsy had to admit, there had been a stunning metamorphosis. Dudley's behavior had turned solicitous and thoughtful, even depositing bagels and other snacks in the break room and asking after the welfare of those he worked with.

Betsy had remained cautiously optimistic that the changes would last. Now she decided that seeing Dudley so stricken and heartbroken, had disabled the common sense of her staff. Those rules that defined an ethical process were in place for good reason. She'd have to fix this and fix it fast.

Betsy sat in her small office off the reception area. She had carefully read the notes that described Andrea's care in the ER and now prepared to read them again. It was considered unethical for doctors to treat their relatives and this particular former wife was especially problematic.

Betsy had inquired and learned that there had, in fact, been another doctor on the premises looking in on a post operative patient. She now wondered why that doctor hadn't been paged and asked to oversee the case until she arrived, and why Dr. Wodsende had not been banished to the doctor's lounge. As far as she could tell, this was the only mistake that was made.

Betsy put the chart aside as Maria brought her herb tea, fixed just as she liked with a slice of lemon floating at the top of the Styrofoam cup.

"I have to say, Maria. I'm disappointed that you allowed Dudley to treat Andrea. I'll have no choice but to write you up for this."

"There was nothing else to do. Andrea was in shock and she'd lost a lot of blood. If I'd waited even a few minutes we might have lost her."

"It doesn't appear that you checked with the nursing supervisor to see if there was another doctor here last night?"

"There just wasn't time. We had a life to save and by the time you arrived the patient would have been on her way to ICU."

"That's not the point. You could have continued to treat Andrea and still made sure the nursing supervisor understood the relationship between doctor and patient. And, as it happens, there was a surgeon on site who could have easily stepped in."

"It's called the ER for a reason, Betsy. The subject came up, but Dudley assured us he would be fine."

"I don't know what it is about Dr. Wodsende. He seems to intimidate my best staff into forgetting who they are. After you add an addendum to your notes, I want to see them. Only time will tell if we'll have a law suit on our hands."

"She'll concoct something if she can. It's unbelievable how Andrea continued to harass poor Dudley."

"Poor Dudley and not Dr. Wodsende? Be careful, Maria. Many of us had a passing acquaintance with Stephanie because she worked here for a time. But the fact is you didn't know either woman well enough to judge."

Betsy recalled the last and only time that she had seen Andrea. It had been at the annual charity auction to benefit the long term care wing of the hospital and she had been dressed faultlessly in a light blue suit with silver piping. Her blond hair and near perfect features seemed more like packaging, a façade behind which to hide.

At that time Betsy had been newly appointed head of ER. She had sold a busy practice that had infringed on family life in ways she didn't like. Working ER allowed a more predictable schedule, which coincided with her wish to spend more time with her grandchildren. Passed over as Director, Betsy had felt Dudley's animosity right from the start.

As she studied Andrea on that long ago evening, she wondered if a cordial relationship with this woman might be a bridge to disarming the obstacles presented by her husband. Betsy watched as Andrea interacted with Dudley's colleagues.

At one point she saw Dudley reach over to kiss her cheek. Later he put his arm about her in a protective gesture. But in both instances Andrea had visibly stiffened and in subtle, but deliberate strategy, positioned herself as far from her husband's reach as she could without putting up an actual hand and pushing him away.

Betsy found these observations to be a revealing capsule. She decided she would look for an opportunity to know Andrea better, attempting to get beyond the stiff formality. She had seen many battered wives in her career, offering her services pro bono to those attempting to rebuild their lives. What she discerned in Andrea's reactions and what she knew of Dudley's difficult personality, made her feel he fit the profile of a batterer.

But the chance to know Andrea never came. Dudley filed for divorce and Andrea was no longer invited to hospital functions.

When Dudley married Stephanie there was a lot of talk. What struck people most was Stephanie's uncanny physical resemblance to Andrea. Dudley had done what many men do. With seemingly little insight he had married a woman some ten years younger who resembled the first wife.

As a board certified plastic surgeon, Betsy's trained eye had recognized the tell-tale signs of several surgical enhancements, but the similarities stopped there. Stephanie was a lacquered version of Andrea; so much more admiring of Dudley, hanging on every word, young and passive.

If Dudley was a wife beater this marriage would end like the other. Betsy determined to watch Dudley more closely and especially because his compulsion to have Stephanie morphed into a clone of Andrea seemed pathological.

Betsy gave Maria a stern look. "We only know Dudley's side of the story, so be careful not to express an opinion. The Wodsende divorce has entertained this staff long enough."

Maria was immediately defensive of her favorite doctor, forgetting that the year before she had called Dudley pompous and demeaning to women. She was about to reply when the phone rang.

"No, Dr. Wodsende is not here... No, he can't be... disturbed just now... Pardon me, what did you say?"

The plaintive wail was so loud that Maria, standing by Betsy's desk, heard every word.

"I've called the police."

"Who is this?"

"This is his housekeeper. Tell Dr. Wodsende to come home immediately; a terrible tragedy. So horrible!"

The next words were nearly smothered under a convulsive sob of grief. "Stephanie is dead. I can't believe it, but someone has murdered that sweet, wonderful girl. Who would do such a thing?"

WOOD'S END

CHAPTER TEN

Detective Jared Shiel stood in the doorway of the bedroom and surveyed the refuse of a violent crime scene spread out before him.

"You can't get creative in this job," his partner, Ed Stuart, mumbled almost to himself. The statement was a call to focus, a reminder they often voiced to one another.

"Why not, I would think that would help?" said the person who would normally be their prime suspect if Andrea Wodsende had not already confessed. The two detectives were clearly disappointed. They had taken an instant dislike to Dudley.

"Because then you're running rabbit trails. No, you have to let the physical evidence tell you what happened. No conjecture, no Hollywood type of reading into things for the sake of plot."

An inappropriate chuckle strangled in the back of Dudley's throat. Jared turned to look at him. It was a practiced stare, famous in police circles, but Dr. Wodsende was patently oblivious. Jared didn't like the man and if asked, wouldn't have trouble saying why.

"In this case, Detective Shiel, your suspect has confessed. I treated her myself barely six hours ago and it's patently obvious, even to a novice, that she has had a psychotic break. My attorney will tell you that I predicted this. Andrea was never stable!"

Jared and Ed exchanged a glance.

"I know what you're thinking," Dudley announced. His tone was both smug and confrontational. "The husband did it! I've watched a few of those crime shows, so I know how you people think."

"Thank you so very much for helping us out here, Dudley. Anything else you'd like to add?" Ed asked.

"Yes there is. Andrea has confessed. Andrea is insane and she'd been harassing Stephanie because she wanted me back. Isn't all this crystal clear?"

"Crystal, huh?"

Jared listened as his partner baited Dr. Wodsende, who had refused to be interviewed without his attorney present and yet, didn't seem to realize he was being interviewed now.

"I'd like you to get finished up here and be out of my house ASAP. And... did you have to wait so long before you let the coroner take Stephanie away. It was indecent of you to leave her lying there with all these people about."

"Interesting that she was fully dressed. Almost like she had intentions of going somewhere." Ed probed.

"Ridiculous. Stephanie was waiting up for me."

"Really," Ed said and caught Jared's eye. They were both thinking the same thing. *Overly confident, arrogant elitist.* The chink in this amour begged for probing.

"Can you tell us anything more about the first Mrs. Wodsende that might help?"

"Stephanie was the best wife a man ever had. Andrea was a huge mistake. So, no, there is nothing else I'd like to say. I'm waiting for my attorney to call back. It should be any minute now. He can tell you all about Andrea. Every obsessive sick detail of how she harassed my family."

Jared watched as Dudley frantically tried to reach his attorney. If he had preplanned this crime, he had forgotten the important detail of verifying whether his attorney, the prestigious Samuel Marstead, was available to take the field when called. Or was his narcissism so great that he couldn't imagine his lawyer having a life apart from his demands?

"We haven't seen the former Mrs. Wodsende have we? We'll get around to that," Jared interjected in a neutral tone and studied Dudley's expression. His face was handsome, tanned from the golf course and weathered slightly from sailing.

Dudley had not asked if Stephanie had suffered. He hadn't asked to see her before she was placed in a body bag and carried to the morgue in an ambulance. He seemed more concerned with the disruption to his house than the loss of a beloved wife.

It was now 10:30 in the morning. Sometime after midnight Stephanie had been brutally murdered. It appeared that she had tried to barricade the bedroom door since a heavy armoire was pushed in that direction. She was attired in street clothes, wore make-up and jewelry. A packed suitcase was open on the floor awaiting the inclusion of last minute items. Downstairs, there was no sign of a break-in.

"What do you think?" Ed asked Jared.

"Looks like Andrea was voluntarily admitted. We'll check the phone records to see if the two exchanged any calls."

"Utter nonsense! My wife opened the door and Andrea pushed her way in. Stephanie ran up these stairs with Andrea following."

"There you go again, Doc, doing our thinking for us?" Ed commented.

They were shamelessly baiting him, and yet Dudley kept the conversation going in a futile attempt at control. There was so much that just didn't fit about Dudley. He stood here arguing when he should be grieving. A compulsion to insert his presence into the mix outweighed any better inclination to retreat, allowing the detectives and crime scene technicians to do their work. He had dressed in a crisp white shirt with gold flashing at his wrists where buttons usually are. The man had actually taken the time to put on cologne before returning home to face this tragic circumstance. Jared wondered why he cared to dress so formally after a long night of wearing scrubs in the ER.

"I need to get back to work and let my staff know what's happened."

"I think they all know what's happened, Doc," Ed said.

"Well, yes. Of course, but I need to clear my calendar for the week. I have a funeral to plan and I need to call Stephanie's mother and sister in Memphis."

"Lots of people behave inappropriately when they're in shock. We understand this," Jared said, not unkindly. "So let me make this as clear as I can. You are free to do just as you please as long as you don't interfere with the ongoing work of this investigation. Isn't there someone you can call other than your attorney, a good friend who can be with you right now?"

"Yeah, get some rest, Dudley," Ed reiterated. "At least until your attorney shows up. Then we can meet at the station to take your formal statement."

They could see that Dudley didn't like being told what to do. He opened his mouth to protest, yet again, but paused to reconsider. The compulsion to speak or wisely remain silent was a visible battle.

"I don't know why this has to be so complicated. Your murderer has confessed. And now my house is totally torn up and disrupted and somehow I'll have to get it back together before Melody returns from school. And then I'll have to tell her that Andrea killed her Mom. My, you people are insensitive."

They had asked Dudley if he had any children and he had said no. There were no photographs of children that they had seen. Jared and his partner exchanged a look, before Ed turned and walked away.

"Is Melody your child, Doctor?" Jared asked.

"Goodness, no. Melody is Stephanie's from a previous marriage."

"Do you have legal custody of this child?"

"No, I imagine her father will come and get her. He lives in Winchester. About thirty minutes from here."

"Have you notified him of what's happened?"

"Well no. Not yet. I thought I'd let Melody call him when she gets home. She likes talking to him and knows his number."

"And how old is Melody?"

"Seven...no, she just had a birthday. She's eight."

"We're going to take care of this for you, Dr. Wodsende. We'll have the child's father notified right away so that he can pick her up at school."

Jared paused. It seemed particularly cruel that it would not occur to Dudley how traumatic it would be for a child to walk into a crime scene like this. Through the years Jared had seen how apparent lapses in appropriate response, too easily excused by others, actually exposed a pattern of behavior that was worth examining for motive. Did Dr. Wodsende have a sadistic streak in him? Time would tell.

"Too bad you didn't tell us this earlier when we asked. Who gets Melody off to school in the morning?"

"My wife usually. I've told her that we have a housekeeper for a reason and she can sleep in, but she will usually make breakfast herself. Stephanie is; she was... a very attentive mother."

There was a derisive quality to this last statement, which begged the question. "Were you jealous of the time and attention your wife devoted to her child, Dr. Wodsende?"

"That's ludicrous. Certainly not!"

Ed returned, flipping back pages of his notebook and reading.

"As we already know the housekeeper noticed nothing amiss when she came in this morning. Her son dropped her off on his way to work because she doesn't drive. Before she entered the house she chatted with a neighbor who told her there had been a woman found shot down the block. They speculated that it was probably a rape. Another woman had been assaulted near here last year."

"Call the attending physician at the hospital and, if it wasn't already done, ask him to run a rape kit on Andrea Wodsende," Jared interrupted.

"What a stupid thing to do. Andrea wasn't raped. She was too busy murdering my wife."

"If you don't tone it down, Dudley, we'll have you removed, and further questioning can wait until we're downtown with a video camera rolling. Do you understand?"

"Okay, then," Ed continued. "The housekeeper said that Stephanie is usually up early, getting Melody off to school. She makes breakfast just as the Doc here said. But this morning the housekeeper did all that and then waited with the child at the end of the drive for the car pool."

"Was she concerned that the morning routine changed?

"Not at all. According to the housekeeper, Stephanie and Dudley had been fighting about how the child was being raised."

Ed looked pointedly at Dr. Wodsende. "He, meaning the doctor here, wanted the child to, quote, 'be strong and raise herself.' He hoped they could agree to send her to a boarding school somewhere in Europe where the Doc here has family."

"That is so ridiculous," Dudley interrupted. "My wife and I never fought and certainly, never in front of the help."

"So the housekeeper is lying when she claims you wanted to send your step-daughter away."

"We discussed it. We didn't fight; we never fought and after some consideration we decided Melody would stay here. She has a perfectly good school, a private day school. The best."

"So," Ed continued. "As we already know, the housekeeper didn't check on Stephanie until she brought her a cup of coffee, knowing she left for the gym each morning after Melody was picked up. Not until she entered the main part of the house did she see the blood trail. And when she did, she thought that Dr. Wodsende had probably been abusive... again."

"That's ridiculous," Dudley proclaimed.

"This is how I see it." In a sweeping motion Jared waved his hand over the room calling attention to the bedroom carnage. "Your wife fought valiantly for her life. Wounded and bleeding she somehow found the strength to rise from the floor, attempting to reach the phone that had been knocked off the table. The perpetrator then wrestled the phone from her, striking her pretty hard. At that point, it's possible, that Stephanie somehow managed to get hold of the gun. She shot her attacker who fled, bleeding."

Dudley could not resist looking at the blood trail. It started a few feet before them just inside the door of the bedroom, trailing down the steps and out the front door. "And that would be Andrea," he whispered.

"We won't know for sure until we do the..."

"It was Andrea," Dudley erupted. "Can't you see that? She killed Stephanie in a fit of spiteful rage."

Ed held up a gun sticky with blood gleaming through the plastic bag.

"Is this your gun, Dudley? Do you own a gun?"

"I've never owned a gun in my life. I'm a proponent of strict gun control. That thing belonged to Andrea. She purchased it while we were still married, and I might add, against my fervent objections. But she never listened to me. Andrea always did just as she pleased."

"From the look of Stephanie I'd say the coroner will report several facial bones broken. Was Andrea strong enough to inflict that kind of damage?"

"She hit me many times and I was always surprised at how strong she was. I could have filed charges against her for spousal abuse, but I was too much of a gentleman to have such a charge made public."

"So, Andrea hit Stephanie several times in the face. Then she fires the gun. Wounded though she is, Stephanie manages to retrieve this same weapon and shoot the fleeing Andrea. Is that your theory, Doctor?"

"That's right," Dr. Wodsende replied. His tone was a halting whisper as he tore his eyes from Andrea's blood trail with apparent difficulty.

"What did you say?" Jared asked.

"I said, that seems right. I'm sorry Stephanie had to die like that."

Jared scrutinized Dudley's face. Aside from anger, this brief hint of regret was all the emotion they would hear.

"Tell me, Dudley. May I call you Dudley?" Ed interjected.

"I'd say no, but you've been calling me that since I arrived home."

"Did Melody's father share custody with your wife?"

"Yes. They shared custody. This wasn't our week to have her, but Stephanie was planning on visiting her parents in Memphis and was going to take Melody with her. They were flying out tonight."

Ed jotted this information in his notepad. He would verify the trip and confirm a return flight. If there were no immediate plans to return to Boston, they would investigate the possibility that Stephanie was leaving her husband.

"What kind of a child is Melody?" Jared asked.

"Melody is an independent child. She preferred her father's home to ours and I think would have eventually lived with him full time. I think children should be where they want to be, don't you? And she actually needs very little parenting, but I couldn't convince Stephanie."

"Really. An eight year old needs very little parenting?" Ed interjected.

"What is this? I'm not having this conversation! You understand nothing! I'm not the one who killed Stephanie. I didn't shoot Andrea..."

Dudley's cell phone rang. "It's about time you called me back, you useless.... We're paying you good money to stay on retainer. That means you jump when I call."

There was a pause. Dudley turned and stalked down the hall. Still in ear shot he continued. "Yes, I've been talking to them. They've been talking to me. I'm being harassed. Yes, Yes... They've been here all morning! I, I," he stuttered.

Jared and his partner watched with deadpan expressions as Dr. Wodsende angrily slammed a door behind him.

"Those first words are telling don't you think?"

"Yes," Jared replied. "It's not about the violent assault on two women he once vowed to love and cherish."

"He was more put out by the overall mess and inconvenience," Ed offered. "Not a shred of empathy for Stephanie's child. It's all about him."

"Seems to me we have a clinical diagnosis for such a person," Jared stated.

WOOD'S END

CHAPTER ELEVEN

One of the crime scene technicians remained working in the dressing room area, but Twanna Adams was bent over something beside the bed. Jared watched as she reached for her camera, snapping additional photographs from several angles. She was one of the best, which is why he had asked for her after arriving at the scene.

"What do you have?" Jared asked.

"Looks like a footprint. It's too large to be the suspect or the victim. Any of you been walking around in here? Take off your shoes so I can rule you out right now."

"This is crazy," one of the uniforms said. "The case is shut. We have a confession and the Doc says she's certifiable. Do you really think any of this evidence matters now."

"Didn't any of you see what happened in the Sam Shepherd case? That doctor was the obvious suspect, the only suspect they saw so they ignored or suppressed good physical evidence. You, too, Dr. Wodsende, take off your shoes," she called as Dudley stepped back into the hallway.

Jared bent over the footprint, seeing it for the first time. The outline was so vague that he had missed it and yet once treated would show up more clearly. Following Twanna's instructions they all removed their shoes.

Jared turned and looked fully at Dr. Wodsende. He knew that Marstead would have advised his client not to talk with the police any further, but here he was back in the entrance to the bedroom where Stephanie had been murdered. His eyes roved restlessly over the room and settled not on the place where Stephanie's body had been outlined, but on the place where Andrea's blood trail began.

"There are a few minor details I'm interested in understanding more fully," Jared said as pleasantly as he could muster. "Your housekeeper told my partner that Andrea was finally happy. She'd moved into a new place and was decorating and settling in. They kept in touch. Did you know that?"

"No, but I wouldn't care."

"So what would prompt Andrea to drive from Woods End Township to Boston in the middle of the night? If this were a crime of passion, as you say, Andrea would have had plenty of time to cool off."

A flush of barely restrained rage crept over Dudley's face. "I told you. She's insane."

"We'll see," Jared spoke quietly.

"You're trying to provoke me. My attorney is on his way. He told me not to say another word."

"Good advice," Ed offered. "You should take it."

"Andrea was a terrible wife. She was selfish and self centered and ignored our needs whenever a competing influence called her away. She wanted me back. Even then she was unraveling. A divorce that should have taken months took almost a year because she fought me over every detail. She was stalking me every chance she got."

Ed gave him a hard stare. "It seems to me that if she wanted to stalk you, she would have stayed in the city."

"She tried, but I got a restraining order. And she moved to Woods End just last month. Every time I looked in my rearview mirror, she was behind me."

"Any proof of that, Doc?" Ed asked. "Because I already called to check and the only restraining order of record was hers against you."

"I don't need proof. Everyone at the hospital knew how she was. I let her have that run down farm in Woods End just to get her away from Stephanie. Andrea couldn't let me go. And you two are trying to make a case where there isn't one. I would think a psychotic suspect that's confessed would be enough for you?"

While his partner continued to bait the doctor Jared took another careful look at the crime scene, cataloging in his mind the many unanswered questions. He looked forward to a quiet moment when he could compare his notes and the crime scene photographs with the forensic evidence provided by the lab.

He whirled about to face Dudley. "I haven't talked to Andrea, so haven't heard this famous confession."

"If you knew the first thing about such things," Dr Wodsende began before Jared interrupted him.

"Saying something doesn't make it so. Ed and I are always suspicious when a suspect tries to do our thinking for us. Bad habit of yours, Doctor Wodsende; that trick might work in your world, but not in ours."

Jared and Ed had encountered this before. Dudley would allow no rest until every detail worth managing had been pressed through the mill of his version of events. That the investigative team of Shiel and Stuart would not capitulate, conforming to his bias of a lazy police force, inferior to his superior intelligence, was forcing Dudley's hand. He was too arrogant to see the damage he was doing to himself.

Jared guessed that if Dudley or his attorney had any favors to call in, the apparatus would start exerting its weight. Samuel Marstead was not to be underestimated. He had a hand in every facet of state politics and could attract large sums of money to a campaign. It was said about him, that he was a master politician in the Machiavellian mold, too powerful to trade what he already had, for the constraints of public office.

Marstead, as Dudley's attorney was curious. Taken at face value, this powerful lawyer appeared to be tethered to their prime suspect, suffering himself to be at the beck and call of a man to whom the word *jerk*, absolutely applied. The first forty-eight hours were crucial in any investigation and Jared felt a particular urgency to get busy before any outside resistance could derail their focus.

"Let me tell you something, Jared. You need someone to do your thinking for you."

"Detective. It's Detective Shiel," Twanna corrected as she bagged the other of the doctor's shoes. "And if you plan on addressing me for any reason, my name is Miss Adams. And I must say, Doc. You don't look like such a prize to me. I can't imagine two women fighting to the death over you."

"When will I get those back? I notice you're not taking anyone else's shoes."

"That's because no one else wears the magic size."

"But you don't have a warrant for those shoes. Oh what the... Take them. I don't care. I have five pair just like them in my closet."

Marstead arrived and promptly removed Dr. Wodsende from their midst. The house was now nearly empty as Twanna packed up the last of her gear. Crime scene tape closed off the bedroom, the adjoining bath, dressing room, and outer hallway.

Jared looked at his partner. "What strikes you as odd about this picture?"

"Nothing. It looks like too many other crime scenes we've seen. But the Doc said he had five additional pair of shoes just like what was taken into evidence for a total of six. He gave us one pair and wore another out the door with his attorney. I found two pair of black shoes and one brown in his closet, leaving one brown unaccounted for. We've searched the house and there is no sign of a break in. With this alarm system there is no doubt that Stephanie let Andrea in. Had to, no other explanation."

"So what are we saying? Once in the house Andrea either forced Stephanie up to the bedroom or the two walked up here at will," Jared mused.

"Or the two ran up here to get away from a third party," Ed offered. "At some point Stephanie shot at the intruder and got Andrea by mistake."

"Thus this heavy armoire in the middle of the room. Stephanie ran for the phone, not knowing the line was cut, while Andrea tried to barricade the door. If there was an invitation, we need to see which lady initiated the invite."

"I'll check the phone records. Could Andrea have retained a key?"

"Not likely," Jared said.

"But Andrea knew the housekeeper. They kept in touch. If Andrea was as obsessed with Dudley as he claims, she might have lifted a set of keys from her."

"Entirely possible, but she would still have trouble getting past security without knowing at last two, frequently altered codes. So, whatever happened had to be planned."

Ed looked at Jared who was younger by twenty something years. While Ed started out taking the lead Jared had, early in the partnership, just naturally assumed the role.

"So what do you think?" Ed asked.

"I won't be happy if we don't do a full investigation, but I can already see the signs," Jared said. "The powers that be will like the obvious fit espoused so eloquently by Dr. Wodsende. Especially because this is going to be high profile. And with Marstead involved..."

"As much as I like the husband as our perp it has to be said that this Andrea may be every bit as unhinged as he is," Ed offered. "And if she did this... It may just be true that she is also insane. Dudley claims Stephanie's murder was fueled by Andrea's psychotic break."

"As far as I'm concerned the jury is out. Psychotic people are not goal driven. This was a goal driven murder."

"What do you want to do next?" Ed asked.

"I'll have a look at Andrea Wodsende and then I'll track down the ER attending and the nursing supervisor. I'll check what lab was ordered; make sure they treated this as they should have. I'm troubled that both victims and Dudley have such close ties to the hospital. A little to incestuous for my comfort."

"I'll make a few phone calls," Ed said as they divvied up the work. I'll call Stephanie's parents and find out if everything was as copasetic at home as Dudley claims. Then I'll track down Andrea's family and get their take."

"And check on that plane reservation," Jared said. "If there was no return flight then maybe Stephanie was leaving her husband."

"Sounds like a plan. We'll meet up in a couple of hours."

Jared waved goodbye to Twanna. "Call me when you have something; call me if you don't have anything."

Jared entered through the lobby and bypassing the reception desk, headed toward the bank of elevators. No one had to tell him where ICU was located. He was more familiar with every hospital in the greater metro area than he liked, but this small private hospital was unlike any other. Plenty of endowed money kept it running at the convenience of those doctors lucky enough to have staff privileges.

Entering the unit Jared paused at the nurse's desk, allowing his eye to scan the glassed enclosures, which encircled the central work station. The charge nurse waved a greeting. He knew her well. They had become the kind of friends who could joke and talk, but never met outside their jobs. She had told him about her children and she knew that he was lonely and hoping to settle down some day. "Not likely to happen," she would tell him, "not for someone as obsessed with work as you are."

"Thanks for the encouragement," he would banter back. But today there would be no such conversation. For the hospital staff, the violent death of Stephanie Wodsende was personal.

"You're here to see Andrea. She's over there."

"How's she doing?"

"She's finally conscious, but we had to restrain her."

"Can I have five minutes?"

"Sorry, Dr. Bloom said no visitors. You wouldn't get anything from her anyway. She's hallucinating. We had to restrain her just to keep her in the bed. She's lucky to be alive. They'll take her into surgery tomorrow after she's more fully stabilized."

"I just want to look at her. No talk, I promise," Jared said and without waiting for an answer walked the short distance to the bedside.

If Andrea had been combative before she was now quiet. Lying on her back she stared up at the ceiling, eyes wide and pupils dilated to black balls. As he watched, she closed her eyes and seemed now to be sleeping.

There was a touching fragility about Andrea. He caught sight of her hands prone at her side as though positioned for a casket viewing. Her nails were perfectly manicured, but lacking polish. Whatever altercation she may have been involved in hadn't been so bad that the nails were broken. He took out his notebook and made a notation. Turning a limp hand over, Jared saw that trace amounts of blood were still imbedded in the lines of her fingers and under her nails. He called his partner's cell phone.

"How are you doing?"

"Talked with the little girl's father. He said Stephanie was afraid of Dudley. Said she changed a lot after they got married. Was guarded and wanted the child to spend more time with him. He thought this was odd. He wondered if Dudley was abusive, but when he asked, Stephanie denied it."

"Anything else?" Jared asked.

"As a rule she didn't confide in him. I got the impression that he still carried a torch. He was pretty broken up. Asked all the right questions and, if it checks out, he has a rock solid alibi."

"Did Stephanie ever mention Andrea to him?"

"No, she didn't." Jared could tell his partner was reading from his notes. "Said she never spoke to him about Andrea; he said she wasn't the kind of person who would have made a point of getting to know the former wife. I got the impression that unlike Andrea, Stephanie was milk toast. Very different from how people have described Andrea."

"Yeah well I'm looking at her now and there are a couple of things we need to do. Get someone up here to test for gunshot residue. I want to know if she actually fired that gun. I also want a tox-screen and there's blood under her nails. Probably hers, but let's confirm."

"I'll call the crime lab and her doctor," his partner offered. "Who is it, do you know?"

Jared glanced at the information posted above the bed. "Doctors of record are Dr. Betsy Bloom and Herbert Smith. I know Herb. He's fishing in Canada, so call this Dr. Bloom. I think she's the new head of ER, so must be filling in for Herb until he gets back."

"Done. Anything else?"

"Not unless you can think of anything?" Jared replied.

"Okay, I'll see you at The Fours on Canal within the hour. In case you haven't noticed we've skipped lunch."

Jared didn't want to discuss the case amid the busy luncheon crowd. "Why don't we meet at my place? I asked Twanna to call with her unofficial take on the scene. We can put her on speaker, lay everything out, and decide where we go from here," Jared suggested.

"With that snake Marstead involved I'm thinking we'll get one shot at Dudley and unless we can charge him, there will be no more access. Let's not forget he has an alibi. How many times did he give us those details?" Ed reminded.

"As anxious as Dudley was to do our jobs for us, I'm expecting to find a few holes. After I leave ICU I'm heading down to ER," Jared said. "I want to check out Wodsende's alibi. If going and coming was possible without anyone noticing. Let yourself in if you get there first."

"Yeah," Ed said.

Jared had inherited a town house on Beacon Hill. Prime Real Estate that tended to prompt jealousy in the department when he first came on board. He didn't have to work, but had taken to police work as a priest does a spiritual calling. After a certain time period of testing and hazing he had earned a respect that couldn't be purchased.

"There's left over roast in the crock pot and some white chocolate cheese cake. We'll make a couple of sandwiches and check in with Twanna."

"What are you thinking?" Ed asked.

"Gut instinct?"

"Gut instinct."

"I'm thinking this woman was set up," Jared replied. He looked again at Andrea and was struck at the sheer prettiness of her classic features. "What do you think?"

"I'm thinking it's complicated," Ed answered. "Not the cut and dried scenario the good doctor hoped to serve up on a tarnished platter. I haven't heard back from the airlines, but they'll be calling soon, and I have yet to hear from the victim's mother in Memphis. So I'm reserving judgment."

"That's good," Jared said. "One of us needs to."

Jared pocketed his phone and slid Andrea's hand into his. There wasn't much lifting room. Both hands were secured by leather bands lined with lamb's wool to the bed frame. He knew that her ankles and waist, though covered by the light blanket, would be just as securely restrained.

He studied her face. In the dim light her white skin had taken on a child-like radiance that made her circumstances seem all the more incongruous. He bent close to her ear. "What happened to you?" he whispered. Her dark eye lashes seemed to lift very slightly. Under the closed lids he saw movement. Jared waited, but Andrea remained immobile.

"No one can speak for you, Andrea. Can you open your eyes and look at me? Can you tell me what happened?"

No answer. No movement.

"Your ex-husband has pretty much fingered you for this crime. If I'm going to help, I'll need to know your side."

He felt certain she was striving for comprehension. Under a wash of apparent oblivion she had followed, if not the actual words, then the intent of those words. Jared realized how much he hoped that she would be innocent so that Dudley would be guilty. Convoluted thinking that was certain to get him in trouble. He needed to keep an open mind. Was he reading more into this than was wise?

"Just give me a sign that you've understood and we'll talk later when you're feeling stronger?"

No response.

"I want to help, Andrea. Can you speak?"

Her grip tightened. Jared leaned closer, preparing to hear whatever it was she would say, certain that he had gotten through to her.

She formed a tight fist into the softness of his palm. Her nails fanned out and dug into his flesh. Simultaneously, she lifted her head, connecting with his chin on the way up. They would both have a bruise. In as raised a position as the restraints allowed, with her eyes unfocused she emitted an inhuman, bone chilling scream that reverberated throughout the unit, freezing all who heard it.

"Okay, time to leave." A nurse rushed in nudging him away from the bedside. "We just had her settled down and now look at her."

Jared glanced over his shoulder as he was ushered out the door. In a semi-raised position, Andrea's mouth was open though the scream had died. Drool slid down her chin and her hands opened and closed, grasping desperately for substance out of empty air. He felt an absurd desire to return and dab at the wetness of her mouth with a tissue.

"Okay, now. That's enough. You're a grown woman. No more screaming." The words were spoken harshly.

Didn't they see the terror? Jared inwardly chastised. He wanted to comfort Andrea. To tell her everything would be alright, but there was nothing he could do. Although banished from the bedside he held his ground outside the door watching.

"We're not equipped for this in ICU," a young nurse complained as they attempted to ease Andrea's rigid body back into a prone position.

"After she's out of recovery tomorrow, if she's stable enough, we'll talk to Dr. Bloom about admitting her to psych."

"The best place for her."

"Good riddance." They all agreed.

"Don't let Dr. Bloom hear you talk like that," the charge nurse said. "She's been pretty clear about what she thinks."

"Yeah, she kicked poor Dr. Wodsende out of here didn't she?"

Jared felt a chill. "Dr. Wodsende was here?" he asked. The three nurses had gathered posse like around the bed. In unison they turned and glared at him.

"Thought we asked you to leave?" his friend scolded. "I did you a favor allowing you in here, Jared."

"I'm going, but couldn't help over-hearing. After Andrea left the ER was Dr. Wodsende here with her?"

"Why not? He's a doctor and she was his wife. He was pretty broken up."

"What did he do while he was here?"

"Sat with her, that's all."

"Did she know he was here?"

"I don't think so."

"But the first time she turned combative, that was with Dudley here beside the bed, right?" Jared probed.

"That's enough," the charge nurse interjected. "Detective or not, friend or not, I want you out of here. And, just so you know, if we had even guessed about Stephanie, Dr. Wodsende wouldn't have been allowed within ten feet of ICU."

The explanation was defensive. Someone had already reprimanded them, and Jared made a mental note to find out who it was and have a conversation. He shook his head. The charge nurse caught the gesture of disapproval. "I thought you were leaving," she reminded.

"I'm leaving. Hey I'm gone, but don't forget. Innocent until proven guilty, so be nice to her. And...my partner is sending a technician over to test for gunshot residue and scrape the nails for blood and tissue. So bag those hands. They should be here within the hour."

"She confessed."

"That's what they say. Any of you hear it?"

They looked at him, evidencing silent surprise at the question.

"That's what I thought. Only Dr. Wodsende heard this famous confession? Am I right? Call me if that changes," was Jared's sarcastic rebuttal.

Still hearing the echo of that scream, Jared walked into the corridor. He felt depressed and guessed he just liked to plant his energy in hopeless territory. He could think of not one good reason why he should take extra care with Andrea Wodsende. He needed to clear his head. Every instinct told him that nothing was what it seemed, and despite all the talk about depending on physical evidence, his instincts were rarely wrong.

For some reason Jared felt a wash of self pity. Why couldn't he simply bite the bullet and settle down, because there were lots of good women out there. Or so he was frequently told. Jared thought of Nora Dilihunt. He had invited her to a showing of his uncles work in which a painting of Nora and her sister, Lydia, had been featured. Lydia Dillihunt had been kidnapped as a young girl and never found; the cold case attracting cobwebs of neglect for over twenty years. But his uncle Burns had known the family and painted a quite charming portrait of the two sisters.

Jared reached for the memory. When he came to the force, perhaps because of the connection with his uncle, he had asked around. The name Marstead had surfaced in the Dillihunt case. Paul Marstead had been briefly considered a suspect in Lydia's disappearance though he was very young at the time. Maybe, after he got the Wodsende case behind him, he would revisit this other because it nagged at Jared. How the high and mighty Marstead had suffered himself to be so talked down to, so demeaned by a fool like Dudley. It didn't make a lick of sense and ran counter to all he knew of the Marstead ego.

Samuel Marstead... Paul Marstead. Jared let the connection jell. The substance of such coincidences, once explored, could unearth a flood of answers one never expected.

Jared made a mental note. If it turned out Dudley was guilty of his wife's murder he would send for the cold case file on the Dillihunt disappearance. He would phone Nora, Lydia's elder sister, and ask if she knew Dudley Wodsende or Samuel Marstead and if she recalled any involvement during the time that Lydia went missing. He was fairly certain Nora still lived up the coast in Rockport, Massachusetts. She would be easy to find. He already knew that she was pretty. Maybe they would click. But that was for later. Jared chastised himself for allowing such sentiment to distract him from the case at hand. He was, he admitted lonely. Maybe it was time to share his life with a woman. To really open himself up to the possibility of love and family.

The elevator door opened. Jared hesitated too long and let it shut. Turning on his heel he looked at his watch. There wasn't time for a detour, but it seemed his course was set. He walked down several corridors before coming to the elevator that would take him to the pent house floor which was entirely paneled in a rich cherry. It was here that one of the best medical libraries in Boston was housed, including many rare books of historical significance. This was a hospital so well endowed it didn't need to court anyone's favor.

But for one librarian busy on the phone, and a snoozing security officer, the premises appeared deserted. Jared flashed his badge in their direction, though it wasn't necessary. They knew him here and it was no mystery why he had come.

Toward the back, in a lighted alcove, he paused before the painting he had come to see. He looked down at his left palm. Andrea had drawn blood. He pulled a handkerchief from his inside jacket pocket and wrapped it around the wound as he calculated the timing of his last tetanus shot. He'd let his partner make the sandwiches while he soaked his hand in peroxide and water.

Jared took a deep breath and studied the large oil painting, bolted to the wall and fitted with a silent alarm system. Painted by his famous uncle, Burns Padgett Shiel, it had been donated by a patron, and was worth a substantial sum. If the hospital was smart, they would hold on to their prize since it would one day be worth millions. Even in his lifetime Burns was considered among the best of American painters.

The colors drew him in. Soft but vivid they reminded him only of good. The farm of the painting stood much as it was pictured on the canvas. He went there, to Western Massachusetts as often as he could. It wasn't Boston he wanted to escape because he loved the city. It was the overwhelming emotional drain of what his senses were assaulted with as a homicide detective that sometimes required respite.

The farm reminded Jared that what he saw and dealt with every day was not the normal stuff of life. His partner had a wife, children, and even grandchildren that kept him grounded. Jared had the farm left to him by his famous uncle. Burns had never been much of a farmer, but used the landscape as rich fodder for his art.

Ever since the first Shiel settlers had made their way south from Canada, descendents had lived in and around Woods End, Massachusetts. If Jared didn't produce a few children, all would end with him after 270 years of carefully recorded history.

Jared knew exactly where his famous Uncle would have set up his easel to paint this scene. Or perhaps Burns had known it so well that he'd painted it from memory. Burns would have hiked to the western ridge that looked across the valley to the place where Woods End was nestled. The Church spire could be seen gleaming, white in sunlight through the sparse autumn foliage with bells that marked the noon hour in a cacophony of pleasant sound. In winter there were overland ski forays along the ridge with brief portages before the slope careened toward the valley floor. At the foot of the ridge the Shiel acreage fanned east and north toward the Vermont border.

Stone walls, built with rocks cleared from the land, encircled three fields, portions of which were captured on Burns' canvas. The orchard and a nineteenth century pound near the road which, in another century, had been used to keep wandering farm animals secure until collected by their owners. The steep roof of the house could be seen, and the barn some distance away with two stone silos appearing like Irish round towers at either end.

Jared had always imagined he would raise a family on the Shiel farm. He would work in one of the nearby towns, perhaps as the Police Chief, where nothing much but the occasional domestic dispute and a few rebellious teens rippled the ease of daily life.

His last visual memory was of the painting that had revived his spirits and quelled the disquiet of Andrea's haunting scream. He felt the pangs of hunger and looked forward to left over roast on sour dough with Muenster cheese and sweet pickle paste.

Much later, when Jared tried to remember beyond these thoughts, he drew a blank. There was no sense of impending danger. No memory of the burning pain that shot through his body as the bullet tore bone from tissue and decimated a kidney. As if that were not enough his assailant had then bashed his skull with a blunt object, perhaps the butt of the gun that was never found.

What followed was a long recovery and, at least for a time, Jared forgot that he had ever been curious about Andrea Wodsende.

WOOD'S END

PART THREE
CHAPTER TWELVE
Two Years Later

ZACH

"Get UP!"

It was Saturday and Zach had no intention of waking before noon. His Saturdays were pretty much set in stone. Sleep as long as possible, call best friend, Vince, whose father happened to be in prison. Smoke a little pot on the way to Wafer Thin's Back Room where Wafer Thin Guido served up beer absent the requisite ID, and fat Uncle Mario cooked linguini with clams, baked penne with sausage, or crab bisque with parker house roles and a pepper salad from the one dish menu recorded on a chalk board over the toilet in the unisex bathroom. Although the entrée tended to change the dessert didn't. Steeped in various fine liquors and chunks of rich chocolate with whipped cream and toasted almond slivers, Mario concocted the absolute best bread pudding in the world.

"The recipe's a secret," Mario told Zach. "If I handed it over, I'd have to kill you. Ha, ha, ha," Mario's laugh was contagious. "Got it doing a deal in Belfast off Queen. Almost got shot crossing from York. A couple of brothers and one was a former chef like me. Of course we had to talk food while Guido talked business. Well, I got the recipe and I never went back to Belfast. In those days, even for me, just too dangerous."

Since the bar itself lacked a liquor license, and was open per invitation only, Guido didn't worry much about a few irregularities. He was more focused on the back room where an apparent game of poker was always underway and occasional taxis deposited travelers from the airport or the bus depot.

Vince would sometimes ask Guido about his father, whose stock reply was, "I haven't seen him, but Mario drove your mother up last week."

Zach wondered why Vince didn't just ask his mother or Mario, but most conversation came through Guido. Sometimes Guido would pass Vince an envelope crammed with bills so his mother could pay the rent and buy food. Vince was wiry and tall with a lock of glossy dark hair that fell over hazel eyes.

Vince had been pretty anonymous until Zach hooked up with him in detention. Zach talked his new friend into joining the newly formed golf team where Zach happened to be a star, since he'd grown up playing at the club. After being quietly expelled from two private schools, Zach was temporarily in the public school system. He'd begun by offering the competition a can of warm beer around the third hole, which happened to be the most isolated. By the ninth hole, Zach's team was most always in the lead and Vince, who had been drinking like everyone else, was as cool and unperturbed as if he'd never actually swallowed. "Just doesn't catch up with me," Vince said. "It's the European in me. Been drinking wine like water since I could walk."

Zach managed to acquire a few dime bags of pot. "For private use," he told Vince, but soon decided to sell. Both boys quickly became the go-to guys, popular with a certain set of girls and invited to an eclectic cross section of parties. Although exaggerated, Zach liked the aura of respect that lent mystery to his expanding reputation.

After a few hours at Wafer Thins, feeling pretty mellow, they would party until Sunday or lately they had been driving from one end of the city to another searching for the best rave. Then it was off to the after party for a fitting end to a night of drugs, dancing, and music so loud his ears rang for the rest of the week.

The bane of Zach's existence was his father. No matter how he tried, Zach could not escape the tape of his father's voice reciting a litany of do's and don'ts, telling him that nothing was ever what it seemed. According to Elias, all people were liars, and the con, the fix; the rush for power in getting it over on someone else lay at the root of most interaction, which was why lawyers were essential to any society. And, Zach decided, not the exclusive domain of shadowy characters like Mario and Guido.

Guido especially seemed interested in his father. The kinds of cases he took and what he'd been working on over the last few years. This didn't seem strange to Zach. His father had been in the news working his magic in the area of forensic accounting and called to testify in at least two very high-profile cases.

Elias Goldfarb taught his son to think for himself. Even when he wasn't present, Elias had a way of sapping the joy out of each act of rebellion. Zach wondered why he couldn't just take his fun where he found it, like every other kid he knew. Except Vince. And, come to think of it, Vince wasn't having all that much fun either. At times he appeared set apart from the crowded mêlée of something like a rave, somber in the midst of fervent gaiety, locked in an aspect of watching, even waiting.

And the drugs, "here, take this, it's a little bit of Heaven." Zach didn't doubt that Heaven might be a real place, located in another galaxy where a more evolved community of God's creation had learned to do everything right, but he knew Heaven could not be found in a pill. Sometimes he took what was offered, but more often he pocketed it, noticing that Vince was doing the same.

Vince's mother always called Zach's mother to ask if he could spend the night and Evelyn Goldfarb always said, "Yes, but next time we'd love to have Vincent. You've been so kind to have the boys. It'll be our turn next," but it never was.

Zach knew that his parents wouldn't like Vince. While his father could be more tolerant, his mother was a stickler for proper English being spoken, and manners, like writing thank you notes for the most incidental gestures. It would be glaringly obvious to her that Vince lacked certain social graces. Apart from that, it wasn't necessary to sneak out from Vince's large apartment. His mother either didn't notice or condoned whatever her son wanted to do. Vince was clearly in charge, while his mother, with her Italian accent and comfortable dress seemed more like wallpaper.

"I've only been to your house once. Why don't we go more often," Vince began to suggest.

"We can, but trust me. No fun to be had at that address." Vince didn't seem to realize that he was being protected from Evelyn's cruel and lacerating assessments and continued to push.

By three in the afternoon on Sunday, Zach was on his way home in time to do just enough homework to maintain his C+ average. He prided himself on knowing his parents breaking point and made a concerted effort to infuse their hopes for him with some well planned words or deeds just before their frustration peaked and they threatened him, yet again, with military school. And yet he had to admit that lately he wasn't doing such a great job of appeasing their suspicions.

Evelyn was yelling again, but now her tone was a nerve-racking screech painful to hear.

"GET UP!"

Zach rolled over and covered his head with a pillow. He had just drifted back to sleep when she ripped the covers from his bed.

"What are you doing?"

"This is Saturday, Zach. Sadly, you are not done with community service. Isn't that humiliation enough for this family? You have to be late, too? Now, get up, get dressed and I'll drive you to the nursing home!"

Zach groaned. He had been imagining life before he was busted, and the intrusion of this present reality was a rude awakening. He opened his mouth to protest, but his mother had already left, leaving the door open behind her. She had broken his one cardinal rule that his bedroom door remain shut at all times. Clearly he had work to do to bring her back in line.

Andrea Wodsende was vaguely aware of movement all about her. The world was in teeming motion, while she was locked in stillness. Most hands that tended her were impersonal. Others were harried and full of tension or sometimes even gentle. For what seemed like an eternity she had known that something was very wrong, but try as she did, she could not say what that wrong was. Right now it seemed to be meal time and she knew this because she recognized the startling sensation and taste of food. Someone was feeding her.

"Okay, now open your mouth. That's right. Tastes good, doesn't it? Swallow, don't forget to swallow. Good girl!"

For Andrea, at that very moment there was an internal shift in awareness. She forced her mind around a concept which teased just at the edge of recollection. If only she could shake that full feeling from her head. It reached down from the top of her skull to flatten her arms and legs, imprisoning her under a mysterious weight. Every fiber of her being reached for comprehension and never, never, never in all her life had she strived so hard to achieve a goal.

"Red Jell-O." She'd choked out the words, barely audible over vocal cords long out of use.

"That's right," a woman's voice said just at her ear and somewhat astonished. "I can't believe it. Looks like I'll have something different to write in your chart today. Do you want more cherry Jell-O?"

Andrea opened her mouth without being asked, to receive the cold, wet, cherry taste.

"Guess what? Andrea just spoke. I can hardly believe it. You did speak didn't you, Honey? Don't make me out a liar. And just now she opened her mouth without being told."

"Really?"

"Say something again sweet heart because if you don't, no one will believe me."

"What did she say?"

"She said red Jell-O." The two laughed.

"I'll take over if you want a break."

Andrea noted the masculine voice, but had difficulty tracking the conversation. The aide who had been feeding her said, "if you insist," and giggled. Andrea's mouth turned up in an unpracticed smile at the sound.

"Will you look at that?"

"Do me a favor and don't write what she said in your notes. Don't say there was any change in her affect; including that smile."

"Why ever not? Her doctor will want to know. This is an occasion. The first time I've ever heard her speak a word. I think we should celebrate."

"If her doctor finds out, he may increase her medication."

"What's wrong with that?" The aide asked.

"What's wrong with that? Look at the poor woman. She's a doped up zombie."

"That's because she's dangerous. She's one of the state patients."

"Andrea doesn't look a bit dangerous to me. You're the dangerous one. Maybe we can have a drink some time after work."

"Oh yeah," she laughed. "Like you wouldn't get carded and thrown out of the first place we entered. How many times do I have to tell you? You're too young for me, Zach. And I do have a boyfriend, as you well know. How old are you anyway?"

"Old enough. Go have that cigarette and I'll feed her the rest of this obnoxious red stuff, but first promise, you won't say anything. It'll be our secret."

As footsteps walked away the person with the masculine voice leaned close. Andrea felt his breath tickle her ear.

"Andrea, can you hear me?" Zach whispered. "I've been trashing your meds. Whatever you do, don't swallow any more of that yellow liquid stuff. You know; the stuff that smells like decaying fish parts."

There was a pause before he spoke again. Andrea had a sense of someone entering the room, the clatter of a tray, his absence, and his return.

"This is what you have to do. Hold it in your mouth and spit it out after they leave. And if you can remember, rinse your mouth with water afterwards. I can't be here every shift to intercept the med nurse. Do you understand what I'm saying?"

The voice stopped. Andrea felt him waiting. "Alright, then. They won't notice if you're careful. You can do that, can't you, Andrea? Because if you don't, you're toast. There can't be too many brain cells left in this ole noggin."

He knocked at the top of her head for emphasis. Andrea thrilled to the sensation, actually feeling and then registering the feeling.

There was another pause. Was he waiting for her to answer? It was all she could do to capture his words. She wrapped her mind around them and held them close like too many skeins of yarn, like squirming puppies, like marbles in white gloved hands. She'd think. She'd do her best to think because she heard the words. She knew the words and yet could only partially grasp the meaning.

"You can do it. I have confidence in you. Don't let them give you any more medicine. It's killing you. Understand?"

Andrea sighed.

"And don't do that either. They're used to you sitting around like a lump of clay. Don't smile, don't sigh, and don't do anything different from what they expect. If I'm going to rescue you, I'll need a little cooperation. You got it? Understand? Are you with me, Andrea?"

Are you with me, Andrea?

She repeated these five words in her mind as meaning hovered in a foggy place beyond reach. Still, she felt a thrill of confidence. She knew. She would know again and so did her very best to keep the stimulation of these five words uppermost in her mind. Understanding was everything and she had grasped *red Jell-O* and for that effort received praise. A little light had penetrated the dark tomb of her imprisonment.

Andrea forced herself to concentrate, but suddenly a tremor of emotion shot through her. The feeling was as alien from the hated numbness that had cradled her in a lifeless catatonic oblivion as it could possibly be, and she was frightened. Tears welled in her eyes as the awkward swipe of a tissue intercepted their descent. There was something tender in that kindness that reached her still more.

"That's good, Andrea. Tears are probably a good sign. That's what my court ordered counselor says anyway, but you can't cry either. You especially can't cry. I'm in counseling. Do you remember me telling you that?"

Andrea found the drone of his words a comforting stimulus.

"The old bag, she's about 120, said she was giving me permission to cry. What can I say? I haven't cried since I was six, so why start now? But as for you, well, maybe this means you heard me and can see the dangerous predicament you're in. Because, if I were sitting in this oversized highchair with a strap around my chest to keep me from falling forward, I can tell you that I would definitely be crying."

Andrea liked the sound of his voice. It was company. It was more than she'd had for a very long time.

"Oh, and in case you've forgotten, my name is Zach and I'm not like these other losers who work here. I didn't choose to be here, so you and I have something in common."

He paused and she could feel his scrutiny.

"And your name is Andrea Wodsende. Remember? Your name is Andrea Wodsende, and since I've been here you've never had a visitor. I'm not supposed to read the charts, but hey... I read yours cover to cover. Maybe it's too hard for your mother to see you like this. Maybe I can understand that. I never once visited my Uncle Sol when he had a stroke, but of course I was a kid. It just didn't occur to me. I'd visit him now if I could. After working here I'd definitely visit him, but he's dead. Are you still hungry? I can get you some pudding or some yogurt. Trust me. You don't want any more red Jell-O."

He put a cup to her lips and she took a sip of water without being coached.

"Good job, Andrea. Making progress. So let's just keep that between you and me, okay? Because the fact is, we have a fight on our hands."

Too many words and now Andrea was tired. It was an unnatural, pervasive kind of lethargy. It was a dangerous state that now, today, at this very moment she must begin to view as the enemy. She would fight.

At the afternoon shift change there was no one to greet him and no nurse to follow at his heels as he visited the one nursing home patient he had come to see. As Dudley approached the door of Andrea's room he felt compelled to finger the contents of his pocket.

There wasn't much time. Once out of staff meeting, the aides would be busy assisting the majority of the residents toward the cafeteria, where they would congregate for an early dinner so as to be settled for the night by eight.

He was noticed, but in no way impeded, and at the end would jot a cursory note in her chart in order to document the required monthly visit.

"Doctor, Doctor. He's back. Ohooo, no!"

"Shut-up, Birdie."

"Shut up, Birdie."

Dudley detoured toward Birdie's bed which was closest to the door, resenting these few wasted steps.

"You are wrinkled, shriveled, and useless and if you open that pie hole to utter one more sound, I'll make you very, very sorry." He grasped the back of her neck and with some force pushed the side of her head, where no bruise would be evident, into the tray table. Birdie straightened herself in obvious shock. He held up the back of his hand as she shrank back, gaining only inches of distance before he leaned in; their faces nearly touching.

"You want more of this?" he threatened, holding up the back of his hand.

"You want more of this?" she parroted, as was her habit, but Dudley was already turning away, focusing his gaze on the reason for his visit.

"Watch out," Birdie whispered. "He's back. Watch out."

Andrea sat immobile and staring at the scene before her. With an abrupt and sudden urgency he kissed her full on the mouth, his tongue penetrating the flaccid space between dry lips, probing the inside of her mouth until she began to choke. He withdrew and studied her intently for a long moment.

"Hello, my darling. Glad to see me?"

Zach didn't mind doing community service. He was lucky not to be doing time in lock-up, but he did miss his time with Vince. They talked on the phone less and less. Vince was not going to be the kind of friend who stayed in touch. Zach heard he had stopped attending school and was helping Guido with the business, whatever the business happened to be.

Zach called his parents by their first names, a detail the family counselor had clearly not approved of. Only his father seemed to be getting into the counseling rhythm, beginning to "unburden" himself, actually relieved to confess that he had been a distant parent, something Evelyn hated since the statement reflected equally on her. Zach hated the confusion of emotions that rose to the surface upon hearing his father's admission.

He didn't mind the twelve step meetings he was court ordered to attend, though it was startling to see grown men confront their frailties until some actually cried. He took note of certain pitfalls to avoid in life and even liked the people he met. It was soon apparent that attending these meetings made him part of some unique and enduring brotherhood.

Leaving a shop in the mall with his mother, he ran into Marvin, a bearded attorney who had lost everything and was heading for a meeting in a different part of town. Zach quickly realized that meetings were conducted nearly around the clock and some people had to go more than once a day. Marvin threw his arm around Zach's shoulder, smiled at his mother, and invited them for coffee which his mother, mortified by the unexpected encounter, politely declined on his behalf.

"That was rude," Zach said as they walked away.

"He's not the kind of person for you to know. I'll be glad when all this is over so we can have our lives back."

"I'm going to ask Dad to help him find a job."

"You'll do no such thing. We'll not involve ourselves in matters that don't concern us."

"Yes I will..." and with those words Zach discovered a new, more potent way to rub salt into the festering wound of their contentious relationship. He would help the downtrodden and insert them into his life. This would disconcert his mother even more than discovering he was selling pot, stealing their liquor supply, and hanging out with a boy whose father was in prison. He could think of no one more downtrodden than Andrea. After he talked with his father about Marvin he would concentrate on her.

Zach didn't think twice about standing up in his required weekly meeting to proclaim, "Hello, my name is Zach and I am an alcoholic and a pot head." "Hello, Zach," the chorus would respond in comforting unison. Of course he didn't believe he was either since now that he had to stay clean because of regular and random drug tests, also court ordered, he didn't miss getting high all that much. What he did miss was his freedom and in particular, not being able to drive. He had prided himself on not needing his parents, who found it easy to ignore his comings and goings until consequences dislodged a cultivated smugness.

Feeling humiliated, Zach stood in front of the nursing home and waited for his mother to pick him up. Phyllis, the charge nurse on day shift stood beside him. Zach liked her drill sergeant approach to management. There was never any doubt about what she expected from her staff and her only concession to that image was when she spoke of her three children and seemingly perfect husband with genuine warmth.

"I'd be glad to give you a ride home," she offered.

"No, Evelyn, that's my mother, she's on her way. Thanks anyway."

"You can't take the subway? It's a quick ride from here to your neighborhood."

"No, I'm not allowed. My mom has to pick me up."

"You could walk."

"I wish," Zach said, "but I'm sort of under house arrest unless I'm here or in school or at an AA meeting. The judge called it strict parental supervision. I sort of got the idea it was as much an indictment of them, as it was of me."

Phyllis laughed. "And you hate it."

He smiled a grim smile. "I do."

She smiled back. "We expected to have trouble with you, but you've worked hard, Zach. The staff has decided to write a letter to the judge telling him what a fine young man you are."

"I really appreciate that, Phyllis. Unfortunately I've already been sentenced. But I'm sure my lawyer would like to have a copy for his file. You know, just in case." *...just in case for the next gig*, he thought grimly. "So if you don't mind doing it anyway that would be great."

"We'd be happy to write it and I know everyone will sign. Even some of the residents. They notice how you take time with them."

Of course she was wrong. He hated the smell of the place and how most of the residents always needed something. The only extra activity he now had time for was an occasional round of golf at his parents club, since he'd been kicked off the high school team. As a condition of his probation, he wasn't allowed to see certain friends, and especially Vince. Out of the loop, he no longer knew what was going on. He felt lonely and dejected and when fall came he'd be going to a conservative Jewish prep school in Western Pennsylvania. His parents had never been particularly faithful, taking him to temple only on holidays. Zach felt particularly betrayed by the decision and guessed the school might be only a hair better than the threatened military academy.

But most of all he was bored, which is how he happened to take an interest in Andrea. He felt sorry for the patients. Many were largely forgotten by their families. Then there were the state patients, whose care was contracted by the commonwealth of Massachusetts to cut costs while alleviating an overcrowded system. Like old Bruce who was doing a life sentence for double murder, only now he had something called geriatric dementia, which transformed him into the docile, lovable old man he'd never been in real life.

The door behind them opened. Zach sensed a new alertness in Phyllis as she watched a tall man approach."

"Hello, Doctor," she called as he sailed by without speaking, presenting a wall of impenetrability.

"That's Andrea's doctor," Phyllis spoke betraying a hint of frustration. "I was hoping to catch him."

"You want me to run after him for you?"

"No. I'll call him next week."

"Too bad, I heard she's overmedicated."

"Whoever shared that with you was being inappropriate," Phyllis commented with some sternness.

"Sorry, but you know its common knowledge, and all you have to do is look at the woman to see the truth."

"Not for you to worry about," she softened. "They said you had trouble with authority and we should watch you. I just haven't seen it. Maybe you've learned your lesson, Zach and you'll have a good life."

Zach almost laughed. With single minded attention he had ingratiated himself to the staff, letting the older ones mother him while flirting with the younger ones. It wasn't long before the nurses and aides were treating him like an affectionate pet. They talked openly in front of him and that's how he learned about the state patients transferred to the nursing home from prison.

"How many are there?" he had asked as he sat in the break room with the two practical nurses that covered patient meds.

"We have five at the moment including Andrea. She came to us from the state hospital."

"Why was she in a mental hospital instead of prison like the others?"

"She was declared incompetent to stand trial. She had what's called a psychotic break," one of the nurses explained. "That means she was unstable and probably masking mental illness throughout her adult life. But we're not supposed to say. We don't let the other families know about the state patients."

"Why not?"

"You know the answer to that, Zach. How would your parents like it if your grandfather was here and his roommate was old Bruce who murdered two people in a jealous rage? Do you think they'd feel comfortable with that bit of information? No, they'd transfer your grandfather post haste. What if the Tyler family knew what Andrea did? Well...it goes without saying. Birdie would no longer be in that room and only someone as out of it as Andrea could tolerate her."

He found out a lot from ease-dropping on conversations. Once when he pulled double duty, working the grave yard shift, he had carried Andrea's chart to the copy machine and copied every page as one nurse and two techs dozed in wing chairs grouped for the night and sleeping through a good number of call lights.

Of course his parents had to check on him. They set the alarm and called the nurses' station once at 3AM and then again at 6AM, and Zach realized that the biggest obstacle to regaining his former independence lay in convincing his parents that he had learned his lesson.

Before he'd gotten into trouble they had taken everything at face value. His father was consumed with his career and his mother with her social calendar, and on the few occasions they suspected something serious they threatened, but failed to follow through. Zach had learned to say the right words and to appear polite and reasonably compliant until it was business as usual and they began ignoring him again. Only this time his parents had juvenile court staring over their shoulder and so Zach was caught between a rock and hard place, trying to make the best of what he considered an impossible plight.

When he was young he felt invisible and wished for his parent's attention. Then when puberty set in, he stopped caring and let those hurtful expectations die, and that was the scariest part of counseling. His parents were actually showing signs of change. Their effort did not feel like evidence of love, but instead a disingenuous facsimile. He felt betrayed. The rules had changed and, as usual, his vote didn't count.

"See you tomorrow," Phyllis interrupted his thoughts as she walked toward the parking lot. "I'm sure your mother will be along soon and don't worry about Andrea. She'll be fine."

It was very clear to Zach which doctors the nurses respected and which they didn't. While the staff displayed deference they were later very frank about what they really thought, and that's how he happened to learn about Andrea. The prevailing opinion was that she was not only over-medicated, but on the wrong medication. Over time this was accepted since none of the usual interventions succeeded in changing her doctor's mind. Zach could hear the resignation in their voices. He hated that. He hated giving up on anything.

Zach looked at his watch and sauntered over to a line of rocking chairs. He made himself comfortable and bit back a surge of impatience. Feigning interest in a game of Chinese checkers, played by two residents, he thought of Andrea and the two words she had uttered. He hadn't heard the words for himself and yet had fully expected that at some point her mind would begin to clear. He looked forward to that day when they could have a conversation. After delving into her back ground and reading what he could find on the crime, he had many questions to ask.

The nursing home had two wings which jutted out from a central area attached to the private hospital. It had been an easy matter to get assigned to Andrea's portion of the long corridor. There was a young man about his own age who suffered severe brain damage in an auto accident. Zach offered to shower and dress this resident, suggesting that having someone his own age around might prove stimulating. Andrea was just next door, placing her room on Zach's assignment schedule. Andrea's roommate was Birdie Tyler, a woman with high blood pressure and chronic short term memory loss, evidenced by a maddening habit of repeating whatever was last said. The frustrations of her condition could provoke unruly, sometimes combative behavior. When the LPN came in with morning meds Zach was ready.

"Are those for Andrea? I'll give them to her if you'll check on Birdie. I couldn't read her blood pressure. She kept jerking her arm away."

"Jerking; not true, not true," Birdie announced.

"Will you try?" Zach asked. "She likes you better than me. You have a special way with her."

"She likes you better," Birdie repeated in sing-song agreement.

"You need to learn to do this for yourself," the LPN chided, but Zach knew she was also pleased at the compliment. "Birdie is not that hard to handle if you talk nice to her. In the five minutes that she's tracking she's not confused as you might think. Don't talk down to her. That's the trick."

Zach took the meds and walked over to where Andrea sat like a dead woman strapped to a port-a-potty. After nearly a month of working in the nursing home, Zach was doing things for people he never imagined needed doing, and now he was getting a little used to the work which really scared him. The judge predicted that working in this environment would provide a sobering experience. His exact words: "You need to be taught that the world doesn't revolve around you. What you need, Son, is a sobering life experience."

Zach put Andrea back to bed. Then, with Birdie watching him over the shoulder of the nurse, he dumped Andrea's medications into the urine and carried the receptacle to the bathroom to measure and record, the contents before flushing. When he returned Birdie was scowling in his direction and pointing a long bony finger.

"I saw what you did, young man."

"You did? What did you see, Mrs. Tyler?"

"I saw you. I saw you take...."

"Take that receptacle to the bathroom, Mrs. Tyler."

"Yes!" she pronounced, scrunching up her face in a parody of intense concentration. "And... You won't get away with it. I'm telling on you."

"You should do that. Right away."

Zach couldn't be there to intercept the nurse on other shifts, but since the serious meds were given in the morning and he was present at least four days a week, this worked in the beginning. But now, more than ever, he needed Andrea's cooperation.

Zach had collected a pretty complete sampling. He sat at his desk and lined up all her medications in neat miniature piles before him. Thanks to the Physicians' Desk Reference, lifted from his father's library, he now had a pretty clear idea of what he was up against. A quick look at the medicine log, while the LPN was in another room, had provided the name of the yellowish liquid, which of all the meds, seemed the likely source of Andrea's near complete withdrawal. Zach was stunned at the cacophony of poison they had her on. She had many of the side effects, neatly called contraindications, but took other pills to counter-act those.

Zach had also discovered a curious detail. Andrea's doctor of record, the one who had transferred her a year earlier from the state hospital, was not the same physician that now ordered her meds and made the required monthly visit. And... it could not be a mere coincidence that he and Andrea shared the same, very uncommon last name. Although he didn't have all the details, and his father didn't practice this kind of law, Zach thought he might have stumbled on a potential malpractice suit.

As he thought about Andrea, Zach experienced an emotion that was only vaguely familiar. He recalled the day his favorite cat had delivered two still-born kittens on the floor of his closet. He had felt empathy for that mother cat as she searched for her kittens just as he felt empathy for Andrea.

After everything she'd been through, she was still attractive. Her features where delicate, her eyes wide and blue and he guessed that if she could wear makeup and dress herself up she could be pretty once again. And then he imagined that Andrea was a nice person assigning her imaginary attributes as though it were in his power to do so, and that's when he decided on a course of action.

Life in a nursing home would be the death of Andrea Wodsende. He'd get her out of that dump if it was the last thing he did all summer.

WOOD'S END

CHAPTER THIRTEEN

"Hey, Elias, another big case that'll fall apart without you? Weight of the world and all that jazz."

Elias looked up. Zach could usually tell when his father was preoccupied with work. He expected to be dismissed with an absent-minded reply, but instead Elias let the light blue jacket fold over the brief he'd been studying. For what seemed an uncomfortable eternity he held his sons gaze before motioning for Zach to sit.

"The counselor would like you to call me, Dad. And I'd like to hear that name once in a while. I understand that you're too old to make it a habit, but being a parent is a privilege, and it occurs to me; well... that maybe I've had my priorities a little out of joint."

His father's words were evenly delivered, almost flat and yet Zach experienced an odd stirring of emotion and felt certain Elias had been thinking of him and just pretending to bury his face in work. Zach took a deep breath and pondered the request as a heavy weight of bitterness settled on his chest. Only because he wanted something would he address Elias as requested.

"Okay, Dad. Now don't get mad. I just want to ask you a legal question."

Elias' smile was faintly condescending.

"There is this patient at the nursing home. Her name is Andrea Wodsende. Ever hear of her?"

Elias cocked his head, suddenly more aware. "I did some forensic accounting a few years back for a client with that name, but she'd be too young for a nursing home."

"She's a state patient, remanded to Crest May from a mental hospital because she had a psychotic break. Well her doctor has the same last name. I'm about ninety percent certain that he is actually her former husband. Is it legal for him to be taking care of her?"

Elias Goldfarb swallowed his first response which under the previous rules of engagement would have been something like: *My advice to you young man is to stay out of it. This is none of your business.* But instead he asked, "Can you tell me why you're so concerned about this woman?"

"Because she's so doped up on psychotropic drugs that she can hardly move. She's frozen. You know, a lump on a log."

"What's her doctor's first name?"

"I don't know, but I can find out tomorrow."

"I might know the case. And if it's the person I'm thinking of, she killed someone, Zach."

"That's what they say. I just don't believe it and that's not my question anyway."

"You see, Son, this is the problem. You imagine that you are the expert. Every teacher you've ever had has called you arrogant and I guess that's our fault."

Elias looked uncomfortable as he edited his own pronouncement. "No, it is our fault. We've spoiled you, indulged you, and according to the counselor, your mother and I have shirked our responsibilities in other ways as well."

"Elias... Dad, please let's not go over this again. An hour a week of this crap is about all I can tolerate."

His father took a deep breath and looked away to buy time and Zach realized from whom he'd learned this same trick.

"I want you to consider this. Her doctor is the expert, not you. The nursing staff is made up of professionals trained to do a job, and I doubt very much that you are allowed to read the private details of a patient's chart. Now your mother and I would have preferred that you do your public service at another location, but we were given no choice. We were lucky the judge didn't put you away. So I need you to keep out of things you can't understand?"

"I believe the old bag also said that you shouldn't lecture me because it's dismissive. Let me think a minute. Ah yes, shuts down the communication. Kind of sums up our relationship, don't you think?"

"I'm not going to see you get into any more trouble, young man."

If he took the bait, Zach would have stormed off, and then father and son wouldn't have spoken for a few days, circling one another like weary dogs until they both conceded something. Now it was Zach's turn to buy a little time. He took a deep breath and looked down at his shoes. He had Andrea Wodsende to think of. She was a big responsibility. If he forgot to feed and water the family cat, his mother would do it for him and not complain. Andrea was a different matter entirely. She was completely helpless and he was all she had.

"So," he charged ahead, "you're not supposed to be dismissive with me, your only son, because the counselor says we fail to communicate, and since you're the parent and I'm the teenager, her words again, you're to take responsibility for kicking things off right. Do you think we could start again?"

Zach could see that his father wanted to argue. It would have been the natural thing to do. The familiar, well worn groove that had become a trench between them, averting pain and any real sort of reckoning. Zach took a deep breath. He felt that in this case he was the parent leading. He was the one better equipped to rub a little sandpaper over the sharp intractable ridges of their relationship.

Slowly Zach released a breath and acknowledged to himself that this was hard. Changing was hard work. The old bag had said this very clearly in their last session. At those words his mother had tightened her crossed ankles and tucked them deeper under her chair. His father had instinctually reached for her hand. Neither of them looked at him. If it weren't for Andrea he wouldn't bother. But...

Zach continued, "If we made a few points at our next session maybe that counselor, older than dirt and probably senile, will focus on Evelyn and give us a break. We could say how we had this conversation, started to fight, and changed our minds."

Simultaneously they smiled, sharing a unity that was rare. If their history had been better they might have laughed.

"I don't know about you, Dad, but I'd like to see that."

"You're right and I'm sorry," his father said. "Now let's see. I'm supposed to listen right? I'll listen and try not to judge. Let me say that your question is a good one, Zach. And the answer? It is not illegal for a doctor to treat a family member, but it is considered unethical."

"Why?"

"The premise is this. A doctor would have difficulty prescribing treatment for someone close to them and couldn't do so and remain objective, so while the intentions might be honorable, the care might suffer. In today's culture this would leave a physician vulnerable to legal action from other family members or the powers that be if something went wrong."

"His judgment would be flawed," Zach reiterated.

"Yes, that's the thinking."

"Should the nursing home insist that another doctor be assigned to care for Andrea?"

"Maybe they have. You do jump to conclusions, Zach."

"I don't think they know. I would have heard. There aren't many secrets in that place."

"We can safely assume that this doctor is another relative. If this was truly her husband, he would have been required to disclose the relationship. A review board at the hospital would have considered the request and I feel certain that, given the circumstances as I knew them, the request would have been refused.

"What circumstances?"

"I guess I can say this since the matter is public record. The Andrea Wodsende that I knew was a battered wife."

"He beat her up?"

"Let's just say, the Wodsende divorce was volatile."

"How long did you know her?" Zach asked.

"My work was limited to a little over a week. Then I turned her over to a colleague who could handle the divorce. But I liked her. She was a nice woman."

"Thanks, Dad."

"You're welcome. Remember, stay out of it! If you don't keep your nose clean, we can't send you away to school. The judge will require you to complete your community service locally and extend the counseling."

"Really?"

"And you want to go away, don't you, Zach? Your mother thinks this is probably best with all the talk. You'd get a clean start with other kids who don't know anything about your trouble."

"Thanks, Dad."

Zach took the stairs two at a time. He walked into his room and slammed the door with such force that the windows rattled in their frames. Pacing a few rounds he dropped into the chair at his desk, placing his hands on the surface of the wood to steady himself. Zach lowered his head and studied the wood grain and the place where he'd carved his initials with a scout knife when he was ten. This had been his father's first desk right out of law school and Evelyn had picked it up at a flea market for twenty-five dollars.

His mother liked to tell how they had been poor and how all the hard work had paid off. Of course, Zach thought, her definition of poor was probably as screwed up as her definition of love. Until his father let it slip just now he didn't know his parents had a choice and believed that his going away to school was one of the conditions imposed by the court. No one had bothered to ask the requisite kid, in existence because it was expected, useful to parade around as long as he was cute and cooperative. They hated him. Solution: get rid of the kid.

What would they say if he blurted all this out in their next family counseling session? If not for Andrea, he would do it.

If not for her, he would pack a bag and leave home, but this wasn't the time to call undue attention to himself. To do so would be to abandon her, and then she would surely die long before she should, with no voice and no way to recover her mind.

Zach reached for the folder he'd begun on Andrea. He felt better when he was plotting on her behalf. She was worth saving, but his parents? Zach sorted the news clippings as well as the nurse's notes and latest updates to Andrea's chart which he had secreted to the copy machine in the work room. He was pondering his next step when there was a knock at his bedroom door. Before he could respond his mother walked in with a plate of warm cookies and milk. She looked like a dark haired June Cleaver with her trim skirt and peach colored sweater set.

"Zach, dear."

The moment was surreal. "Yes, Evelyn?"

"Your father said you had such a nice talk. If you can call him Dad, is it just possible that you would call me Mother?"

Zach realized that Elias must have sent her up to his room. He felt protective of his space and especially didn't like her occupying any part of it. He reached for the milk, grateful for the distraction of the cold glass.

"Mother and not mom or mommy?"

Evelyn's look changed. Her moods were mercurial. When he was little he would pay rapt attention, wondering if being really good, really quiet, really entertaining could in some way keep life steady. Why must he think of this now? Zach didn't like thinking about how he had felt as a child or that some part of him still needed these particular parents.

"We've been instructed to re-parent you," she said as if she'd lifted the word from his mind. "I'm only following doctor's orders, so whatever you like, Zach."

What I'd like, Evelyn is for you to leave my room and never, ever come back! He screamed the words, but didn't say them. Working at Crest May had changed him and he was surprised to discover that co-existing alongside the more immediate anger was a stab of compassion for his mother.

"If you don't mind, I'll stick with Evelyn."

The cookies smelled good. He reached for the plate. With her hands free she crossed her arms over her chest. Zach bit off a chewy corner and savored the warm chocolate.

"Thank you," he said.

She shrugged and furrowed her brow. This was unfamiliar territory. Her invading his room, even with a plate of cookies, would usually elicit an angry outburst.

"You're welcome," she replied as if balancing on the edge of a high wire.

In that precise moment Zach saw the pattern for what it was. Evelyn had expectations and he didn't meet them. She was profoundly disappointed and complained to his father. Elias commiserated and comforted her, being far more invested in keeping her happy since an unhappy Evelyn was a lot to trouble with. Zach was the quotient they ignored until consequences came to roost. Forced to react he was no longer invisible and gained a modicum of revenge.

No one despised the necessity for counseling more than Evelyn. She hated that Zach had gotten into trouble in the first place. The humiliation had frayed the smooth, predictable facade of her life. For one thing, she had to drive him everywhere. People wondered what he was doing for the summer and she couldn't lie since the defining event had found its way into a short paragraph in the metro section of the Boston Herald: *Local Boy Sells Drugs at School.* It was enough to set the gossip mongers off on an investigation that would outshine the worst tabloid.

She couldn't say, "So nice of you to ask. Zach's at soccer camp or Latin school," or some such stupid activity that fit her idea of what a perfect son would be doing with his spare time. When everything was distilled to nothing, even her anger was impersonal and directed more toward the inconvenience than at him.

Zach smiled at his mother. She looked perplexed. They weren't fighting. If they weren't fighting what was there?

WOOD'S END

CHAPTER FOURTEEN

After much deliberation and many false attempts, Zach was fairly satisfied with the letter. He had typed it on his father's home computer and thought the duplication of the signature about the best he had ever managed: *Elias Z. Goldfarb, Esq.*

Dear Detective Shiel: I'm writing to you about Mrs. Andrea Wodsende, a state patient at a nursing home where my son is employed. Her doctor is Dudley Wodsende. You were the lead detective on the Wodsende murder case and will recall...

Zach studied the two pages written on personal stationary with his father's name in raised letters on a bisque vellum background.

Zach wondered if he could persuade his mother to make the drive to Wingaersheek Beach. Earlier that morning he had helped fill the one bird feeder she couldn't reach and she had made him a large omelet with turkey bacon and toasted bagel. Forced to spend more time together they had affected a kind of uneasy truce. Despite the beautiful summer day, Zach's thoughts turned compulsively to Andrea. She had begun to emerge from her chemically induced fog and could no longer mimic her former zombie state without constant reminders.

The most striking change was her demeanor at meal times. While previously an aid had fed her, she now was aware of taste and consistency and would chew and swallow without reminders, meaning that a new, more normal diet had been ordered. Zach felt some urgency to come up with a plan before the next monthly visit by her doctor. Writing to the detective who had led the murder investigation was the best he could come up with.

"Zach, pick up the phone. It's for you."

"Who is it?"

"Guido from the library. You have an overdue book."

Before saying hello Zach waited for his mother to hang up.

"Hi, Zach. Hold on. Someone here wants to speak with you."

"Hey, Man."

"Vince." Zach knew there was too much joy in his voice, but he didn't care. "What's going on?"

Zach didn't intend to tell Fat Mario, Wafer Thin Guido, and Vince all about Andrea, but she was on his mind and so he did. His mother had dropped him off at the library so that he could return the nonexistent overdue book and brush up on European History for an advanced class she had optimistically signed him up for at the new school. What she didn't know was that there was not a chance of his going. She'd be packing and just as quickly he'd be unpacking. Zach had already written the judge a letter and told him he didn't want to go away to school. He reported that his parents were merely trying to get rid of him and he liked working at the nursing home and was considering a career in geriatric medicine.

Zach reflected. If he really applied himself, maybe he could get decent grades in chemistry and biology. Maybe he'd give up his career as a famous movie star and study medicine. Why the hell not?

Zach sat at the bar and sipped a cold beer, his first in over two months. He could smell the bread pudding as it baked in the oven. He and Vince repeatedly turned their gaze in the direction of the timer wishing they could hurry perfection. It was comforting to see that in his absence, nothing had changed. There was a card game going on in back. A creamy pasta sauce simmered on one burner while a pan of bruschetta sent forth a palatable herb aroma from another. Mario speared a lamb chop from the pot of bruschetta and dropped it on a bed of greens and grated cheese. Then he rubbed some kosher salt and garlic juice from the press into the meat vigorously with bare hands, finally pouring a generous shot of Jamison's into the pan juices and spooning that over the meat. Zach expected the plate to disappear into the back room, but Mario dropped it in front of him with a clatter.

"Eat up, kid. Since we seen you last, you don't look so hot. You look a little puny. Too much routine dulls the soul." Mario laughed. He wasn't at all obese, just solid, wide body, big hands.

Mario hit the back of his head and wrinkled his forehead. "Why should you care so much about this Andrea Wodsende? They didn't send you to that boot camp for gang bots, and believe me, if you hadn't had some legal weight behind you, they would have. Your father probably lunches at the club with the judge. Right?"

Zach didn't answer.

"You won't always be so lucky, kid. So take my advice. Stay low. Be the rich, intellectually superior elitist you were raised to be and in a few months you're back in the game all the wiser."

They had moved from the bar to a small table in the corner. The door to the back room opened and the participants wandered out. Two men exchanged brief cases while all discarded their cell phones into a waiting bread basket before picking up new phones lined up in readiness at the corner of the bar.

Zach had observed this curious dance once before and for some reason Guido and Mario had allowed it, inviting him to ask questions which some instinct warned would be a miry pit into which he must not step. And yet today curiosity gripped him more than usual. He watched closely as Mario ushered the stragglers out the door, saying goodbye in several languages. Zach recognized Spanish and Italian, but there were short bursts of phrases in languages to which he had no hint of recognition.

Mario returned to the table, allowing a brief hiatus of silence into which Zach was invited to ask the questions that any other normal person would have already asked on previous occasions.

"So what's the deal, kid?" Guido broke the stalemate. "Enlighten us. Tell us why you care what happens to this woman?"

For the first time since meeting Mario and Guido, Zach felt a little intimidated. He swallowed his first smart answer and watched as Vince took a last bite of bread pudding while his own sat untouched before him, the whipped cream melting into a moat around an island.

"You going to eat that?" Vince asked.

Suddenly Zach realized he was not hungry. The lamb chop, the best lamb chop he'd ever eaten sat on his stomach like a hard brick. Why, all at once, did he feel so sad? If Andrea was the kind of responsibility that caused sleepless nights and loss of appetite, shouldn't he rather trade that for the carefree self obsessed kid he used to be? Zach slid his plate across the table toward Vince. Mario and Guido exchanged a look.

"You're pretty broken up about this?" Mario prodded.

"If you could see her, you would care, too."

"She must be a knock out."

"She must be rich."

"It isn't that she's pretty, which she is. And I doubt she has a penny."

"So what is it?" Vince asked.

"She's helpless. And she's not playing me because she barely speaks, and I'm not playing her cause she's not much younger than my mother. There's nothing to be gained here and maybe that's it. Maybe you sometimes just want to help because everything and I mean everything," Zach repeated for emphasis, "is stacked against her."

He looked around the table and saw that he had their attention. "We're talking about her. We're saying her name, but no one outside that nursing home ever says her name. If I stop paying attention, that's it. She might as well be dead. For all intents and purposes she is dead, and we can bring her back to life. Do you get what I'm trying to say?"

"Yeah, I get it," Mario said. "It's a power trip without a pay off. You're a dumb kid, you know that?"

There was no evidence that anything he said had made a difference. All they cared about was work, whatever that dubious work happened to be. He'd considered lots of possibilities from bookies to jewel thieves to money laundering. Why should they care about a woman who sat in an oversized high chair much of the day and exercised only when someone took the time to walk her up and down the hallway?

Suddenly Zach felt very alone. He had felt drawn to these three. They were colorful and quirky and seemed to share the common ground of alienation, the angst of being misunderstood. And yet, he would never choose to be part of their tight inner circle.

With growing awareness Zach had begun to suspect a subtle game of seduction. They wanted something from him, or maybe, what they really wanted was access to his father. This thought and others just as odd had entered his mind and been quickly dismissed. The trouble was, like a bad penny, they resurfaced.

Not for the first time Zach wondered if Guido and Mario had wives and children. He'd never seen Mario outside the bar, but had once glimpsed Guido leaving a neighborhood church.

"He goes to mass every day," Vince had said.

"Really, he's religious?"

"You could say that," Vince replied and looked at him then, expecting the next obvious question. But Zach had held back, choosing not to probe the layers of secrets that held them fast in some mysterious bond of dysfunctional brotherhood.

"Okay, kid," Guido interrupted his thoughts. "This is what we're going to do. And only, I might add, because we like you and because you didn't roll over on Vince when they dragged you down to the precinct and interviewed you for three hours."

Zach wondered. How could they know how long he had been interrogated about some imagined ring of kids selling drugs at school? He had passed around a little weed and pocketed a little money, but nothing like what the detectives proposed. It was fortunate that Elias had suspected he might actually be guilty and had the good lawyerly sense to wrest him away until after the arraignment the following morning.

"You did us a favor because we told the kid's father here," he thrust a thumb in Vince's direction, "that we'd keep him out of trouble until he was free."

Wouldn't have been good to have one in juvie and another in Bridgewater," Mario commented.

"So, about this Andrea Wodsende," Guido asked. "You say she has no family?"

"Only a mother who never visits."

"And her doctor is Dudley Wodsende." This was a statement, not requiring an answer.

"How did you know that?"

"You told me and I told them," Vince offered.

Zach was fairly certain that outside the hospital, his father was the only person to whom he'd spoken that name.

"I'll tell you what we're going to do, kid. Guido here is going to get a haircut and shave and put on his favorite outfit. He's going to saunter into that place and say he's a relative. What you want to be Guido? Her older brother or her uncle?"

"I'll be her uncle. She looks like a WASP right? Blue eyes, classic Anglo features and very pretty."

The description of Andrea was accurate. Was that merely a guess? Zach opened his mouth to question, but Guido and Mario turned frigid looks in his direction. Zach wished he could imitate the strength of those looks and decided he'd go home, look in the mirror, and practice because with that tool, he'd never have to use his fists again.

"And Guido here is calling the shots," Mario stated. "If we stick our necks out to help this woman, you are to sit tight until we tell you otherwise. No move in any direction. Are we clear?"

Soon Vince was driving him back to the library in his newly restored tan and white Corvette, circa 1967. Zach decided he wouldn't question the sudden wealth that could have purchased a dream car like this. His plate was pretty full dealing with Andrea.

"See that mail box up ahead. Pull over," he directed Vince.

Zach hesitated. Now that he had Guido and Mario on board, maybe he didn't need Detective Shiel, who was after all an unknown quantity that could just as easily hurt Andrea as help her. But something about the exchange back at the bar nagged at Zach. He had a sense of walking through a play without knowing his lines. It might be a good idea to have someone involved who knew more about Andrea's history than he could find when he did a search for old records.

And yet, Mario had told him to sit tight. Zach decided to cooperate. Vince sounded the horn and as he did so a boy on a Moped rounded the corner, nearly clipping him; far too close for comfort. As Zach jumped out of the way his fingers let go and the envelope, bearing the red and black crest of his father's firm, with their home address written in Zach's hand on the outside flap, fell beyond reach. Fate had intervened and any decision not to mail the letter was taken out of his hands.

Zach comforted himself with the thought that, even if Detective Shiel arranged for Andrea to go back to jail, she'd be better off thinking for herself. This was the true outrage. Dr. Wodsende had taken her mind captive with a powerful cocktail of chemicals. He had all the necessary credentials, but was every bit as dangerous as a drug dealer, hiding in the shadows near a middle school and selling heroin to children.

Zach slid onto the caramel colored leather.

"What took you so long?" Vince asked. "Looked to me like you couldn't decide if you wanted to mail that letter. Who was it addressed to?"

Embedded in the question, if it didn't seem ridiculous to think so, Zach detected a note of desperation in Vince's tone.

"That kid would have slammed into me if you hadn't leaned on the horn," Zach deflected.

"An important letter?" Vince queried, not letting it go. "I noticed it had your father's name and crest on the outside."

Caution stopped Zach's reply. He turned to study Vince's profile. When it was known he wouldn't be returning to school, Vince had dropped out and now Zach wondered if that was a mere coincidence. A growing distrust, an unsettled perception of being played by experts, wormed into the forefront of his thinking.

"Let me ask you a question?"

"Shoot," Vince replied, but his demeanor had shifted. He was no longer the unsettled high school youth acting out because he missed his father. He suddenly looked older than sixteen. Twenty two or three, Zach thought.

"What did your father go to jail for?"

"It had to do with programming. He's a cyber genius. Let's just say that he designed some programs that put other programs at risk."

"So his trial is a matter of public record. I could look it up if I wanted to."

"Sure. If you knew where to look."

"So what is going on?" Zach demanded forgetting his earlier decision not to be drawn in.

"It's not what you think and that's all I can say. Any more questions, you'll have to ask Guido."

"One more. Your father's not in jail anywhere in Massachusetts is he?"

Vince looked straight ahead.

"Is he even in this country, because there seems to be an international focus to what you're doing?"

Vince gunned the engine, careening a half turn around the fountain before screeching to a halt under the shadow of the library's gothic edifice.

"Last question and I'm not expecting an answer to this one either. Will I ever see you again?"

A pretense had dropped away. Vince was distant and stoic, causing Zach to question the sincerity of the friendship they'd shared. He felt oddly hurt.

"Well if I can do anything to help you..."

To no avail Zach waited.

"If someday you find yourself on the run or need a lawyer, because I may go to law school, or if you need some money. You know where to find me," Zach ventured and paused, waiting. "And if Mario and Guido are involved in anything illegal," Zach continued... "And that happens to catch you on the down turn..."

Again no response.

"And I guess I can speak about this, since the three of you contrived to let me see the murky outline of whatever it is you're up to."

Vince stared straight ahead.

"Don't forget we were once friends. You don't have a brother and I don't have a brother. So if it comes to that, if you need to break free and start over, all you need to do is ask," Zach said surprised at the changes in himself that inspired such an offer.

"I did. I did break free."

"Free from what?"

"If I told you, you wouldn't believe me."

"Give it a try. I'll keep an open mind."

"Can't. But... you should know. The time is coming when you'll look back on our association. When that day comes, and there will be no other day like it, nor has there ever been, you'll see things differently. And if you begin to regret that you didn't ask more questions when you could have well; don't waste the energy. There has always been a plan."

Vince reached across and unlatched the passenger door, giving it a forceful shove.

"I get the hint. We're not going to talk about this. At least not without Guido here, telling you what to say and think. Is that the way it is?"

"No," Vince replied. "I'm my own man. I'm helping out because it's the right thing to do. The only thing to do."

"You're crazy," Zach said. "I see that now. You're all crazy."

As he exited the car, Zach no longer felt conflicted about mailing the letter to Jared Shiel. He was out of his depth. If he was going to save Andrea, he needed practical assistance and not from some insane conspiracy addicts.

WOOD'S END

CHAPTER FIFTEEN

"Dr. Wodsende, please."

"This is his service, may I help you?"

"I'm calling about Andrea Wodsende. We'd like..."

"You say Andrea Wodsende?"

"Yes."

"I'll have Dr. Wodsende call you right back."

Phyllis had heard this before, but in her changed way of viewing Andrea, who everyone noticed was coming out of her stupor, she was suddenly processing differently. She was suspicious.

"Don't you want to know why I'm calling?" she asked.

"This is the Crest May Nursing Home. I see that on my screen. Dr. Wodsende has left strict instructions to notify him immediately, should anyone from your facility call about his niece."

Phyllis replaced the phone and considered. Whatever Dr. Wodsende was to Andrea, she doubted very much that this could be the relationship. If he felt the need for deceit, what else was he hiding?

Of late Zach had been a broken record, casually interjecting his opinion about Andrea at every opportunity. "Dudley Wodsende? Is this the same Dudley Wodsende who was once married to Andrea? My Dad, he's an attorney, and he says a doctor shouldn't treat a relative." Zach's two new favorite words were unethical and problematic and Phyllis was sick of hearing them.

"Well, NO they are NOT related," Phyllis had countered.

Zach hadn't responded, but then, by apparent coincidence, several old clippings of the Stephanie

Wodsende murder investigation showed up in the nurse's lounge and she had asked around.

The evening before, when reaching for her keys, Phyllis had discovered a clipping in her own purse and a housekeeper had brought another from the ladies room commenting, "Doesn't seem right that he should be treating her. She's so doped up. You all say so, and you can't get him to reduce her meds. So what's the deal with that?"

"What indeed?" Phyllis now thought.

It was required that doctors make monthly visits to see their patients. Because Andrea was Dudley's only patient, he was able to come and go with minimal conversation. Most orders would be called in by his nurse after his departure, placing even more obstacles between him and the staff that cared for Andrea.

On a routine basis the care and therapy of each patient was reviewed. At nearly every staffing the subject of Andrea's meds were addressed, but they had given up suggesting any alternative care procedures. There was no persuading Dr. Wodsende to more conservative measures.

Phyllis pulled the clipping from a folder. She had a pretty good idea who was leaving these around, and when Zach showed up to work, she planned on confronting him. She was fond of Zach and didn't want to write a critical update for the court. But for now he was stirring up too much trouble.

Pouring coffee, she reflected on the conversation with Dr. Wodsende's service. What could she say that might elicit an admission of his true relationship with Andrea? When she asked, she'd been told that Dr. Wodsende had once held a staff position in the ER, which might explain how Andrea came to be a patient here.

Phyllis stood at the window in the break room deep in thought. Old and stately oak trees were perfectly spaced over the well kept lawn, as city traffic flowed by, just beyond the decorative iron-gate. Her talent for recognizing a resident in trouble before the symptoms fully developed was well known. She was a skilled nurse with all the right instincts and right now she was feeling very uneasy about Andrea. Something was wrong.

"Did you know that Dudley Wodsende was married to Andrea?"

Three employees had joined Phyllis in the break room. She answered truthfully. "Not until recently. I thought he might be a distant relative."

"I knew. When the murder happened I was working here. Everyone felt sorry for him."

"I just figured management cleared it for him to treat her. Even though..." the other aide paused for effect. "Andrea killed his new wife. Many people still remember her."

"Why didn't we know about this?" the LPN interjected.

Phyllis chose her words with care. "Andrea was declared mentally ill and incompetent to stand trial and went right from one locked psych-ward to another."

"What if Dr. Wodsende has a vested interest in keeping her so doped up she can't string two words together."

"Maybe you've all been watching too many cop shows." Phyllis retorted. "I'm tired of this talk. I want it to stop."

She walked down the hallway to the nurse's station and selected Andrea's chart from the circular rack. "I have a call into Dr. Wodsende. If he calls back, tell him I'm busy with another patient. Tell him that my question is incidental and I'll call him back as soon as I get a chance."

"We can page you."

"I know you can page me, but first I want a little quiet time with Andrea." Phyllis tucked the chart under her arm. "I know it's his day off, but if Zach comes in for any reason, I want to see him right away."

"Zach's in trouble," echoed a childish sing-song voice. Phyllis turned on her heel and saw that the three from the break room had followed her to the nurses' station.

"All of you," Phyllis reprimanded. "Get back to work."

She would have smiled to see them scurry off in different directions if she were not so concerned. Andrea was one of those patients forgotten by her family and friends. No one ever visited and Phyllis had never met the mother. Did the mother realize that Andrea's former husband was the doctor of record? Well, yes, Phyllis reasoned. Administration would have required the mother's permission. They might have closed ranks around Dr. Wodsende, but they were not entirely stupid.

It irked Phyllis that an underage, court ordered adolescent was able to figure out what should have been evident from the start. She would have to write a report and discuss this sensitive issue with the hospital administrator and she could guess what would happen next. They would transfer Andrea rather than risk keeping her. The next facility, with the prospect of a generous contribution from the Wodsende Trust, might require even less from Dudley.

The receptionist studied the priest as he walked toward her with unhurried steps, almost graceful in the way of an athlete. "Hello Father, may I help you?"

Guido smiled, "I'm here to see a family member. Andrea Wodsende."

Under his arm was a box covered in decorative gold foil with raised letters in a language she didn't recognize. He held a bunch of what looked like wild flowers, their spidery stems poking through wet paper towels. She concluded that he had picked them himself, and was touched by the gesture and curious about the box.

"I don't see your name on the approved visitor list. I'm sorry Father, but Mrs. Wodsende is one of our special residents. For this reason we're required to record the comings and goings of all her visitors. You understand?"

Into the pause that followed she decided she liked this man. He looked a little lost, his manner polite which made her immediately want to help him. He was far too handsome to be a priest and she couldn't help thinking what a waste. A lock of salt and pepper hair fell boyishly over his forehead and belied the unlined appearance of his skin. When asked later, although she made up a number, she knew she couldn't accurately guess his age. He could have been thirty or fifty.

"Your flowers are beautiful," she said, delaying the inevitable delivery of bad news. Keeping to strict policy for state patients he was precluded from visiting Andrea.

"I picked them myself. Just this morning."

"Queen Ann's Lace and Black Eyed Susan. And what are these?"

"Delphinium. Andrea's favorite."

"They're lovely," she agreed and wondered at the effect this stranger had on her.

"May I ask? Are not pastoral visits encouraged?

"Yes, of course. But the state patients are different and the only person listed is her mother, Sybil Bryant." A tone of disapproval crept into her tone. "As far as I know, she has never once visited."

"And just between you and me and the lamppost, that's why I'm here. We know her mother never visits." He dropped his voice. "I told a friend of Andrea's that I would come and see her for myself. We have some concerns," Guido confided and looked forlornly at the box under his arm, shifting its weight as though it were very heavy.

"I brought Andrea some candy," he said. "I guess if she can't have them, you might as well share them with the staff."

He handled the box as though it were very valuable. "Italian," he whispered and lay it on the desk. "You can't get these in the United States. They make them in a little sweet shop in the shadow of Vatican City. I'll be disappointed not to see Andrea. Can you tell me? How is our girl doing?"

The receptionist smiled, approving his concern. "Andrea is doing better. She might actually recognize you. We feel she's noticing so much more." She turned the book to face Guido and handed him her pen. "I tell you what," she offered. "You go on in. If anyone asks, I'll say you're here to see her roommate, Mrs. Tyler."

"I'm sure Mrs. Tyler needs prayer too. We all do." He sounded buoyant. "What's the roommate's first name?"

"Birdie." She lowered her voice to a conspiratorial whisper. "She has short term memory loss. It won't matter if she doesn't recognize you. If the charge nurse comes in, just talk like you're old friends. No one will be the wiser."

"God Bless you, my dear."

"You did it again. I'll report you. I saw...I saw you get up and wall, no walk, no..." Birdie was on another tangent. She pointed off in the direction of the bathroom. Her hand dropped when she saw Phyllis.

"What's wrong, Birdie?"

A bewildered look came over Birdie's face. There was an angry intensity to that look, focused not at those around her as often seemed the case, but at the bitter warfare within to salvage her cognitive functions. Phyllis felt compassion and even admiration. The fighter she'd been in life, the stubborn individuality that a loyal family described for the staff, was serving Birdie even now.

"Don't you worry, Birdie. Andrea will be fine," Phyllis said and bent to share a warm hug. "I'll take over from here."

Phyllis pulled a chair up, sitting at eye level across from Andrea, who sat slumped forward with her tray table locked in place. For long moments Phyllis studied her patient. Andrea's color was good. No one had brushed her hair, so Phyllis took a comb and began to smooth the tangle of short brown strands. Her head remained down, her chin settled between the upturned fold of her robe. If she felt the pull on her scalp, there was no indication. Now that she had seen the clippings, Phyllis knew that Andrea's hair had once been colored a honey shade of blonde. She had been quite beautiful and it was said that, despite the mental illness she would have successfully hidden from the world, she had dressed fashionably and been active in several charities.

"Andrea, I want you to look at me." There was no response. "I understand that you're improving. The staff tells me that you're eating better and that you seem more alert."

A side effect of Andrea's medication was dry mouth, but drool slipped from the corner of Andrea's mouth and lodged on her chin. Phyllis had a sense that she and Andrea shared the significance of this, which begged the question. Was she organized enough to be spitting out her medications?

"Andrea," Phyllis tried again. "This is serious. I'm trying to help you, so if you're pretending to be sicker than you actually are, please, just give me a sign."

No response. Phyllis breathed a sigh of frustration. She waited with no real hope that Andrea would respond, if in fact she was at all capable of doing so. And yet, some of the staff insisted they had heard her speak. Just a word here or there that could have been Birdie or a sound from another room tossed about in the hollow acoustics' of the hallway. Had Andrea successfully feigned mental illness to avoid doing hard time for murder?

Phyllis chided herself. No one could play the part this well, sustained for over two years. Not without help. Help such as strong drugs to maintain the façade. But even so, these drugs had taken their toll and the long term risk would be dear.

Phyllis began to rise. She would go back to the nurse's station and write the carefully crafted notes that would address the legal risk of keeping Andrea, giving a copy to the hospital administrator in the morning. That action alone would be enough to get Andrea's presence reviewed.

Phyllis rose to go, but stopped when she felt a gentle restraint. Ever so slowly Andrea's right hand had curved over the edge of the plastic tray, and caught the sleeve of her uniform. Phyllis sat back into the chair. She took Andrea's thin hand and squeezed. Andrea turned her palm up and returned the pressure. They sat that way for a long moment. Phyllis thought she might cry. Andrea was holding her hand.

"I can't help you unless you talk to me, Andrea," she whispered. "I understand you've said a few words. Is there anything you want to say now?"

Andrea's expression changed. Slowly she lifted her head. For a long moment she held Phyllis's gaze with her cornflower blue eyes. *Windows to the soul.* The words flashed into Phyllis's mind as she tried to decipher the wealth of emotion that resided there. Something in the complicated mesh of Andrea's long absence from self had shifted. Behind the façade of mental illness there was a woman present, and in that brief interlude of wordless exchange, Phyllis saw intelligence and even sanity.

"Well hello, Doctor. Come right in. Let me tell you about my.... I need a doctor. I need..."

Phyllis turned to see Dudley Wodsende. He was handsomely dressed in a dark pin stripe suit and a pastel colored tie. Phyllis distrusted those negligible colors on men. How long had he been standing there?

"I was in the neighborhood when I got your page. How's our patient today?"

"No change, Doctor." The lie rolled off Phyllis's tongue so easily it surprised her.

"Yes there is. There are lots of changes, Doctor. For one thing she walls. Walks to... Well hello. Hello, Doctor. I need a doctor. I need..."

"How are you today, Birdie? So Andrea is walking is she?"

"I'm walking too. She's walking." Birdie pointed an accusing finger at Andrea, before turning back toward Dudley. A gathering expression of intensity locked her face in a near spastic contortion of fear. "Don't hit," she commanded. "No kissing. Don't hit."

Dr. Wodsende chucked. "No one is hitting anyone." His voice was evenly pleasant, but Phyllis had caught the significance of what was said.

Birdie might make little sense to outsiders who didn't know her, but the character of her confusion had its own language. There were always nuggets of truth, and glimpses of how she really felt buried in her conversation. She liked who she liked and was consistent in her rejection of those who grew impatient with her frailties.

"None of the staff have witnessed Andrea walking on her own, Doctor Wodsende. It would be impossible for her to do so without us noticing."

"Really?"

Dudley's tone was faintly sardonic and Phyllis experienced a rush of panic, unusual for her. He gestured toward the chair she sat on, expecting her to vacate so that he could take her place. Andrea's hand tightened over hers, but her head was down and the appearance of withdrawal firmly in place. Phyllis removed her hand, feeling faint resistance that tugged as her heart as she did so. She had a sense of how helpless Andrea was as she struggled for awareness. Turning her attention to Dr. Wodsende, Phyllis had the impression of a vulture in human form perched at eye level and taunting his prey. Like Birdie it would seem that Andrea had enough sense to be afraid of this man.

"You can go now, Nurse," Dudley directed, his look transfixed on Andrea.

Phyllis resisted the invitation which came to her as a kind of odd temptation to fall into lock step with his wishes, no questions asked. "I'll stay," she replied and moved from behind Dudley to stand at the side so that she could better observe.

"Get me the chart," he demanded, giving her a plausible reason to flee and thus avoid confrontation. He wanted Andrea to himself. How often had the staff, herself included, left Andrea defenseless with a man who had every reason to hate her? "I happen to have the chart right here, Doctor."

"Get me a glass of water, will you please?" Now he did look at her. His smile was charming. He was inviting the camaraderie of their mutual profession, but Phyllis wasn't buying. She walked to the intercom and called to the nurse's station for water with ice, deciding that whoever brought it would stay.

By the time she returned to stand again at Dudley's side his smile had vanished. The pretense of acting out their mutual roles was gone. Dudley took Andrea's hand, feeling for her pulse.

"My, but your pulse is rapid today. I do think that if you could, you would throw off the shackles of this chair that confines you and run. And is that perspiration I see on your upper lip? Nervous are you?"

No response. Was he attempting to provoke Andrea into giving herself away? Please, God, Phyllis prayed. Don't let her respond. *Don't do it, Andrea. Don't fall for his tricks.*

Phyllis watched as Dudley picked up Andrea's hand, the one that had so recently tightened over her own, and dropped it limp and yielding to the surface of the tray. Taking a stethoscope from his pocket he listened to her heart.

"For someone who is thought to be nearly catatonic your heart is racing pretty fast, my dear. Is that equally true of your mind?"

Tearing his eyes from Andrea, Dudley regarded Phyllis for what seemed an interminable length of time. He couldn't take an employee's pulse to determine the level of anxiety, but that he sensed it and even enjoyed her discomfort seemed clear.

"I think we'll try a new medication. From now on it will be administered IM."

Baiting her, he shifted position, allowing Phyllis to see what he was doing. From somewhere he had produced a syringe and was pulling a dosage from a medicine bottle. He held up the syringe, going through the motions in deliberate pantomime. He was making a point, putting her in her place. He was the doctor, she his subordinate.

Dudley glanced at Phyllis, flicking air into the top of the syringe and squirting out a little fluid. "This will stay in her system for several weeks and eliminate the possibility that Andrea could be spitting out her oral meds."

"Oh, I don't think so, doctor, I..."

"Oh, *but, I do* think so and I hope you'll question your staff because it seems perfectly clear that someone has been circumventing my orders, which we both know is grounds for dismissal."

He opened the chart and took a pen from his pocket. He wrote with a flourish and held the open chart out to Phyllis. "I've ordered this medication stat. I do believe I'll administer this first dosage myself. If you'll just prepare the patient..."

He had his hand in his pocket. As he turned to regard her directly, Phyllis caught an image of yet another syringe, thicker than the first and fully loaded with a whitish fluid. Would he explain this second medication or just administer the dosage without documentation.

Phyllis read what he had written. "And I see you've come prepared knowing that, since we are not a psychiatric facility, we wouldn't have this medication in stock."

"How kind of me to anticipate the need."

"Even if we did have this medication in stock, I would not be able to carry out your order, Dr. Wodsende."

"And why is that?"

"Because there is some question about whether you should be treating your former wife."

"Until that's decided I am her doctor, acting with the full approval of her mother who happens to be the only family she has. Now I've had enough of your delay. Get the patient on the bed and positioned for this injection in her right buttocks.

Voices were raised in anger, the most insistent belonging to her mortal enemy. Andrea willed herself to speak, having finally realized that unless she could push the words from her mind and past vocal cords long out of use they would not be heard. Following instructions from Zach she had been careful to keep her voice low as she practiced on Birdie. At first she had felt a flood of insecurity, wondering if the sounds were truly hers. When she asked, Birdie had replied in the affirmative; "yes it's you, it's not the bed post... the post; I need to post a letter."

From across the room, perched on the side of her bed with a waist restraint keeping her from moving very far, Birdie held Andrea's gaze. Though no one noticed, the two roommates concentrated, feeding on one another's attempt to break free of what entrapped them. Andrea liked that Birdie noticed her. No one but that boy who whispered clandestine instructions and warnings in her ear appeared to care that she was emerging from a death like state of inertia. Andrea tried again and failed and Birdie seemed to be saying, "I dare you. I dare you to speak." Birdie lifted her hand and pointed again at Andrea, looking between Dudley and Phyllis, but failing to capture their attention.

"Watch out! Watch out!" Birdie announced. "There she goes. There she goes! She's going!"

But doctor and nurse were otherwise occupied as they faced off.

"I happen to have several trial doses of this medication." Dudley held up two vials. "Lucky for us they were given to me only yesterday, by a pharmaceutical rep. I'm not going to ask you again, nurse. Prepare the patient or I'll be forced to do so myself."

Phyllis hesitated. He was Andrea's doctor. He was within his rights to order any reasonable medication, but this particular med was not familiar, of the type used for those with severe mental illness. Andrea was not out of control and there had never been any indication that she hallucinated or heard voices. For the first time she was somewhat participating in her own care and feeding. She was more aware, but cooperative and there now seemed little doubt that Andrea had been secretly spitting out her meds. The only question that remained was to discover who on her staff had been assisting this process, something Phyllis must leave until later.

"If you don't mind, Doctor, I'd like to look up the medication and be prepared for any side effects," she said buying time.

"All the information you need is right here." With impatience Dudley pulled the insert from his pocket. As he did so the larger barrel she had glimpsed earlier caught the corner of the insert and tumbled to the floor. Before he could respond Phyllis scooped up the fallen instrument, noting that it was the type used to irrigate a wound. On first glance the substance appeared cloudy and Phyllis wondered if this was intended to be an oral dose, another psychotropic medication that, given to someone who was already overmedicated, would guarantee the catatonic state Andrea had evidenced.

Phyllis considered. It was her job to anticipate and be prepared for any allergic reaction that might occur. This meant that she must know the medications, their side effects' and what symptoms of toxicity might manifest. It now seemed clear that Andrea's ex-husband was administering medicines without the requisite documentation. Dr. Wodsende must no longer be allowed to treat Andrea.

"I'll take that back," Dudley said, holding out his hand as Phyllis sidestepped away, wrapping the barrel in her handkerchief before tucking it deep into her own pocket.

"You may not have noticed that the plastic cracked when it fell," she offered, feeling a sudden threat at his presence. "I'll dispose of it for you, Doctor, since the contents are now contaminated and unusable."

Phyllis had no doubt that his next step would be to take the syringe by force if, in fact, he did have anything to hide. She determined to fight him off if necessary, to scream, and make a scene that no one would quickly forget. She glanced at Andrea, reminding herself that her first duty was to protect the patient.

"I'd like to call her mother," Phyllis delayed as he held out his hand for the barrel and stepped closer. "I'd like to confirm permission for you to treat this patient before you make any significant changes in her care," Phyllis challenged and moved so that Andrea's tray chair was an obstacle between them.

"Her mother is out of town. On a singles cruise I believe and trolling for new fish." He unlocked the wheels of Andrea's chair and none too gently, slid it out of the way. "Even if you reached her, she wouldn't be at all interested in your opinion. The fact is Andrea has no family. I'm the only one who cares; the only family Andrea has. Now I'm not going to ask you again! Get this patient on the bed and on her side now!"

Buying time Phyllis bent toward Andrea as if she had every intension of removing the tray that, until now, had kept Andrea restrained. Phyllis wondered where the aide was with her request for water and ice. If ever she needed a witness, it was now.

"Andrea," she whispered, feeling desperate, her hands now on the release to the tray table as she feigned cooperation, but feeling Dudley's eyes on her back and hating that she could no longer see his face. "Please, you must refuse this medication. You must say the words."

Dudley was ranting, his words a stream of threats. "Clearly you have failed in your responsibilities. The blood work I'm about to order will show that Andrea has not had her meds for some time and as charge nurse you'll be held accountable for this lapse. I'm ordering a urine specimen and I'll take both blood and urine with me when I go. I don't trust any results you might submit. Insubordination is a serious infraction. I'll see that you lose your job. I'll have that syringe you stole from me before I go. I'll..."

Forgetting caution Phyllis placed two firm hands on Andrea's jaw and turned her face up toward hers. Abruptly Dudley stopped talking. She could feel his stare drill into her back. Phyllis swallowed a mounting surge of fear and tried again.

"Andrea, you have to speak." Seconds passed with no indication that she was heard. "No one can speak for you. Do you want this man to treat you or do you want a different doctor? Andrea you have to say so. You have no family to speak for you. So please..."

Andrea opened her mouth as a sound, no more than a soft unintelligible whisper, floated into the air.

"I hope I'm not intruding..."

"Hello. Hello. I'm Birdie. I need a doctor. I need..."

Phyllis and Dudley turned in unison. A priest had entered the room and now bent to kiss Andrea's cheek.

"Well, hello, pumpkin. How are you? Sorry it's taken me so long to get here."

He put his flowers on the tray in front of Andrea who followed the gesture, appearing to study the bright confluence of color. She breathed deeply and Phyllis realized that her intent was to catch the scent of the bouquet. This one act revealed the degree of remarkable progress that Andrea had made.

She and others had failed to be Andrea's advocate until the need was thrust in their faces by Zach. It had to be true that Dr. Wodsende was right and someone on staff had interfered with her receiving medication that, it was now clear, she never needed. Phyllis felt shame that she hadn't taken a stand far sooner.

The priest took Andrea's hand and Phyllis noticed that her fingers closed over his in warm response. With his other hand he smoothed the longish bangs back from her scalp. Whoever he was, he seemed perfectly at ease as if he may have been faithfully visiting each week.

"I liked you better as a blond, pumpkin. Now that you're feeling better, maybe we can get someone up here to do your hair. Would you like that?"

"I would," Birdie chirped. "Thank you, I'd like that very much."

The priest smiled at Birdie before addressing Phyllis. "Who says Andrea doesn't have any family. I'm her family, right pumpkin?" Andrea actually lifted her face and looked at him. She then lowered her gaze, content to study the flowers. "See," the stranger said. "You were arguing. Maybe I can help?"

"And, you are!"

"A member of the family." Guido looked intently at Dudley; a look that Phyllis found disturbing for its intensity. "I believe we have a relative in common... one I choose not to recognize. But you would know that better than anyone."

"I was married to Andrea. I knew everything there was to know about her. I knew her history. I knew more about her than her own mother."

"Then you will recall that she once took out a restraining order against you. That being the case, if she could speak for herself, why would she let you within forty feet of her?"

Dudley's color had turned as pale as his tie. He straightened his shoulders and glared at the visitor.

"Her mother appointed me to care for Andrea. And since you claim to be related to her, perhaps you can tell me exactly who her father was, because I'm fairly certain Andrea never met him, nor did she know his name. I, on the other hand..."

Phyllis listened to the exchange and was filled with hopeful optimism. Finally there was a family member who would speak for Andrea and a priest no less.

"I'm waiting. What was her father's name?" Dudley demanded, unable to tear his eyes from Guido's clerical collar while avoiding eye contact."

No reply.

"And it looks like I'll be waiting a long time. You have no idea. Do you Mr. ...? You're probably not even a priest and this is just a disguise to get past the visiting restrictions. What did you say your name was?"

Although he should have expected it, Guido was surprised to encounter Dudley. He had long been curious to lay eyes on his infamous uncle, who was closer to his own age than his father. Standing at the door and listening to the heated exchange between nurse and doctor had made him decide to risk a confrontation in order to see Andrea for himself. She was, after all, the reason for his visit, and like Dudley she was a pawn around whom much plotting and drama had circulated.

Though engaging Dudley was a risk, he and Mario were now finished with what they had set out to accomplish. Slipping his hand into the inside pocket of his jacket, Guido felt for his cell phone. Dudley's eyes were riveted to each gesture.

Guido probed to see if his uncle were a reader, an intrinsic with the ability to discern the subtext, the underlying truth of people and circumstances. He was startled to find that Dudley lacked this gift, a gift necessary for any that ascended to his high position within the family. It could only be true that Dudley was a decoy, a paper tiger, a Trojan horse.

Fingering his cell phone, Guido punched the code that would send his brother a prepared text. Within minutes the process of destroying all traces of their present life would begin, until finally the house was torched and the final details of this last operation completed by others.

The drill was familiar, and yet Guido felt sad. Working in the Boston area, his father had been in close proximity. More than once Guido had followed Henry, fully expecting to be noticed and secretly hoping for another conversation. He was disturbed to see that Henry was no longer the confident, quick witted man they had met in Paris. There was an aspect of weary despair in his demeanor which alarmed Guido, who desired nothing more than to see his father's eternal soul rescued from the cultish enslavement of their shared heritage.

Coming to see Andrea was a rash move and if he did run into Dudley, well then... dressing as he did was a provocative challenge.

Guido thought of Zach. More than likely they would never see Zach again. They had arrived with every intention of marking his father, Elias, as the recipient of certain information, some of which Vince had already loaded as a sleeper program on the Goldfarb's home computer. Having handled the accounting details related to Andrea's divorce, it was hoped that Elias had seen enough of the cult finances not to be terribly shocked by what future events, Bible prophecy, and the sleeper programs would reveal.

After getting to know Zach they settled on a change of plans. The son was young and tenacious with a sense of morality and a love for justice, though he lacked a compass. The Holy Spirit seemed to be working in Zach's life, drawing him to the truth. Vince had been adamant that Zach could survive what was coming and especially if given a little help by way of valuable cyber tools and information. When Mario objected, bringing up Zach's age and behavior, Vince had quoted St Paul, both in support of what he felt God had showed him and in hopeful vindication of Zach. *Let no one look down on your youthfulness, but rather in speech, conduct, love, faith and purity, show yourself an example of those who believe (1st Timothy 4: 12).*

Guido looked at Andrea. Seeing her inspired his compassion and a new commitment to pray for emotional and physical healing.

"Well!" Dudley demanded. "I'm waiting. What was her father's name?"

Guido opened his mouth and was about to speak...

"Clarence." The name was barely discernable. The unused vocal cords of Andrea's throat hardly got the sound out, but they had all heard and understood.

Phyllis felt a thrill of joy. She bent over Andrea and placed a comforting hand on her shoulder. "Go on," she encouraged.

"My father...., his... name was Clarence. I... I was named after his mother, Andie Rose. I'm Andrea?" She turned her head and looked at Phyllis as though for confirmation.

"That's right, Honey," Phyllis pronounced with glee. "Your name is Andrea Wodsende and this is your uncle. Father, what did you say your name was?"

"You can call me, Guido. Dr. Woods doesn't remember, but he and I have met."

Andrea raised her head and looked at Guido. Their eyes locked and he felt a connection. Though pale and shrunken, with dark circles under her eyes, he sensed her true spirit. Zach had been right. There was something special about Andrea. And he knew. She would never deliver the child the family awaited, the son of prophecy, the man clothed in the demonic power of perdition. She was as much a decoy as Dudley, meaning that he and Mario were not only working in the wrong city, but on the wrong continent. Milan, Italy was next on their list.

"This is your Uncle Guido," Phyllis said, reminding Andrea, helping to orient her further. But Andrea appeared to have retreated. *Oh, not now,* Phyllis thought. *We need your help. You must help yourself!*

"See, pumpkin, I brought you some flowers." Guido picked up the flowers and put them close to her face.

Andrea blinked, breathing in the scent. She concentrated and breathed again. Reminded of other places, other times, comprehension filled her face. She could no longer contain the smile. It came infectious and innocent and had the effect of disquieting Dudley even further.

Phyllis grinned, feeling triumphant in this success.

Once more Guido took Andrea's hand in his. As he did so his gaze locked on Dudley and Phyllis made a decision.

"I'm sorry Dr. Wodsende," she said. "It looks like you're off the case. You understand what I'm saying? Andrea has three witnesses. She rejected that injection and asked for a different doctor."

"She said no such thing."

"Oh, but she did. I heard her clear as a bell. This priest heard, didn't you?"

Guido was silent. He could not engage in dishonesty. To do so negated his spiritual calling.

"And I imagine your third witness is that pathetic excuse for humanity in the next bed," Dudley sounded incredulous.

In unison they turned to look at Birdie who smiled back at them, grateful for the attention. Phyllis nodded in Birdie's direction. "That's right. You heard, didn't you Birdie?"

"I heard. I heard and my hair, I need a haircut."

"If you imagine I'm done with you, you're sadly mistaken. This isn't over. You'll be hearing from Andrea's mother this afternoon."

"For now, Dudley, it is over, and if the policy of this hospital is that a certain doctor can't treat his former wife, then it won't matter what a lost *witch* of a *false mother,* might say or not say."

There was now a clinical aspect to Dudley's bearing, a cold and menacing leer behind the eyes. He had alerted to the seemingly intentional use of the word *witch, lost witch, false mother,* as a wolf intent on its pack and threatened by an outsider. Hackles of suspicion jelled in Dudley mind.

In response Guido lifted his chin and squared his shoulders watchful as Dudley's thoughts moved to their obvious conclusion.

"It must be true that we know one another?" Dudley acknowledged, scrutinizing Guido's features for further recognition.

A force rippled beneath the structure of Dudley's face, stretching the skin tight over jaw and cheekbones. A visible shape-shift had taken place. When he spoke there was an echo, evoking the impression of words arrived over a cavernous void. Leaping through a dank chasm, they dropped into the room, having a physical weight and cloying attachment. An unmistakable odor of decay, of burning sulfur contaminated the air.

From across the room Birdie gagged and vomited, bile staining her white shirt. Phyllis covered her mouth with one hand, and picked up a towel for Birdie with the other. She had every intention of rushing to Birdie's side, offering help, but for now she was struck immobile, stopped in her tracks by some visceral shock of confusion. There was in the room another entity; not human, threatening and evil.

"We know you... You are a Henry son, first son, traitor," the gravel tongued voice spoke.

Outed by a demon. So this is why Dudley is still alive, Guido thought, feeling compassion for the humanity that was lost as he fell into that mode of protection against such exchanges. He spoke audibly in controlled even measure and in the strength of his gifts, sending forth the command of a weathered exorcist.

Holy Spirit, please burn all evil spirits present with your fire. Send Your mighty heavenly host to arrest and escort all spiritual entities serving Satan and the power of darkness to Your throne to receive Your righteous judgment. Cancel their orders concerning us forever and send them to the abyss never to return.

At this moment, for all intents and purposes, Dudley the man was gone. Though not yet totally and completely lost as his father, Guido and Mario's grandfather had been. The dark side had lost valuable chattel when, in an act of vigilante revenge, old man Woods as he was known, had been gunned down on the streets of North Adams.

In the name of Jesus Christ of Nazareth who came in the flesh and by the power of the cross, under the covering of His blood, I command that any back up spells, curses, or unholy ties be broken and all satanic forces responsible, be sent to the throne of almighty God to be judged and consigned to hell; never to return.

"Dudley. I'm speaking to Dudley. Would you like me to escort you out, or are you going on your own steam? Because I'd be pleased to help," Guido said and removed the principal weapon, a weathered Bible from his pocket. He read several key verses and then...

Let all ties, interaction, and communication between demonic spirits within the body or outside the body be cut off. I pray a canopy of protection over this room, under the covering of the blood of Jesus Christ and pray for God's will, protection, and purpose over the actions of all persons present."

"Andrea is my wife. She'll always belong to me."

The voice was Dudley's. The odor had retreated, but Guido knew better than to open a dialogue with his cousin. This wasn't the place. He opened his Bible.

I ask for the protection of the shed blood of Jesus Christ of Nazareth who came in the flesh. I ask for the protection of powerful warrior angels to guard Andrea, to protect others in this room, and to aid in this ongoing battle for healing, deliverance, and freedom. Our Father, who art in heaven...

Phyllis felt confused and conflicted. Should she stop this? Could she stop this? In answer a single word filled her mind. *"Faith."* She knelt down and silently began to pray for this priest who had arrived on the scene just when she and Andrea were most vulnerable. If he hadn't come she didn't want to think of what might have transpired.

"Andrea belongs to another and only arrogance blinds Dudley to this reality," Guido announced and began reading through a Psalm, finishing and turning the pages in order to read another passage. His movements were patient and unhurried. He had produced a vial of holy water, continuing to read the words he'd memorized and yet returning to the page.

Dudley stumbled. He had lost time, but had grown familiar with this internal shift in autonomy, over which he no longer exercised control. He gathered himself, pulling together the tattered shreds of his humanity, not seeing that more of that precious cloth had been lost, the scars beneath ever more visible, a calcified barrier; a living death.

This was Guido, servant of the Christ, demon slayer, exorcist, former cult member, but no longer enslaved to the evil symbiosis of the Wood Son heritage. There was no claim, no power to be had over Guido's soul that was not of his Savior, Jesus Christ.

For his part Guido had seen the face of his enemy and once again the enemy had laid eyes on him. Every dark intrinsic, directly conversant with a familiar on the eastern seaboard, would be sending out their feelers in search of him. But Guido knew that nothing would transpire that Jesus Christ did not allow.

With war openly declared, he and Mario would find periods of rest few and far between. Thus was the nature of such warfare in the closing down of an age that was all too swiftly approaching its end.

WOOD'S END

PART FOUR
CHAPTER SIXTEEN

JARED

For though we walk in the flesh we do not war according to the flesh, for the weapons of our warfare are not of the flesh, but divinely powerful for the destruction of fortresses
(2nd Corinthians 10: 3, 4).

Jared rolled onto his back. The sheets tightened and further constricted movement. He kicked wildly, shivering as the morning air hit his skin, lifting the sweat from his body. The night-terror was unlike anything previously experienced. Every perception of touch and smell became an intrusive assault that even now lingered like a cloying substance to cloud his thinking.

Despite having slept, he felt he had just plowed a field with a hand held tiller, his limbs weighed down by fatigue and exertion.

Don't sleep, a voice warned from the empty place beside him on the bed. D*on't sleep,* was the second fading echo. But already his body was drawn deeper into the soft warmth of the mattress. The strain in his neck, supported by a favorite pillow, eased as he sank into an ever widening crevice. Despite his resolve to fight for wakefulness, Jared drifted off toward that dangerous rim of unconsciousness where horrors await.

Seconds later, rescue arrived with the merciful chime of the coffee maker preset the evening before. Almost simultaneously and better than any alarm clock was the sound of Thor's truck crunching gravel as it took the turn from the drive to the barn faster than was safe and the rooster, his rooster, though the thought never failed to amuse him, crowed from the wood stump.

With sudden abruptness Jared came fully awake. He threw two pillows against the headboard, easing his body into a sitting position and tried to recall the nightmare. He stood on a darkened stair case needing to move forward, but entangled by a mysterious opposition. On that stair with him was something intangible. It was a space-less presence that tapped at the natural defenses of his mind, hating the mere humanness of his existence. The step he occupied was bloodied by the wounds of those who had fought a path up those stairs before him. He felt the refuse of suffering and defeat through the soles of his shoes, the emotional angst of which was a heavy burden of cinderblocks. The conflict loomed, or perhaps the fight was done and lost, and what he felt was his own blood underfoot.

He wouldn't think about it. To do so was to give the dream power beyond what was reasonable. "Enough!" Jared spoke aloud into the stillness of the room. He swung his body to the side of the bed and pulled on a pair of jeans before heading to the kitchen for a first cup of coffee.

But then he stopped. Though an inner restraint warned otherwise, he succumbed to an inexplicable compulsion and turned back, pausing at the threshold. Morning shadows crisscrossed the room with sunlight, a dappled glow over the floor and bed. Even the cream colored bottom sheet had come loose and all appeared a tangled mess.

Jared reminded himself that this was just a dream, but then the vision came, leaping into his mind, a brazen assault as it materialized before him in the room. Gray grasping hands, bloody around the oversized nails, reached up through the broad sinkhole of the bed. Locked in terror, afraid to blink, afraid that doing so would provoke the apparition Jared turned, running wildly from the room.

It took only a few minutes to regain his composure. He could not explain, even to himself what he had just experienced and yet felt a clear challenge to face his fear or be forever adversely impacted. Doing so was necessary, even imperative to his future health. Jared walked back into the room, standing firm in a patch of sunlight. Nothing of the vision remained to challenge logic and the bed was just as he had left it with the sheets twisted into the tight restraints they had become during the long, restless night.

During that first year of Jared's recovery his world had narrowed and centered almost entirely on gaining back mobility and stamina. As he faced the second year Jared was increasingly depressed feeling he had reached the plateau his doctors predicted.

A turning point came as Jared was about to enter the pool for aquatic exercise. He was told that because of the complicating brain injury he would progress no further and was now merely fighting to maintain. There would be a new treatment plan and one more surgery. The young man beside Jared scowled. When they were alone, he in his wheel chair and Jared balancing on a cane, he said words that Jared never forgot.

"Don't you listen to those kinds of statements, you hear me? I call them doom-statements and they be nothing more than word curses. How does he know what God will do for you in the future? You keep working, praying and believing. You understand what I'm saying, brother?"

The following day Thorson Dillihunt, Thor for short, showed up for a long overdue visit. Thor saw immediately that his friend was dangerously depressed. Scoffing at doctors' recommendations he returned Jared to Wood's End Township and home to the Shiel farm that once belonged to Jared's famous uncle. This was the hardest work Jared had ever done, but there was something restorative about working outside that stimulated acuity, which left him feeling grateful for life itself. Life no longer being a state he took for granted.

Thor divided his time between pastoring a small country church and acting as farm manager on the Shiel's acreage. As

Jared and Thor inventoried the farm equipment, idle for two generations, Jared took on the job of cleaning away rust, sharpening blades, and making additional purchases from the farm implement dealer. And then there were the repairs to the barn, portions of which had been converted by Burns to an art studio, fully insulated, and wired. The stalls were reclaimed for the two new geldings and the chicken coop needed to be cleaned, painted, and reinforced against the nocturnal visits of foxes and weasels.

As the season's work came to a close Jared felt infused with a deep satisfaction. There was something about the bales of hay, rolled pale amber under the sun, awaiting the cattle he had yet to purchase. When he stood back and surveyed the land cleared of brush and fences previously left to ruin, he was happy and guessed the reason was a kind of genetic imprint, the culmination of so many Shiel farmers contributing eons of life's affinity to the gene pool.

He sometimes met up with the few remaining farmers of the area for a dawn breakfast at the local diner. The shoptalk proved an education and he enjoyed swapping the occasional story with local law enforcement when they meandered in between shifts. More welcome still was the kind of tired he felt at the end of a day filled with such activity. Questions from the past haunted him less and less and, except for the occasional panic attack, he felt his old self.

As he spooned hot bacon grease over eggs sizzling in the pan Jared decided the apparition had been a kind of warning. Bothered by the ambiguity of that conclusion, he then determined to concentrate on forgetting the entire episode, keeping physically active all that long day, sorting those areas of the barn that he and Thor had yet to explore.

Together they dove into dark forgotten corners filled with items his uncle would have shuffled to the side as he carved out a studio for himself over what had once been the milking floor. They quickly found a surprising number of papers that had not been archived by the estate, which Jared found disturbing. He wondered what else may have been over looked by impersonal attorneys, closing out the estate.

Fear had fueled the manic busyness of the day. As dust rose amidst mildewed boxes the nightmare seemed less intrusive. Tired and satisfied with what had been accomplished Jared felt foolish for elevating his experience to such importance.

It was the hour of supernatural clash and preternatural heights, 3am, when Jared hauled the mattress and bedclothes out to the gravel drive. On his third trip he hoisted the solid wood headboard onto the burning pyre, feeding the flames with the last of the kerosene from an old lamp base. Thinking nothing of the expense, he watched the fire as it spread greedily over the pillow top fabric, eating black holes between the springs and curling fingers round the frame of the bed. He had taken the precaution of pulling the garden hose around front. A spiral plume of smoke, whitish gray and then a darker black against the night sky rained large shreds of ash, coming to land amidst the tall grass gleaming with dew.

Jared sipped whiskey unceremoniously from the open mouth of a Waterford decanter and watched over the flames, finding hidden fuel amidst the ashes and dying hard in the wind which had picked up and made a soft piping whisper through the trees.

He wasn't thinking of the vision when he fell into bed exhausted from the long day's activity. His muscles ached and he'd taken an over the counter sleep-aid, which in retrospect he considered a mistake. The medication had left him with fewer defenses to fight his way fully awake and thus escape the... He couldn't say it. Not now anyway.

Reclining as best he could in the porch rocker, Jared fought sleep. He had just closed his eyes when he came alert to the distinctive sound of Thor's pick-up barreling down the drive and screeching to a halt between the glowing embers of the fire and the porch.

"Hey city boy, I almost called the fire truck. If the wind changes direction your house will be burning. You want to tell me what's going on?"

"What are you doing up so early?" Jared asked, buying time, trying to think of a response that wouldn't leave him sounding entirely insane.

"Brenda was up with Victoria who couldn't sleep. They saw the flames and woke me."

Jared offered the decanter, but Thor waved it away and sat heavily into the rocker beside him. "What is that mess, a bed?" Thor asked squinting into the dying embers.

"That's right."

"Whose bed?"

"Mine."

"You burned your bed?"

"Yes, I did," Jared spoke decisively, a slight slur to his words.

"Why?" Thor asked studying his friend.

"At the time it seemed like a good idea."

"And now that you've had time to reflect?"

"Let's just say I had a nightmare and that bed was the weapon of choice. You wouldn't remember, but it was like the Scollay Square subway entrance before renovations. Entering that tunnel would have ended in the grave. My grave, just to be clear and there was this bloody gate keeper. I was supposed to ask it for help, but if I had, I'd be a goner. Can't negotiate with the devil you know, and he was a devil. So you see..."

"Perfectly, what else could you do?"

Jared sensed the smile behind the words. Thor was humoring him.

"The dream seemed real. Hell, it was real." Jared spoke in his own defense. "I'm not crazy. I didn't imagine this."

They sat in silence for a few minutes and Jared guessed that it was Thor's turn to gather his thoughts.

"Okay then. You saw something and you thought it was real, and now you think it was a dream. Do I have this right?" Thor ventured.

"Yes, it was both. I saw something in my dream and it was real. Yesterday morning I saw something when I wasn't dreaming. I was wide awake, but I convinced myself at the time that I was still half asleep and conjuring up the memory of this nightmare."

"Forget it.   That's my advice.   We're known for such things in this corner of Berkshire County.   That's the reason we attract outsiders at certain times of the year, and let's just say some are the kind of drop-ins from another culture one doesn't really want around.   They light fires, farm animals disappear, and sometimes worse things happen.   Leaves too much to the imagination, if you get my drift."

"Well, that's news to me.   I didn't know Woods End had such a reputation.   And I imagined nothing."

"Right, I understand, but maybe there are reasons."

"What reasons?"

"I wouldn't know.   I'm just saying, forget it, and try not to burn another bed.   Adds fuel to the fire so to speak, invites what you don't want to see.   You understand what I'm saying, Jared?"

"Ever have a similar experience?   Ever see something that wasn't there.   Because what you saw couldn't possibly be real and yet... you weren't dreaming and darn sure weren't hallucinating because you're not mentally ill and well past the age for onset of schizophrenia."

"Are you drunk?"   Thor asked.

"Drunk is a plausible explanation I could live with.   But, sorry, won't fly tonight.   Maybe in the morning."

Thor studied his boss, deciding.   "Here goes," he said.   "I saw something once; my last year of high school."

"What was it?"

"I thought it was a ghost.   I was at this abandoned farm house that has a long history.   A group of us went there, egging each other on.   The place was said to be haunted and we were brash and stupid and wanted to prove that we were fearless.   If I hadn't been dating Brenda and she didn't live on the same road, I would not have gone anywhere near that place ever again. When I told her she wasn't at all surprised."

"What did she say?" Jared asked.

"She said that God wasn't careless. He didn't leave people behind and just forget them for a few hundred years, and especially little children."

"Was it a child you saw?"

"I saw a man walking across the lawn toward the barn. He was dragging a reluctant child behind him, and she looked back at me with dead eyes. I still remember those eyes... they were black holes. My wife and I talked and her explanation was that they were demons impersonating dead people."

"I've never heard that explanation."

"I know that God is stronger than any demon. He defeated satan and all his hordes of fallen angels and cast them down to earth; Revelation 12: 7-9. That veil between men and evil creatures sometimes lift. Matthew, Mark, and Luke did a pretty good job of telling us what to do when we encounter them or discern their activity. As for me, I don't worry anymore. I have Jesus inside me. What about you, Jared?"

"What about me?"

"Are you a Christian? Do you have Jesus as your Savior?"

"I don't know."

"That answers the question, doesn't it? This isn't something to wonder about. Got a Bible anywhere about?"

Something about Thor's matter of fact solution buoyed Jared's spirits. It all seemed too simplistic, but he'd take whatever he could get for now.

"Not that I'm aware of."

"I'll bring you one."

"Maybe I'll sleep with it under my pillow."

Thor got up to leave. He had the truck door open when he looked back. "Here's an idea. Try reading it. Your uncle read his Bible every day."

"No, he didn't." Jared was astonished.

"Yes, he did."

"Burns wasn't religious," Jared said, surprised to find another false assertion about Burns which needed his defense. "And how would you know?"

"Cause I knew him better than you did. You dropped in on holiday with your parents. You were here for a month or so during the summer, and when you got older, you found better things to do with your time. My dad worked for him like I'm working for you now. And no, he wasn't religious, but he was a believer and had a deep and meaningful prayer life. He was an intercessor, an intrinsic."

"A what?"

"It's a word we use around here. Burns considered prayer his vocation and if he'd been Catholic, he would have been permanently ensconced in that monastery in Kentucky he visited, like doing so was a kind of vacation. And I guess for him it was. He could pray and meditate without the pressure to paint and without the demands of fame."

"This is changing the subject, but I've always wondered. Do you have an opinion about why he never married? They say it was his art; some have even suggested he was gay."

Thor leaned out of the truck. "That's a lot of hooey. He would have married his high school sweetheart. They would have had a family, and might even have moved away from Woods End. His agent was always trying to get him to live in New York or paint in Europe."

"What happened to the girl friend?" Jared asked.

"The long and short of it?"

"Why not?"

"Old man Woods kidnapped her. She was absorbed into that cult, married off, had two babies and disappeared. Burns never recovered. End of story. They say she was exceptionally beautiful, which I guess drew attention." Thor turned the key in the ignition, precluding the possibility of more discussion.

Next to Ed, his old partner, Thor was the most practical, down to earth person Jared had ever met. He thought that if he had a bed that wasn't a portal to hell and didn't have a fire to watch over so close to the house, he might actually be able to sleep without worrying about the next nightmare.

WOOD'S END

CHAPTER SEVENTEEN

The previous year working the farm had done a lot for Jared and he had even delved into his former profession as a kind of unlicensed private investigator turning his attention to the Lydia Dillihunt disappearance. This was an old case close to him; an unsolved abduction that had touched the Shiel family since the child was a first cousin to Thor. The mystery of what happened had inspired Jared's career goal of joining the police force and fighting crime.

What Jared concluded from this foray into the past was that no crime was unsolvable. More significant, he was unlucky in love, and third, had not totally lost his sleuthing skills. Two out of three were odds he could live with.

When he thought about the other major unsolved case of his career he didn't suffer from any similar inclination to dive right in. To do so was like bringing up old ghosts. Stephanie's murder and the Andrea Wodsende case was a trauma and a loss too close to the actual events. Against his will and without his say so, the Wodsende murder had completely altered a carefully planned life-trajectory.

Jared paused between the barn and the house and followed the flag attached to the roof of the mail jeep, all that was visible above the golden stalks of wheat until it turned up his drive.

"Hay, Jared, got your mail. What a mess," Scotty said surveying the fires debris. What'd you do? Have a late night bonfire? Cook marshmallows without me?"

"Something like that."

"Well, you picked an odd place for it. Should have dug a pit in the back yard. Next time let me show you how to do it right, cause you're lucky," he lectured, "that this didn't burn your house down."

"Thanks, I'll remember your kind offer," Jared replied having grown immune to the idiosyncrasies of his postman.

Jared put out his hand to receive the folded newspaper with his mail enclosed. "Is there anything worth reading?" He asked, since both had dispensed with the pretense that Scotty didn't examine each piece of mail before consigning it to the mail box.

"Utility bill. Everyone's complaining at the rate hike. Usual stuff and then... this here letter." Scotty handed him the one letter he'd withheld. The reason he'd driven up the long drive. "Expensive paper," he commented. "Law firm in Boston. Looks like it might be important. Embossed crest. You want it?"

Jared smiled as he received the letter.

"Oh, yeah. And the New York Times and Washington Post. What's the deal with that? Everything worth knowing is already printed in the local papers."

"They sometimes write about my uncle. Have to keep up with the art world, you know. Pays the bills."

"Yeah right," Scotty laughed as if he almost believed such an occupation could so generously provide. "I'll be off. See you tomorrow."

Dusk settled a muted haze over the landscape. Off in the distance a clap of thunder, but here on the farm precious solitude. Jared wondered if the storm was heading in his direction or would those heavy black clouds disappear over the ridge behind him? Wondered, but didn't care.

The letter lay open on the table beside him. He had read it now countless times, hoping to discern something more. Jared placed a hand over his shirt, over the place where the bullet had exploded. Neat going in, but tearing a raged hole in its deadly path out the other side. He recalled leaving

Andrea in the ICU unit and deciding at the last moment on a detour to the rare book section of the hospital library where his uncle's painting was on display.

Jared was sick of these useless circular thoughts. He had spent his career in the pursuit of answers, but the long road to recovery had left him impotent and helpless, needing to accept the dead end of the Wodsende case, and yet fighting the ingrained habit of a lifetime. It wasn't his style to walk away from an investigation.

The letter was either a curse or the gift of an invitation. All the excuse he needed to shake off the cloaking comfort of brooding immobility. He now had every reason to take a second look at the case that had nearly cost him his life and yet, he hesitated.

Jared could almost say that he was fully healed. There should be nothing to undermine his confidence. He liked his old self far better than the invalid that had nearly trapped him. With no other choice he had finally come to grips with the risk-taking, addictive personality that had driven him to extremes. It was the reason he was alone, allowing little more than work into his life.

He thought about the nightmare, thought about the attack that had nearly taken his life. The two weren't related, and yet they vied for space in the forefront of his mind as though they were. Was God really in control, allowing painful, life-threatening circumstances to bring his creation to an epiphany of self awareness as Thor had preached the previous Sunday? *...return to me for I have redeemed you.*

The little church was nestled off a rural blacktop. Shaded by tall oaks and flanked on one side by a sunflower field and on the other by forest, was attractive to Jared for its very lack of a permanent pastor and whatever intrusion he imagined that might bring. The pulpit had been intermittently filled with theological students on spring break or summer hiatus, practicing what they'd learned in class, sometimes tentative and hesitant to offend and other times brash and forceful to a fault. He liked best the retired pastors who spoke their minds, for the first time free of committees wielding misplaced power.

Only now the few aging members had offered the job to Thor who had quickly said, yes, assuring Jared it wouldn't interfere with the paying job that made this one possible. But Jared saw the handwriting on the wall as he sat between Thor's wife, Brenda and their fifteen year old daughter, Victoria. He had counted the number of younger families. They almost outnumbered the elderly regulars and if this continued new seating would be required.

Thor had come in early to tend the animals, and then taken the day off to be with family. Jared was sleeping on the couch, though he'd ordered a new mattress and box spring, new sheets and blankets, which he expected to arrive that afternoon. He had kept busy shuffling boxes from the attic to the dining room and had spent the morning stacking them in chronological order while leaving a narrow path to maneuver.

Before his partner retired, Jared asked that the Wodsende case files be copied and delivered to him. A moving van was parked across from the fenced square of his Boston townhouse when Ed drove up; pulling a small trailer.

"Making a permanent move I see."

"I don't know how permanent, but for now it's the principal residence. I'm officially a farmer." Jared acknowledged and introduced Thor who had been loading several boxes of favorite books.

"Got room for more?" Ed asked.

"Perfect timing," Jared said. They transferred the boxes and slammed the heavy doors, sliding the bolt into place. "Thanks for doing this. I know it was a chore."

"Yeah, well, it's probably a mistake. Doctor's orders are you're to concentrate on this white-bread life they want you to accept. Me? I don't see it happening. We are what we are and a farm in the middle of no-where won't cut it for long. Not enough potential mayhem and crisis."

"Thanks for the observation."

"As you know, I could get into trouble, but I had enough help. They'd have to fire everyone in archives and the evidence room and at least a couple of secretaries. As of today every scrap pertaining to the case is copied to those boxes including hospital records and Andrea's first court proceeding. We also had the photos reprinted. I'll send you a bill for that."

"Anything new?"

"Nothing," Ed said. "Last I heard Wodsende bowed out of ER medicine. Sees a few patients, but mostly devotes himself to recreation. A few months ago a girlfriend filed an assault charge. When they went to question her, she dropped the charges and moved to California. No forwarding address."

"Sounds like Marstead's work."

"Precisely."

It seemed fitting to Jared that Ed would retire about the time he was released due to permanent medical impairment. It grieved Jared to think he was never going back, but the department wasn't about to accept liability if he lost the second kidney in some future altercation.

By afternoon, Jared had extended the table and begun organizing the contents of some of the boxes into neat piles. He felt a thrill of expectation and was strangely heartened to see his pre-injury handwriting, a cross between print and incursive.

As he worked, Jared listened for the mail truck, hoping that Scotty had something worth hand delivering, but ready to flag him down if he didn't.

"If you're waiting for something, it's not here. I've already looked. Just a few bills and catalogs. No more fancy letters," Scotty said when Jared met him outside.

"I don't know how I survived before I had a mail man slash secretary on the job."

"Are you trying to be funny?"

"Not at all, what I need is directions."

"Shoot."

"To the Wodsende Farm. Where is it precisely?"

"You mean the Woods farm?"

"I mean Andrea Wodsende. She received the farm in a divorce settlement and moved there about three years ago."

"That the woman who shot you?"

"She couldn't have shot me. At the time she was in restraints in ICU."

"She could have hired it done." Scotty wrinkled his brow in a serious frown. Scotty had given this a lot of thought. It was impossible to change his mind once an opinion was arrived at, but Jared plunged ahead regardless.

"Yeah well, the prevailing opinion is that it wasn't the Wodsende Case at all. It was another blast from the past with a grudge. Last I heard they were hoping to turn a jail house snitch. So, back to the subject at hand. Can you point me in the right direction?"

Jared picked up the narrow black-top running parallel to the ridges rough upland plane, once an old Indian trace still used by hikers. Ridge Road meandered over rock lined river beds cut by steep valleys edging the occasional stone ringed field. These were the forgotten boundaries that memorialized the labor of long dead landowners.

Jared looked forward to contacting Elias Goldfarb; hearing what he had to say. He delayed only to familiarize himself with the details of the aborted investigation. Aborted first when he was brutally attacked and then by Andrea's diagnosis of mental illness and the confession that only Dr. Wodsende ever admitted hearing.

One telling detail had galvanized Jared's thinking. Somehow Dudley Wodsende had managed to get himself appointed Andrea's physician. Jared felt outrage for Andrea, and wondered... in whose best interest was this significant piece of bureaucratic injustice?

Jared thought of Andrea. If she was innocent, she was no threat to Dudley as long as she resided helpless in a nursing home. In jail she would have been beyond his reach. So why hadn't Dudley killed her? Why take such a risk when there was always the possibility that Andrea might awake from her catatonic state and declare herself innocent?

Jared tightened his hands on the steering wheel. He could feel dormant anger rise from some place deep within. This was not merely about the murder of Stephanie Wodsende and convicting the right person. This was personal. Someone had wanted him dead and, although others disagreed, Jared had never believed the crime was connected to any other case.

After he was shot, the Boston PD had looked at old files cross checking for any recent parole releases and verifying the whereabouts of each possible suspect with a grudge against Jared. Soon fewer resources were allocated as they awaited the break that would jumpstart the investigation. Eventually someone would talk and news would filter back. But, at the time, it was clear that Jared and Ed were looking hard at Dudley Wodsende. They weren't buying the ex-wife as the only viable suspect. Someone had seen that as a monumental threat.

Slowing the pick-up Jared crested a steep incline and began a descent into the valley, his eye catching sight of a tractor pulling bales of hay off in the distance. He drove past the occasional abandoned farm house marking the places where families once lived. Impatience mounted as he scanned the roadside for the unmarked turn described by Scotty. He was determined not to return home without a firm visual of the last place where Andrea had lived.

The only possible turn was an overgrown trail heading off into a darkening wood. Established fir trees hemmed the path, and the grass grew thick in neglected wheel tracks. Dismissing the drive as too narrow, he inched along the blacktop, searching for the drive with little success.

Jared imagined the anonymous gray Buick, covered with a tarp, and parked forlornly in a stall of Burn's barn. If he were really going to pursue solving the Wodsende murder case, he'd be driving that anti-crime mobile, as Ed used to call it, the one with vinyl seats, and the lingering scent of long stake-outs. Under the hood was a custom engine that climbed from 0 to 60 in five seconds flat, with hidden storage for his shotgun and basic surveillance equipment. The car would need a tune-up, new tires, and a good cleaning. He'd make the arrangements, and then, at least for a while, it would be the truck parked under the tarp in the barn.

The tractor he had first seen off in the distance slowed and then came to a stop alongside the pickup.

"Lost mister?"

"I'm looking for the Andrea Wodsende farm."

"She's not there anymore. I heard she died in prison."

"Sorry to disappoint, but she is very much alive. I'm here to check on the property, but can't seem to locate the drive."

"You were just there. You should have no trouble getting in, but watch out for the dog."

"What dog?"

"Mrs. Woods had a Doberman Pincher that's gone wild. Animal control can't catch him, and my Dad hasn't been able to shoot him. He's a wily creature that one."

"Is the dog dangerous?"

"Yes, he is. He's a Doberman for gosh sakes. Killed a calf last spring. All they found was bones and hair."

Jared smiled and introduced himself.

"I know who you are. I'm Jake Brown. My sister, Brenda is married to Thor and everyone round these parts knew your uncle. Most famous resident we've ever had. My literature teacher had us write a paper on him in school last year."

Jared was touched. He wondered how Burns would feel about his old high school paying him such homage.

"He put us on the map so to speak, but seems other towns in Berkshire County benefit more than we do. My Mom's on a committee to get a visitor center on the old property. Burns did most of his painting in that rickety old barn. They plan to take it over, selling prints and local crafts and all kinds of things."

Jared cringed. *Over my dead body...*, he thought. The art was enough and stood on its own. It took a bevy of attorneys to protect the name from copyright infringement.

"For that to happen I'd have to sell the property, and the last I checked that wasn't likely."

"No problem," the boy grinned. "My Mom and her friends say you're not really Woods End. When you get tired of farming you'll move back to the city. Expect a visit in the next week or so. Fair warning."

Jared's refusal to cooperate with the indiscriminate branding of his uncle's legacy had frustrated many. "Thanks for the heads up," Jared smiled back. "I'm in the book. I'd welcome a call if you notice anything odd about the comings and goings on the Wodsende property?"

"Happy to oblige. Is she going to sell the place?"

"Don't know."

"They'll never sell it to a local."

"Why's that?" Jared asked.

"The land is cursed. No one living there has ever come to any good. Look at Mrs. Woods. She seemed nice enough, but suddenly she up and murders this other woman. And the family before her moved out in the middle of the night and never came back. How do you explain something like that? And there's more..."

"I'm curious. You called her 'Woods,' not Wodsende?"

"She can call herself anything she wants, but it doesn't change who she is."

"And who is she exactly?"

"She's one of them. She married the son of a devil. That means she belongs to that cult and even if you leave, if they don't kill you, they keep a hold. After what happened they changed their name. Did it legal-like, so they could avoid notice. But memory dies hard in Woods End. Everyone remembers."

"What do they remember?"

"They were satan worshippers. There's a group that still gather there and especially around the summer solstice.

We've tried to catch them, but the State Police won't investigate."

"Maybe they killed the calf. Maybe it wasn't Andrea's dog at all."

"My Dad says it was the dog."

"So why won't the State Police investigate?"

"It's a local matter. I think they're afraid to get involved after the last incident."

"What incident?"

They were in the middle of nowhere on a rural black top with no traffic about, but Jake lowered his voice. "Old man Woods kidnapped this girl. She was still in high school. He picked her up while she waited for the school bus and then she just disappeared. They couldn't convict."

Jake had Jared's attention. "Not enough evidence?"

"Plenty of evidence, but everyone knew a jury would be too afraid to cross that family. The old man could put a hex on animals and a curse on people. Cows wouldn't give milk and plenty of families moved away. But he got his."

"What happened?"

Jake hesitated. He put one hand on the steering wheel and the other on the gear shift.

"We're alone," Jared offered. "I won't repeat what you say and no one can hear us."

"Most of the people involved are now gone."

"There you go," Jared comforted. "No one to complain."

"Okay," Jake agreed, shifting in the tractor seat to better converse. "After the jury came back with that chicken verdict, a group of upstanding citizens decided they couldn't risk this happening to one of their daughters. He got away with it so they knew it would happen again."

"So what happened," Jared prompted.

"They ambushed him when he stopped at the Hardware Store at the corner of Liars Spot and Ridge Road. Murdered him like a rabid dog in the street. That's what my grandpa said anyway. Like the rabid dog he was."

"Did they find out who did it?"

"Not a chance. That group of citizens I mentioned. They had this choreographed down to the last detail. They knew who had time to get into town ahead of that devil and they knew who had good reason to make time. Three men had the hood up on their truck, pretending repairs. Others were positioned on the roof, in the drug store, or in the back of the hardware store. Some even arranged for vacation so they could be hanging out at Mullin's Tavern when the call came."

"So, they were tipped off?"

"Yes, they had someone inside who let them know he was coming to town. Alone. He rarely came without his posse. But this day... it all worked out."

"Did he suspect anything?"

"They think he did. He was a warlock of the highest order, or so they said, but plenty of ladies were home in their kitchens praying that there would be confusion in the preternatural realm of evil spirits."

"And you believe all this?"

"I sure do, Mister. You don't live in Woods End Township and not believe."

"So what happened? I'm fascinated," Jared coached.

"Don't be too fascinated. They latch on to that. We never say his name for that very reason."

"Who, latches onto what?"

"The bad spirits. They're thick on this stretch of road. You need to listen better."

"I'm no longer fascinated. Not even a little. So, what happened when the elder Mr. Woods pulled into town?"

"He must have sensed something amiss because he looked around very cautious-like. They say he sat in the pickup for a full ten minutes studying the lay of the street. But then he opened the door and the minute he was away from the truck and on the sidewalk they took aim. Over forty men had him in their sites. My father said he was so riddled with bullets the Coroner threw pieces into the body bag."

Jared was amazed. He had been exchanging stories with some of the local law enforcement at the diner, but no one even hinted at what must certainly be the most notorious crime Berkshire County had ever seen.

"What happened next?" Jared asked.

"My Grandpa said that a Catholic Priest, the Methodist and Presbyterian ministers and even the Mayor took part. Your uncle was there, though he was my age at the time and they wouldn't let any of the other kids near this."

"There was no one to point the finger." Jared stated.

"That was the plan. In all honesty no one could say who fired the fatal shot, and they all denied having anything to do with it."

"What about ballistics. Couldn't they match the bullets to any of those weapons?"

"The weapons were collected and disposed of. I told you, every detail was planned. All were guilty and all had a score to settle that died in the legal system for lack of money and fancy lawyers. But the outcome was that no more girls were picked up at the school bus, forced into marriage, brain washed and raped. Country justice long overdue is what my Dad called it."

"That's quite a story."

"It's no story, Mister and it gets better. The Woods clan moved away after that. They had three farms at the time which they'd bought cheap from people they harassed and threatened. They sold most of the land, but kept the original ninety acres. No one in their right mind goes near the place. And you shouldn't either. It's cursed and it's haunted."

Jake was completely serious. Jared didn't want to insult him by arguing the point. In the future the boy might prove a valuable resource since he seemed more than willing to talk about what others wouldn't bring up.

"I'm here," Jared said. "Might as well take a quick look around."

Jake shrugged. "It's not my job to convince you. I just said something because it seems you won't be warned off and Thor says you're a good person. So now you know."

"Fair-warning. Thanks for the heads-up."

"Happy to oblige, and now I've got to be going," Jake said. "My Mom will have dinner ready and she gets mad if I'm late. You've got about an hour before the light dims. Don't over stay."

"I won't. Stop by some time. We've done a lot of work to that rickety old barn. I'd love to show you around."

"Do you have any of Burns' paintings in there? I'd like to see some of those."

"No. The ones he didn't sell stay on permanent loan to museums. That's the safest place for them."

"Do me a favor. When my Mom and her friends show up to pitch their proposal for economic development, please don't say I told you the old Woods story. I'm not supposed to talk about what happened. They all agreed not to."

Eventually Jared would get around to interviewing everyone that Andrea had known during the short time she lived in Woods End. But for now talk of Andrea's farm being cursed seemed strangely connected to the apparition he had seen. With every bone in his body and every fiber of his soul, he knew that what he'd seen in his bedroom had been real. Somewhere in the dilemma of what that presented, denial had fallen away. But this was not the time to be thinking about curses or, for that matter, vigilante townspeople driven to desperation. There were answers to find and he needed them as much for himself as for Andrea.

Jared resolved to take a quick look at the house and see what it told him about Andrea. Then he'd head home, stopping first at the Mennonite grocery for the specialty steak this particular family was famous for. He'd fire up the grill, bake a potato with mushrooms, shreds of cabbage and leek wrapped in foil, and afterwards he'd settle down with a warm brandy and a new stack of reading from the Wodsende case files. Then tomorrow he'd return for a closer look.

Jared hesitated with the truck door open and one foot sinking into a soft layer of shed pine needles. The thick wall of trees seemed imposing. Although not logical, an instinctual certainty entered his mind. The trees could not grow fast enough. There was nothing natural about how the branches grew taunt and perpendicular, more upright than they should have been and doing a good job of obscuring the drive from people like him.

Jared decided to walk in rather than risk the paint job on his truck. Taking the semi automatic from under the seat he retrieved pepper spray for the dog and a flash light from the trunk. After walking some distance he emerged into the clearing. Even uncared for and lonely, the property had a charming appeal with a sense of being remote and further beyond the hamlet of Woods End than it actually was.

As he came to the center of the bridge Jared paused to look at the flowing water beneath. Mountain clear over the rocky surface the water appeared black in those places that it pooled over the bedrock. Continuing along the drive Jared could see where the barn had once stood. If this were his land, he would have cleared the fallen timbers long ago, and he wondered why this had never been done. The barn's site seemed somber, almost eerie, and in some strange illogical perception, far less abandoned than the house and adjacent property.

Even before he stepped from the bridge Jared felt a trail of eyes locked upon his progress. He un-holstered the police issue automatic and let his hand curl around the grip, deciding that as weapons went, he'd opt for the tangible, impersonal feel of cold metal to the Bible that Thor had dropped on his kitchen table with instructions to start reading at the Gospel of John.

Approaching the graceful sweep of the porch, with every intention of mounting those steps, Jared found instead that he had shifted direction, circling the house to begin his investigation at the back. He tried the handle of the mud room entrance before removing the locksmith's tool from his pocket and to no avail, he jiggled the rusted bolt. Oil was needed, but he had left the can behind and the light was beginning to dim. It was then that he heard the low guttural sound of an angry dog, too close for comfort. Jared turned slowly and saw the black form nearly lost against the gathering twilight.

"Calm down; not to worry. I'll come back tomorrow with a little left over steak. How does that sound?" he cajoled.

Jared reached into his left pocket for the can of pepper spray. If the dog lunged at him, he would start with that. Focusing his attention he remained still and waited. He took a step forward and squinted through the dusk for a closer look. The dog growled again, sounding every bit the aggressor, and then, with a whimper of pain he plopped down in a ragged bundle. Jared bent over for a closer look, shinning the light over the dog's emaciated body.

"You're a mangy bundle of bones, now aren't you?" Jared soothed. The animal was covered with burs and what had to be a few satiated ticks. Still he sought to make a last valiant effort in defense of his master's home, and with teeth barred snapped at Jared, but this time the performance was unconvincing.

"If animal control showed up right now you wouldn't stand a chance. But if I'm going to help, I'll need a little cooperation." Removing his jacket, Jared extended it, allowing the dog a good sniff. He then patted the head, feeling the scar tissue that shortened one ear, while making a futile effort to coax the dog to his feet. "You're just too weak. You stay and I'll get the truck," Jared soothed.

Jared jogged over the bridge and, preoccupied as he was with the dog, felt again that sense of his progress being marked by unseen eyes. Soon he returned with the truck, driving around the house toward the back where the summer kitchen was. As the head lights guided his progress he scanned for any sign that someone else was loitering about the property, but saw no such evidence.

In his absence the dog had curled into his jacket as though it were a bed. Lethargic beyond caring, he barely lifted his head when Jared lifted him onto a pile of seed sacks, into the back of the pickup.

WOOD'S END

CHAPTER EIGHTEEN

"Do you go to church?" Guido asked.

Phyllis nodded her head. She felt exhausted, as though she had just worked a double shift with no rest.

"Go and see your minister and discuss what happened. You'll need people to be praying for you over the next few weeks. If your pastor doesn't know what you're talking about, find one who does and especially if you have nightmares, can't sleep, or become physically ill."

"Andrea is all that matters," Phyllis said, focusing on the one outcome she did understand. "Thank you for helping me get rid of Dr. Wodsende. I'm sure he would have hurt us."

"You realize Andrea has to be moved. And moved now! I understand she's been court ordered here rather than a psych ward. She'd be better off under lock and key. You have no security to speak of and Dudley can waltz in anytime and give her any lethal dose of whatever he chooses."

"It's impossible to move her without permission."

"If you value her life, get it done."

"That's not so easy," Phyllis replied now defensive at his tone. "There's a procedure in place. Not even her mother could make such a decision. Someone would have to petition the court. She would need an attorney. If one was present at her competency hearing, we wouldn't have that name in our records. Until you came along, Andrea's had no one to speak for her."

Guido turned his attention to Andrea. He bent close. "Andrea we're discussing a move for you. You may need to be transferred for your own safety. Do you understand?"

She was no longer looking between them as if following the conversation. It was apparent to Phyllis that she was exhausted. Her mind had shut down in order to recoup the tremendous energy expended in their earlier exchange.

"She's too over loaded with sensory input to track. We'll get her back to bed so she can rest," Phyllis said.

"And she'll be fine as long as you're here, but as soon as the shift changes, he'll be back."

"He wouldn't dare."

Guido gave Phyllis a knowing look. "Of course he will. He has limited time and opportunity and he knows it. For some reason we can't guess at, Dr. Wodsende has allowed her to live. Consider that we're not dealing with the normal, run of the mill sociopath. He operates by a code you can't understand. So forget logic and just concentrate on doing everything necessary to keep your patient safe."

"What will you do?"

"Nothing. I'll make a few recommendations to the person who sent me and then you're on your own."

"What do you mean? You're not a relative. Are you at least a priest? After what I just saw you have to be."

"I am a priest." Guido was at the door when he turned back. "You *are* going to have the contents of that syringe tested, right? I saw you put it in your pocket, and it looked like a dose of something more fit for a horse than a human."

Phyllis fingered the edges of the handkerchief that enclosed the barrel of the syringe. "You think I need to?"

Guido said nothing. Just gave her a knowing look.

"I wouldn't know where to send it. I can tell you right now that Crest May wouldn't pay unless I made a written request and filled out an incident report, and by the time I had approval, it might be too late to help Andrea. I guess I could call the police and offer it to them."

"You don't have enough to involve the police. They'll delay, and later a good defense attorney will complain about the chain of evidence and imply the contents were contaminated. I'd get it someplace fast. Here," he said peeling bills from a leather money clip. "Call one of the precincts and ask which independent lab they recommend.

Have the results copied to you, the hospital, and the Wodsende Case File. The longer you wait the more danger."

"Me, in danger?"

"You're a threat to him. You're on her side. And don't think for a minute he isn't worried about leaving that syringe behind. Dudley was either trying to silence her or kill her. If it's the latter, you're holding the murder weapon. Be smart or be dead. There's no other way to look at it."

With that parting refrain Guido was gone. His words played in Phyllis's mind dislodging the last shreds of complacency. Could this strange man be right?

She made a decision. She would shift the contents and residents of two rooms to get Andrea within site of the nurse's station. Andrea wouldn't notice, but hating change, which tended to confuse her, Birdie, would be difficult to manage. It would be days before she would accept the new room, and the move would not be popular with the staff; especially with the evening shift. When they came in at three she would have them begin packing the personal effects of four residents, and the following morning, before breakfast, the night shift would move the beds.

Phyllis had yet another idea. If a resident experienced medical crisis, they were immediately transported to the ER and then a medical floor. She would invent a set of symptoms tied to the medications. This would get another doctor involved who would render an opinion, drawing attention to the dosages prescribed.

Phyllis considered phoning Andrea's mother, alerting her to the pending change, but decided against it. After the deed was done there could be no further debate and she didn't need to ask the mother's permission. Other than that her hands were tied."

"Smart or dead," Birdie sang. "Be smart, be dead. That's what I say." Uncharacteristically she began to cry.

"Don't you worry, Birdie. Let's change your shirt and get you cleaned up and comfortable again."

"Get a haircut. The demon needs a haircut."

"There are no demons, Birdie," Phyllis assured, keeping her voice steady and calm. "Everything is fine. Maybe we'll give you a sedative. This has been hard on you, too." Phyllis undid Birdies restraints and lowered the bed. "How would you like a change of scenery? We could see each other more often if you were closer to the nurse's station. Would you like that?"

"They're after her," Birdie whispered.

"Who?"

"The demons. They hate her. Because she left, she left them and never went back."

"No," Phyllis soothed. "Everything is fine, now. Soon you'll have something to help you rest and you'll take a little nap and feel better by the time dinner is served."

"They own him," Birdie persisted.

"Own who?" Phyllis couldn't resist asking.

"Don't let him back. I need a haircut. I'm moving."

"Would you like a drink of water," Phyllis offered instead. Although Birdie was physically strong, Phyllis helped to lift her so she could drink, talking to her, soothing and seeking to distract her mind onto a more pleasant topic."

For Zach the real trick had been getting the garage door back up. He waited patiently for his father's nightly ritual of locking the doors, checking the thermostat, the windows, and the garage. He had already turned on the maid's kitchen radio, started a load of laundry and waited until Elias walked into the butlers' pantry with the mewing cat shuffling around his feet. With the descending clatter of cat food into the well of the stainless steel bowl, Zach pushed the button that allowed the garage door to open.

"Did you hear anything?" Elias asked his son as he came out to the keeping room from the pantry, a bag of cat food swinging by his side.

"No. Just a utility truck going by outside and that avalanche of cat food. We need to get a plastic bowl, don't you think?"

"Your mother says that plastic doesn't disinfect like stainless," Elias said switching off the radio. Tomorrow there would be a note for the maid who would insist she hadn't left it running. "As you know, she's not overly fond of anything plastic. I'm surprised it's not crystal." The two laughed. Another inside joke at his mother's expensive taste.

It had utterly surprised Zach that the old bag had taken up for his mother during their last family session. Evelyn had complained that Elias undermined her authority by marginalizing her status with a steady barrage of subtle, but erosive sarcasm.

"Is that true?" she asked Elias who sputtered nonsensical platitudes and laced his fingers together, pressing them into his chest. Zach watched intently as the counselor leaned forward to give Elias an open look of calculated appraisal. The pause before she finally spoke was painful. Zach and his mother both shifted in their chairs, turning their bodies slightly off center, away from the two between them.

"I'd like you to listen carefully when you speak. Keep track of how often you may undermine your wife's credibility and especially where your son is concerned. Will you do that Mr. Goldfarb?"

"Of course," Elias replied in a practiced tone of lawyerly capitulation.

Zach doubted the count would be accurate so, unbeknownst to his father he had a tally sheet running upstairs and the bit about the crystal bowl would start the second page of his notes. He guessed that in the future he needed to refer to the counselor by name. After all, it did seem that she deserved that dignity.

The LPN on nights was the only trained nurse. She read the order. "Is she crazy?"

"What's wrong?" the aide asked.

"Phyllis wants us to shift the residents and contents of two rooms, starting at 4:30 AM. She wants the move completed before breakfast and says they've already packed up the personal belongings." She gave the room numbers.

"That's Birdie, right?"

"Yes."

"Great Scott! Birdie will wear us out. There'll be no rest for the wicked tonight."

"Well, it can't be done. The day shift will have to do it in the morning. I have one aide who called in, probably with a hangover and another that just started."

"It's decided. We'll leave it," the aide replied clearly relieved at the reprieve.

"She doesn't say why she wants this move, so any call lights from there need to be answered immediately. And I want the intercom left on."

"Got it."

"I wonder if I should phone Phyllis," the LPN mused.

"She'll be in bed asleep."

"Right, this can wait."

Around midnight Zach put his mother's car in neutral and with one hand on the steering wheel and the other on the frame; he guided the vehicle into the street. By the time he started the engine he felt fairly safe knowing that the hum of the air conditioner on and off would muffle any wayward sounds from the street. He picked up Storrow Drive, running parallel to the Charles River until nearing the Mass Avenue Bridge. The humid air threatened rain while a low cover of fog inched forward from Boston Harbor into the streets and byways of the city.

In sight of Crest May Hospital Zach hooked a sharp left. If you didn't know any better, you would think the auspicious brick façade sitting back from the street on a patch of manicured lawn, an upscale condominium complex. Following his plan Zach pulled the car around back toward the residential care section. He chose the entrance closest to Andrea's corridor, checking his pocket for the master security key that very few people were intended to have and certainly not a lowly orderly doing community service.

Zach replayed the phone conversation with Guido in his mind. He had felt both excited and disturbed by what was conveyed.

"Hi, kid. It's me, Guido. Are you ready for an update?"

"You were there? You went to the nursing home?"

"Just as we discussed. And I had the distinct pleasure of meeting the very capable nurse, Phyllis. See if you can book her in advance if I should ever need such care. I have no children, so I'm putting you on notice."

Zach laughed. "You got it. What happened?"

"The ex-husband showed up with a syringe full of some designer voodoo something. It was either going to kill her or plunge our girl back into a coma. Phyllis squared off with him, but was losing ground. I'm glad I was able to be there. Your assessment was dead on. For now, the doctor's been banished, but not for long. He'll be back. He's out of time."

"Out of time, how?"

"The nursing home will make a report to the court and ask to have Dr. Wodsende removed from the case. But first they'll call several meetings. Maybe a week goes by, maybe two while they assess their vulnerability. They might make an ethics complaint to the AMA so they can appear to be taking the high ground should anyone hold them liable. By the time they finish talking the subject to death, your lady will be chilling in the morgue."

"I don't understand." Zach felt overwhelmed by what he was hearing.

"The worst scenario is they may decide to pass the buck and let the ex-husband transfer her so he can kill her somewhere else. But I don't think Phyllis will stand for that. She'll make them act, but it will take time. Time is what Andrea doesn't have."

"He'll kill her?"

"Wake up, kid. You know exactly what is going on here. Weak people convince themselves it isn't what it is. Are you a man, called to complete what you started, or will you remain a boy? Your choice."

Zach was silent.

"She's cooked. That's what I'm saying. As of right now you are all Andrea has. You inserted yourself uninvited into this little drama, which means you've assumed a certain level of responsibility. Knowledge makes you culpable, Zach. If you do nothing and she dies you're culpable; get it?"

Zach felt a sinking feeling in the pit of his stomach. He had playacted his way through every bit of trouble he found himself in, and except for this last time, circumstances had eventually worked out to some advantage. This was different. Someone he cared about could actually die. Death equaled permanence. Zach felt scared.

"I'm still operational because I've spent most of my life working alone, and there have been times when Mario or I had to cut our losses. If I didn't have confidence in you, Zach, I might risk staying a little longer. Timing, kid, it's all about timing. You'll think of something."

"For a criminal you're pretty good at moralizing."

"Criminal? Now, that's a relative term. Thought you gave us more credit than to accept the simplest, most obvious explanation for what we let you see. Thought you asked no questions precisely because you knew what we did was something else, something better. Fact is, you don't know."

"That's true. Forgive me. I really do appreciate your help with Andrea." Zach liked that Guido treated him like an equal. As if he belonged to an earlier time, he referred to almost everyone under fifty as a kid, so the moniker wasn't personal.

"I'd like you not to involve Vince in whatever you decide to do next. Another eight months and his father will be free, but until that time Mario and I have this debt to repay. More than that really, it's an obligation. You got that, kid? You read comic books; play video games? You understand brotherhood, loyalty and honor, right? And, if I could make a suggestion, study the history of your own people."

"What history?"

"You're Jewish. So read about the noble characters in the Old Testament and model yourself after them. You should know all about David, Joshua, and Daniel. Then you might read the work of a few other Jewish rebels who rocked the establishments of their time like Matthew, John, and Paul."

Zach nodded his head in agreement, as though he might actually follow Guido's suggestion of a revised summer reading list. Fact is he had no plans to read the Bible. Not in this century anyway.

"Thanks again, Guido."

"May Jehovah God bless you, my Son."

Zach was taken aback. The words were clerical, the tone official. He wouldn't have been surprised to know that Guido had crossed himself in the manner of a Catholic priest pronouncing a kind of blessing.

From that first day that he began holding her meds, some strange feeling of obligation bound him to Andrea. Was that the honor Guido spoke of? He guessed it was a knight of the round-table or a Luke Skywalker kind of thing. Luke protected his sister...only he didn't know she was his sister, and he was in love with her for about two minutes. It felt different with Andrea. For one thing he never imagined that he cared for her in that way. Rather, it was her utter helplessness and the injustice of her circumstances that brought out in him a sense of duty that felt foreign and alien to his character. He could give up and retreat into childish modes of operation, or he could do what Guido challenged him to do. Zach didn't see himself as a quitter.

As he drove, Zach thought about his parents. He would never be habitually cruel to someone he had vowed to love. He'd just say what needed to be said and be done with it. Not his father's slow drip of Chinese water torture disguised behind seemingly innocuous humor. Although Evelyn was the target, he could see now that he had been affected. He had heard that disrespect for his mother and been invited to feel the same. If not for the counseling, if not for Andrea, he would not be seeing it now.

Zach felt a sudden confusion, a nonverbal, emotional surge that suggested he reject the analogy that was teasing at his brain. He would have appreciated the luxury to think, to dredge up buried emotion, and assign those feelings a name, but he was already at his destination and there wasn't time. He wondered why these potential flashes of insight arrived at such inconvenient junctures with so many other competing distractions to lure his mind off the scent. Maybe he'd ask the old bag. Zach corrected himself. Maybe he'd ask the counselor, for her professional opinion. ...or not.

As the chemically induced fog began to lift, Andrea was able, by increments so small no one noticed, to insert that growing awareness into the fabric of the life around her. The conversations of the staff drew her in. The talk revolved around whom they liked or didn't like, their husbands or boyfriends, children, the weather, or a discount sale.

Of late her favorite exercise lay in guessing what would be served for dinner based on the smells that emanated from the kitchens. Bacon meant BLT's for lunch and sauerkraut meant the German cook was preparing pork for dinner with baked apple as a side. All this and more entertained her senses and motivated her to strive harder each day.

Tonight was different. Thoughts came to her like sharp, lacerating pellets always ending with a question. What happened? How am I so different? Why can't I walk, talk, think with the same quick ease that was my former self? And Dudley... Was Dudley truly here, or had she imagined that dark menacing presence?

Andrea turned her head toward the window and caught site of the large oak tree silhouetted in the glare of an oncoming headlight. Cars on this end of the drive were rare at night. The observation, proof that her memory was getting sharper pleased her greatly. She smiled and felt a surge of pride. If the memory of Dudley was accurate, then her life depended upon this new and burgeoning ability to think, process, and remember.

Sleep would come soon. Twenty-one, twenty-two, she counted rain drops as they hit the window and imagined rivulets of water falling over the ledge and onto the ground beneath. Movement caught her attention and suddenly, confused by the unexpected, she stopped counting. She turned her head in Birdie's direction and was startled to see a dark shape cross into the room. The soft tread of footsteps were not announced in the customary way of aides making their night rounds. Fear gripped her as a shadow inched over the bed covers. A cry escaped, but was cut off as a hand covered her mouth.

"It's alright. Andrea, it's just me."

"Dudley?" The mere utterance of that name jolted her to full awareness.

"No, it's me, Zach. Remember?"

She did remember and felt such relief that tears sprang to her eyes.

"Listen to me very carefully because your circumstances have changed and you're in serious danger."

She asked the question that had been plaguing her. "What is wrong with me? Am I sick?"

"No, Andrea you're not sick."

"Was I in an accident? Was I paralyzed?"

"You get up when no one is around. The staff walks you up and down the hall. You know this? "

Zach was the person who told her not to take the medicine and especially that liquid, poisonous substance that coated her tongue and burned her throat long after it was swallowed. She peered up at him, trying to make out his youthful features in the defused light from the hallway.

"This is good, Andrea. More lucid conversation than I've heard in a while. So maybe you can understand me. Listen carefully."

She nodded her head hoping to encourage him to tell her what she most wanted to know.

"It's about Dudley," Zach began.

"It's about Dudley?" Birdie parroted.

Andrea wanted to tell him that she had been thinking about her ex-husband. This afternoon when Dudley had come and the nurse, and another man who was a priest. It had suddenly become too much and she felt helpless to track and process anything more than Dudley filling the room with his black heart and the buzz of insensible words. Despite her fear, she had fallen asleep, waking once or twice, but unable to keep her eyes open for long. How dangerous, she thought, to doze like that in Dudley's presence. Her being in this place, incapacitated as she was and nearly unrecognizable to herself was Dudley's fault. He was the enemy. He was the reason.

"It's a long story, Andrea and I'll tell you all about it later. For now, all you need to know is that your ex-husband is trying to kill you, so I'm removing you from this nursing home."

The reservoir of memory from which she had such difficulty retrieving images was stirred. Her eyes sought Birdie. Birdie didn't like Dudley, and when he came to visit, even as she parroted nonsensical phrases, she noted his presence with every ounce of concentration she could muster. Andrea turned her attention back to Zach.

"Nursing home? "Am I old?" she asked.

"Let me put it this way," Zach hesitated. "You're pretty old, but not older than dirt."

She was propped on the side of the bed and fell against him as he pushed her arm into a coat sleeve. He caught her and helped her stand. Her legs had grown stronger, but it took a few minutes of standing upright to subdue a first wave of dizziness. Once or twice she had fallen, and Birdie, a one woman cheering section, had urged, "Get up, get up. I'll tell, I'll tell."

"Let's go. You have to be really quiet. Is this kidnapping? I mean you are a grown woman. Do you want to go with me? Look at me and say so," Zach instructed. "Just say, yes."

"Yes," Birdie said.

"I heard a yes. That's good enough for me."

Zach smelled like the outside world. Like newly cut grass, summer rain, and the city smell of car exhaust. Andrea recalled the flowers her visitor had brought that afternoon and how they had so artfully filled the space of her tray table. She had wanted to be alone with those flowers, to admire them, allowing whatever thoughts were prompted by their presence to inform that vacant absence of memory. As the two argued and Birdie interjected her senseless commentary, Andrea realized that the flowers were wilting. No one had thought to put them in water.

She imagined herself unlatching the tray and rising from the confines of the chair, a move she had grown quite practiced at executing. Walking to the bathroom and filing a vase with water, she would look back over her shoulder and say, "Excuse me. I must attend to my flowers."

The words in her mind seemed an echo of a normalcy that had been lost... stolen. She wanted nothing more than to reclaim the simplicity of courteous exchange and interaction; back in the land of the living.

After everyone was gone and fighting exhaustion, she had managed to slip out of bed. Before gathering the stems and slipping them into the water carafe on her bedside tray she carried them to Birdie, who had greedily buried her gray head into that mass of color.

"It's not right to be so deprived," Andrea had whispered feeling an angry surge of injustice.

"It's not right," Birdie agreed her nose dusted with yellow pollen.

Thinking of this now Andrea reached back, her fingers touching the makeshift vase. The boy, Zach, was speaking to her, his hand on her elbow when the metallic clatter of the carafe shattered the silence as it tumbled across the tile floor.

Zach froze against her and she felt his fear. The sound galvanized Birdie. "Hello, hello," she called as though answering a phone.

"Everything okay there?" The voice echoed from the intercom.

"Hello, hello," Birdie called.

"Everything okay, Birdie?"

"Yes," Zach whispered.

"Yes," Birdie repeated.

"Everything is fine," Zach coached.

"Everything is fine."

"Alright then. Go back to sleep before you wake Andrea."

"She's awake, he's awake."

"Then be quiet so Andrea can go back to sleep. I don't want to hear another word from you? Got it?"

"Yes," Zach coached.

They waited in breathless silence until the stillness of the nightshift let them know the threat had passed. Zach let go of Andrea and she fell onto the bed.

"Look at me," he whispered peering intently into her face. "Do you want to leave this place?"

"Yes."

"Why?"

"Because of Dudley."

"He's a demon," Birdie pronounced, sounding more together in that simple statement than Zach had previously heard.

"You think so, Birdie?" Zach looked over his shoulder.

"I need a haircut. I need a doctor."

"She doesn't like him," Andrea said. "I saw him hit her. He wants to kill me."

"Here's the deal. I want to be able to say you asked for help and I was just some dumb kid who didn't understand you couldn't leave the nursing home whenever you wanted and hopefully, if push comes to shove, someone will buy that explanation."

What was so wrong? Why couldn't she leave this place if she chose to do so? Andrea was decisive. "I need your help. Please get me away before Dudley returns."

Having said the words, she felt a mounting urgency. There was Dudley to escape, but there was also the more immediate possibility that soon she might be outside, standing under the night sky with moisture laden clouds swirling overhead and wonderful, precious rain on her skin. For five minutes of that she would say almost anything.

"It's a good thing I'm still a minor and my father is in the business," Zach mused, shoving her other arm into Evelyn's borrowed raincoat as he helped her toward the door.

"Goodbye," Andrea called to Birdie. "I'll not see you again. I'll not be back."

In that moment Andrea was convinced in every fiber of her being that it was true. Fate called to her. Unfinished business awaited and what's more, she was anxious to interact in all the messiness and joys implicit in the stuff of life. Whether the chains were chemical or relational, Andrea knew, she would never be imprisoned again. Never!

WOOD'S END

CHAPTER NINETEEN

Zach intended to rise before his parents, getting some snacks from the kitchen and raiding his mother's goodwill bag for a few things Andrea might wear. He heard the water running in the master bath and realized it was too late. Elias was in the shower, which meant that Evelyn was in the kitchen cooking oatmeal and steeping the morning tea. He only hoped that nothing would happen to shatter the illusion that all was unchanged.

Disengaging himself from the sleeping bag, Zach kicked his feet clear and looked over at where Andrea lay asleep on his bed. The night before, he had wasted time, unsure of what to do. Plans and strategies had always come to him and he expected this magical formula to work again. Only this time it wasn't so easy.

Upon leaving the nursing home, feeling lost and scared, Zach tried to phone Guido, only to find that service had been suspended. Although he agreed not to involve Vince, he rang that number as well. Vince's mother had attended to the phone as if doing so were her one vocation in life, but even she failed to answer. As a last resort he tried Mario's cell. That too had been shut off. Where were they?

Andrea had rested her head against the seat. She turned in his direction and he read the question in her eyes.

"Unfortunately our options are limited," he replied in answer. "I'm taking you home." He hadn't known this simple, logical solution until the words were off his tongue. But, once spoken, this seemed the only alternative. He was just a kid. Where else could he go?

"Home," she reflected and smiled. Zach wished he could be as unconcerned.

With the fog whirling around the tires of the car and separating before them like sea spray before the bow of a ship, Andrea had seemed transfixed, almost joyful. He returned her smile and lowered the windows so that she could feel the damp summer air on her face. She laughed. This was an occasion. He had never heard her laugh before. Zach watched as with the abandon of discovery, she pushed her head out the window letting the wind and rain pelt her face as if there were no greater entertainment.

By the time he pulled into the drive it was not yet light. He was relieved to see that the garage door remained open with nothing disturbed. Elias had not gotten up in the night to discover him and the car gone.

"Now you've got to be really quiet," Zach told Andrea.

"This is good exercise," she whispered back, struggling a little with the incline of the stairs.

Zach cringed and put a finger over his mouth. He would not relax until his bedroom door was firmly shut behind them.

He showed her where the bathroom was, and cautioned her never to lock the outside door or his mother would use that as an excuse to enter his bedroom in order to unlock the hall entrance. Andrea seemed to understand all his instructions, following his words and nodding her head. If she remained cooperative just long enough for him to come up with a more permanent plan, everything might actually work out.

Zach thought about the letter. Two days to get there and one day to respond; he'd expected to hear back before now. What if the letter was lost? What if Detective Shiel had moved without leaving a forwarding address and the letter was returned?

"When are we going home?" Andrea interrupted his thoughts.

"We are home. This is it, but no one can know you're here. It's a secret."

"This isn't my home." She sounded faintly disapproving. Did she remember living somewhere?

"No, it's mine."

"Why?"

"We can't go to your house. If in fact you still have a house."

Andrea thought about it. He could tell she was reaching for a memory, on the threshold of realization. He waited.

"It's a farm house with the ruins of a barn and a summer kitchen. I wasn't there long enough to see the apple trees bloom in spring." Her voice trailed off. For long moments she stared into the distance. When she looked back at him, her eyes glistened with tears. "I was looking forward to that." Her tone had gone flat, resigned.

"We can't help that right now."

"Why not?"

The question caught him by surprise. Andrea had never asked for any kind of an explanation before. Whatever he could offer would lead into a labyrinth of highly charged dialogue. This was not the time to risk such a discussion.

"If they find you, Andrea, you'll be sent back to Crest May. And then Dudley will have access. You don't want to die, do you?"

"Like Stephanie?"

Zach was startled. "Do you remember Stephanie? Do you remember what happened to her?"

Andrea bent her head. The tears, pooled to overflowing. They coursed down her face as she turned away in confusion.

"Not to worry, Andrea. We'll figure this out together. For now you have to trust me. You're safer here where no one will think to look for you. Now go to sleep."

She lay on his bed and curled into a fetal position. By the time he had his sleeping bag out of the closet she was sound asleep.

He had seen it many times before. Too much change, too much stimulus, and her eyes glazed over as she fell into a trance-like exhaustion. Deep sleep would follow and the cycle would begin again. She hardly stirred as Zach removed the hospital slippers and then the rain coat he'd taken from the hall closet. He tucked the bed clothes about her and felt an almost paternal pride in seeing her safe.

Zach startled his mother when he came into the kitchen. It was so rare that he was up without being called more than twice and eventually threatened. She smiled to see him.

"Hi, Evelyn. How are you this morning?"

"Fine, dear. Did you sleep well?"

"I did. Have you seen my skis?"

"No water sports today, Zach. You're on the schedule at Crest May. Thank goodness that embarrassing community service is almost over with. We don't want to upturn that applecart now do we?"

"No, we don't. Not at all. But Vince called and asked if he could borrow them. I think there're in the garage, right?"

"Yes, they are. But you're not to have anything to do with that boy," she said in a rush of panic. "The judge was very specific."

"I know. He's just dropping by to get them, but I'll be at work and won't even see him, remember? I'm leaving them on the back patio," he called over his shoulder. "You won't even notice, and knowing Vince, he may even forget to come by and collect them."

Zach was moving fast. He was into the keeping room, beyond the butlers' pantry door, and peering into the garage just hoping Elias was still in the shower. He had his hand up, ready to close the outside garage door, so that the loose ends of his night foray wouldn't find him out.

"Now why must you look for those now?" his mother startled him. He didn't realize she had trailed him from the kitchen. "My goodness. Was that door open all night?"

"No," Zach lied. "I opened it just before I came to ask where my skis where."

"Open your eyes, Zach. There they are right in plain sight," his mother pointed.

"Thanks, Mom."

She smiled. He recognized a softening of her expression as he used that name more and more. He hoped it would distract from the subject at hand. He hated to give her false hope that their relationship was improving, but the fact was that things were better. He liked her more and was only sad that he liked his father less. When he thought about it, he felt confused, almost emotional, but couldn't say why. For now he pushed the feeling down.

Zach suffered his face to be kissed. The last thing he needed was Evelyn barging in on him with a plate of cookies as an excuse to talk. To his chagrin the counselor had told her that doing so was her privilege, her prerogative as a mother to check on Zach for no good reason and especially if her instinct suggested something was wrong.

Zach thought about staying home. He weighed the option of calling in sick and attracting attention to himself when it was discovered that Andrea was gone, against trusting her to remain silent, concealing her presence from Evelyn and the housekeeper. The choices seemed equally fraught with danger. He wished he could be in two places at once.

"Now, go on. Get ready for work and I'll drive you."

"Is the oatmeal ready? I'll take a bowl with me and eat on the run."

Evelyn fixed it for him just the way he liked with brown sugar, cinnamon, fruit, and warm milk. She bought her oatmeal and a Swiss version of Ovaltine from a New Hampshire catalog company and liked to cook. For good measure he tucked a banana and a wheel of crackers into his bathrobe pocket and hoped Andrea would eat the oatmeal and not mind if she had to make do with the other for lunch.

"Don't forget to bring the bowl back down when you come. I don't want empty food bowls attracting ants."

"I won't," he called making a mental note to hurry Andrea along as he showered and dressed.

Phyllis wasn't happy to learn that Andrea and Birdie had not been moved as she had ordered. She delivered a harsh reprimand at the staff meeting, but Zach hardly listened. He was too preoccupied, wondering when Andrea's absence would be discovered. It was then that Phyllis announced he would be assigned to bed changes, having minimal contact with patients. The reasons were clear to everyone.

Zach nodded his head and said nothing, but one of the female aides jumped to his defense. "You think he was taking her meds? I think she was doing that herself."

"I don't think she was ever as sick as she claimed," another chimed in.

"She was easier to care for. She was more alert and never combative. Someone did her a favor. I say, good job!"

"We'll have none of that talk," Phyllis countered. "As you all know, withholding medication is a serious offense, the consequences being immediate dismissal. It is unfortunate that we will now need to investigate this possibility. For that reason Zach is better off. This is for his protection, and not at all a punishment."

No one believed her, but Zach nodded his head and picked up his room assignments without comment. He was stacking his cart with linens when a commotion and whispering were heard. With sudden abruptness Phyllis raced down the hall, with others following.

The police were quick to arrive. First a car with two uniformed offices' imagining they would find that an Alzheimer's patient had wandered off. When they learned the identity of the missing resident, it was another matter entirely and fell under the authority of the state police. Within the hour two plain-clothed detectives arrived. Andrea was a murderess and insane and her escaped status reflected poorly on a new program designed to alleviate overcrowding in the prison system.

Zach took comfort when he realized he was not the first person interviewed. They started with the nursing home administrator, then Phyllis, and various persons on the night shift called back to work, including the employee that recorded a commotion in her notes. Under duress she now admitted that she had ignored orders and been too lazy to walk the short distance down the corridor to investigate. She also admitted that the intercom had been left on, and she may have heard whispered conversation which she thought was Birdie talking to Andrea. She left the interview room in tears, which did nothing to allay the anxiety of those who waited their turn.

When pulled from his duties, Zach wondered if he should call his father, but immediately discarded the idea. He would approach this like everyone else. If he were defensive, attention would immediately focus in his direction.

"Did you see anything unusual, son?"

"No. I was off yesterday and the day before that, I worked the evening shift."

"And now you're on days. Is that your usual schedule?"

"Yes. I work when they need me."

"Are you paid like everyone else?"

"Any money I make goes to pay court fines. I'm doing community service." Zach figured the investigator already knew this and the admission looked better coming from him. He told himself he had nothing to hide. Repeating this lie eased some anxiety and almost made him believe it was true.

"And what exactly did you do that landed you in trouble?"

"Some people thought I was selling marijuana at school."

"And were you?"

"No, I was giving it away. But you know how it is. Gossip gets started. Things get blown out of proportion."

"You were dealing drugs and this is where they send you. A nursing home!"

"No, I wasn't selling drugs and it was only a little bit. And the judge believed me. It's not likely I'll have any time left when I start school in the fall, but if I do, I'll be tutoring kids in math."

The detective gave him a hard stare. He shook his head in disgust. "And I suppose the judge ordered counseling?"

"Yes, sir, he did, family counseling to be exact. And he also said he wanted me to learn the seriousness of life, and a nursing home was a good place to learn some of those lessons. Fact is, I'm grateful to be here."

"I should think so." The detective made no attempt to hide his contempt. "They say you're a good kid. Everyone likes you, you work hard. Would you say that's true?" he asked, skepticism cloaking his words.

"I work with some nice people. I like the patients. And, yes, I've learned a new appreciation for the meaning of life. Three residents died this summer. None of them my assignment, but I knew them." Zach could almost hear Guido whispering in his ear. *'Keep it simple.'*

"Save it for the judge." The investigator paused, waiting for him to expound further, to compensate for his guilt by saying too much. When Zach failed to take the bait, he asked, "Any plans for the future?"

"I have another year of high school and then college. I'm thinking pre-med."

"Did you know why Andrea Wodsende was here?"

"Yes, sir. Everyone knew."

"They suspect that someone was stealing her meds? Are you a drug addict, son? Was that you?"

"No, sir. I wouldn't do that."

"When you leave this room you'll be handed a specimen container. We'll be checking your urine and will know the truth within minutes. So you might as well fess up right now."

"My answer is the same. And since you don't know, and because this is where the judge had me doing my community service, I have to pass a court ordered drug screen more comprehensive than any quick pee-in-a-cup test. It's random, so I have no idea when my mother will get a call to have me at the lab within the hour. Results show I haven't relapsed since I was sentenced."

"I hear her doctor, the former husband, had her overmedicated," he pressed. "She was a zombie according to everyone we've talked to. Maybe you took pity on her? Decided to take matters into your own hands?"

Zach looked the detective full in the face, resisting the urge to look away and then back. "No sir."

"In your opinion was she well enough to walk out of here under her own steam?"

Zach pretended to ponder the question. "I don't know. She got dizzy whenever she was exercised. She could walk, but you had to assist or she'd fall."

"People said she was talking to her roommate and getting up when no one was around."

"I never saw that."

"Did you see this visitor she had? This Guido; this Catholic priest?"

"How many times have I told you, morons? She doesn't have an Uncle Guido! She has never had an Uncle Guido!"

A grating screech could be heard clearly from the next room, which had been commandeered for similar interviews. Word had it the police planned to speak with everyone from the food delivery men to the staff doctors. For now, Zach's own interview had stopped, both jarred by the level of outrage and anger that radiated through the wall.

"No one related to me would ever name their child Guido. Do I look Italian to you, you jerk. How many times do I have to tell you? No Uncle Guido. He's probably abducted her. He might even be her lover. They're in this together!"

The door burst open and immediately Zach found it difficult to reconcile Sybil's small size with the assault of her voice. He could see that every disparaging comment he'd heard about Andrea's mother was true. Clearly in her sixties she had dropped in their midst wearing too much makeup, with her skin shriveled from forty years of tanning and the color of mustard. Her unnaturally bright hair was frizzed in the eighties style and her open toed, three inch heels caused her to wobble like a two year old playing dress-up.

Zach couldn't help wondering what it would be like to have a mother like Sybil, and for the first time in his life he was truly grateful for the one he did have. He could take Evelyn anywhere, and while no one would dub her cool, she was what every teen wanted, an anonymous mother icon blending into the back ground in soft unassuming authority.

The intruder's hands flew up in exasperation and she crossed the room in three easy strides without the shoes flying out from under her, a feat of skill Zach had to admire.

"Is this him? Is this the one?" She accused punctuating the last word with a stab of her finger which, if she had been inches closer, would have connected.

Zach stood, as did the police officer interviewing him. "You're not allowed to be in here, Ma'am. If he knows anything at all he'll tell us."

"Really?" A dark expression scrunched Sybil's eyes and nose low over her mouth. "You were in and out of my daughter's room two or three times a day for two months. You ought to know something! I have a feeling about you! So cough it up! Where is she?"

Zach had his own instinct and was not at all intimidated. He looked into Sybil's eyes and felt outrage for her passive complicity in Andrea's suffering. By the time he was through with her, she'd be putty in his hands. The woman was a vain hedonist. He could tell. She had no self-control for anything that counted and had actually cleared the way for Dr. Wodsende to be the physician of record.

Unbelievable, Zach thought. *I bet Dudley paid her.* If he wanted to he could find out. He would find out.

"I'm so sorry, Ma'am. I just took care of her. I didn't really know her all that well, cause she couldn't talk. Hey, I like your shoes." He blinked and held her gaze, waiting until she blinked in return. "You have pretty feet."

WOOD'S END

PART FIVE
CHAPTER TWENTY

CHARLIE

Properly trained, a man can be dog's best friend. Corey Ford

As a rule Jared forgot his dreams, and the few details he did recall evaporated quickly in the seconds after waking. But now there was a change, and though it wasn't logical, he came to think of this change as having something to do with Andrea's farm and even the dog he'd rescued. Not only did he remember his dreams, but most would qualify as nightmares, details of which haunted him into the daylight hours.

The previous night he had stood frozen before his uncles' oil painting in the dim windowless light of the library alcove. He knew what would happen and yet was locked in fear, helpless to respond. Any minute the flash of the gun he had failed to see would ignite an excruciating pathway through his body. Bathed in sweat he kicked the covers free and under the swirling blades of the overhead fan shivered as the stickiness jelled on his skin.

The dog whimpered. The closeness of the sound startled Jared. He sat up with a start to find the animal beside him, his head lifting lazily from the pillow, black dog eyes peering into his.

"How did you manage to get up here in your condition? I fixed you a nice bed right over there," Jared lifted his chin toward a pile of old blankets in the corner and the dog seemed to follow the gesture, looking back with disdain. He whimpered again, sneezed twice, and with proprietary assurance nestled his head back on the companion pillow.

The house was dark and still, but there would be no going back to sleep and it was never, Jared believed, a wrong hour for good coffee. He swung his feet to the plank floor and heard the dog drop to the floor behind him with a cry of pain.

On impulse Jared issued a command. "Sit." The dog sat. "Lie down." He obeyed, looking at Jared with expectant eyes as though a treat might follow. "Heel," the dog walked in measured stride beside him into the kitchen and then, rather than dart off at the first opportunity, he waited for a release command.

"Someone's done a good job training you," Jared said and busied himself opening a foil wrapped tin of liver pâté that had arrived per mail with wine and cheese as a housewarming present many months back. Jared covered the pain pill and antibiotic with a generous scoop from the tin. "As far as I'm concerned this stuff qualifies as dog food," he said. "Bon appetite."

In only a few days the dog had made good progress. Upon first seeing him Thor had pronounced, "This sorry bag of bones needs to be in a hospital."

"Yeah, but he's not going unless you say he needs surgery. I want him here with me," Jared countered. There had been little he could do for Andrea. The least he could do was look after her dog.

"He may die on us."

"I've seen you work. You're as good as any vet, and this animal has suffered enough. I won't have him experiencing any more traumas, and if we leave him in the impersonal atmosphere of a kennel, he'll think he's been abandoned again."

"We'll see what we can do," Thor agreed.

It was fortunate that Thor kept the farm well stocked with medical supplies and had been trained by Burns and his father to doctor animals at a time when calls to the vet were reserved for real emergencies. They fixed the dog up with an IV of fluids and pumped him full of antibiotics and pain medicine before pulling several swollen ticks from his famished body. Now, three days later, the dog was clearly doing better though he had lost good bits of his fur, and until it grew back and he gained a little weight, the signs of neglect would be clearly visible.

"Nothing that a little rest and food won't fix," Thor had finally pronounced. Having made this investment in the dog's care, Thor felt as attached as Jared and stopped by the house each morning to check on his patient, sometimes bringing a toy or two, which the dog took proprietary ownership of right away.

Jared couldn't imagine what it was the dog could tell him, but felt there was something to know. A connection to Andrea and a reason he had hovered about the old farm house with such stubborn resolve.

The half light of morning had seeped into the rooms, dimming the artificial glow of the kitchen lamp. Jared ground the coffee beans, pouring them into the French press. When the tea pot sounded a full boil he added the water, letting all mingle until rich and strong.

While he waited, he called the dog to the open door and without immediate success coaxed him outside.

"It's okay, boy. I know you've been homeless and need some temporary digs, but you're with me now." *You're with me now!* Since when had he decided to care so deeply for this animal that he would consider keeping him?

The dog limped his way over to the one tree he'd commandeered as his spot. He looked back as he relieved himself, ready to make a feeble dash for the house if it appeared he might be abandoned, yet again. It hurt Jared to see such raw anxiety.

Coffee and newspaper in hand Jared settled into a cane rocker on the back porch. The forecast predicted rain, but at the moment there was no evidence. An amber sun inched above the horizon and sent golden rays through the straight trunks of pines lined up like sentinels at the back property line. Jared caught site of two deer investigating the horse trough and saw that the dog noticed as well, but gave no sign that he considered this an invasion of their territory, too busy finding a comfortable position close to Jared's leg.

"When you're stronger, we'll go back to your place and poke around a little. What's your name anyway? What do they call you?"

In answer, the dog stood and dropped a heavy head into Jared's lap. With ears pressed back he gazed mournfully up and into his face. "Yeah, I know. You've been through a mess, but you've survived. You're going to be just fine. Can you trust that?" Jared smoothed the mottled fur on the dogs head and scratched his one good ear. Apparently satisfied, the dog lay back down, pushing his body over Jared's feet before closing his eyes.

Andrea became familiar with the rhythms of the house. The air conditioner off and on, letters dropped into the foyer from the front door. Then late afternoon the Washington Post hitting the front stoop and sliding down to land on the step with a hollow thud. Zach was good about letting her know when the housekeeper would be present. Most days Evelyn was gone at least part of each day and he communicated her schedule as accurately as possible.

The change of environment was good, and yet she chaffed at further confinement. She had taken to exercising up and down the stairs when the house was empty. Today she might venture beyond the landing and look for the kitchen. The mere anticipation of this adventure caused a grin to break over her face as the unfamiliar muscles that produced that expression strained to accommodate.

The phone rang shrill and hollow. Jared ignored it, busy pouring through the case files. He felt in no hurry to do anything more, and was glad for the excuse of the dog's recuperation that allowed him to postpone the trip to Boston and the overdue interview with Elias Goldfarb.

Again the phone. Jared counted the rings, hoping there would be no message requiring a response. When the cell phone erupted he thought about answering, but in the end hesitated too long. He was on his way to the kitchen for another cup of coffee, the dog following at his heels, when the house phone sounded once more.

"Hello."

"Hi, Jared, why don't you answer the dang phone?"

"Hi, Ed, where are you?"

"I'm fishing off the pier in Naples."

"Caught anything?"

"Nope, and fortunately that's no longer the point."

Jared laughed. "So you're not missing the city?"

"Not at all, this is the life. But I am calling for a reason."

Jared and his former partner had spent a lot of time in one another's back-pocket. It was easy to pick up as though they had just separated the week before.

"This isn't why I'm calling, but if I don't ask the wife will make me call back."

Jared laughed. "Shoot."

"She heard a little gossip from one of her friends back in Bean Town. Did you apply for a marriage license? It was in the paper. She's perturbed... that you're planning a ceremony without her input."

"Never. Must be another Jared Shiel."

"Thought so, you couldn't get so lucky. Anyway I'm calling to be sure you've heard the news. Andrea Wodsende took a hike."

Jared paused. "No, I didn't know that. I thought she was hopelessly catatonic."

"Not exactly. It seems the commonwealth ran out of room and contracted with a few nursing homes to take some of their criminally insane. Andrea was thought to be so debilitated that she fit the criteria."

"So what happened?"

"She walked off into the good night so to speak. They think she had some help. So here's what I'm getting to. If she's well enough to engineer an escape, she's well enough to say what happened the night that Stephanie was murdered. And, if the attack on you is at all related to the Wodsende case, this might make a certain someone a little nervous."

"Dudley Wodsende."

"Yeah. If you recall Dr. Dread was shaping up to be our number one draft-pick."

"Funny this should come up at this particular time."

"Why's that?" Ed asked.

"Because I received a letter from a Boston attorney who suggests that Andrea is innocent and more important still, guess who he claims is the doctor of record?"

"Who?"

"Her ex-husband. Seems he's been allowed to treat her."

"Not true!"

"Evidently it is true, but I'll need to verify. Hard to believe Dudley could get away with that," Jared replied, "unless this nursing home wasn't aware of the relationship."

"I don't know how they could not be aware. It's Crest May, the same hospital he worked at when the murder occurred."

Jared was silent so long that Ed felt compelled to interrupt his thoughts. "All I can say is I hope that hospital has a good law firm on retainer. So what do you think partner?"

"Wodsende was a master manipulator. Power and control were his drugs of choice, so I guess on some level we shouldn't be all that surprised. I'm planning a trip into the city to look up this Elias Goldfarb so I can hear his story. Does the name sound familiar to you? Maybe a connection to the case after I was out of commission?"

"Not that I recall," Ed replied

"I've run into a little delay," Jared said, looking at Charlie who was hovering over a plush toy, his paws holding it in such a way that he feared it might escape. "I'll be back at full speed tomorrow."

"Keep me posted. And call if you need me. I can always hop a plane and be up there pretty quick."

"Thanks."

"Don't forget. Watch your back."

"Don't I always?"

"Well, no! You forgot once and nearly died for it. Put an early end to your career and tanked my last year on the force. I might as well have been doing desk duty. You're not back to full throttle, Jared. So don't act like you are. Capish?"

Andrea's gaze roamed the confines of the room. She bit into an apple retrieved from the kitchen after first watching Evelyn's car back out the drive. Andrea was almost envious of this other woman's life. She guessed that Evelyn was off to do errands and hoped she'd pick up more of the artichoke cheese spread. Helping out, she had jotted the item onto the grocery list, clipped to the calendar and placed just so on the Jacobean desk tucked into an alcove of the kitchen.

Andrea opened the window and left the apple core on the ledge. She had successfully teased a blue bird to drop by periodically for little offerings of food. She could tell that Zach had an orderly mind, and despite the teenage decorating sense, everything had its place. She bent to roll up his sleeping bag, tucking it under the bed.

The memory of a town had begun to emerge, morphing into mature maple trees and even older oaks which lined a rural lane. There were carefully tended lawns separated by narrow strips of fields gone wild. In contrast the city sky line at Zach's window had replaced the deep valleys and rock lined riverbeds of her memory. And a farm, and something urgent related to that farm that she had newly recognized and resolved to confront before her life was interrupted by... she reached for the memory.

Stephanie had called with an urgent request and Andrea had given in. Against her better judgment she had postponed, something. Something she had intended to do, related to that farm. She had put Stephanie's needs above her own and in doing so incurred Dudley's wrath. Was that survivor guilt?

Andrea let her eyes drop to Zach's desk and aimlessly opened a drawer. Her fingers fell on a folder and played over the bulky surface. Driven by restlessness, she lifted the heavy contents from the drawer, dropping it with a thud on the desk top.

Copies of newspaper clippings fanned out from between the pages. Even before she looked she felt the stabbing intrusion of anxiety as her muscles tightened and the pain began, creeping up her neck, hinting at the headache that would later rend her incapacitated with pain.

With tentative fingers Andrea slid an article out from among the collection. She felt wracked with ambivalence, the avid desire to know it all and the equally strong desire to hide from that first searing assault of truth. But her gaze had already absorbed the first words and there was no turning back. As she read, she allowed her thin frame a gradual slide into Zach's worn desk chair, afraid to break her concentration, afraid that in doing so the clippings would disappear with the truth forever beyond her grasp.

Shifting pages she recognized her own image, the woman she had once been. Tears came as the wall of ignorance cracked, each sentence ushering in a little more light until she felt blinded by the intensity of a harsh reality.

Evelyn Goldfarb pushed her grocery cart through the aisles of the organic foods market. As usual she had enjoyed the diversion provided by an afternoon of bridge. Although she would confide the level of pessimism she felt about her son to no one, there was always comfort to be found in the distraction of being in the company of women she had known and played bridge with for almost thirty years.

She checked off each item, placing them carefully into an organized cart and thinking about the peaches she had just lifted from the scale. Perfectly ripe and smelling like the Georgia orchard they had come from, she decided to make a cobbler instead of the usual coconut cake her family expected. Good to vary routine, she told herself, selecting a quart of cinnamon vanilla ice cream to top the warm crust.

A current of alarm raced through her body. Written in an unfamiliar script were the words, *artichoke dip - the kind in the green container.* Was her maid telling her what to buy? Evelyn didn't think so, but as often happened, when anything seemed wrong, she thought of Zach. He was fine; helpful around the house, waking up without being called, polite and even considerate. *Hmmm, considerate?*

Was this denial? Was Zach hiding behind a shield of compliant behavior? He had lulled them into a false sense of security with just this maneuver before. Was he associating with Vince in flagrant disregard of the court's order to break with old friends? If so, that boy could be taunting her, eating her food, and sneaking into the house when she wasn't home. Worse still, the two could be doing drugs in the house.

The counselor had told her not to fret. She was to think through her feelings. To decide in a rational way if the suspicion she felt warranted a second look. The fact was that Zach had passed his last drug screen. He had not relapsed and just as Zach had predicted Vince had never showed up to borrow the water skis.

Of late Evelyn had harbored hope for her son. After giving birth to Zach she had experienced ambivalence complicated by shame at not feeling an immediate attachment for her child. It didn't seem possible that she was the only woman in her circle of friends who had faced motherhood with feelings of regret. She would like to have discussed this with other women, but bringing up such a topic was anthemia to everything she'd been taught.

Evelyn had always felt Zach was in on her secret. This in turn stripped her of a mothers' right to assertive intervention so that she alternated between permissiveness and indulgence, withdrawal and anger.

In some perverse twist of self-fulfilling prophecy Zach had continued to be a handful, acting out in rebellious disregard of her feelings, as if he knew all along that he was never truly loved as he had a right to be.

Tears pooled in Evelyn's eyes. The counselor had also coached her to be involved no matter how intimidated she was by Zach's reaction. She would start by asking him a few direct questions, and just to be certain, she would search his room for any telltale signs of drug use. Knowing was better than fretting.

"Guess what? I met your mother today. What a witch...." Zach stopped.

Andrea was on the floor with all his carefully cataloged newspaper accounts, and sheets from the internet describing her medications, spread about her on the floor. Their eyes exchanged a kind of mute understanding. Later Zach would describe his response to the tumult of Andrea's anguish as so rehearsed that he felt instantly transposed to the painful reality of her shock in a heightened cavalcade of sensation.

Was this empathy? He took a step forward, but Andrea held out the palm of her hand like an assertive crossing guard holding back a flood of children.

"Don't you worry, Andrea, its okay," he soothed, keeping his distance. Suddenly she dropped her arm and hugged herself tightly, bending at the waist in silent agony. She rolled onto her side and began to sob, hyperventilating huge gasps.

How often had he wished to be older? So he could drive sooner, drink sooner. So older girls would notice him and like him, but never did he anticipate rushing youth for such an occasion as this. He felt inadequate and even scared, and could only be grateful that they were alone, his mother not yet returning from her afternoon of bridge.

Zach went to Andrea and put his arms around her. This was instinct on his part and it came to him. He had good instincts. He could do this. He could do more than manipulate and contrive. Maybe he'd make a good counselor.

With startling abruptness Andrea's sobs fell silent. He helped her onto the bed and she crossed her arms tucking her hands under her arm pits. He stroked damp hair back from her face until she curled into a ball, falling instantly asleep.

Surveying the disorderly contents of the folder, carefully gathered proof of his investigations, Zach accurately guessed that she had read it all. He felt the import of the moment, a kind of inevitable reckoning. She needed to know the truth, and yet he was fearful of telling her. Doing so had now been taken out of his hands and Zach was relieved. Moving forward in any kind of success meant that he needed her cooperation.

Zach sank to the floor, his back against the bed. He kicked out at the files further scattering the mess. Where, he wondered, was Detective Shiel? If he didn't hear back very soon, they would need a back-up plan.

The last thing Zach wanted to do was confide in his parents. He was, he guessed, an all or nothing kind of guy. *Is that a good thing or a bad thing?* Or, as the family counselor would say, "Is that a healthy strategy? Remember, Zach," she'd said time and again. "Healthy people ask for what they need."

Enough is enough! If I don't hear from Detective Shiel very soon, I'll talk to Elias.

Following Guido's instructions, Phyllis had dropped the barrel of the syringe off at a private laboratory the day after their confrontation with Dudley. When interviewed she had described what happened to the police, giving them the name and address of the lab, and so was surprised to get a call a week after Andrea's disappearance.

"You should be calling Boston PD," Phyllis said.

"You're the name of record."

"The police haven't called you?"

"No. That makes this your report. Do you want to know the results or not? There's a notation here that we should fax the result to the police, but no fax number and no case number."

Phyllis looked at her watch. If traffic wasn't heavy, she'd be at work in time to intercept the fax before anyone else picked it up. She gave the nurses' station fax number before curiosity got the better of her.

"Were you able to identify the medication? Just give me the shelf name and I'll take it from here."

The answer was short and cryptic and she was certain she hadn't heard correctly. "It's what?" Phyllis asked.

"Sperm."

"Not medication?"

"I'm afraid not."

"Can't be." Phyllis was stunned.

"Plain old fashioned sperm. The kind used to make babies," was the sarcastic rebuttal.

What flashed to mind was how Dudley had wanted Andrea to himself, but when Phyllis refused to leave, he insisted she be on the bed lying on her side and ready for an injection. Phyllis recalled how he had found excuses for her to leave the room until, with Guido's arrival, he had finally given up. Very little time would be needed for Dr. Wodsende to accomplish his purpose. Knowing the schedule as he did, Andrea would remain in bed, in a prone position for at least an hour before the patients were removed to the dining room for the evening meal. This would assist in the process of insemination. The mere thought of anyone attempting such a perverted assault was hard to fathom.

"No crime to have a baby," the lab technician offered.

"More likely, a certain obsessed former husband was trying to get someone pregnant against her will."

"Excuse me?"

"Never mind," Phyllis said. "Forget I said that. What I want is a DNA profile. And when it's completed I want a copy sent to Boston PD." Maneuvering in traffic she fished a business card from her purse. "Here's the address, name and badge number of the detective to whom you can address the results."

WOOD'S END

CHAPTER TWENTY ONE

The aborted investigation into Stephanie's murder was on Jared's mind as he broke into Andrea's locked house. It seemed a kind of fateful symmetry that events had returned him to this juncture. The dog was at his heels, urging him on as he shifted the dead bolt free, the stump of his tail wagging in jubilant excitement. Did the dog imagine they would find Andrea inside?

Steady meals, antibiotics and a medicinal bath had accomplished a lot, although the patches of missing hair were evident. Not wanting him to be exposed to the morning drizzle, Jared had stopped to buy a yellow rain slicker on the way over which the dog had off before they arrived at the farm.

"Guess your health is improving," Jared said. In answer, the dog gave him a look which Jared interpreted to mean, *you think I'd wear a sissy coat? What am I, a toy dog?*

To stress the point he proceeded to wrestle the rain slicker in ferocious abandon, tearing it to shreds. Despite this, Jared thought him almost handsome in a new red collar and engraved medal that announced Jared the proud master.

"We didn't plan on this, boy, but I guess we're a team." Jared put his shoulder to the door giving it a final shove. The dog bounded ahead and Jared almost felt betrayed at his reaction. This was home and he remembered it well. Racing from room to room he barked as if to say, *I'm here, I'm home, where are you?*

Did he imagine that Andrea was somewhere about or soon to return after such a long absence? Two years later he was still hanging on, refusing to leave even when neighbors and the local dog catcher tried to tempt him with prizes of food. And when he did venture away to forage for leftovers in garbage bins and barns, he was shot at and lucky to have survived as long as he did. Jared was impressed. He admired stamina. He admired loyalty. The dog had heart.

No footfall appeared to have preceded his or the dogs for a very long time, perhaps even since the day Andrea left home, never to return. Jared gave each of the ground floor rooms a quick walk through. He then headed for the basement, doing the same and finding a root cellar with a lean-to like roof and a door leading outside. There was also a winter apple room with barrels lining the wall.

Back on the ground floor Jared continued his investigation, peering behind doors, into closets and cupboards. From habit, expecting nothing, he lifted the lid of a metallic trash can tucked into its place under the kitchen sink and felt a stab of exhilaration. The contents were undisturbed.

This was, what his partner liked to call, providence and yet Jared was troubled. If he read this correctly, his contemporaries had failed to search Andrea's home in the first days after he was shot. Was it so clear from the very beginning that Andrea was not only guilty, but so deranged that there would never be a trial? And if so... what else was left to chance?

Jared stood in the light from the kitchen window and pondered. Abused women were usually isolated by a possessive partner who viewed every potential friendship as a threat. Andrea and Dudley had been separated for over a year and divorced for several months. It would take Andrea time to reestablish what was lost, and even more time before she trusted herself enough to resume much of a social life.

Jared prepared to take the trash with him. He unfolded a paper evidence bag and let the thought nag at him. Why wouldn't an investigator have come here to confirm facts, check for inconsistencies? He hated laziness, hated ineptness and he didn't trust the obvious; especially when so neatly wrapped for consumption. If he hadn't been fighting for his life in the intensive care unit, he would most certainly have come, if only to close out the case, with every possibility examined. Stephanie had been a vibrant young mother. Both she and her surviving child deserved better.

When there was no earthly justice, Jared liked to imagine an eternal price. Behind the scenes was a god of weights and measures who delivered whatever retribution was required. He had committed his life's work to finding resolution for the families and loved ones left to suffer in the wake of such outrage, his primary motivation always the faceless future victims he hoped never to hear of. Without a doubt, Dudley would still be victimizing other women.

Interesting, he thought, that at these times of philosophical reverie he could give a God he didn't trust credit; almost as if God were known and understood as they partnered in a battle for good to overcome evil.

Despite the presence of items lovingly placed and once cared for, an aura of emptiness permeated the house. There was a hollow, unsettled quality to the environment that transcended the material sense of Andrea's possessions. Places were stamped by the personality of those who lived there. If Andrea had recovered enough to plan an escape, she might have an opinion about him being here, walking abandoned rooms in search of answers she had been too sick, at the time, to provide.

Jared shook off these thoughts and reminded himself that he had yet to explore the second floor and the attic. Instinctually he lifted his head toward the ceiling and simultaneously felt an irrational fear steel over his mind, which he immediately suppressed. There was work to do.

Jared placed the tall brown evidence bag with Andrea's trash by the door and noticed a pad of paper partially hidden by an old newspaper sitting at the edge of the kitchen counter. He replaced the sterile gloves, now dusty and contaminated. The first page was yellowed and dried and yet the next revealed faint lettering.

The morning rain continued and the sky was overcast. With no electricity, there was no better light. Jared slanted the page toward the window and, with the added glow from the flash light, his heart skipped a beat. Andrea had written: *Stephanie! What could she possibly want!!!* Impatience was evident in the script and Jared could almost feel her ambivalence as she pressed down hard with her pen. Attracting Dudley's attention would be the last thing Andrea would want to do.

There was a phone number. Although he would need to check, Jared knew in his gut this would be Dudley's home number. Stephanie and Andrea had talked, confirming what he and his former partner initially suspected.

With care he flipped back the newspaper and read the date. Andrea's notation had been written the day before Stephanie was murdered. It was assumed that sometime around midnight Andrea drove to Boston, ostensibly to commit murder. But now that purpose was in doubt.

Jared squinted and made out additional faded letters. It looked like, yes, it was.... Two words, *left open*. There were one or two indiscernible sentences that would require the expertise of a forensics lab and two other final words born down on the pad with a heavy hand... *needs protection*.

Jared walked across the kitchen as the dog continued to nose about, his olfactory senses working over time. He removed additional evidence bags from his knapsack as well as a role of red labels upon which he would write date and contents and then seal the bags.

The note seemed to indicate that Andrea did not go to Dudley's home in a fit of jealousy as was presumed. More likely she was invited by Stephanie Wodsende. Perhaps the plan was for Andrea to help Stephanie get away from Dudley. This new theory undermined the prevailing, more obvious scenario that the murder had been premeditated. More significant still, it seemed that when Andrea left her home around midnight, or shortly thereafter, she had been rational enough to plan and write cohesively. There was no evidence of mental illness.

Making a spontaneous decision, Jared lifted the cell phone from his belt and punched in a number.

"I'm calling for Dr. Betsy Bloom. Tell her its detective Jared Shiel."

"Detective Shiel. I can't believe it. Are you actually back on the job?"

"No, I'm retired. But thought the detective part would jar your memory."

"I couldn't forget you. I guess congratulations are in order. I hear you're getting married?"

"Not me. Has to be another Jared Shiel. It's good to hear your voice. You sound well," Jared said.

Betsy had treated him in the ER on the day he was shot and visited him during his recovery several times after. He always appreciated her thoughtfulness.

"I imagine this is about the Wodsende case?"

"It is."

"I figured. You didn't strike me as the kind of person who could let loose ends flutter about."

Jared could hear the bustle of the ER in the background. "You sound busy so I'll make this quick. What would cause a pretty normal person to have a very sudden psychotic break?" Jared waited patiently and listened as Betsy issued an order that would send a patient to x-ray.

"It's not my area, you realize," she said coming back on the line. "But in my opinion no one experiences mental illness as a sudden event. Symptoms are there that people close to the patient don't see. Maybe they become numb to the pathology because they live with it every day. They are in denial or lack the tools to connect the dots."

"I'm in Andrea's house right now. It appears undisturbed since the day she left, meaning no one came here to tie up those loose ends you just mentioned. Everything I see tells me that Andrea was pretty rational."

"I certainly thought so. But, there may have been some compulsive features to her illness that we didn't see and yet, finally drove her over the edge."

Jared looked around. He didn't think so. The lay of Andrea's things were neat and tidy but not neurotic. A used tea cup sat on the kitchen table and the pad of paper and

233

newspaper had not been put away. He was about to say so when the dog suddenly froze in place. His ears went back and he stood at attention, the tiny stub of his tail that had been waging in exuberance moments before was now tucked close to his body.

"You there?" Betsy asked.

The dog lifted his head, and in that precise moment Jared heard the noise. Not a thud or a step exactly. More like a swoosh, followed by a crackling sound.

"I'm here," he told Betsy and let the palm of one hand drift toward his gun. "What else could cause a psychotic break in an otherwise normal person?" Jared kept his tone even as he moved across the kitchen toward the hall. As he did so a dragging sound from overhead accompanied his progress. He stopped. The sound from above ceased.

The dog whined and remained where he was.

"Sorry, I've got to go. Can we talk later?"

"Sure, but here's a thought for you," Betsy offered clearly on the move herself. "Psychosis can be chemically induced."

"Say again?"

"Don't look at catatonia as a state, but as a set of symptoms. Andrea could have ingested something toxic. It might have been something in her environment, perhaps even a drug reaction?"

"Yeah, but wouldn't that clear up if she was normal to begin with?"

"Not if the agent is still present. Adults can develop allergies. Did anyone look at that? I have to go, too. Maybe we can talk later in more depth."

"Wait. What if she was drugged?" Jared asked.

"Anti-psychotics administered to an otherwise healthy person could induce catatonic withdrawal, hallucinations, or erratic, even aggressive behavior. I shouldn't pose this question, but I will because it's been on my mind since the day of the murder. Ask yourself, Jared. Who had immediate access to Andrea when she first arrived at this ER?"

"Dudley."

"And who sat with her in ICU for at least an hour between the time we transferred her and the time we heard that Stephanie was murdered."

"Did you suspect something at the time?" Jared asked.

"I was too busy managing the potential risks caused by Dudley's poor judgment in treating Andrea when it wasn't necessary. There was another doctor in the hospital that night who could have taken over within the first fifteen minutes of her arrival. So I guess you could say it's come back to haunt me. But then I ask myself, if Dudley had given her something that induced psychosis, how could he keep it up? Andrea has been in lock-up for what? Over two years?"

"What if I told you Dudley continued to have access to Andrea? For the last six months at least, she's been in the nursing home wing of your hospital."

There was a heavy pause. "I didn't know."

"And if my information is correct Dr. Wodsende is still treating her. And since Andrea's mother gave that permission, we don't know what access he had before she was transferred to Crest May. My guess is he manipulated something. Power and control were his drugs of choice."

"I'd say that's a crying shame because Andrea hated her ex-husband. I wouldn't trust any decision he made for her. Given the circumstances, no one in their right mind could."

"You didn't hear that one of the state patients escaped from the geriatric unit?" Jared asked Betsy.

"Was that her?"

"Yes, it was."

"Names weren't released and it was very hush, hush that we offered a home to people who would normally be in prison. We're a small facility and there's a lot of competition for space, with pressure to keep the beds full or lose them. The research side has especially been agitating for room to expand since they received a generous grant in the last year. I guess geriatrics found a way around that, didn't they?"

"Yes and lucky for Andrea because now she's out of his reach."

"Unless he took her?"

"Let's hope not," Jared said keeping his eye on the dog who was now cowering under the butcher block. "Dr. Wodsende would have been the first person they considered so I'm sure they've explored that. I've got to go," he said. "Next time I'm in the city we'll have lunch and catch up. There are a few more possibilities I could run by you."

"I'd like that," she said. "Call me anytime."

Slowly Jared lowered the phone back to his belt, his face turned toward the ceiling, alert and listening. He might have dismissed the overhead noises as mice or a raccoon making use of an abandoned house for shelter if not for the dog's reaction. Animals had good instincts and this one had honed his in the crucible of hard survival.

Jared chided himself for not doing a thorough inspection of the premises when he first arrived. He had lost his edge and been away from this work too long and the time he spent on the Lydia Dillihunt kidnapping over the previous winter didn't qualify since there were no new forensics in that very cold case.

Jared focused. The fine layer of dust over the hardwood floors showed no disturbance whatsoever, but that meant nothing. Someone could have gained entry via an upstairs window. Jared searched his memory of the property. There were two large oak trees, though he failed to notice if one of the limbs extended toward the roof or any of the upstairs windows. Yes, he certainly had lost his edge.

The dog whined and cowered. "Sorry, boy can't help you with this one."

Jared took a step. A louder, more distinct dragging sound from overhead stepped with him. Too deliberate, he told himself; *otherworldly* deliberate? The word had just popped into his mind and he suddenly regretted the conversation he'd had with Jake Brown. All that talk of the preternatural and the farm being haunted had unsettled him.

As he moved into the hallway the dog abandoned his hiding place and followed. Facing them was the entry and front door. Jared couldn't help but admire the curved arch of the staircase with the beautifully carved banister and newel posts. As he paused at the bottom of the stairs he noticed that the dog, only a moment ago following so closely they might have tripped over one another, had fallen behind. He looked accusingly at Jared.

Jared motioned for him to follow, slapping his thigh, and whistling low. The dog whined, ran two quick circles in place, sat abruptly, and shot a warning look at Jared who almost smiled. He tried again, now his foot on the third step, but the dog refused to budge. Giving up, Jared stepped higher into the darkness. He took the flash light from his belt and turned it on, shinning the beam into the gathering gloom of the upstairs hallway.

And then he felt it. A cold like nothing he had ever felt before. It wheedled its way through the atmosphere around him, sought entrance beneath his clothing and through the pores of his skin. Jared felt every muscle in his body tense. His jaw locked so tight his teeth hurt. "Breathe," Jared reminded himself and, though it was summer, he was startled to see his breath visible in this closeted pocket of frigid air.

He ran various references through his mind and discarded each until he was left with only one. Had that first nightmare been a premonition? He had dreamt this, or at least the kernel of this which came to him now with a shock of recognition. As if it were a physical obstruction Jared thrust the panic aside.

Think! This was nothing like the dampness that seeps past clothing when snow is moist and heavy; nothing like a wind driven rain that tightens the chest triggering a cough and a chill. His mind searched for an explanation, but found instead that no quotient of logic could calm what he now knew to be true. The boy he'd met on the road was right. The farm was haunted and whatever it was that inhabited this space had been expecting his arrival.

Jared was practiced at shifting detachment into place like a shade that settles distance between fear and outrage, allowing him to function professionally. But, this was different. He felt his body react to what his mind rejected.

The hair stood up on his arms and tickled at the back of his neck.

Both he and his partner had agreed that at many murder scenes they could feel an aura of evil. Violence, they decided as they philosophically explored these impressions, could sometimes be an energy that lingered and especially when innocent human life was lost. It was the aura of anger, the intensity of passion gone awry to horrible outcomes. Was this all there was to it? Was there something more that he'd been socialized to ignore? Jared felt and thought all this as tentacles of coldness teased at his skull and, despite the danger, he stood frozen on the stair imprisoned in a kind of extreme sensory-shock.

With sudden abruptness the dog abandoned his winning and barked wildly, somehow freeing Jared to move forward toward the upstairs hallway. Once there he turned back. If dogs could talk, this dog was doing so. Come back, come, back, back baaaak, bark, bark.

Once more Jared called the dog to him, but the animal had gone as far as he was willing. Giving up Jared shifted his attention to the work at hand. He was in Andrea's house for a reason and there was no thought of leaving until he accomplished what he came for. Through a great expenditure of will he succeeded in cloaking himself in that practiced facade, that clinical detachment common to police work. And yet that frigid intelligent liquidity remained and now shadowed him deeper into the heavily shadowed dusk of the hall.

To escape it, Jared turned abruptly into the first room that opened onto the hallway. Though this room was closed and stale from lack of use, the temperature was in keeping with what one would expect, and felt a welcome sanctuary from whatever it was that had opposed him in the hall outside.

The gun was in his hand; every muscle in his body poised tight to react. He had failed to maintain this alertness once and nearly lost his life. It wouldn't happen again.

"Jaaa red Shiel...."

Jared whirled around. The whisper was husky with a raspy sort of intonation. It had emanated from the hallway, faint and yet distinct. The challenge moved him to action. He was here to do a job and nothing, not even a ghost, would send him running from this house and yet, Jared had to admit, he felt dread at the prospect of entering that hallway. To feel otherwise would confirm his status as a fool.

The thought of an alien spirit seeking habitation crept into his mind and lodged there like mold, like mildew, like the insidious residue of boyhood horror stories shared over camp fires. Jared shook off this impression, which seemed not to have been generated from within his own mind.

It occurred to him that if a return visit was required, he would need more protection than a lackluster, philosophical pretense of faith. He thought about buying a crucifix, investing in holy water and one of those catholic medals that his partner Ed had worn on a chain around his neck. It had been given to him by his wife who had it blessed by their parish priest for protection. Did such things really work? While he would have laughed at these superstitious accessories twenty minutes ago, any one of them now seemed like a good idea.

Thor's advice resonated in a way it hadn't when the words were first spoken. *Here's an idea. Try reading it. Your uncle read his Bible every day.* He would take that advice. Now desperate, he would search for answers in God's word.

Jared walked swiftly from one bedroom to a second and then a third, grateful that he felt nothing more from the hallway. The fourth bedroom ran the length of the front of the house with five tall windows and a fire place at either end. Beyond the drive was a stretch of uncultivated meadow with a low stone wall rimming the boundary that marked the entrance to the orchard.

The view was familiar. Jared was intimately acquainted with all of Burns' work, and now it came to him in dawning surprise that Burns had painted this scene. Not merely the subject, but the precise view from this very window in a group of ten paintings dubbed, *The Orchard Series.*

When he left that morning, there was a soft drizzle of rain just as Burns' had captured on two of the series. The gray backdrop was in striking contrast to the waxy blossoms, a pink and white haze amidst the green leaves. In the foreground of the painting, donated to the Adams Public Library, Burns had depicted a straw hat caught on a low hanging branch with a red ribbon trailing in the wind. He had called this painting *The Ribbon Red Hat.*

Jared considered. After being at the farm he no longer saw this painting in the same light. The contrast of such a beautiful subject, juxtaposed with whatever evil the house and grounds were used for, convinced him that Burns had used artistic expression as a way to work through a deeply felt conflict, perhaps even grief.

The painting, donated and then displayed as it was in such a public place now seemed to him a message to those that lived in the vicinity, a statement of something Jared didn't understand. He had believed he knew everything there was to know about Uncle Burns. Now he felt the greater weight of what he didn't know as a failure on his part, seeing just what he wanted of their shared family history, and little else.

On impulse Jared lifted the needlepoint rug and was not at all surprised to see a few dots of paint fallen from a brush or the edge of a pallet knife. The very particular tone of green was one of the colors Burns was in the habit of mixing for himself.

Jared was now curious. What had brought his uncle to this house, made him aware of this bedroom, the striking beauty of that orchard in spring? He felt a familial connection and knelt to touch the droplets of paint. Carefully he scraped them into a glass tube. When the matter of Andrea Wodsende was settled, he would have them tested, verifying a match to the original art.

Jared accurately guessed that Andrea would have commandeered this room as her own. She'd decorated in feminine pinks with a floral red duvet, a comfortable chaise with a Chinese lamp and a simple curtain treatment that in no way impeded the outside light. He picked up a book from the table, a pair of reading glasses nearby. *Haunted Houses of Berkshire County and Other Such Phenomena* by, Kearin Richmond. Andrea's place in the book was marked by a decorative paisley ribbon, though he could see she hadn't made much progress.

Returning the library book would give him an excuse to appease a growing curiosity to take a fresh look at his uncle's painting. He felt certain that after visiting the house and hearing the story told by Jake Brown, he would see something different in the painting, something that had never presented before.

Had Andrea believed the place was haunted? Had she felt the presence on the stairs and in the hallway and come to believe she was not alone?

By the time Jared was ready to leave, he and the dog were both tired and hungry. The exhaustion they felt was emotionally oppressive, a draining heaviness brought about by the exposure to whatever energy they had felt in that house. It was time to go, and though it irked him to back down from any fight, he felt certain there was danger in staying. Whatever clash was coming, would have to wait for another day. Right now, he simply was not prepared. He lacked the necessary defense, the tools provided by a genuine faith. Of this Jared was now certain.

Jared wondered if he would have trouble getting the dog away. His loyal instincts had been to stay and protect the property, certain his master would eventually return. Jared opened the passenger door and placed the various items he'd collected into a storage box brought along for that purpose and without coaxing, the Doberman followed. With a sigh of relief he curled into the blanket on the back seat, put his head between his paws, and let out a plaintive whine.

Zach woke with a start. The sound was somewhere between a protestation and a scream of intense outrage.

Andrea called out again and simultaneously Elias was knocking at his door.

"Zach, are you alright?"

"I'm fine. Just a bad dream," he responded hoping she would not call out again. He reached up from the floor, shaking Andrea awake even as he gathered the sleeping bag with his free hand.

"Are you alone?"

"Of course."

"Doesn't sound like it. Open the door, Zach."

"Just a minute."

Andrea was sitting up. As rehearsed she dropped between the bed and the wall and he covered her with the sleeping bag. He hoped she would cooperate and remain silent. As time went by Andrea was less likely to act inappropriately, but could still exhibit moments of confusion, struggled to articulate her thoughts, and occasionally over reacted when she substituted the wrong words for simple everyday phrases.

Zach opened his door.

"I thought I heard a woman's cry." Elias looked over Zach's shoulder, letting his eyes scan the room with suspicion. As far as he knew, Zach had never had a steady girlfriend, but it wasn't too farfetched to think he might sneak a girl up to his room. That was just the kind of brash, disrespectful exploit his son was famous for.

"I'm sorry, Dad, I was having a nightmare. Someone was chasing me. I guess I was scared."

"You want to come to the kitchen and I'll heat you some warm milk, just like your mother used to make when you were small?"

"With Karo Syrup and vanilla?"

"The very same, but maybe this time we'll add a shot of brandy to help you relax," Elias winked.

'Thanks, but I'm tired. I think I can sleep now and besides. Don't think the judge or my ten step buddies would approve," Zach chided wondering if the counselor would call the offer of alcohol a kind of sabotage. As far as Elias knew he really did have a substance abuse problem and from what Jared had learned about addiction from listening to numerous stories in his meetings an apparently harmless offer of any potentially addictive substance could set him ten steps back to the very beginning; in danger of suffering a new life threatening bottom with all the mess that implied.

"Alright, Son. Wake me if the dream comes back. Sometimes they do."

Feeling conflicted Elias studied his son, wishing he could take Zach's explanation at face value. With startling abruptness he walked toward the bed, pulling back the covers and half expecting to find a naked girl hiding under the blankets. He then walked across the floor and pulled the closet door open, separating the clothing. Finally he charged through the bathroom door.

Zach remained where he was listening as the shower curtain was yanked aside none too gently. "Had to check for myself," Elias said as he stepped back into the room slipping his hands into his bathrobe pockets. "I'd like to trust you," he said. "In fact Son, there is nothing I would like more."

"I understand. I haven't given you much reason to trust me. I would have done the same."

Elias hesitated, until Zach walked around him, opening the door wide, inviting an exit. But Elias stood his ground, letting his eyes rove over the room one last time. As he turned to go he cuffed the back of Zach's neck, bringing his head close and placing a kiss on the forehead. Not since he'd been a little boy, had Zach been kissed by his father in this way. He didn't know what to feel. Guilty for the lie he'd told, happy for the attention that arrived years too late?

What he couldn't feel was relief. If Andrea were discovered, Elias would know what to do. He always did and the temptation to confide in someone was growing.

"What's wrong," Evelyn asked and turned on the light as Elias sat on the edge of the bed.

"Zach had a nightmare."

"How do you think he's doing?" she asked.

"I don't know. These days you see more of him than I do."

"It's been a very long time since he's had a nightmare, but maybe we wouldn't know. He doesn't confide in us, does he?" she asked. "Do you think it's real?" She turned to her husband, worry evident in her expression.

"What?"

"He's doing well. Getting up without being called and hasn't complained in weeks. I just have trouble trusting that the changes are sincere. I'm waiting for the other shoe to drop. Tomorrow I thought I'd search his room."

In answer Elias reached over and hugged his wife. It was a tender gesture that had been absent between them for a very long time.

"I think he's on the mend," he said.

"I'm sorry," Andrea said and crossed her arms tight across her chest.

Zach was at the door checking the dark hallway. He could see the light under his parent's door. "He's gone now. Do you think you can go back to sleep without dreaming?" he whispered.

"I don't think so."

"Afraid?"

"Yes, and curious. I've either had that dream before or I really experienced the events. It was just too real."

"You want to tell me about it?"

"I was at my house in Woods End. My dog wouldn't come up stairs with me."

"Why not?"

"There was a demon on the staircase."

"You mean a ghost?"

"No, I mean a demon. It was a demon. And I was so scared. This thing was empowered to kill people who came there, but for some reason it couldn't kill me. It was inviting me... Inviting me to be part of something hateful and horrible. So horrible," she spoke haltingly. "There aren't words and I couldn't say, even then, what it was."

"You had a bad dream," Zach said, feeling a residue of fear attach to him in a curious kind of transference. He pushed the physicality of the fear down, denying what he had just felt.

"No, it was more than a dream. I'm scared, Zach. I don't want to go back, but I need to. Will you take me there?"

"No," he whispered with some assertiveness. "That's the first place they'll search."

"I think it's possible that someone has already come and gone from there. Someone with an important role to play. In my dream, I found myself praying for his protection."

"Yeah, the police when they investigated Stephanie's death."

"No. Recently. Today."

"How could you know that?"

"I dreamt about that, too. I felt him walking through the rooms and I feared for his safety."

"And you still want to go back?"

"It's not that I want to. It's that I have to. There's a reason I need to go back and it has to do with Stephanie and Dudley and even my mother."

"I can only promise to think about it. We'll talk later; no more tonight."

"Do you have a Bible?"

"We're Jewish remember?"

"Yes, but you have the Talmud. Do you have a copy of that somewhere?"

"Maybe I can find one. Tomorrow."

"No, I need it now. I can't sleep unless I can read it now."

A soft pinkish light filtered from under the door. His parents were still awake, probably digesting every detail of what his father had thought and felt about the cry he'd heard, and his mother would be avidly listening. He didn't have to see the expression on Evelyn's face to know that tension would be building until she had sufficient excuse to verbalize her worst fears which would allow a kind of cathartic release. Then life could get back to normal for a few weeks.

Without ceremony, Zach opened the door. His mother looked up startled. She wore a satin night shirt, with a tone on tone pattern, which fell below her knees. His father hadn't removed his bathrobe. They sat on the foot of the bed framed by an upholstered headboard, the matching brocade cover folded on a bench by the window and a white goose-down comforter askew over the linens.

Either he didn't have their attention, and months went by in which he felt insignificant and unnoticed, or they were shining the glare of their suspicions in his direction, every one of their accusations a kind of perverse invitation to overreact. As always Zach felt like an intruder, which in turn made him feel defensive. This was the ingrained routine the counselor wanted them to dispense with. "Go with it," she'd said. "Express what you're feeling and talk about it." Only now didn't seem like the right time.

"Anything wrong?" Elias asked with concern.

"Do we have a copy of the Old Testament around here somewhere?"

Elias and Evelyn looked at one another, clearly stunned by the request. Zach was pleased at catching them off guard.

"It's on the shelf in your father's library," Evelyn replied. "Why do you want it, Son?"

"I just want to read it. I don't think I can sleep unless I do," he said, feeling a little dorkish as he repeated Andrea's words to him.

"I'll get it for you," his father said as Evelyn stood, ready to do the same. The three walked in single file downstairs, into the hallway and into the study.

"Do we have any rabbi's in the family?" Zach asked, suddenly curious.

"We did," Evelyn said. "We've told you, but you've evidently forgotten."

"His name was Thierry Abram Goldfarb," Elias said. "He studied in Paris and died when the Germans invaded Holland. All his children died in concentration camp with the single exception of your grandfather who escaped capture and worked with the resistance. He died when you were a baby."

"What was he like?"

"My father was very devoted," Elias said. "He worked hard and was active in supporting the state of Israel and the return of our people after the war."

"He was opinionated and full of energy," Evelyn picked up. "So intense he was hard to be around. During the time that he lived with us we went to Temple every Sabbath. It wouldn't have been possible not to do so. And... maybe that's why we got out of the habit after he died."

Elias took the heavy book from the shelf and put it in Zach's hands. "This belonged to your great grandfather. My father carried it with him on the boat to this country. Maybe we'll go to Temple next Saturday," Elias offered.

"Would you like that, Zach?" Evelyn asked her voice full of surprise at the turn the night had taken.

"I would," Zach said, feeling a surge of emotion. There was something ceremonial about standing in the dim light of his father's study with one parent at each side and this book, heavy with the weight of history in his hands. This was the oldest book known to man, and his copy had come from a synagogue in Holland, rescued by his grandfather when the Nazi's invaded. He'd heard the harrowing story but, now felt a sudden hunger to know additional details.

Maybe, Zach considered, he would study the religion of his ancestors and be a rabbi. If that was what he was meant to do, then this banishment to the orthodox Jewish school in Western Pennsylvania might be part of some larger cosmic plan.

And what was it Guido had suggested? Study the history of... Moses, Joshua, and Daniel. It would shock Elias and Evelyn if he did, challenging their lackluster affirmation of a rich heritage with a personal commitment that they lacked.

The radical notion resonated. They were accustomed to the irreverent, rebellious son. A religious substitute might shatter their complacency with far more effectiveness than the risk taking, negative behavior whose consequences Zach was deciding he could live without.

WOOD'S END

CHAPTER TWENTY TWO

Andrea studied a photograph of Stephanie. Had she hated this woman enough to murder her? She thought not. These were not the circumstances that would prompt her to take a life. When she escaped Dudley she felt sad for the loss of a dream, but even more so she was relieved to be free. She wasn't jealous of Stephanie. On the contrary, she was grateful for the distraction that Stephanie provided. Even without her faculties fully restored, she knew that Dudley wasn't worth fighting for and certainly not as defined by the newspaper clippings, which characterized Stephanie's brutal murder as a crime of passion.

If only she could hurry the process of recovery. When she tried her vision blurred and an overwhelming lethargy forced retreat. Most memories were prompted by incidental tasks or thoughts that turned out to be bread crumbs leading to the path of more recovered memory.

"Charlie," she smiled at the thought of her dog. His good ear up and the other standing sideways, he eyed her bribe of a gourmet package of soft food mixed into the dry that, in normal circumstances, provided a treat he couldn't resist. But, as usual he had read the preparations and knew that she was leaving, hopeful that he was going, too. Charlie turned in an excited circle as she collected her purse and a bottle of water. Finally he stood at the door, his nose pressed into the crack. If she would let him, he would race ahead in a burst of joyful energy. Andrea hated to disappoint.

"Charlie." As in Charlie Brown or just because she liked the way these two syllables rolled off her tongue? She didn't know. "Be good," were her parting words. She bent her face close and felt his wet kiss, his brown eyes sad and questioning.

There was some reason why he didn't like being left alone in the house. Some reason she didn't like leaving him and had gradually, by degrees, come to an awareness of, which left her frightened. She was carving out a life for herself in that house and she imagined it now. The long reach of the afternoon sun and she, admiring the view as dusk settled down the shadowed slope of the mountain as the last chorus of birds rang to silence. Except for the kitchen, which was the original cabin and out from which the rest of the house was built, the rooms were large and spacious.

Was it possible this home could be waiting unchanged since the day she left? Andrea forced her mind back to the night that she had driven into a blackness that was only now beginning to lift.

Charlie had been more troubled than usual, and she wondered what had happened that may have prompted his anxiety. In her mind's eye she saw herself attempting to reassure him. "I'll be back before you know it. Be good," she said and latched the door behind her, hoping he would settle down and fall asleep in the overstuffed chair they both pretended he didn't retreat to when she was gone.

In a hurry to be off she had timed her arrival to coincide with Dudley being at work, and yet was irritated that going was necessary at all. Against her better judgment she had given in to Stephanie and with a pretty sure idea of what Dudley was up to. Whatever that something was, well, she could not now remember except that it had the power to spill over into her own life if not contained. It was this urgency that beckoned her forth and once committed, there was no turning back.

Andrea recalled walking to the car. She closed her fist around the imaginary keys lifted from her purse. She had a picture in her mind of the night sky, a low ceiling of running clouds back-lit an iridescent gray. It smelled like snow and she only hoped the coming storm would hold off until she was back at home, safe and sound.

Tears moistened her eyes. She had lost more than time.
The mere hint of what might have been was an ache of loss
so powerful it threatened to swallow every hard-won-gain.

Jared drove to North Adams and dropped his car at the
garage. With over an hour to wait and the dog at heel, they
walked to the library. He paid the fine and decided he liked
the idea of Andrea owing him money. When he saw her
again this would be a light way to begin their first
conversation.

Jared detoured into the larger reading room where
Burns' painting hung above a rustic stone fireplace with
comfortable chair groupings. He found a place to sit where
he could easily view what at first glance, appeared a beautiful
pink and white confection against a rainy backdrop with the
ribbon a bright splash of contrast against the gnarled trunk
of the apple tree.

Jared's gaze was drawn into the row of trees, their black
trunks saturated in rain with vivid new grass at the base and
the scattered cycle of fallen blossoms. Gone was the idyllic
country scene of former imaginings. The very subject matter
was now and forever tainted and he would never again see
this series of paintings in the same naive light.

Jared considered the owner of that hat. He imagined
how she had turned to flee in terror, running from the house,
the ribbons flying and catching on a low branch, testimony to
the fact that she had lived and maybe died in that orchard.

In the next instant, what snapped into place was a visual
reframing of what he saw; the suggestion of an outline. He
shut his eyes tight. When he opened them again the form of
a man, dressed as a farmer from a previous century emerged
from the shadowed depths of the background.

Now the black-green foliage of a branch became the brim
of a hat, and two linear shadows that logic told him should
not lie as they did, became suspenders. It was a trick of sight
that when he looked, the man was gone and all he saw was
the tangled stand of trees. But when he squinted with the

knowledge of what he'd experienced at the farm there was a perceptual brain shift and he saw the clear and lurking figure of a man.

And then he realized. The hidden image of the painting was a statement and one must not accept the surface, superficial context of what the image implied. This was both a message and a reminder from beyond the grave.

Intrigued Jared wondered about the other nine paintings of the *Orchard Series.* All but three were in private collection. He thought of this as he untied Charlie from the bike rack and headed for the drug store counter restaurant. There he ordered a milkshake, and for the dog a bottle of water with three cheeseburgers.

Jared walked back into the street and found his eyes fixated on the abandoned storefront opposite. Thinking he would sit on the bench and feed the dog the hamburgers, he read the cracked lettering with the once bright base-color bleeding through and a four leaf clover stenciled above the letter "I"; *Mullin's Tavern.*

And in that precise moment he experienced the first and only vision of his lifetime, which arrived without any preamble whatsoever. Much later, when he was invited to agree that he was often the recipient of such supernatural occurrences, and it was suggested they came like a seizure one has cognitive warning of, Jared could only say that it was nothing like that. This had never happened to him before and he hoped it never would again.

There was a vague awareness of water running, which for lack of a better reference made him think of putting a conch shell to his ear and listening for the submerged sounds of a running tide. He was a twig caught in a strong current, helpless to say he would go or stay since he was already there, instantly transported back to a time that he had never lived.

The dog whined, forgetting the uneaten hamburgers. He pushed his body against Jared's knees with his ears back and his brown eyes pleading.

"This is for her."

Jared smelled exhaust from a truck idling nearby with the hood turned in toward the parking meter. An elderly man sat within, both hands on the steering wheel in a desperate white knuckle grip, oblivious to all but his own pain. Slowly, by increments so measured that it was hard to be startled, Jared watched the careful uncoiling of a snake like presence. Though he tried to make out the details, tried to discern the contours of what he saw, he realized there was no separating the substance of the man from the demon spirit that possessed him.

The dog barked and then whimpered, now cowering under the bench, pushing his body against the back of Jared's legs. The presence lifted slightly from the man until with startling speed it lunged at him, able to traverse the distance without relinquishing its grip on the possession in the truck.

"I'll take what I like and leave the rest," was the gravelly intonation of a voice that was all too familiar. What ensued was a kind of mental rape, a flagrant, heartless riffling of feelings so deep and private that Jared was left stunned and nearly paralyzed at the lacerating affront to his personhood. And in this weakest, most helpless of moments came the invitation, the intimation of what repelled and horrified him, and yet on some base level attracted with a trance-like drawing together of what was never intended to meet.

The choice was clear. The choice was his. He could open himself even more and be what; a vehicle and not a person? Lost forever? By a fight or flight instinct, self protective and visceral, Jared knew something more than his twenty first century mind, at first rejected.

Oh, God, help me, Jared pleaded. *Jesus, fill me. Cast this other out. Oh, God... In the name of Jesus Christ...* Love drew him as words of confession flowed from the depth of Jared's being. At last there was a wash of release, a feeling of being clean. Prostate before the throne of grace, enveloped by praise and wonder, filled with gratitude for an undeserved forgiveness Jared knew that, until eternity, he could never fully grasp the scope of God's love and power.

Jared turned his attention back to the truck. The man within appeared to be an ordinary farmer come to town for errands. But a new awareness revealed something very different. Jared understood that all communication between the demon and the man was blocked by prayer and this was experienced as an abrupt loss, a physical and psychic agony of withdrawal from a diabolical, symbiotic enmeshment.

In the cessation of communication with the primary demon, the handler familiar, old man Woods was utterly alone as he grappled to act within the humanity of a God decreed autonomy, a forgotten volition; the gift he had traded for darkness and death.

Jared wished he could encourage the man; cheer him on in laying claim to the lost territory of his soul, but it was too late. He could only wait for the demon to command, barreling in to fill the void of stolen territory in the predatory battering of a grasping, greedy interloper. Demon spirits had been fully operational in the stolen physicality of the man, and to lose that object, even for the hair breath of seconds, enraged the infectious horde.

"This is for her," came the thought.

Jared shifted his attention to the overhang of the drug store entrance out of which he had just strolled with the dog at his heels. A young man of sixteen or seventeen crept to the entrance and hunkered down. He was a lanky boy coming late to maturity and physically unremarkable.

He held his weapon with the ease and confidence of one born to hunting pheasant and deer in lean winters. But this was no prey destined for the dinner table. Unflinching, poised, and ready he lifted his weapon and Jared felt, rather than heard the weight of the bullet as it dropped into the chamber.

"This is for her."

Jared heard the shift of the truck's handle and felt the air displaced. Even more palatable was the weightier expectation of unrequited revenge watching in hushed anticipation for this one, inelegant opportunity to act. Jared looked between the old man, as he stepped from the truck, and the boy, understanding that there was no power at his disposal to stop the vigilante justice that had been carried out before he was born.

Even in overalls and work boots, old man Woods bore a striking resemblance to his youngest son, Dr. Dudley Wodsende.

This was the pivotal moment upon which so much hinged, the circumstances of which Jared was intended to see and understand. The old farmer glanced back at the gun secured in the rear window rack. Left to his own forfeited resources, he was too depleted to exercise that weak and atrophied element of choice. He left the gun and yet, in this fateful decision, was more human than he had been for many long years.

Familiar tentacles of icy air clashed with the hot cement of the sidewalk as that dank cloud of shrieking scorn sought to be heard. "You excreting little whipped whore of a creature, listen to me. Listen to meeeee. Get in the truck and fly like a bat escaping the flames. The weapon, you forgot the weapon! Oh I, we, so liked eating. The carnal knowledge of men and woman... The pain inflicted; the screams. Stop or you'll be burning in the caverns of hell before I can; you, you, you will ruin. You are ruin, you worthless... you!"

Deaf to the shrieking voice the old man walked toward the overhang of the drug store, unaware of thirty plus rifles and guns marking his progress from every conceivable angle.

The eruption of gunfire converged. The scent of graphite burned the delicate membrane of Jared's nostrils.

The father of Dudley, Sybil, and Henry spun about, his body flailing like a doll before gravity sucked his lifeless form to the hard cement in the harsh aftermath of a deadly silence. Blood spurted and for an instant, just before he fell, Jared felt a jolt of fear as he locked eyes, not with the man, but with the demon now stripped of habitation.

"Later," came the gravely intonation.

Jared had seen the demon vanquished. He had seen the demise of the human shell that gave physicality to its power and in the seeing, in the context of that mental clash he knew himself marked for a battle that had begun with a nightmare, moved to the dark staircase of its' current lair and would conclude at a later time.

The boy, Burns Padgett Shiel, walked to the body and kicked the lifeless form with the toe of his boot as if disbelieving that the monster was really dead. With deliberate care he leveled the gun and fired one last shot.

"That's for her," he said. *"That's for her!"*

Down the length of the street men left their hiding places, by prearrangement stepping out of the roles that had been carefully choreographed. An SUV glided by as men jogged along to toss their weapons into the open back before departing the scene, some fleeing town entirely, while others faded into the normal activity of small town life. Only Burns broke with the plan and stood transfixed over the body. Two rushed to his side, one grabbing his rifle, sprinting to catch up with the SUV, while the other urged him toward a waiting car, as a first siren pierced the air.

As he was hurried away Burns kept his eyes glued to the place where Jared sat. He didn't see his nephew, but sensed the import, aware of a witness being there.

. "And that's why you never married," Jared said aloud addressing Burns as he looked back one last time before being pushed into the waiting car. "And that's why I'm here to break the hold of this generational curse."

Jared came alert to heavy dog paws pushing against his chest. Charlie had picked up the bag containing the hamburgers with his teeth and deposited them on Jared's lap.

"Hungry are you?"

He opened the bag, surprised to find that the food was still warm. Whatever had happened, all that he had seen, had taken seconds and not the minutes that real time required. He thought of Andrea. Somehow they were connected by these events. They were the next generation charged with a task to heal. It wasn't that he would help her; rather he was compelled to do so. And now he realized that without faith, healing could not take place.   Only a supernatural infusion of Godly love and wisdom could repair the longstanding erosion of institutional evil upon individuals, upon families, and even towns.

Soon the last house nestled at the crest of a sloping hillside, disappeared in the rear view mirror and large oaks entangled their branches overhead in a canopy of green.
The dog thrust his head out the window, catching the early afternoon breeze.   When they hit the turnpike, picking up speed, he pulled back and rested his chin on the seat.
The day before, Jared had phoned his former housekeeper, asking her to stock the shelves with a few essentials, putting clean sheets on the bed and towels in the bathroom.
"I ordered you a bed. It'll be waiting when we arrive. It's about time you had a name. What will I call you?"
The dog looked interested.
"How about, Charlie? No point in being original," he said and turned around in time to catch a wet tongue across his chin.

"Charlie." She whispered the name.
"Who's Charlie?"
"My dog. I only hope he's found a good home."
They were sitting on the floor, their backs against the bed and a 5lb box of chocolates between them.   Zach was accustomed to her changeable moods. She could be nearly overwhelmed in the sadness of a memory and a short time later, after processing and then distancing herself, she could be hoping for the next cavalcade of sensory over-load in a hurry, she said, to arm herself for whatever lay ahead. Some of the memories were good, but bittersweet in the captured recollection of what had been stolen over the last two years.
Zach scrunched a candy wrapper into a tight ball and hooked it into the waste basket placed strategically for that purpose.

"Won't anyone miss this candy?"

"Are you kidding? My dad gets so many presents and especially around holidays. This was left by one of Elias's clients at Easter, which we, of course, don't celebrate." He looked at her then. "What were you thinking? You had that look on your face."

"What look?" she asked.

"That capturing a memory kind of look. You shouldn't keep it to yourself." He hated being shut out. "I could probably fill in a few blanks."

Andrea pondered his words and took in the boyish features, still forming into the man he would be. Warm brown eyes and darker hair; straight nose balanced to wide cheekbones. He had recently suffered a growth spurt, so he was always hungry, always eating. Even before she had heard Evelyn comment from the hallway that his trousers needed to be replaced before school in the fall, she had noticed too, proof positive that she was less focused on herself, looking outward, hungry for whatever the future might bring.

"Just tell me what you were thinking," Zach prodded.

"I was thinking about Stephanie. I don't think I knew her very well."

"Probably not," Zach agreed.

"Even before I arrived in the emergency room covered in blood, as the clipping says," she thumped the old newspaper with the back of her hand. "Dudley had already drugged me. I have a vague recollection of running in the snow and then not being able to continue. I just couldn't keep my limbs moving and dropped to the ground."

"So you think my theory is correct. He was at the house that night?"

"On the surface he had an alibi, but when Dudley and I were married, it was possible to slip away to check on me. We lived close enough to Crest May, and don't forget... The hospital had a significant endowment thanks to Dudley's family. The ER operated more like an after-hours clinic. Unless it was a true emergency, walk-ins were sent elsewhere and if it wasn't the hospitals night for overflow, patient traffic was fairly predictable."

"Nice job," Zach remarked.

"And there's something else. I have to say, I'm surprised, even suspicious that Crest May agreed to take state patients."

"Like maybe Dudley engineered that so he could have greater access to you?"

"All that money gifted to Crest May... It's why Dudley was never censored before Betsy Bloom arrived on the scene. Even before he filed for divorce he expected to be made head of ER. When Doctor Bloom got the job he was incensed, but finally had to see how his treatment of people alienated them. And Stephanie working at the hospital didn't help. They didn't like Dudley, but they loved Stephanie."

"And you?"

"They only knew what Dudley told them. I was always the scapegoat. Dudley wasn't someone to forget a slight, no matter how trivial."

"So, you think Dudley could have left the ER and returned without the staff noticing. Did he go home intending to murder Stephanie? Or was he merely planning to confront her about leaving him, found you there and flew into a rage which ended in murder?"

"I don't know how much he knew. Dudley didn't trust me to be alone, and I imagine he felt the same anxiety about Stephanie. If she was planning on leaving him, he might have guessed. He had an uncanny ability to read people."

"Think for a minute," Zach said. "You ran from the house. Stephanie was dead or dying. What happened next?"

"Just what I told you. I was outside, running. Once I was off his property, he had to let me go. He couldn't risk having a neighbor recognize him, and he would have been keeping a close watch on the time. If a patient came in and they couldn't find him right away, there goes the alibi. At the time I thought he was behind me, breathing down my neck, reaching for the sleeve of my jacket. I was so scared."

"I'm sorry."

"And there's something else."

"What?"

"As scared as I was, I remember thinking. And... I'm just recalling this now as we talk."

"What?" Zach could hardly contain his curiosity.

"As scared as I was, I was thinking that Dudley was at least an enemy I could see."

"What does that mean?"

"I have not a clue. But I do believe Dudley won't let me live, which is why I have to leave here. He must be worried that my memory is returning. And if I recall enough to defend myself..."

She touched his arm. "I simply won't have your family endangered, and especially your father after what he's already done for me. In light of our prior connection, no one would believe your parents innocent of hiding me. I simply couldn't live with myself if any of you were hurt."

"I strongly disagree. Dudley doesn't want you dead," Zach asserted, recalling what Guido had told him. "He could have killed you any time and made it look like you died of natural causes. There is a big piece to this puzzle that we don't have and it centers on Dudley's warped motivation."

Andrea reached for another piece of chocolate, but just as quickly put it back.

"And I have to say I don't know that woman." She pointed dismissively at the old newspaper where her image peered back from the upper corner of page six. "I don't believe I would have killed Stephanie, and I know I wasn't jealous of her. The truth is I was grateful to be free of him."

"I believe you," Zach said, recalling the complaints of the staff.

"I'm leaving at the end of the week," she whispered.

"Not without me."

"You've done quite enough, more than anyone your age should. For that I'll always love you like a dear friend. My house must be somewhere outside North Adams. See if you can find the address for me." She gestured toward the photo of herself. "I'm so changed I won't be recognized if I go back."

Zach reached for the clipping and studied Andrea's image. Not a hair out of place, intelligent eyes looking directly at the lens in poised formality.

"You're not as pretty as you used to be."

"Thank you very much," she responded.

Zach looked at her. "You've recovered pretty fast. It makes me worry for you."

"I'm fine."

"A month ago you were imprisoned in an oversized highchair with your hair uncombed. You sat where they put you and only exercised up and down the hall because it was ordered twice a day. It's remarkable really. A few more weeks and you could be completely well, making trips to get your hair colored and getting your nails done just like my mother. Heck you could get your driver's license back. You might even have a driver's license. So...unless they find you and send you to jail, you could be living a full life."

"Jail?"

"You didn't have a jury trial, so I'll have to ask my father where you stand. A judge declared you incompetent to stand trial after several doctors agreed. But if what you say is true, then Dudley went to considerable trouble to get you out of the system. He wanted access to you for some reason."

Andrea studied Zach. "I'm ready for this to be over, but first I have to return home. There's something waiting for me at Wood's End. It's the key to understanding Dudley's agenda, the purpose of all this."

"What could be there?"

"I'll know after I re-enter that house."

"I'll drive you."

"No, I can't have you involved any more than you already are. But if I'm in that house alone, it will be easier to remember. I need to know the truth so I can defend myself. I'm done with being a victim."

"If what you say is true, then remembering will make you even more a threat to Dudley."

"You said yourself he could have killed me, but didn't. So what does he want from me?"

"Are you hungry?" Zach changed the subject, counting the days until she would leave. He'd have to tell his father, light a fire under Jared Shiel, and see what kind of help he could pull together. What he couldn't do, was put her on a bus, and watch her disappear. As far as Zach was concerned Andrea had far to go before she was fully recovered and until that time, she could hardly be expected to defend herself. In Dudley's site she was a sitting duck.

"Evelyn's made macaroni and cheese, herb chicken, garden peas and coconut cake for desert. I'll go check on the status of dinner," he offered.

"Good idea. But no more chocolate." Andrea put the lid on the box and slid it under the bed. She looked at Zach. "She's made either a cobbler or a pie."

"Really?"

"I can smell it baking." Andrea gulped and put a hand to her mouth.

"What's wrong?"

"I feel nauseated. Too much chocolate, I guess."

"You threw up yesterday," he reminded her. "Are you getting sick?"

"I don't think so. I'm not as dizzy and unsteady on my feet as I used to be. Except for that full feeling in my head. It's like my brain is wrapped in cotton batting. When that goes away I'll be back to normal."

Zach got up to leave. His hand was on the door knob when she called him back.

"One more thing."

"What?"

"I know Dudley killed Stephanie. She was my proxy, forced on him and entirely dispensable; never really what they wanted, but a suitable substitute for... something."

"Listen to yourself," Zach challenged. "You said 'they' and not he. You said, 'what *they* wanted.'"

So who is *they?*" Andrea asked.

"You should know. You brought it up."

A wounded look wrapped Andrea's features in concentration. "When Dudley gets what he's after, he'll kill me. I may not remember everything just yet, but I do know that if you and your family are to be safe, I have to leave. You should forget you were ever connected to this mess."

"Impossible," Zach replied, already out the door. She listened to his step bounding down the stairs.

If I ever have a son, she whispered. *I'd want him to be just like you, my friend.*

WOOD'S END

CHAPTER TWENTY THREE

Jared did not phone ahead, preferring the element of surprise. As he reached the city limits the threatened downpour washed over the streets in a lineal sweep of gun metal gray. He turned on the wipers, liking the sound against the soft hum of the engine. Jared had fond memories of this car and felt energized behind the wheel.

The rain stopped just as he turned into the gated community looking for Weymouth Street, a narrow road with cul-de-sacs and even narrower lanes stemming off, creating an enclave of old world suburbia in the midst of city life.

The houses were stately, not quite mansions, but large enough to house help. In decline and then serious decline, they had been converted to duplexes and small apartment buildings to accommodate the influx of students at nearby colleges. In the last three decades, the historical significance of the area had precipitated a reawakening to single family residences beautifully restored.

Elias and Evelyn had been among the first to see the potential, completing their restoration twelve years earlier. Number 18 boasted an arched doorway with two Grecian style benches on either side. Ivy trailed about the glassed enclosure as a side portico, deep in shade, wrapped toward the back of the house. Jared rang the bell.

"Yes?"

"Hello, Mrs. Goldfarb. I'm Jared Shiel. Your husband sent for me." Jared held the letter conspicuously, allowing her to catch a glimpse of her husband's embossed crest and singular script.

"Really? I'm so sorry. He neglected to tell me."

"Is he at home, Mrs. Goldfarb?"

"No, but I do expect him soon." She hesitated, not quite sure what to do. He waited as she wrestled with the dilemma, hoping she would opt for courtesy over safety.

"I'd be glad to wait outside," Jared offered knowing from experience that the longer the hesitation the more likely he would not achieve his purpose.

"Certainly not." She glanced at Charlie who sat beside him, chin up, nose in the air and clearly anxious to be released from the sit-stay command. Evelyn crossed her arms. She took in the missing clumps of fur with a perceptible wince of revulsion. "We have a cat. I'm afraid you'll have to leave your animal outside."

"That's no problem at all. As you can see he's been recovering from an illness of sorts, but I'll just put him in the car with the windows cracked."

Jared felt her cautious eyes on him as he walked the dog back to the car. He patted Charlie's head. "Might be useful to have you around," he whispered. "She was so worried about you she forgot to worry about me."

Andrea paced the room, too restless to read. Finally she paused at the window. Below the ledge, a show of dragon flies darted upon currents of moist air. Even they had a freedom denied to her, and she chaffed at the limitations imposed by a spectator status, becoming more a prison each day.

As the chemicals were flushed from her body, memories returned like errant stragglers hauling along the baggage of even more, far older memories which seemed to clamor for an audience. As each was unveiled, Andrea struggled to overcome a powerful inner command not to think or delve too deeply into what had been... artificially sealed. An image had come to her of a dark fortress being dropped into her mind and becoming the collection site for secrets which protected others. She was done living life under the punitive control of people like Dudley, like her mother. In her way she had been fighting for freedom from such personalities since she was a little girl, but no more.

Of late her home in Woods End became a persistent image that occupied her thoughts. More and more it had come to her... It felt as if.... Seemed entirely possible that, despite all Sybil's protestations she, *baby girl...* had known the house and farm long before she acquired it in her divorce settlement.

"Andie Rose at Woods End, of World's End, Wodsende Farm, you'll be a princess, you'll be a queen. It's your family; your fate, your destiny."

"No, no, Mom. I don't want to go back there." She had stamped her foot. Everything around her loomed large, her head reaching just above the counter top.

"Don't talk back to your mother. I don't have time for that now. Come over here and let me get you dressed."

"I hate that dress. It smells bad and it itches and if you make me wear it, I'll run away," she proclaimed and turned to go, shuffling her small feet as fast as she was able toward the door before rough hands wrenched her back.

Andrea heard voices. A car was in the driveway, and she was irritated with herself for having been so engrossed in this latest memory that she'd missed its arrival. A man stepped from the shadow of the front entry, escorting a dog along the walk. He opened the car door wide, ushering the animal onto the back seat before retracing his steps.

She observed his way of moving with a wayward lock of hair falling across his forehead, and wished she could see his features with more clarity. Just as the thought formed full in her mind, he stopped abruptly, pausing to let his gaze sweep across the second floor windows. She remained immobile, and when he resumed walking, she felt disappointment at not being seen in return. As the light from the house fell over the deepening green of the lawn, she shifted her attention to the dog, standing like a sentinel in the back seat, alert with an air of expectation, waiting for his master to return.　His demeanor seemed to mirror the confining predicament of her own status, and Andrea wished she could stroke the dog's black coat, offering comfort and being comforted in return.

Jared decided that there was something distinctive about Evelyn Goldfarb.　She was dressed in a straight skirt and man tailored shirt with a paisley silk cummerbund cinching in a narrow waist.　He clicked off the details; nice jewelry, expensive sandals, understated manicure, and just the right daytime scent.　Her gray eyes conveyed a no-nonsense air of respectability, and he realized, small in stature as she was, she didn't need the uniform.　First impression told him that she ran deeper than her comfortable life would seem to indicate with the cloned accoutrements that had become, in Jared's mind, a cliché for the uselessness that had briefly tempted him.

He could have taken his uncle's money and never worked a day in his life.　For a brief time he tried, but owning every toy he never wanted and ending up with a hangover he couldn't shake until mid afternoon, when it was time to start again, quickly lost its luster.　The futile aimlessness went contrary to his Yankee upbringing. Pursuing a childhood dream, fueled by the memory and unsolved kidnapping of Lydia Dillihunt; the girl that had, along with her sister, been the subject of one of Burns' paintings, Jared joined the force.

That he was named the largest single beneficiary of Burn's estate hadn't been a surprise, but the combined value of the assets were, and especially because his Uncle had led such an unobtrusive, nearly Spartan life.　The money came with strings attached and soon he understood the responsibility of protecting Burn's legacy as the most important American artist of the 20th Century, requiring a public relations firm with several litigators and copyright infringement attorneys on permanent retainer.

Paying for all this necessitated the Burns Padgett Shiel Endowment Trust, which paid the bills and at the same time doled out monetary gifts to worthy causes which in turn required a Board of Directors. Jared declined the chairman title and attended six of the eight meetings held each year. With the exception of two trusted friends of Burns, he rotated the others off every three years and always included several of limited means, but somehow attached to the art world as curators or employees at auction houses, including the security guard who presided over Burn's wall at the Museum of Fine Arts in Boston.

"We're about to sit down to dinner. Would you care to join us?" Evelyn asked, relieved to have the issue of the dog settled.

"I don't want to impose."

"Not at all. I don't know how long Elias will be, so we won't wait. When he's late he's very late. Are you hungry?"

"I am actually. I tried to get lunch while waiting on my car to be fixed, but those plans went astray."

She gave a nod to her maid. "Would you call, Zach?"

"That boy won't eat a thing," the maid complained. "He took a plate to his room, came right back asking about desert. I slapped his hand and told him to wait."

"Thank you. Now if you'll be so kind as to call, Zach. Boys are a bottomless pit at this age," she said turning to Jared who noticed the boy had shown up on cue. He stood behind his mother, eyeing Jared with veiled curiosity.

"Zach, this is a friend of your father's, Mr. Shiel?" She looked at Jared for confirmation. He nodded and extended his hand. She continued. "He'll be joining us for dinner. Your father is late, but we won't wait," she said already turning away.

Alone for a moment with Zach, Jared felt himself being sized up with a guileless curiosity. He smiled. The boy failed to smile back.

"After you, Sir," Zach said, covering the silent exchange with glib politeness. He was his mother's child, Jared decided.

The dining room held European pieces from the early nineteenth century, and filled the room more than Jared liked. He sat across from the boy and his mother with a place setting empty at the head of the table.

"Nothing special. I hope you don't mind, Mr. Shiel."

"I'm sure it will be delicious, Mrs. Goldfarb."

"Macaroni and cheese," the boy offered sounding sincere. "She makes the best and not that store bought stuff that comes in a box."

Jared studied Evelyn's expression for any sign that she appreciated the compliment. There was none. What would it be like to have this woman for a parent? Perhaps if born into the present generation, when such a decision was more acceptable, she would have chosen to pass on children altogether. He guessed the boy had another year before he was out of the house and she would be counting the days.

They made their way through freshly baked bread with honey-nut butter, a green salad with sprouts, avocado, and mushrooms before the peas, macaroni and herb chicken was served.

"You're an excellent cook," Mrs. Goldfarb.

"Thank you. May I ask your business with my husband?"

"An old case I worked when I was with the department."

"Cambridge, PD?"

"Boston."

"I must say I'm quite surprised. My husband doesn't do criminal work and no litigation in years."

"Well, he evidently had an interest in the Wodsende case. I won't know the connection until we have a chance to talk. It seems clear from his letter that he believed the person charged was innocent."

"Remarkable. May I read the letter?" she held out her hand.

"Did you come with a dog, Mr. Shiel?" Zach interrupted. "I heard my mother mention a dog at the door."

Jared looked at the boy. He could tell that Mrs. Goldfarb didn't approve the interruption. She sat straighter in her chair while Zach, who would be practiced at reading her body language, ignored the message.

"More salad?" Zach asked and slid the art glass bowl across the table.

"Yes, thank you. There is something special in this dressing. What is it?"

"The mushrooms were marinated in lemon juice and fresh tarragon," Evelyn offered.

"I must remember that. About the letter," Jared returned to the subject.

"She's made a cobbler for desert," the boy offered. "She usually makes coconut cake on Tuesday's. That's really good too."

For the first time Evelyn's face softened and she smiled at her son. "Why yes. I stumbled on some late peaches at the market."

They finished the second course with no more mention of the letter. The maid came to remove the plates. "Before leaving for the night, would you bring Zach and Mr. Shiel a serving of cobbler with the cinnamon ice cream? You were saying, Mr. Shiel? This case my husband has a curious interest in. I can't imagine really..."

"Oh, so sorry," Zach said in perfect sync with an almost full glass of milk creeping a white pattern across the table to the edge of Jared's linen placemat. Zach and his mother stood in unison and began to blot the milk. Jared helped by contributing his napkin when, amidst the distraction Zach raised a finger to his lips. They sat again as the maid served them.

"I hope you like it?"

"This is actually a favorite of mine. Mrs. Goldfarb," Jared turned in his seat to face her fully. He could feel the boy tense at what was coming. "Can I move in or maybe just show up occasionally for dinner?"

She laughed, pleased. It was a nice laugh that he guessed was not often heard. Was the kid the problem? Jared decided he'd speak her language and see what came of that.

"When I'm in the city I stay at my home on Louisburg Square. We're almost neighbors, so I can jet on over any time you're making this cobbler."

As he expected, her interest shifted. When she saw the car she'd written him off, but this was prime Boston real estate and only people of means could afford to pay those taxes.

"So I was saying. It was the Andrea Wodsende case. Ever hear that name?"

"Yes, I think so."

"Two years ago, and briefly I might add, you would have read about it in the papers. She was charged with murder, but never stood trial."

"No, I've heard the name more recently." She poured steaming coffee into a cup so delicate that Jared could see the liquid through the porcelain. "But I don't normally follow local crime," Evelyn added. "What happened?"

"Stephanie Wodsende was shot by the husband's ex-wife. This was the last case I worked as a homicide detective."

"Is this Andrea Wodsende in jail?"

"No, she's..."

"Mom can I have some more cobbler?"

"Of course. You know where the kitchen is. So you were saying, Mr. Shiel?"

"Andrea never stood trial. She was declared insane. I was shot while working the case. My injuries were serious enough that I was placed on permanent medical disability, so I was never able to return for a second look. Until now that is."

"Now?"

"Let's just say that your husband's letter has revived my interest. He expressed what I always thought to be true."

"Which is?"

"That Andrea was framed, that she was innocent of murder." Jared could see Zach's growing alarm. He considered backing off until he could get the boy alone.

"Why now?"

"It seems that Andrea is missing."

"Well! I'm just so amazed because my husband has not mentioned a word to me, which isn't like him. And as I said, it's not his area. He's a tax attorney, corporate law and some forensic accounting. They sometimes call him as an expert witness in white collar fraud cases."

"Is it possible he has a personal interest in the case?"

Jared watched her face. She felt his scrutiny and rose abruptly to retrieve fresh napkins, replacing those they had contributed to clean up the spilled milk. She didn't like the idea of something significant happening without her knowledge. Jared thanked her for the napkin he no longer needed and scraped up the last bit of cobbler dipping the flaky crust in melted ice cream.

"Best cobbler I've ever had. You made the crust yourself. I can tell."

"Yes, I did. The secret is no water. Ice-cold vodka instead."

"I'll remember that. You were going for seconds," Jared reminded, Zach. "Did you change your mind?"

In answer, Zach glared at him and Jared knew his pushing was about to yield dividends. He liked that expectant feeling of satisfaction that came from drawing details from people, which they had no intention of sharing. Often they were details forgotten or not thought significant, but could tighten into sharp relief bringing clarity when it was least expected. Is this what Zach feared? That his mother's suspicious mind would deduce a scenario he was not ready to have known?

"So what occupies you over the summer?" Jared asked.

"Zach goes to school. He'll be a senior this next year," Evelyn offered.

"Really. Play any sports?"

Once again Evelyn answered for her son. "He's quite good at golf and soccer," and Jared knew that her modest pronouncement meant that he was not just good at these sports, but very good.

The boy shot his mother an irritated glare. "And I have a job."

"What do you do?"

"Really, Zach, our guest isn't interested."

"I work at a nursing home," he interrupted his mother. "Crest May Hospital and Research Complex. Ever hear of it?" he asked not waiting for a reply. "I'm doing Community service. Court ordered. I'm almost done."

"Really, Zach! Mr. Shiel is not interested in your life story."

"I'd like to see your dog. What kind is he?" A sardonic tone had crept into Zach's voice and Jared realized the boy had been listening from the top of the stairs and was now needling his mother. Jared had issued a challenge and Zach was pushing back.

"That dog is not coming in this house," Evelyn asserted, anticipating where her son was going. "For one thing he's sick and for another we have a cat."

"The cat's sleeping on your bed upstairs and honestly, Evelyn. If the dog is sick, he should not be closed up in a hot car. Maybe he needs water. What kind of a hostess are you, anyway?"

Jared felt sympathy for Evelyn.

"Well, we must see him." The boy spoke in a contemptuous parody of her vernacular and stood abruptly.

"Zach, you are being horribly rude and I won't have it. Perhaps Mr. Shiel would like another cup of coffee while we wait for your father?"

"Call me, Jared."

"And if you must see the dog, you can put him in the garage and, yes, by all means, get the poor animal some water."

She turned to Jared. "Is that a good idea?" Her expression was a combined apology for her son and for the dogs' unsympathetic reception. Jared had to admire the boy. He knew how to push buttons and had his mother practiced at jumping through the requisite hoops.

Jared turned to Evelyn and smiled, inviting her to smile back. He had already decided that any woman who could make such common fare taste like a gourmet meal deserved the benefit of the doubt.

"I'm not at all offended, Mrs. Goldfarb."

"I'll get the dog," Zach interjected. "What's his name? My friend had a Doberman once. His name was Charlie."

Jared stood, preparing to follow Zach outside and noticing that Mrs. Goldfarb had the pained expression of a mother who had just lost control of a strong willed toddler.

WOOD'S END

CHAPTER TWENTY FOUR

Andrea pressed her ear to the door, but heard nothing. She turned the handle, feeling a thrill of excitement at the risk she was taking with Zach's mother at home and company downstairs. Footsteps entered the foyer. Seconds later the front door opened and then slammed shut. Andrea walked to the window to see what she could.

Jared caught up with Zach as he approached the car. Charlie, who had settled down to wait for him was back on his feet anticipating freedom.

"So," Jared said, pulling the letter from his pocket. "Do I owe this kind invitation to you, or to your father?"

Zach opened his mouth to speak and closed it again. Why couldn't Jared have called first? Dinner with his mother wasn't what he had in mind. It did not bode well for Andrea that this former detective hadn't cooperated with his warning to remain silent.

"You said at dinner that you thought Andrea was framed," Zach probed.

"Andrea... the two of you are on a first name basis?"

"I knew her at Crest May. She was on my end of the hall so naturally it was my job to sometimes feed her. She was over-medicated. We didn't know that Dr. Wodsende was actually her ex-husband. I guess you could say that someone at the hospital helped Dr. Wodsende conceal this information from the staff."

Charlie thrust his head through the open window and sniffed at Zach, his stance alerted, his one good ear fully upright.

275

"Why didn't you call first? I thought you'd call first," Zach continued.

An ear piercing bark shattered the silence as Jared prepared to answer. He looked curiously at Charlie, wondering what was wrong. If there was room, he guessed the dog would be turning in his usual quick circles, which he did when excited, or in this case agitated. If Charlie kept this up, Jared knew he might have to interrupt the interview and attend to his dog.

"I don't understand why you came if all you're going to do is make things worse. I'm not the criminal here, and neither is Andrea."

"Do you know where she is?"

Zach ignored the question. "Over dinner, you said that Andrea was innocent so cut the bad cop routine because I'll tell you what you came to hear, but only if I think you can help us."

Jared smiled, inwardly. He'd accomplished what he wanted. "I'll do what I can. I promise you that."

Zach lowered his head and leaned his body back against the car where he was once more in direct sniffing distance of Charlie. The dog thrust his head through the window and buried his nose in the collar of Zach's shirt.

Zach jumped forward clearly startled. "Something is seriously wrong with your dog."

Jared was about to move Zach away from the car, when they both heard the sound of the garage door opening. A silver BMW glided by. Elias exited the car, giving Jared and Zach a wave, before he was confronted by his wife at the inside garage door. Both watched uneasily as the two talked, their heads together, finally casting Jared a puzzled stare.

"Times running out, Zach. You got me here, so whatever it is you have to say, you need to make it quick. We're about to have company."

Once more Charlie pushed his head out the partial opening of the car window, this time erupting in a desperate cacophony of whines and barks, stopping only to give Jared a pleading glare.

"Rin-Tin-Tin or Lassie or whatever is going crazy. You said he was sick, sounds like he's in pain."

Before Jared could stop him, Zach opened the car door and Charlie bounded out. He moved fast with focused purpose his nose intermittently pressed to the ground.

The visitor's body language had seemed at first angry to Andrea as he waved a piece of paper inches from Zach's face. But for now the conversation was halted as both turned in common pursuit of the dog. Andrea heard the man call out with some authority in a loud voice. "Charlie!" At the sound of that name budding cognition teased at her mind until the thought came. *Was this her Charlie?*

Andrea felt a surge of excitement. She imagined it was a squirrel the dog was after. She had seen their agile red bodies running up and down the trunks of trees, disappearing among the lush summer branches. Sometimes she heard them on the roof, scampering overhead, and once heard Zach's mother call out to her husband from the hallway, "Elias, I think we have another squirrel in the attic." Andrea wanted to contribute her opinion ..."No, just on the roof," but wisely resisted.

No longer able to see the dog, Andrea turned from the window.

Charlie made a frantic dash for the open garage, running toward the door leading to the hallway and kitchen where Elias and Evelyn were conversing in low voices. Evelyn screamed as the dog flew by, his compact body brushing Elias who was thrown off balance. "What the blazes."

Zach sprinted through the door.

They could hear the dog's feet scurry over the hardwood, slipping and gaining traction when he hit the Persian runner in the hall leading to the foyer. Jared caught Evelyn's astonished look as he raced after Zach.

The two sprinted up the stairs nearly catching the dog, their fingers making brief contact with his collar. With sudden abruptness, as though this were his intended destination all along, Charlie stopped and pressed his nose into the opening at the base of Zach's bedroom door.

Less concerned now that Charlie had come to a standstill, and fairly certain of what he would find when the door was opened, Jared scrutinized Zach's face. "Got anything in that room, Son?" he asked gently. "Anything you wouldn't want your parents to find?"

Zach gave Jared a defiant look. "Is this a police dog?" he asked and searched his memory, but didn't believe there was any marijuana in his room. Even before the court hearing he had cleaned out the little that remained and flushed that last stash down the commode. Maybe in a forgotten pocket somewhere, but how could the dog possibly pick-up a scent so far away? It wasn't possible, Zach concluded. There had to be another explanation for Charlie's odd behavior.

"Open the door, Son," Jared instructed.

"Don't you dare open that door" Elias demanded as he rounded the threshold and approached the two with long strides. "I don't know who you are, I never sent you a letter, and right now you are in my home uninvited. My wife tells me you're a cop. If so, I expect to see an ID and a warrant."

"Please, Dad. This isn't what you think!"

In unison all three adults turned expectant eyes in Zach's direction. In that moment he struck them as somehow taller; less like a boy and more like a man.

"Don't say a word, Son."

Evelyn groaned. "Are you going to protect him again? I can't take any more of this. Zach, if you've done something illegal, if you're selling drugs again, I've had it. No more trying to rescue you, and I don't care what your father says. I'm finished! You don't appreciate a thing we do for you!"

"Not now, Evelyn," Elias said failing to look at his wife, his eyes riveted on Jared's face.

"As usual you are both over reacting," Zach said, looking earnestly between both parents.

Charlie still had his nose pressed to the crack at the foot of the door. Now he jumped his full length, scratching the paint around the door handle as he came down barking in excitement.

Elias reached for Jared's arm. "You're leaving right now. And if you refuse, I'll call the police. Evelyn," he directed. "Go into the bedroom and call the authorities."

"No, Dad. I have to tell you what's going on because I can't handle this by myself anymore." Zach looked between his parents confessing, "I wrote the letter. I asked Mr. Shiel to contact you and I'm glad he's here. We need his help."

"Please Zach. Not another word. We'll talk confidentially and I'll do all I can," Elias pleaded. "Maybe you need a rehab facility and if so, your mother and I will find the best."

Evelyn groaned as if struck.

"We don't need to involve a stranger. This isn't the time," Elias concluded.

"You're just afraid I'm in trouble; worried about how that will tarnish your precious reputations. Well, I am in trouble, but not because I've done anything wrong. At least not morally wrong."

His mother stumbled and put out a hand for ballast against the wall; her famous poise shattered. Zach turned to her. "You always think the worst. Did it ever occur to you how hopeless that makes me feel? Like I'm doomed no matter what I do. Like why should I try, because this is all you think of me?"

"Open the door, Zach. Open the door or step aside," Jared declared. He'd heard enough of this domestic dispute, noting that Charlie continued to paw at the door, alternating with his nose at the base and clawing at the handle as if he understood that in turning the knob a last obstacle would be breached.

Zach reached out a hand.

"Wait," his father cautioned, ambivalence lacing his words.

Taking that hesitancy for permission, Zach pushed the door wide. The dog bounded through as the others caught a first glimpse of Andrea who sat cross legged on the bed. She was dressed in red jeans with a tailored short sleeved shirt, which Evelyn immediately recognized as clothing newly added to the donation bag. Her brown hair was caught with a frayed head band that Evelyn had discarded weeks ago.

As though he were jumping into open arms, Charlie landed on the bed, knocking the woman to the floor. His black form stood over her, licking her face, the nub of his tail wagging in unbridled joy. She attempted to sit up and not quite making it, wrapped her arms around the dog's neck pressing her face into the glistening coat with a cry of recognition.

As they walked into the room the dog turned and growled. "It's alright, Charlie. Sit," Andrea commanded with assurance.

In practiced obedience, as if a long separation could never be an issue, the dog turned and sat, positioning himself beside his master as she stood to face them.

Jared felt a stab of jealousy. Charlie was home.

WOOD'S END

PART SIX
CHAPTER TWENTY FIVE
Four Months Later

Anton: A Dead Son; A Wood Son

Woe unto them that call evil good,
and good evil; that put darkness
for light, and light for darkness;
that put bitter for sweet and sweet
for bitter (Isaiah 5: 20)

Anton Kollyn was sixty-eight, but in the right light could pass for forty. He spoke five languages, had a doctorate in romance languages and archeology, and a law degree from Yale. It was not widely known that he could trace his ancestral roots to the early Hapsburg dynasty and connection with many royal houses. He was accepted in places few citizens would risk going and conversely into the most exclusive and diverse scions of society.

Today he wore a silk shirt of dove gray over ragged canvas shorts. Though he looked like he might be vacationing in the south of France he lived in Milan; a place known for its dismal weather patterns. His penthouse, which overlooked the finance district, was lavishly decorated. From here Anton ran his many concerns some of them conveniently situated in office space on the floors below him. Bypassing his butler, if he happened to be in the vicinity, he was known to answer the door completely naked throwing security and decorum to the wind.

Anton rarely left his home and when he did go out it was at night and usually to the opera or a private flight to Paris, Hong Kong, or London. Business associates from New York or Los Angeles, places he had once called home, came to him. He avoided sun damage and was addicted to colonic cleansings. To say that he had an exaggerated fear of death and an unhealthy preoccupation with youth would be an understatement.

His home, of which this was only one, was filled with masterpieces of museum quality many acquired during the largest transfer of wealth the 20th century experienced; World War 11. He even had a few pieces stolen from the vaults of the Vatican; cherished talismans that he considered vested with preternatural power.

Anton expected to live a long time. His youngest son was not so fortunate. Ryan Kollyn, an American athlete and former Olympian had been murdered the year before and though he had rarely seen his son, Anton was increasingly enraged at the thought that Ryan had been taken from him. Something, belonging to him... had been stolen! The families had invested in Ryan, placing him in a media position where he could do them considerable future service. Someone must pay!

"Your call, sir."

Anton switched on the ear piece as his gaze rested on the framed image of his deceased son. His fingers drummed over the latest investigative report which addressed the circumstances surrounding Ryan's murder. It had been compiled in strictest confidence by the security detail at a large bank of which he was an officer and in this report Anton had stumbled across a familiar name; *Shiel*. And now a Jared Shiel was interfering in their attempts to contain Andrea.

"Hello, is this you, Dudley? Are you secure?"

Normally, dealing with a problem like Dudley Wodsende would be beneath Anton. He was too important to embroil himself in the details of family rivalries and their innumerable paranoid exploits. Dudley had long since outgrown any benefit to the families and seeing him as a liability Anton would have ordered him dispensed with. But, he could not ignore the apparent tie between his son's murder and Jared Shiel. Conspiracy had shaped his life and asserting real and made up conspiracies had allowed him to reach the pinnacle of success in both his apparent and hidden fields of endeavor.

The telephone call from Anton Kollyn had the effect of putting Dudley in his place, making him feel vulnerable and small. When they were still living under their father's roof, his elder brother had wielded such power, but no more. Back then Henry had been the golden boy, the heir apparent, but Henry was now a broken shell of what he used to be. There were times, Dudley acknowledged, when Marstead could intimidate and unnerve him, but this man, always.

"Did you hear me, Dudley?"

"Yes, I did. But I can handle this. I can get Andrea back."

"You've put yourself and others at risk. I want you to pack a bag and catch the next flight to Milan. We'll send someone to meet you."

"If I run away, I'll look guilty."

"You already look guilty. Your reckless behavior has focused too much attention, putting your family at risk." There was a sharp intake of breath. "And that spills over as we've seen time and again. We happen to know you're about to be questioned for the assault on this police detective, Jared Shiel. We'd just prefer you not be available."

"Between Marstead and me we have the Andrea situation under control."

"And we'd also like you not to be anywhere near Andrea when her hearing comes due. If something happens to her... well then. It will be easier to reinforce the disintegrating premise that you had nothing at all to do with Stephanie's murder."

"No problem. I won't go near the court house."

"Marstead agrees that you can't be trusted where Andrea is concerned. We need to rein you in."

Dudley was stunned. He hadn't expected Marstead's betrayal.

"You realize he botched the divorce," Dudley went on the attack. "Because of him we could not observe Walpurgis Nacht at the farm. I don't need Marstead's help! He answers to me and if he's not loyal I'll fire him."

"He'd laugh in your face if you tried. Samuel Marstead answers directly to the council and has long since stopped being principally your thing. Now focus, Dudley. Because I do think you are over-wrought. We told you some time ago to get rid of Andrea if she didn't come around to our way of thinking, and you deceived us into believing she was fully cooperative. You're lucky to be alive."

"I am head of this family. I say what will happen and what won't," Dudley tested.

Anton shifted topics. "There may be another viable candidate."

Silence gathered momentum as Dudley digested this unexpected news, proof that his secret fears could be realized, hypersensitive to the idea that another could follow in the footsteps of the perfectly possessed, laying claim to unfathomable power in this world and the next.

"If you're talking about my brother, the judge..."

Dudley thought of the priest in Andrea's hospital room. In a clash of wills he had been humiliated and with lost time, could not recall all that had taken place. That he had been driven out, while the priest remained, still unnerved him.

Dudley assuaged his anger with the knowledge that someday he would see the tables turned. It would no longer be his kind hiding in the shadows, living in fear of exposure. During a time to come, persecution of Jews and Christians would be accepted, even encouraged. In that altered reality, in a changed geopolitical climate, Christians and Jews would no longer be the powerful instruments of restraint and opposition. Evil would reign.

Dudley knew that some Christians believed they would be rescued in what was called the Rapture of the Church. Those with a mere intellectual attachment would be left behind, easy pickings, fair game.

Rumors abounded about people escaping the cultish influence of the families. These men and women, in numbers not known, had formed a network of dissention, laying the groundwork with resources and tools intended to arm those people who would come to faith after the Rapture of the Church. Dudley had been present as some were captured and sacrificed. He had heard their outlandish claims shouted at the moment that they were neutralized, believing their last words the mere pain ravaged retort of lunatics.

Only now, having come face to face with Guido, having been on the losing end of a skirmish, Dudley was no longer so complacent. He had underestimated the opposition. In the name of... he wouldn't say that name wielded by Guido. But, against his will, it slipped beyond every defense, program, and device planted in Dudley and resonated with a soft power that for a second... just a second, constricted his heart in bitter-sweet longing. At the name of *Jesus Christ of Nazareth who came in the flesh*, demons fled. That Jesus traversed time and space to become the substance of humanity, while remaining every bit the divine... did that give God's Son and therefore the priest Guido an advantage? His god could do no more than indwell flesh already created; flesh with the potential to choose life and light over death and darkness.

The way of the righteous is like the first gleam of dawn, which shines ever brighter until the full light of day. But the way of the wicked is like complete darkness. Those who follow it have no idea what they are stumbling over (Proverbs 4: 18, 19).

"What else can you tell me?" Dudley asked, swallowing his discomfort, frightened by his thoughts and hoping they hadn't been discerned by the person on the other end of the phone.

"Your father would not be proud. Sybil has been a huge disappointment. Henry is useless, and because of your obsession with a woman, you diminish the mantle you were born to wear. If not for Marstead, your family would have sunk back into the lackluster worship of gnomes, reading tarot cards and holding the occasional séance. I can only say that I expected more from you, Dudley."

Something had shifted in the power base of blind support Dudley had always enjoyed. Had Marstead, who wasn't bloodline, taken over? And how was that possible?

"Have you forgotten that Andrea is not just any woman?"

"I forget nothing," Anton said, his statement laced with salient malice.

Many of Dudley's ancestors had been burned at the stake for practicing the dark arts. Satanists, they worshiped the templar's Baphomet and the Dragon and awaited the third piece of an unholy trinity... the antichrist of mammoth power. They believed in a form of reincarnation that placed them back in their own families in the following generation. Each family revered the blood line traced back to the Middle Ages and the knight's templar and some even further back to pagan roots; boasting connection to the Hebrew tribes of Dan and Ephraim, which were overcome and swallowed by the detested practices of the people Yahweh had told them to destroy.

For this reason the twelve prime families were invested in protecting inherited wealth. They chose their women for breeding and their careers for accumulating more of the same. In the advent of technological advantages, with communication no longer a hindrance, the various families had seen this as proof that the current age would soon end while the "little age," their age begun. What else did the caller know that he didn't?

"You said that Andrea would be the mother of my child. You told me she was destined, handpicked," Dudley continued in the tone of a petulant child. "Our son would be the architect of the last great battle, perfectly possessed like no other the world has ever seen."

"We thought so. The charts proclaimed it."

"For the last six hundred years, the various families, previously united in agreement, are suddenly wrong? Is that what you're telling me?" Dudley did his best to contain his emotions. It wouldn't do to lose control now.

"The new theory is that pi is arbitrary. So naturally we applied this trianglature formula to astrological and family charts, with the idea of taking a fresh look at previous calculations. This is still under review, but the revised data does indicate that events are lining up faster than we thought. Wrong is right, bitter is sweet, and now it seems a triangle is sometimes a circle or a square; the fixed pi no longer sacrosanct. We can only wonder. What will fall next?" Anton laughed. His voice was a gleeful cackle of derision.

"Meaning what?" Dudley demanded.

"If the new data is correct, and we are still examining the charts, then the prince of perdition would need to be older than any child you could produce. He would need to be either approaching manhood or already grown into the vehicle he will soon be."

"I don't think so," Dudley proclaimed in a menacing tone.

"What if I told you there *is* another child, soon to be fourteen and not the child of a demon handler, but virgin space? The next best thing and perhaps, all along, the plan we could never quite fathom," the gravelly voice entombed the words in a parody of reverence.

"What are you saying?" Dudley demanded.

"With no help from the families, with no accompanying sacrifice of the mother, he was born at the summer solstice on the precise hour."

"I don't believe this can be true," Dudley asserted.

"You know Mario's lineage. We have carefully examined the mother's. She is descended from eastern European royalty; my branch of the family tree. I doubt even she knows to what family she belongs and yet, cosmic forces worked to comingle two powerful families in producing an heir apparent. We could not have planned it any better ourselves," Anton replied. "In fact we tried and failed with Andrea, now didn't we? Time to cut our losses," he finished not sounding in the least perturbed now that a new candidate with such impeccable credentials had dropped into their laps. A boy connected to his own family tree.

As intended, Dudley took the last words personally.

"May I remind you that Andrea's child would be a descendent of the Gog and Magog kings? It remains to be seen, which child has the stronger claim. In my mind it could only be the blood closest to the perfectly possessed."

"Be careful, Dudley. Be very careful."

Dudley shifted subjects. "And if Andrea dies before she can have such a child, all that work and generations of planning die with her. I want her!" he demanded.

"And therein lays the crux of your problem. Arranged marriages rarely fail, but yours did. More often than not, our people marry without ever divulging their true identity. Spouses are kept in the dark while we maintain the upper hand, operating with full impunity behind a shield of normalcy. You've never learned to cut your losses. Ours is a life of accommodation. We fit in; we blend and behind the scenes we launch armies and manipulate currency, commodities, kings and sultans. We control communication avenues and prefer a military dictatorship on the assumption that no one else can hold the world together. Why do you think we are such proponents of the UN; our invention. Only occasionally do we encounter a leader we can't bring around to some portion of our agenda. So you see Dudley, this myopic fixation of yours has derailed your usefulness."

"You gave me Andrea and then you pawned off a pale substitute in Stephanie. Was that so I wouldn't catch on about the possibility of another child?"

Anton was disgusted. Dudley Wodsende was a complete liability, entirely expendable. He was so obsessed with Andrea that not a word of what he'd said had penetrated. If not for his need to learn more about Jared Shiel and any connection to his murdered son and this very odd confluence of Dudley and Jared Shiel being focused on Andrea, well... Anton would allow Dudley to live just a bit longer. Anton shifted tactics.

"You failed to get rid of Andrea as directed, and now she's seeing a psychologist we have no sway over. We can't even get Sybil through the front door. Soon Marstead will have two or three people on site, but all this takes time."

"Is this doctor religious?" Dudley asked.

"He goes to one of those useless churches that trade power for social acceptance and status. We've hacked into his computer, keeping up with the therapy notes. Andrea must not be allowed to remember earlier connections to Wood's End Farm or to the family. But, this Dr. Martin is more inclined each day to trust what she tells him."

"Is she close?" Dudley asked.

"She's very close and this Dr. Martin is quite skilled at working with recovered memory; with those alters that hold the key to too much information. If she'd been kept away from that farm she wouldn't have made contact, been stirred up... You lost control of Andrea and you lost sight of your first responsibility."

"First of all..."

Anton hated sentences that began with this juvenile phrase. Dudley had no superior talent for conversation.

"First of all I didn't lose the farm. Marstead gave it away. I wasn't even in the room!"

"And whose fault was that?"

"Not mine. And second, it remains to be seen if I've really lost Andrea. And lastly, if you've ordered her death, you'll have to cancel the contract." Dudley paused, letting suspense build. "Andrea is having my son. Not even you could risk the dragon's wrath if this child is the intended host. And the fact is, until history reveals the true son of perdition, no one knows. It could be you. It could even be that exorcist priest, Guido."

"What have you done?"

"I wasn't the only member of the family who invested heavily in Andrea as the dragon's choice. If I'm wrong, you're all wrong."

"What have you done?"

"What I was told to do by my father before he was executed on the streets of North Adams. What you commissioned me to do with dual ceremonies on two continents. Andrea is to have the child that will stand firm in the firestorm to come, supreme architect of the last great battle. We all agreed that she met each qualification with impeccable accuracy. She's having a son; my son."

There was a sharp intake of breathe from the other end of the phone encouraging Dudley to press what he foolishly imagined an advantage.

"I can tell you it will not be Mario's fourteen year old whelp of a bastard."

"Make no mistake," the voice on the other end proclaimed. "The other candidate is every bit a Wood Son and could very well be the incarnation of your father... the perfectly possessed."

"Henry forfeited his rights when he lost his wife. He insulted all of us when he let her slip away with my nephews, the last two potential candidates. This leaves only me. I was the one everyone discounted until it was clear Henry wasn't up to the challenge. I am what you made me."

"Oh, Dudley, what can I say? Always you go too far. You'll come to Milan. We'll talk when you get here." The words were conciliatory, the directive no request.

Paranoid suspicion that had always existed where his elder brother was concerned raised hackles of anxiety. "Does Henry know about the child?"

"We think not. However, we have newly assessed his status. Readers have picked up the scent of a possible treachery. Marstead will be watching him closely."

"I could call, Henry. Feel him out for you."

"We'd prefer not."

"Is Mario aware that he is the father of such a child?"

"He makes an annual drop of funds. He's done so, ever since he took up company with the exorcist traitor. Very soon Mario and this other, whose name will be forever trampled in filth down the chronicles of time for his chosen path, will be found and dealt with."

Dudley's face contorted in an expression of focused intensity. He would join the leadership in Milan. Clearly he needed to reestablish himself and there was now the issue of Mario's son.

With Mario and Guido hunted, and Henry not long for this world, the boy would need a family member to mentor him. Should there be a tragic accident resulting in an untimely death; well, there was always he and Andrea's son to fill the vacant throne occupied by a long line of oppressive, sadistic dictators. Each one, including Herod and Hitler, hoped the prophetic mantle of universal authority would fall on them. They schooled themselves in the arcane arts, connecting with powerful occultists, assigning signs and devices only to discover in the end that they were mere prototypes, a vile foretaste of what would come.

To squander the Wood Son inheritance and all that exquisite, concentrated power, with legions of demons and willing vassals to command, was to leave a vacuum that Dudley felt only he was strong enough to fill, or so dictated the ravenous Wood Son ego.

Dudley and his caller each made the profane gesture, hanging up the phone in near unison.

"It's me," the caller announced with no preamble of hello. Momentarily shaken, Henry anticipated what the caller wanted, buying time to settle surprise.

"You should know why I'm calling," Dudley tested.

Henry reached for the most obvious reason. "I've had correspondence from Marstead, letting me know you're in Milan on extended hiatus. Per instructions I've assigned myself to Andrea's hearing. I'm ready for tomorrow."

"How's security at your house?"

"I could care less. They can listen and spy to their hearts content," Henry admitted.

"I'm not calling about tomorrow's proceedings, although I will be interested to know how my wife looks."

"What is it that you want?" Henry asked his brother, deciding not to remind him of his current marital status.

"It seems that Guido and Mario are alive and well."

"The family would know better than I."

"In all these years you haven't heard from them?"

"No," Henry lied, fully aware that Dudley's talent as an intrinsic was almost nonexistent. It was he that had inherited their father and grandfather's "reader" abilities.

As the eldest, with the pressure of all that concentrated attention focused in his direction, Henry had only wished to fade into the background, concealing the power at his disposal. In an odd twist of genetic caprice, those gifts had passed to Guido who had sought solace and answers in the one Christian denomination that offered the celibate life he felt obligated to adopt.

The irony was not lost on Henry. Guido was a powerful exorcist; all he'd inherited turned from the inverted, to the Christ side of light."

"What about your wife?" Dudley persisted.

"I feel certain she is dead. I have no other sense of her."

Henry was filled with disdain for his brother who could no longer discern the difference between ego driven enticement furthered by demons and his own thoughts. Henry caught himself. He had been born into the dysfunctional imprisonment of a cult, and now ambivalence had erupted into a dangerous rebellion. A jaded skeptic, he could no longer say what he believed.

"I have it on good authority that you're a grandfather."

"How would I know such a thing?" Henry questioned. He was unsettled at the possibility and invited the image of a grandchild to settle, to germinate and take form. He would need to probe for the truth of it.

"You do realize that if there is a challenge to Andrea's child through a pretender, and neither of us has exercised a guiding hold on that boy, the lesser families could gain strength and we might become obsolete. We might even die out."

Henry hoped their blood line would die out. Some of Hitler's extended family and the descendents of high ranking Nazi's had made sure they never reproduced. Guido clearly felt the same. Isn't this the reason Guido was so committed to celibacy? And now this! *Could it be that Mario has been less than honest?*

Preparing to say goodbye, Dudley made the profane gesture which, unless they were in public, was always returned. From long habit Henry moved his hand, but then inexplicably he dropped his forearm to his thigh, feeling a sudden revulsion. Slowly his fingers uncurled, palm open, waiting. For what?

There was a sudden change in what Henry felt from Dudley. An enticing familiar had dropped a maggot of truth into the quagmire of Dudley's mind. "The council, including Anton Kollyn, has questioned your loyalty. A little advice, brother. Beware of sentiment. Old age inclines one to such extremes. I sense ambivalence. You've grown weak."

"Weak? I'm an old man," Henry deflected. "In the last years I've aged faster than is normal. My hearing is faulty, I have arthritis, I can't sleep and I don't always make the bathroom in time. You can do me a huge favor, Dudley. Tell Anton, I'm ready to die."

"No one is ready to die," Dudley asserted.

Dudley hadn't told Henry about the clash of spiritual forces at Andrea's bedside. Nor that he had lost this first round or that Guido looked very much like his striking mother and nothing like their side of the family. Why hadn't he known immediately who Guido was? Why hadn't he recognized his nephew, as the dark powers he supposedly possessed should have revealed?

Doubt was a ravenous worm. Henry's wife had succeeded in escaping the cults' control and, if leadership could be trusted, this was a rare feat of accomplishment. But, after seeing Guido for himself, Dudley wondered if such defections and escapes had been under-reported. A close observer of Marstead's dealings for many years, he knew that outcomes were often concealed and bad news repackaged for consumption. It wouldn't do to let others get similar ideas. Freedom of thought and human autonomy was a powerful intoxicant, its value only fully understood by those seriously threatened with the theft of such liberty.

The gardens at dawn were shrouded in mist which hovered above the grounds in a whitish haze. Henry stood in the light of the door, cutting shears in hand and watched until the stone wall grew clearer and the emerging color of his roses took on shape.

Despite the promised Indian summer, Judge Capra shivered. He knelt in the wet soil, his pajama bottoms immediately soaked at the knees. Henry selected each stem with a view in mind for the vase that would perch on his desk at the courthouse. With care he laid the flowers on a newspaper spread out beside him. Soon he would be pruning in preparation for the long New England winter. He'd cover the mounds with new mulch and a fine layering of cheese cloth.

Today would prove difficult, and his roses, the cultivation of which gave him pleasure, would be a reminder that as hours closed off the day, the gardens would remain to welcome him home. Henry was no longer as confident in his skills and abilities. More and more he forgot important dates and tasks, and felt he was finally living up to the cults' perception of him as seriously impaired by conscience.

Intent on cutting each stem and slightly deaf he failed to hear his name whispered. Nor had he heard the hollow snap of dry milkweed stalks from across the wall that heralded the approach of an intruder.

"Hello, Father, didn't want to startle you. Tried to make a little noise."

It could not be. "Guido?" Henry squinted trying to focus.

"Yes, it's me."

"What are you doing here? This can't be safe."

"I wanted to see you one last time, to give you this."

Guido extended an envelope which Henry accepted. "You could have posted it, you know. And if you didn't trust the mail, there are other avenues."

"You're not as sharp as you used to be, Father. I've been in the city for the last six months with my team. Each time I followed you, you failed to notice."

"Don't tell me. I don't want to know."

"There's something I need you to do for us."

"I can't. It's not safe."

Henry's greedy eyes scrutinized his son, almost disbelieving the unexpected gift of his being there. The body was toned as he remembered, and he wore jeans and an all-weather jacket, though his hair was graying prematurely at the temple.

Henry felt awash in self-pity. He felt certain he would not be welcomed in heaven or the bottomless pit where the cult taught he would stay a year worshipping satan. He would then be reincarnated back into his own family. In his revised way of thinking Henry could not imagine a worse fate. There was so much to regret and so much to fear. He had believed that Heaven was vastly over rated and his coming year in Hell just a continuation of the same frightful existence, but on a larger, more fascinating cosmic plane.

"You have a case ahead of you today, I've come about that," Guido interrupted his fathers' thoughts.

"If I make any recommendation, other than what they want, I'll raise too much suspicion. What little trust I enjoyed no longer exists. They'll think of you and Mario."

"This concerns Elias Goldfarb. We need him to retain a certain position over Andrea's finances. This is a small risk, one that will be understood given the larger concessions you shouldn't hesitate to make. You'll be given a convenient excuse at the suggestion of one, Jared Shiel."

"Jared Shiel? Of the Shiel family in Woods End?" Henry asked, somewhat astonished.

"The very same," Guido replied.

"Well, there is a seamlessness to that, don't you think?"

"I've not heard the full story," Guido responded.

"Your mother never told you? She didn't speak of such things?" he mused. "I miss her, you know. I think of her each day."

"I wish we had time to talk about the past, Father, but we don't. There are a lot of questions I'd like to ask, but it's nearly time for you to get showered and dressed for the day ahead. You've had someone watching the house. They've gone for now, but they'll be back."

"What can I do?"

"Just don't kick Jared Shiel out of your courtroom, even if invited to do so by something Sybil says. He won't have an essential reason for being there, but I need you to overlook that."

Stiff after kneeling on the damp ground, Henry stumbled and Guido reached a hand out to steady him. The two regarded one another for a long moment. Henry felt the greater connection with Guido. Mario had been so young when they left.

"Where is your brother right now?" he asked.

"We'll meet up again in a few weeks," Guido answered.

"Dudley called me. He dropped a bombshell so I have to ask. Could you possibly be the father of a child?"

"As you know, I've taken a vow of celibacy. I've not known that kind of intimacy, so not likely."

"What about Mario?"

"I asked him before we disappeared. There was a woman he was quite attached to. I never met her. As far as I know he never looked back."

"Can you investigate the possibility of Mario and this woman having a child? The boy would be about fourteen. Can you do so without telling Mario of your interest?"

"Sadly, if you're taking this seriously I must do the same."

"I feel it is true. And of course the families would be salivating at the possibility and especially because Dudley and Andrea were such a disappointment, unable to produce the child they expected; until now that is. Dudley called last night testing and prodding, jealous of any competition. If Mario does have a son, that boy might not have long to live."

"I'll look into it right away. I've made arrangements to keep Andrea's child safe, at least for a time," Guido offered.

"Could you bring yourself to kill a child?" Henry asked.

"I believe in a God who is powerful to rescue, heal, and deliver. I would never take a life if I could help it."

"If that boy exists... well, you can't let them..."

"If it's true, and I can hardly believe Mario would conceal something so important," Guido cut off his father. "This news would complicate my plans, but I'll figure something out. They won't have him."

"Do you trust Mario?" Henry asked.

"There is another, more important reason why I've come," Guido said, not answering his father's question. "Whatever you've done that you imagine cannot be forgiven, is a lie of satan. Jesus Christ can forgive anything. I want you to take the contents of this envelope very seriously. If you ever loved me, you'll read and consider every word. I'd like to think we can be united in Heaven as we haven't been on earth."

"I'm feeling my age, Guido. Death approaches. How can I refuse my son when I've dreamed you would someday need my help? Yes, I'll read what you've written."

"Thank you."

Henry changed topics. "I'll let Jared Shiel stay in the courtroom and I'll do what I can to be sure Andrea has access to those funds. But you should know. The family considers every penny theirs. And for reasons you know very well, they'll fight tooth and nail to get that farm back."

Before Henry could protest, Guido moved to hug him, his brittle bones melting into the embrace. Henry withdrew first.

Guido tapped the envelope still held by his father. "I want you to know that I'm grateful for what you did for me and for Mario. I know the power of the various families and the hold of that generational curse. You were brave once. You fought for our freedom and sacrificed yourself. For the prize of eternity you can be brave again."

"You have your mother to thank for all that."

"It wouldn't have been possible without your help. As an intrinsic attached to her by love, you had the power to find her anytime you wanted. I know more than you think, Father. I love you."

Henry watched until Guido was out of sight, melting into the tree line beyond the field. He held the roses in one hand and with the other he clutched the envelope tight to his chest, tears coursing down wrinkled cheeks.

Jared startled when he opened the car door. He had come to retrieve a worn canvas satchel and found a large manila envelope waiting on the seat. Only a professional, in the truest sense of the word, could have come and gone from the garage of his Boston townhouse as he slept upstairs. It was a clear failure of both alarm and dog. If there had been time, he would have reviewed the security tape, but felt certain there would be nothing to see that he could use. This would have to wait. He was due at Andrea's hearing.

Moving briskly, Jared carried the envelope back into the house. He laid it on the kitchen counter and gingerly peeled back the flap, shaking out the contents, shifting them with the tip of his pen for a first cursory look. Inside there was an investigative report and several files. Jared smiled halfway through the first page. Laying this aside he found a marriage license and what appeared to be a ring box. Inside was a diamond wedding set and a man's matching band. Engraved on the inside were the words, *forever yours*.

Jared considered what he had before him. He guessed the rings had been picked up at a pawn shop which meant there was a likely record of the purchase. Jared flashed back to two previous comments made by Ed and Dr. Betsy Bloom. Both had asked if he was getting married and referenced a listing in the paper. Someone had gone to considerable lengths to mark him a pawn in quite the elaborate scheme to solve Andrea's immediate problems. Trouble was they failed to consult him. Whoever it was didn't know him very well.

Charlie came over, his nose on a level with the counter and sniffed about. "All the good you did us last night," Jared said. Sensing something amiss Charlie barked. "A little late don't you think?"

Jared gathered the contents of the folder and slipped all into the satchel he used as a kind of brief case. Inside was a gun and license to carry permit. He now went to a wall safe well hidden from view and removed a stack of bills.

On his way out the door Jared stopped and eyed the ring case. He balked at the idea of being used by someone more skilled at macro-gamesmanship than he was; someone who had contrived quite the creative solution to Andrea's immediate problem and with blind confidence that he would cooperate. He picked up the marriage certificate and judged it legit, right down to the forged signature. He wasn't likely to be anyone's pawn.

Then, almost against his will Jared wondered what Thor would be up to later in the day and if he'd ever performed a hasty marriage ceremony. Just as he had the Miranda shebang down he imagined Thor, in his part time job of minister, would have his bit of, *do you take this woman to be your...* memorized.

Jared had alternately avoided and also wished for the right woman to come into his life. He'd only been in love once and that was with Nora Dillihunt; water under the bridge, lost love, heartache and pain. Falling in love with Nora had been safe since it was clear she was in love with another man. And here was another sham-excuse to get his toe in the water. Jared appreciated the irony.

Alert and wary Jared backed his car into the ally and turned into Beacon Hill traffic. He had planned to walk. It was a beautiful Indian summer day and only a short jaunt to the Court House. But now... change of plans. He would need the car because there was quite the brilliant plot about to unfold. He was cast in the unfamiliar role of marinate while a stranger whom he hoped to soon make the acquaintance of, played that of puppet-master. A role reversal was in order.

WOOD'S END

CHAPTER TWENTY SIX

The wicked, through the pride of his countenance, will not seek after God; God is not in all his thoughts (Psalm 10: 4).

The chill of autumn lay trails of gold and auburn ankle deep in the gutters, framing the city sidewalks in the season's last show of decaying splendor. From the window of the high-ceilinged conference room, on the third floor of the Suffolk County Court House, Andrea studied the near barren branches. She wore an ankle length skirt with a loose fitting bolero jacket that did little to conceal the fact that she was pregnant.

A nurse, out of uniform and yet distinguishable for the name badge draped around her neck, guided her charge toward the center of the room. That Andrea was fragile or in need of such hovering assistance was not the impression Elias wanted the judge to have of his client.

Feeling the same, Jared stood to greet Andrea. He kissed her cheek and shutting out the nurse escorted her to a seat next to Elias.

Henry was anxious to get started. He lowered his gavel, the act itself supercilious in these proceedings, and yet setting the tone for what would follow. The resounding echo had the desired effect, calling the state's psychologist and Andrea's mother from the far corner where they had been arguing in low tones. The doctor took a seat beside Andrea, a chair that Sybil had attempted to claim for herself. Affronted, she looked around the table before settling on the one remaining choice which placed her across from her daughter with the narrow expanse of the conference table between them. The court reporter, at a small table to the left of the judge, straightened in her chair. All was ready.

"Ms. Wodsende, do you understand why we are gathered here today?"

"Yes, Your Honor."

"In your own words, can you state the reason?"

Andrea looked directly at the judge. "To determine if I am no longer in need of supervision and hospitalization."

"And... to determine if your release would pose a danger to yourself or others. Is that your understanding?"

"Yes, it is."

"Mr. Elias Goldfarb is here on your behalf. In my view this is unnecessary in such an informal hearing only to determine competency. Do you want Mr. Goldfarb to remain?"

"Yes, I do."

"We are not here to determine your guilt or innocence in the matter that brought you to the attention of the criminal justice system in the first place. You cannot be tried twice for the same crime, even murder. However, for the record, are you indeed responsible in any manner, for the premature and violent death of Stephanie Wodsende?"

The question caught Elias off guard. He opened his mouth to protest, but Andrea was already speaking.

"I remember very little of that night. I recall leaving my home in Woods End and being concerned about Charlie. I didn't want to leave him alone in the house."

"Charlie?"

"My dog, Your Honor."

"What else do you recall?"

"I don't know. Running from the bedroom with someone chasing me. Fragments of things, but nothing significant. Dr. Martin," she turned her head and smiled at the psychologist that had been treating her over the last few months. He was a godsend and she liked and trusted him. "Dr. Martin assures me that I'll remember everything in due time. I have a kind of selective amnesia, the effects of which were compounded by the drugs I was given and didn't need.

Contrary to speculation, I am certain I was not jealous of Stephanie. I was glad to be divorced from my former husband."

Judge Henry Capra prepared to speak, but Andrea continued and Elias wished he had warned her better not to volunteer information, but to say as little as possible.

"I'm hoping to continue my treatment with Dr. Martin." Andrea cast Sybil a defiant look. "He's an expert on recovered memory. We talk about recent events, but also repressed childhood memory."

Elias spoke up. "Your Honor, if I may, I believe I can shed some light on your original question. Phone records clearly show that my client never harassed her former husband as claimed. She also did not phone Stephanie Wodsende in the days prior to her death. On the contrary, it was Stephanie that called my client, ostensibly to meet with her in order to shed some light on the danger Dudley Wodsende posed to herself and her minor daughter."

"As I said, we are not here to rehash the guilt or innocence of Andrea Wodsende in regard to that crime." The judge shifted his attention.

"Doctor Martin, you submitted a report which I have read. You recommend that your patient be released from the care of the State Hospital and returned to society. You recommend no supervision and yet I have a petition submitted by her mother requesting temporary oversight of her daughter. Would that be an amicable arrangement, while her counseling progresses? Because, considering the heinous nature of the crime, I'm reluctant to see Ms. Wodsende entirely unsupervised?"

Elias spoke up again. "Your Honor, Mrs. Bryant never visited her daughter at any time that she was in the state's care. She turned every decision over to Dr. Dudley Wodsende who we believe was administering anti-psychotic drugs she did not need in order to induce..."

"Yes, well," the judge interrupted. "That would be information for the civil case of which we are not concerned today." He shuffled some papers. "Furthermore these allegations seem preposterous. Dudley Wodsende is a well respected doctor whose generosity to worthy causes is well known."

"Yes, and Dr. Wodsende has fled the country rather than be questioned about new allegations regarding the murder. He is also wanted for questioning in the assault on former police detective, Jared Shiel, who is with us today. Boston PD has reopened that case."

But, Judge Capra appeared not to be listening. He had found the document he was looking for.

"I am in possession of a letter from Samuel Marstead, attorney for the widower. He explains that due to the stress of various personal losses and the recent attack on his client's character, Dr. Wodsende has sequestered himself in a sanatorium in an attempt to restore his well being. Sounds reasonable to me after everything the poor man has suffered."

Judge Capra turned to Sybil. As he engaged her in conversation, Jared looked carefully between the two. He noted a remarkable physical resemblance. Characteristics that may have set them apart in youth were now much diminished with age. For the occasion Grace had dressed in a tailored suit with felt hat perched at the back of her head, and without the distraction provided by overdone makeup, Jared was certain a familial connection was worth exploring.

"Mrs. Bryant is it?"

"Call me Grace, Your Honor. Everyone does."

The judge smiled for the first time. "Grace, did you see any evidence that your son-in-law was harming your daughter in any way?"

"Dudley loved my daughter. I was like a mother to both of them. Even after the unhappy divorce my son-in-law continued to care for me, an old lady. He and Stephanie had me to the house for dinner on numerous occasions. A week did not go by that Dudley didn't call to ask how I was doing or if I needed anything. I don't believe he would have harmed my baby girl."

Until now Andrea had followed Elias's instructions. He had warned her that she needed to communicate an impression of confidence. This was important to achieving their mutual goal of winning her independence, and especially from Sybil. But now, at her mother's words Andrea shrank back in her seat, adopting a childlike pose of withdrawal. Jared smiled at her in an attempt at reassurance, but if she saw him at all, it was no longer evident.

Sybil continued. "Dudley offered to act as her doctor, simply to ensure my baby girl would receive the very best care and to save any additional expense, which I could not afford."

Andrea stole a hand to her face as though to ward off a blow. She shifted in her seat, turning away from Sybil and Judge Capra, until she was almost leaning against Dr. Martin's shoulder.

The judge turned in her direction. "Is it true that you and your mother are estranged at present and that you are refusing her visits to the state hospital where you are currently remanded?"

It was clear to Jared that the Judge was doing his best to insert every negative phrase possible into the record. If no one corrected him, it would seem that all agreed, giving credence to the intimation of Andrea as not only guilty of murder, but also impaired. Judge Capra's direct question forced Andrea to turn in his direction. Her positioning no longer shut out her mother.

"Well," the Judge demanded. "Is it true that you and your mother are estranged at present?"

"Your Honor, I do believe I can clarify," Dr. Martin spoke up.

"Please don't interrupt unless I address you directly. Now Ms. Wodsende, are you refusing your mother's visits and her attempts to work out this family squabble?"

"Yes, Your Honor, I am."

"Why?"

"I was afraid of Dudley. That my mother continued a relationship with him against my wishes and then concealed it, made me certain she did not... does not, have my best interest at heart. And then...well...she let my ex-husband treat me, though I was completely helpless. This is hard to reconcile with..."

"Do you recall that Dr. Wodsende ever harmed you during that time?"

Andrea seemed surprised by the question. "I don't actually remember anything from that period."

Elias's impatience was evident. He looked at the Judge expecting to be acknowledged. The judge ignored him. In pre-hearing correspondence it was made clear that anything Andrea might contribute would be considered unreliable due to her faulty memory, in which case she didn't need representation. Elias had gotten the Judge's message, but felt more damage could be done without his presence. Andrea was strong in some areas while remaining fragile in others. She needed representation.

"Do you have something to say, Mr. Goldfarb?"

"Your Honor is aware that my client was dangerously overmedicated to the extent that she was in a chemically induced, nearly catatonic fug state for almost two years. As the medication was withdrawn she improved at a remarkable pace, proof that she did not need such aggressive treatment."

"And your point is?"

"My point is *access*, Your Honor. Dr. Wodsende had access to Andrea in the emergency room immediately after the murder, access to her when she was transferred to the State Hospital, and even greater access while at Crest May Hospital and Research Complex. Mrs. Bryant insisted on his involvement which interfered with the state's oversight. This, despite the fact that, while still in good health my client filed an order of protection against her former husband and expressed fear and distrust of him on numerous occasions."

"I read your brief, Mr. Goldfarb and I find that your allegations make fascinating reading. Your son's claims support the equally fantastic allegations of a charge nurse who was fired from her job for mismanaging the circumstances surrounding Ms. Wodsende's escape from the nursing home, but..."

"She was not fired."

"Did I ask you to interrupt me?"

"No," Elias replied. "But we wouldn't want erroneous information impugning the record. The employee in question left her position due to sudden illness, but has signed a notarized statement to the effect that..."

"Information of that nature does not concern this proceeding." The judge regarded Andrea. "I read here that you are pregnant. How is that possible when it is claimed you were catatonic?"

Andrea's hand drifted to her belly in a protective gesture. "I can't answer that, Your Honor."

"I imagine you'll be filing a law suit against the nursing home and the state? Is it your claim that you were raped?"

Elias interjected. "This is the twenty first century Judge. I think you would agree that intercourse without the consent of one of the parties does qualify as rape. There will be a DNA test which must be postponed due to the unstable pregnancy and the level of drugs administered during the first few weeks of gestation. We're told that Ms. Wodsende should experience no undue stress. For that reason there are no plans to push her just now to remember what doesn't come naturally."

"Helpless? So you say, counselor. We don't know the length of time that her meds were withheld. And, as we all know, recovered memory is notoriously unreliable," Judge Capra mumbled this last under his breath, causing the court reporter to pause in the midst of typing.

Andrea's psychologist spoke up. "We have yet to determine when and who fathered this child. We won't know until the baby is born, since her obstetrician has insisted we not risk the procedure that would allow an early DNA test."

"And who, may I ask would you be testing?"

"Dr. Dudley Wodsende for one. We'll test Zach Goldfarb merely to rule him out, although he has passed a lie detector test."

"That would be your son?" the Judge inquired peering over his reading glasses with furrowed brow at Elias.

"Yes."

"And you do not consider it a conflict of interest that you now represent Ms. Wodsende."

"I naturally wouldn't, Your Honor, if charges were pending against her or my son. I am here today as Andrea's financial advisor and friend and to be sure her claims of mental competency, as supported by her psychologist, are given full consideration."

"And why wouldn't they be?" The judge looked at his watch before turning toward Sybil.

"Yes, Your Honor?" she answered as though avidly awaiting her turn to speak.

"Are you able to provide a safe and suitable home for your daughter?"

"Yes, Your Honor. We have a house in Woods End. We would live there and I would cook and clean for her. I'd make sure she takes her medication and does not get into any more trouble. And when my grandson comes, I can help there also."

"I can see from your letter to me that, although paternity is in doubt, you're looking forward to being a grandmother?"

"Oh, yes, Your Honor. I'm thrilled. I've been buying baby clothes and thinking up names for the little man." She almost giggled.

Jared looked down the length of the table and studied Sybil's profile. For the first time she appeared not to be acting a part. A woman with no maternal instinct, who would not allow her daughter to call her Mother lest someone think they were not sisters, was positively gleeful about welcoming a grandson. Furthermore she had named the sex of the child when not even Andrea had that information. Jared made another mental note to an already growing list. Upon leaving the court room he had a lot of work to do.

"You have proposed the idea that you will be your daughter's court appointed guardian?"

Sybil spoke in a little girl voice. "I'd be her Mom and she would be my baby girl. We'd get reacquainted. Without the interference of these other people, she would love me and learn to trust me again. They've turned her against me; her one and only mother. Instead of helping to reason her fears away, they've encouraged her to think of me as..." Sybil gulped back a sob.

"Take your time, Mrs. Bryant."

"To my face, just now while standing at that window," Sybil pointed to the corner where she and the state's doctor had been conversing before Judge Capra opened the hearing. "Doctor Martin called me toxic. He said I have a toxic relationship with my baby girl! I'm not stupid. Everyone knows that toxic means poisonous. So I ask you?" Sybil looked around the table, pleading for sympathy. "How is that possible? What can that mean except that he intends to come between a mother and her child?"

Sybil glared at Dr. Martin. "And not *that* doctor. I've arranged for a new woman doctor. That one invited me to pour my heart out to him, acting like he agreed with every word, and then he encouraged Andie to shut me out, her own mother! I wasn't even allowed to visit my baby girl during normal visiting hours."

"Your Honor," Elias interrupted again. "The house spoken of belongs to my client. My client has considerable financial resources and can provide for her own needs."

"And, please if I may?" Dr. Martin interjected. "As you can see, Mrs. Wodsende, is neither a baby or a girl. She is a mature woman who..."

"All in good time, Doctor. It will be your turn to speak when I say so. Not a millisecond sooner." He turned back to Sybil. "I apologize for the interruption. Now, be so good as to tell this gathering. In your opinion, what is the best course of action for your daughter?"

"I would like power of attorney to pay her bills. I love my baby girl," Sybil asserted, appearing tearful. She fished a lace edged handkerchief from her purse and dabbed at glistening cheeks. "She needs me. I'd like nothing better than to drive her to doctor appointments and protect her from herself. I think I can do that as well as anyone at this table. Better than anyone. The new doctor won't cast my baby out into the hard, cruel world before she can stand on her own two feet."

Sybil looked across the table at Andrea. "Okay, baby girl, my Andie Rose. I'm your mother; don't you remember the good times we've had?"

Jared could now see that each time Sybil uttered the endearment, *baby girl*, Andrea winced. He had been counting the number of times that she inserted that phrase inappropriately into the conversation, as if seeking out opportunities to do so.

Dr. Martin had explained that in attempting to hypnotize Andrea, he had discovered a deeply imbedded resistance. A firewall had been erected and until he had the key phrase used to erect those mental barriers there was no penetrating that iron clad resistance. On pure instinct, an instinct born on the wings of recent experience on the streets of North Adams, Jared scribbled the words *baby girl,* on the page before him. He folded it, wrote the doctor's name on the outside, and passed the note down the table.

Sybil had inched her hand across the table, pleading now for "baby girl," to reach back. The Judge had engaged Elias in discussion as Doctor Martin listened closely toying with his note, but failing to read the contents.

"Baby girl," Sybil whispered again. The simple words were laced with compelling significance as Andrea's gaze now locked on her mother's hands. Snake-like, palms open with the fingers curling; Sybil's arms inched across the space between them.

"Come on, baby. I love you, baby girl," Sybil reiterated.

Andrea had locked her fingers in a white knuckle grip. In an attempt to distract herself from her mother's pleadings

Jared could see that she had lifted her eyes to study the mural behind Sybil. The effort appeared to cost her a great expense of energy. As much as she might like to enter that mural and escape her mother, the programmed lure to give in and appear to have reconciled was too practiced, too embedded in her psyche.

Jared watched as the fingers of her right hand disengaged from the left and in that moment he knew what he was seeing. As though they had a life separate from her conscious will, the hook of that hypnotic key to programmed control was causing Andrea to reach a hand back across the table, connecting in a show of reconciliation that would play into the hands of a mortal enemy giving the judge the one excuse he needed.

Jared had nothing to lose. He had played the fool for far less. "Baby girl," he spoke as Andrea, having lost the battle had just begun to surrender her hand toward the curling fingers of her mothers' which, if it were possible, resembled even more a claw with the blood red nail of the middle finger pointed abnormally in a spastic caricature toward her daughter's heart.

"Andrea!" Jared let his voice take on a tone of command.

Startled, Andrea looked at him. Her eyes were hooded, nearly closed.

"It's okay, Andie... Baby Girl," Sybil asserted.

Conversation stopped. All eyes were on Jared as he stood and walked around the table. He bent toward Andrea feeling the brush of her soft hair against his mouth. Close now he whispered in her ear, his eyes all the while engaging Sybil across the table. Though quiet his tone was forceful.

"You don't have to do anything you don't want. The power of Jesus Christ releases you, from *Baby Girl*. God gives you the power to resist the command of a witch. Do you understand me, Andrea?"

Andrea's eyes snapped fully open. She lifted her face to look him full in the face.

"Do you understand? You're free to be yourself. In Christ you are released from the supernatural bondage of the past."

Both Jared and Doctor Martin had seen an instantaneous transformation as Andrea stepped back into the power of a human physicality that was never intended to be the possession of another.

Sybil directed her full attention toward Jared, the force of which felt like an electric shot of palpable malice. Her head was held at an unnatural tilt, a dolls head on a turnstile, eyes wider than normal in skin suddenly stretched tight like shrinking leather across blushed cheekbones. Oozing from her pores was the subtle, but distinct sent of decay as her expression betrayed what Jared hoped to never see again. An "It" was back.

"Your silence hurts me," Sybil addressed her daughter even as she continued a ruthless scrutiny of Jared. The helpless, little girl voice was gone. Had Dr. Martin suspected this? Is this why he had invited the mother's wrath when he denied access to the daughter? And why had Judge Capra allowed this to go so far?

"But I forgive you, baby girl."

The sound of the court reporter's tap, tap, taping had fallen to silence and even she seemed unsettled by what had just transpired. Judge Capra appeared oblivious to the exchange between Sybil and her daughter, between Jared and Andrea. The time allocated for Sybil to reassert her influence had not worked out as planned and any verbal reprimand Judge Capra might issue would only call attention to Jared's actions, finding its way into the record for others to read at a later time.

A self conscious silence had descended as Jared made his way back to his seat. The Judges silence was confirmation enough for Jared that far more was going on here than might be imagined.

Picking up the exchange as though nothing had happened Judge Capra addressed Dr. Martin. "Please be brief about any thoughts you have. I've already read your report and found it sufficient."

"Your Honor, I do not recommend you release Andrea Wodsende into the care of her mother. Mrs. Sybil Bryant has consistently violated her daughter's health and well being. She has not respected boundaries and I believe is motivated to care for her daughter, not merely for financial gain, but to assuage guilt over past abuse."

"You traitor," Sybil was back in human persona. "You let me think you were on my side."

The judge pounded his gavel. "Please be quiet, Mrs. Bryant. You may continue, Doctor Martin."

"I believe Mrs. Wodsende is able to care for herself. The outpatient plan allows for her to take an apartment near the hospital so we can continue our work together. I'll maintain oversight, making reports to the medical board and to this court for a period of one year if you so order. If Andrea can stay in Boston, she can more readily participate in the ongoing investigation of the Stephanie Wodsende murder as well."

There was no pause of reflection before Judge Capra cleared his voice, ready to announce his ruling. Nothing that had been said would soften what was coming. Jared was certain of a connection between Dudley and Judge Capra, between Judge Capra and Sybil. And yet his suspicions seemed unbelievable, tempting him to dismiss his own assessment. The wealth of influence, even the level of conspiracy implied, was a can of worms staggering to consider.

"I'm reluctant to let Ms. Wodsende live by herself. I therefore..."

"Excuse me, Your Honor."

"And you are?"

"Jared Shiel retired Boston PD. I worked the original case. I do not believe Andrea Wodsende was ever guilty of that crime."

"I guess you didn't hear me earlier, so let me repeat myself. We are not gathered in this place to discuss the murder of Stephanie Wodsende."

"I'm sorry, Judge, but I have vital information to share. I'm certain you'll thank me for saving you the trouble of having your ruling reversed when this is brought before another judge."

For mere seconds Henry appeared discomforted. "I've made my decision and must now ask that all parties around this table desist from further comment."

Judge Capra looked directly at Andrea. "Ms. Wodsende, you were declared incompetent to stand trial and that is the ruling we live with today. Although," his tone was rehearsed, "it seems we have a miraculous recovery of sorts; all the more mysterious because it is unexplained."

"I think, Your Honor would be prudent to hear what I have to say," Jared persisted. "Since we have established that there may be a civil trial after the baby's parentage is established, I don't think anyone wants to see something significant overlooked in today's proceeding."

Judge Capra was visibly irritated. "Get on with it."

"Mrs. Bryant is a gambling addict." Jared slid a folder down the table. "You give that woman power of attorney and every asset Andrea has will be gone before the year is up."

Jared slid another folder down the table. "Dr. Wodsende pays Mrs. Bryant a sum of money each month. This generous payout is more than adequate for her living expenses." Another folder. "Casino records also show that he pays her gambling debts, which begs several questions."

"Because he loves me," Sybil interrupted the simpering little girl voice back in play. "I'm like a mother to him! And I can't imagine where you would have gotten that information."

"Dudley paid first for your silence, then for your absence, and now for your interference."

The sharp report of the gavel silenced Sybil's retort. Judge Capra made a show of scanning the folder's contents before speaking. Jared thought he saw a flicker of something like amusement cross his face.

"We'll have no further discussion. A life was lost for which Andrea Wodsende confessed. A ruling in this case was made quickly. There was a rush to judgment and not enough time elapsed to assess the apparent mental condition of the accused. And now we have this questionable recovery."

"Your Honor," Elias interrupted.

"You would be wise not to speak again counselor. This is the state's show, not yours."

The Judge looked at Sybil as he spoke his next sentence. "I find that this mother knows her daughter and is realistic about her recovery. I order that Andrea Wodsende be released to the care of the mother, Mrs. Sybil Bryant. The mother does not have power of attorney, although the court will be willing to reconsider that option at a later time. For now Andrea Wodsende's financial resources will be managed by the firm of Elias Goldfarb as suggested by him in pre-hearing correspondence."

He continued. "The patient will be carefully monitored for a period of eighteen months while she re-acclimates to society. Both the mother and referring doctor will make monthly reports via a social worker from Berkshire County who will visit on a routine basis. Andrea Wodsende continues her counseling. I'm not concerned with the choice of psychologist once the accused moves back home to... he glanced at his notes. Woods End, is it?"

"That's right, Your Honor," Sybil's tone was triumphant.

"Without the permission of her mother or assigned social worker, Ms. Wodsende is not to travel beyond the borders of Berkshire County."

"Your Honor," Dr. Martin spoke up. "I was hoping to continue working with Andrea. Under my care she's made considerable progress. Trust is not easily established with someone of her background. Additional recovered memory will shed light on significant issues of interest to this court. I feel very strongly that Andrea have limited contact with her mother and no contact at all once the child is born."

"That certainly seems extreme. What are we talking about here?"

Sybil was alarmed, casting her brother an angry look. The old courtroom adage of, never ask a question one doesn't know the answer to, had been broken. A year ago Henry would never have made such a mistake.

All eyes were focused on Dr. Martin. "I'm glad you asked," he said. "A cult-like group, to which Mrs. Wodsende was born into, has shared a bond for generations. Some members are committed to bizarre religious practices that include ritual abuse. Recovered memory of my client and..."

"What are you talking about?" Impatience burst from those few words as once more Henry pounded his gavel.

"Possible SRA. That is..."

"That is quite enough! We will not introduce such an inflammatory subject into my proceedings. As a professional you should know that the moment you broach that topic we have a highly charged atmosphere not at all conducive to rational thought. You undermine the veracity of your profession and taint your testimony as an expert witness, Doctor."

"I request that this court consider what Doctor Martin has to say," Elias interjected. "It's not what any of us like to hear, but the facts are really quite..."

"There is no such thing as Satanic Ritualistic Abuse. Not in my courtroom! And recovered memory is notoriously unreliable, more often than not categorically disproved. I won't allow justice to be circumvented by useless conjecture. I ask you to retract that statement, Doctor, or we'll strike it from the record."

"I cannot, Judge. And you can see why I need to continue treating Ms. Wodsende," Doctor Martin added, with a calmness that belied his expression. "We've only just begun to touch on..."

Judge Capra turned to the court reporter. "Please strike Dr. Martin's last statements and everything thereafter"

Henry could not resist glancing in his sister's direction. In barely perceptible agreement she nodded her approval. A point had been scored for their side. Once they might have laughed and rehashed what was said. But inexplicably Henry was filled with deep feelings of shame for what he had just facilitated. He remembered Andie, the little girl. How could God forgive...

Soon they would all be gathered at the farm. Individual members of the twelve family groups, some emissaries from far off places, had vied for the privilege of attending. Come the feast of Winter Solstice they were prepared to dedicate the hoped-for soul transfer of a child and the required blood sacrifice of its mother. Thinking of this Sybil looked at her daughter with a leering smile. Observing her closely Jared cringed. To him, that red slash across her face was nothing less than predatory.

Judge Capra did not plan on attending. Ten feet onto the property and he would be marked for the traitor he was. Concealing the core of his thoughts from Dudley and Sybil was one thing, but many powerful intrinsic readers would be gathered at the farm. They would finger his betrayal and tortured ambivalence with the swift, inhuman assessment of the conscienceless reprobate, and they would do so with unbridled glee.

"Judge," Dr. Martin attempted to continue, but Henry cut him off.

"I doubt you'll want to commute four hours to Woods End for a fifty minute counseling session. If Andrea fails to cooperate with the stated restrictions, she will be returned to the care of the State Hospital's ward for the criminally insane for further evaluation. At that time, if this happens, you may continue her care. But for now we're done. My ruling stands! You are all dismissed!"

Henry had thrown Dr. Martin a bone. Had Sybil noticed? She lingered as the others filed from the room. For a moment Henry was afraid she would make the mistake of speaking to him, but what did that matter now? Although stronger than Dudley, she had allowed a life of feeding her appetites to marginalize her dark gifts of divination. Henry told himself there was no way Sybil could know he had an entirely different view of today's proceedings. He had done what Guido asked and he felt stronger and more vital for that effort.

Why should he care what Sybil thought? In the last few years he had straddled a fence. Even he knew there was no redemption in that. Slowly, by increments, Henry opened his heart feeling a release of desperation. He'd pried loose the corner of a mental block. The internal space of inward territory would make room for Jesus Christ; the only true force powerful enough to deliver freedom from slavery.

Shocked, Sybil furrowed her brow in focused concentration, unsure that she had read him correctly.

If Guido was right, then Jesus Christ could forgive, *even him*. It seemed impossible and yet, Henry felt a strong spiritual drawing of his soul and knew he could no longer vacillate. There was no longer the luxury of time.

"I've dismissed this court, but you linger for a reason." Henry studied Sybil. He was no longer concerned with who might overhear. "You are free to join me in what we both know I'm about to do."

As he said the words Henry felt a deep and profound shame for how he had lived his life. How could he reconcile the abundance of his sin? If he thought of each detail of every sin, he would be so overwhelmed he would never succeed in praying for forgiveness.

"*God knows,*" was the assurance that filled his mind. And Henry knew this was true. The dragon did not know everything. Satan was fighting to alter the substance of a history that had been firmly ordained. Satan was a created being and was not now, nor had it ever been, co-equal with God. Contrary to the cults teaching, that evil presence could not be everywhere at once as the triune author and finisher of all creation was; sovereign and omnipresent.

Sybil did her best to threaten him. Hex's, spells, the all too familiar weight of confusion filled the air. *Did he know what he was doing, what he was up against if he turned his back on everything he'd been trained to be?*

Others might point the finger, claim to see satan in every agenda, in every dark corner, and be marked a fool or even mentally ill. But an insider of Henry's level and rank might garner a new crop of Christians to acknowledge a network of cooperation reaching into every strata of life. Before that happened they would kill him. Was he willing to die?

Consider, Sybil seemed to threaten. *Do this and you will surely suffer far more than death!*

With sudden abruptness Henry felt strangely immune. As Sybil stood her ground, he did his best to communicate the light of hope he felt. He stared into her eyes, allowing compassion to flow from his expression. Was this prayer? Henry smiled.

It was more than Sybil could tolerate. She turned and raced from the room fleeing upon the very fantails of hatred, trailing the detested smell of decay, all of which Henry was no longer numb to.

Do not I hate them, O Lord, that hate thee? And am not I grieved with those that rise up against thee? I hate them with perfect hatred: I count them mine enemies. Search me, O God, and know my heart: try me, and know my thoughts: And see if there be any wicked way in me, and lead me in the way of everlasting (Psalm 139: 21-24).

In that empty courtroom Henry sat before the greatest Judge of all. He bowed his head to confess his sins. He forgot time as he prayed and asked for the gift of faith; that Jesus Christ would rescue his soul from the torments of hell, rebirthing him to life eternal. Romans 10: 9-11

THE END

"The Guarantee of Our Tomorrow Is Today's Persuasion That We Do Not Exist"

22626212R00171

Made in the USA
Charleston, SC
29 September 2013